Special Needs

SUE VICKERMAN

CinnamonPress

INDEPENDENT INNOVATIVE INTERNATIONAL

Published by Cinnamon Press, Meirion House, Tanygrisiau, Blaenau Ffestiniog, Gwynedd LL41 3SU
www.cinnamonpress.com

The right of Sue Vickerman to be identified as author of this work has been asserted by her in accordance with the Copyright, Designs and Patent Act, 1988. © 2011 Sue Vickerman. ISBN 978-1-907090-33-2
British Library Cataloguing in Publication Data. A CIP record for this book can be obtained from the British Library.

Designed and typeset in Garamond by Cinnamon Press. Cover design by Jan Fortune-Wood from detail of original artwork 'Man and Woman' © Dileep Kumarvs agency dreamtime.
Cinnamon Press is represented by Inpress and by the Welsh Books Council in Wales. Printed in Poland

The writer and publisher acknowledge support from Arts Council England Grants for the Arts and the writer acknowledges support from Creative Scotland towards the writing of this title.

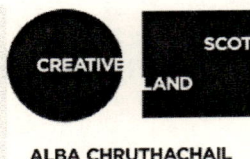

LOTTERY FUNDED

ALBA CHRUTHACHAIL

Thanks to the following friends, acquaintances and professionals who may by now have forgotten that they read and made helpful comments on all or part of one of the several drafts of SPECIAL NEEDS in the long period since its inception. These include the writers John R. Gordon, Tamar Yellin and the University of Northumbria's Penny Smith (alias Penny Sumner); Caroline Dawnay and the late Pat Kavanagh of PFD Literary Agency; former Diva Books editor Helen Sandler; Eileen Laurie, Francesca Rhys, Cath Brookes, Marilyn Anthony, Susan Dunne, my dad, my brother Mike, Stuart Field, and Friederike Debus. Special thanks to John Gordon, Alison Marshall, Jeannie Williams and Jean Harrison for reading and commenting on the final manuscript. Thanks too to Becca and Isobel Clare, Libby Baxter-Williams and Nic and Ruth Carlyle for votes on Best Page 1.

Part One:
Behavioural Problems

To the gifted writer who makes my magic pencil
leap out of its pot at me.

And to what started gently with porridge,
all the way to the end.

Chapter 1

The woman leads the way into a cramped, overheated room. The fringe of her vast smock offers glimpses of mottled ankles. Her wiry orange hair is caught back loosely in a silk scarf. Polished stones dangle from her neck and ears; more are set into silver rings that sink into the flesh of her fingers. She is perspiring profusely.

'I need a head massage,' says Joan.

The woman closes the door. 'Let's have a quick look at your cards first. See where we are.' Shifting a pile of magazines from the coffee-table she sinks to the floor, her garment puffing out then deflating like a hovercraft powering down.

Joan seats herself on a floor-cushion opposite, clunking her steamed-up glasses onto the table. They are heavy-framed, functional, masculine. An incense stick is smouldering oppressively in front of an ornamental Buddha. Joan undoes her double-breasted blazer, then the top button of her shirt, wondering at what age hot flushes start.

The woman's hands flit over the colourful cards, sorting them, flipping them up and down. 'Here.' She flashes one. 'Same one as the last two sessions. There's a special somebody out there, Joan.'

'You said medical, last time.'

'I did, didn't I? Ah yes. There it is. Someone in the medical field.' The woman closely scrutinises a card. 'Or horse-related. Someone with a lot of money anyway.'

'I'm not bothered about money. I just want someone who...' Joan trails off. 'If one of these teaching posts comes through in the States, I could have a new life by September.'

'Have you heard anything yet?' The woman continues flipping cards up and down in the vague manner of someone ironing whilst watching TV.

'They're doing a search for me on the west coast. Where you suggested.'

'Hmm. It could be the west coast of England,' says the woman casually, unthinkingly. 'Well, Wales, is what I'm saying.'

'Oh yes?'

'It's all about the water, and your relationship to it. You need to be on a land-mass with water to the west. There are a lot of ley-lines where you have that situation.'

'So why am I paying this American agency? You told me...'

'Ah.' The woman remains confident, unflustered. 'So I did. Hang on –'She hastily flips a few more times, then stabs a card decisively. 'There we are. Definitely the States.'

Joan looks reassured.

'And I can see recognition for you, over there.'

'Will that be my artwork taking off?'

'Definitely. America is definitely where your opportunities are.' The woman sweeps the pack together, bringing the card session to a swift end, and comes around the table on her knees to position herself behind Joan. 'Just stay there and I'll do your head for you.'

Joan stares across at herself in the mirror-doors that line one wall, watching the woman's large hands cup her skull, smelling her sweet deodorant and sweat. Her eyes wander over the Native American chief's head-dress hanging on the back of the door, the collection of crystals arrayed on a shelf unit.

'So, Joan. How've you been?'

'You know me. Never stop. I'm busy with a party this weekend. A friend's, not mine, but I do all the running around.'

'And how's your daughter?'

'Pshsh.' Joan jerks her head.

The woman's stones clink. 'Stay still.' Her fingers press and knead beneath Joan's hair. 'You're blocked up. You two been having problems?'

'No problem. Absolutely no problem whatsoever. She's just at that age.'

The woman closes her eyes and places her hands above Joan's head, palms down. 'You're sounding a bit defensive.'

'She's a very independent young lady is our Caroline.'

The woman starts to feel the shape of the air, as though examining the texture of a sponge. 'Your aura's dented, love.'

'Is it? You're good at this, you are. That's why I keep on coming.'

'It's in pretty bad shape. It's in long-term bad shape. I've never yet felt a healthy aura on you, have I?'

'Haven't you?'

The woman stares intently at Joan. 'You never let me in. I can't help you if you don't let me in.'

Joan folds her arms, curling in on herself, scowling.

The woman heaves herself to her feet, clinking like a bag of marbles. 'Get on the couch so I can do you properly.'

Joan looks alarmed. 'You know I can't cope with a body massage.'

'I *know* you can't cope with a body massage.' The woman's smile gives form to three chins. 'Not with your block. You're *well* blocked. You can't bear to be touched. I just want to do your head properly.'

Joan removes the lace-ups that she gets through Colin's police-uniform outfitters and lies back on the black leatherette.

'Good. Now just relax.'

Joan's arms are still folded, her toes in tan pop-socks point to the ceiling, her eyes fixated on the Artex swirls.

The woman begins by making slow caresses around Joan's chin, the broad sides of Joan's cheeks. 'There's a stranger out there waiting for you. Someone who wants to look after you.'

'I do worry about how Colin's going to take this.'

'Oh! You've never actually mentioned before that you have a...'

'Husband.'

'A husband? Ah. Well, what I mean is –'

'It's okay. The cards are right. Although–' Joan frowns, 'the bit about being looked after: that's not really me. I'm the looking-after type myself. It's my job. That's what you're doing when you're teaching children.'

'That's typical of your star-sign.' The woman's thumbs circle on Joan's temples. 'When I say "look after" you, I'm saying he'll be *there* for you.' Her fingers slowly trace Joan's hairline then work their way back down to beneath her neck. 'You should go onto once a week with this, your chakras aren't functioning.'

Joan has become very still. Outside it is starting to rain. In next-door's yard a woman swears. In the distance, someone is shouting for their children to get inside.

'We should be true to ourselves, shouldn't we?'

'I knew you were thinking that thought. Shall I book you in for Saturday?'

'I'm helping with that party next Saturday.' Joan's tone is resigned. 'I think I'll leave it and book when I feel ready.'

The red-brick terraces of Henry Place, Henry Walk, Henry Avenue, Henry Rise and Henry View descend from the ring-road in parallel, as orderly as cigarettes in a packet. Number 47 Henry Place is owned by Mr Hassan, who conveniently lives next door at number 45. Number 47 has three doorbells. The wind has blown a sodden heap of crisp-packets, polystyrene containers and free newspapers against the front door's rotten wood. The top bedsit has been rented out for the last few weeks to a nice American couple, two teachers called Howard and Beatrice. The other parts of the house are awaiting repairs. For the time being they have boarded-up windows. One day, when the council gives this postcode-area its turn for regeneration grants, he'll fix everything up.

Just after six that Sunday evening Howard and Beatrice leave their bedsit and hurry in the drizzle towards the city centre. Within minutes they have passed half a dozen curry houses. Howard finally steers them into the Star of India.

It is empty. Three young waiters murmur peaceably behind the bar. A sitar twangs thinly.

'You have a knack for finding good places,' says Beatrice.

Howard, nestled in a velvety corner, is already lost in the menu.

'I *think* that's Prince Arjuna.' Beatrice nods at a painting above his head, of a monarch riding on an elephant. 'I had to read the story with a class.'

A waiter places a large aluminium water jug on the white table-cloth. Beatrice notices Howard noticing the slow, beautiful sweep of eyelash against cheek. The waiter's eye meets Howard's for a fraction of a second.

Beatrice stabs a utensil into some green, gelatinous chutney. 'You've lost every bit of your tan, you know. You're going a sort of British grey. We could both use some sun.'

'We need to recuperate financially.' Howard leaves a finger in the Speciality section, turns a page. 'You gotta admit, it's dirt-cheap to live here.'

'Dirt being the operative word.' Her menu is lying unopened across the cutlery. 'This semester's really dragging.'

'Term.'

'How come we've been here since January and we don't know a soul? We made tons of friends in London and Cambridge.' The poppadum arrive.

'Well, London's just London. And don't forget our Cambridge social life cost us a fortune.' Howard reaches for a shard of poppadum.

Beatrice's head drops into her hands. 'Cambridge was *fun*. Jerome and Jeremy. Fenella.'

'But too nice to be inspiring. This city's really stimulating my writing.' Howard keeps another finger in Seafood, turns a page again.

'It's depressing.'

'Look, it's just a totally different cultural experience here. You have to pick things out.'

'Like what?'

'Well, the curry houses, obviously. And bhangra discos.'

'We don't go to discos.'

The restaurant slowly fills until the sitar is drowned out by hubbub. Howard tucks into every dish, tasting Beatrice's vegetable korma, pulling a large chunk from her untouched peshwari nan. She eats barely half of her meal, instead turning it listlessly with her fork.

Howard finally clatters his knife and fork onto his fully-cleared plate and dabs at his mouth. 'Use it, Beatrice. Like I do. I'm *using* these shitty school experiences. It's great material. You've gotta view teaching purely as a means to an end.' He drops his crumpled napkin. 'For art.'

Far beyond the hump-backed horizon at the city's northern fringe, the vast green expanses of the Yorkshire Dales National Park will be bathed in evening light. The emerald landscape will be breath-taking, latticed with silvery walls like old-fashioned tatting and planted with barns pale as egg boxes. Genteel. Photogenic.

Meanwhile, close at hand, an iron bracelet of blackened villages encircles the industrial city. The villages took root more than a century ago around isolated mills. The walls twisting around the settlements are black with soot, the moors scarred with lesions where old works sites brought the earth's innards to the surface.

The residents of the mill villages will tell you that their moors have a unique character, and will point out that, being still within the metropolitan boundary, they are particularly well-provided with litter bins and loos. Furthermore, converted barns here are half the price of those in the National Park. Add to that the easy commute to the city, the attractions of living in the 'Dales proper' pale. There's a bit of graffiti, but that's the real world.

Down in the mill village of Weatherhope, in one such barn conversion, the bald head of Professor Walter Fox is just visible through a small window. The window is set into the bricked up former archway, as is the front door, plastic for durability, featuring a stained glass peacock. Through the window is Professor Fox's study. In the bedroom above the study, Baldev and Caroline are helping each other to revise.

Caroline's legs are two poles on the bed. Baldev is glad that she's scrawny rather than overpoweringly fat. A body that was bigger than his wouldn't feel equal. Although she's all bone, her angles soften when they lie this close.

'Twenty-four days to my French,' calculates Caroline.

'My first one's chemistry,' says Baldev. 'We'll do some revision in a minute.'

Although Caroline is flat-chested she wears bras. Baldev can see through her blouse that today's one, laid across her sticky-out ribs, is pale blue lace with a little bow between the cups.

Caroline sits up and fiddles impatiently with the laces of her shoes, which she then throws onto the rug. Pointing her toes like a ballerina she slips them under the duvet, her skirt scrunching up around her waist.

Baldev finishes undoing Caroline's blouse. She is as thin as a sapling. His hands creep like ivy over her ribs. Her hollowness reminds him of Easter eggs. He bounds out of bed – 'Forgot,' flicks the small bolt at the top of the door and comes back in awkward strides, his trousers descending round his thighs.

His underpants today, notes Caroline, are horrid, the kind mothers buy. They are filled out by a large diagonal trapped stick. She examines the ceiling until the duvet settles back over them. 'Is there any of Aunty Darsh's vodka left?'

'I need to pop down and purloin some. You should see the booze she's already bought in for the party. The most massive stash.' Feeling Caroline's hand reach the top of his underpants then scurry inside the elastic, Baldev hooks his fingers into her bra-cups. Her nipples pop out like blunt pink crayons. At the same time the waistband of his y-fronts slips from her grasp, the elastic snapping back against his penis. 'Ow!'

'Sorry.'

As usual on a Sunday evening, Darshana is ensconced in her personal sitting-room watching television, enveloped in a velvet sofa. The barn has been stylishly furnished by her own hand. The sitting-room is the cold room that she made warm. On each side of the pot-bellied stove, stacks of perfectly-cut logs fill the cavernous fireplace. The stove is exuding a cosy heat and a whiff of wood-smoke. There's a tiny mullioned window taken from some church, a bureau with a green leather top and a chair with elaborately turned legs. On the bureau is her ceramic retro telephone painted with little pink roses and gilt touches: a landline, so much less stressful. Her husband's non-pristine and therefore resented Chesterfield is pushed back into a corner, its distressed leather concealed under a chenille throw. The white baby-grand, the only thing of any worth from her brief first marriage, stands like a princess on an island of Persian carpet. Up above, the original roof-beams arch crookedly towards the heavens.

Darshana is running through the 'to do' list of her Crystal Wedding Anniversary-cum-Celebration of the Holi Festival of Spring, as she wrote on the invitations. She expects the vicar will ask her detailed questions about Holi in that respectful, interested way. She has done her research on it.

People like to come to her home, to her 'do's. She has it so nice. She caters beautifully. She is their exotic friend. Her gaze wanders over the mantelpiece; at one end the large brass statue of Shiva Nataraj dancing in a circle of flame, at the other Walter's carriage clock. She bought the statue on a hippy market stall years ago. In a way it goes with her horse brasses. She bought it because it's the kind of thing that visitors to her house expect. On Saturday they'll all ask her its name and what it represents. She says something different every time.

The empty glass on the table catches the light. The TV shows a woman's stockinged legs emerging elegantly from a car door, then cuts to a man screeching away in a black sporty number. When Darshana gets up, the sofa contracts. She takes the vodka from the drinks cabinet, pours some out, holds the glass up to the wall-light, stands the bottle on the stone floor and attempts to tip some back. A puddle appears round the bottle's base. She holds up the glass again, scrutinising the liquid, picks up the bottle and once again tops up the glass. She puts the bottle back in the cabinet. A mini-fridge, like the ones in hotels, is hidden in a small cupboard. She pulls out an opened carton of orange juice and tips it into her drink. A last dreg dissolves into the vodka.

Darshana slams the fridge closed and heads out of the door in search of more juice, tripping on the rug. Damn. In the hall her heel catches on a flagstone. Shit. On the threshold of the kitchen, her shoe falls off. Fuck.

At the far end of the kitchen is Walter's study. Through the stained glass door his bowed head shines in the glow of his angle-poise lamp.

The kitchen fridge is also empty of orange juice. Shit.

Walter shuffles through, wearing his leather birthday slippers from the boys, folding his spectacles in speckled hands, his back still hunched from poring over a text.

'No need to come through.' Darshana tries to speak steadily.

'I suppose you've been thwarted fixing a drink?'

'Orange-juice,' Darshana retorts.

Walter reaches stiffly into a top cupboard, pulls down a carton, locates the kitchen scissors and makes a precise snip. 'Where is your glass?' He turns, holding the juice, offering to pour. 'You've lost one of your shoes.'

Darshana grabs the carton. 'I'll take it through.' Juice slops onto the floor.

Walter stands, inert. 'Where are the children?'

'Doing their prep.'

'When's Baldev's first exam?'

'Three weeks.'

To avoid seeing how his wife looks at him, Walter is focusing on pulling at a string tucked inside his buttoned-up cardigan. A small gold watch without a strap appears. 'Does he seem ready?' He scrutinises the timepiece closely.

'You've seen his reports.'

Walter carefully tucks the timepiece back out of sight.

'I believe Holi is a festival of spring. Won't your party next week be a little early?'

'Why do you always have to be so bloody pedantic? Anyway, it's also for our anniversary, in case you'd forgotten.' She walks out.

'But not in fact our Crystal one,' says Walter.

In the slick, runnelled arteries of the Henrys, close to the city's heart, the TVs and electric fires have been switched off but are still warm to the touch. As midnight approaches, a tyre screeches on the wet tarmac of Henry Place. Some glass shatters, followed by a shout.

Beatrice scrambles over the bed and peers out. The tops of the lampposts are haloed with drizzle. The lamp directly outside the window is flickering. Near the shop a volley of angry words is funnelling out of a passage, the way slogans expand through a loud-hailer. There's movement; some figures, half-concealed by parked cars.

'It's something down by the store,' says Beatrice.

Now there is running; a crowd beginning to take shape, spiked with elbows.

'Something's going on, Howard.' Beatrice's face is tilted against the window, straining to catch the detail.

'We live downtown,' Howard shrugs. 'Neighbourhoods like this, stuff happens.'

A vehicle kerb-crawls into view below Beatrice's elbow, seeming to hover like a space-craft, smooth and silent. Its luminous paintwork catches the light.

'It's the cops.'

'If things hot up I can write a piece on it,' says Howard. 'It's time I wrote something on the race issue.'

Chapter 2

It is Friday. Tuesday and Thursday Darshana Chatterjee-Fox stayed at home, having phoned in with a migraine. Today, however, she must make a special effort to get in to work – not so much due to the inspection as to the possibility of tomorrow's party being ruined if colleagues think she is ill and don't show up. A little before seven-thirty in the morning she is leaning wanly against the doorpost of her barn conversion like a runner after the end of a marathon. Her sari is as blue as the stained glass peacock. The tyre of olive flesh at her waist is goose-pimpled with cold but her forehead is beaded with sweat, and her eyes are narrowed to partially filter the painful daylight.

Eventually an extremely thin teenage girl appears at Darshana's shoulder, her school uniform hanging off her like an empty sack, her pallor chalky.

Darshana forces a smile and draws Caroline to her beneath a huge umbrella. They run out into the rain and get into the people-carrier on the drive.

A football rolls in front of the vehicle. A blond, freckly little boy, also in school uniform, comes running from the house.

Darshana rolls down the window - 'Luke – don't get wet!'

He casts his eyes to the heavens – 'It's only spitting,' grabs the ball and races back indoors.

Baldev appears on the threshold, lanky, golden, eating a bowl of cereal. Through the study window, Professor Fox can be seen at his desk. As the ungainly vehicle begins the climb up the steep side of the fell, hands wave from within, and Baldev waves his spoon.

*

At around the same hour on Friday morning, the door of 47 Henry Place opens. The heap of detritus that has collected in the wind overnight slumps over the threshold.

'Ugh.' Beatrice's neat Italian boot shifts back the litter. She and Howard step out into the damp air. Beatrice has stayed home Monday through Thursday, mostly reading Catherine Cookson novels about the poverty of the north of England and feeling as miserable as the weather. Howard, on the other hand, keen on saving up money, has cheerfully accepted the supply agency's offers of work every day this week.

Three teenage boys are approaching from the direction of the shop. They are a familiar sight on Henry Place. They never seem to go anywhere else, such as school, or work. Outside the shop, the Pakistani woman who works there is gesticulating after them like a small, mad nun.

'Her nephews,' Howard informs Beatrice. 'They give her a hard time.'

Beatrice hurries round to the passenger door under her half-opened umbrella and fumbles with the key. The youths draw alongside the car just as her behind disappears into it. One makes a remark, and the others push his shoulder and laugh. They swagger on, sucking their teeth.

'Curry sauce. Disgusting.' Beatrice dabs at her boot with a Kleenex. 'I thought you'd been scooping that stuff up.'

'It's the wind.'

'There wasn't that kind of wind in London.' She rearranges her hair in the wing mirror.

As usual, Howard stops the car outside the corner shop. Beatrice jumps out with her purse. The shop is peeling, unpainted for years, with sacks of rice heaped unaesthetically in the window. The lady behind the counter habitually shakes her head and mutters in her own language, concluding with 'Terrible, terrible', inviting her customers' agreement. Often she will pop an extra bhaji into Beatrice's paper bag.

Howard watches Beatrice returning to the car. Designer boots, well-cut trouser suit, heavy shapely eyebrows, angular jaw, strong red lipstick. What attracted him was her androgyny.

She gets back in and hands him a bag. He starts the engine, dipping his face into the bag's contents. 'Another thing that can be said for this town,' he enthuses, making crumbs fly. 'Fresh samosas for breakfast.'

'Makes it all worthwhile,' says Beatrice heavily. A Bollywood soundtrack rollicks from a passing taxi's window. She peeps into her own bag. 'God, I miss Maria's bagels.'

Darshana's cherry nails rap nervily on the wheel. She checks her watch again. The people-carrier careers past gaudy shops, cardboard boxes and thrown-out furniture. The shops' awnings, which later on will shelter vegetables and TV sets from the rain, are printed with lettering and motifs. Shabab Jeweller's is gold on burgundy. Nafeez Homewares is red on white. Sri Ganesh Sweet Home is yellow on yellow. Joan will be coming by the Sri Ganesh later to pick up the catering order for the party, not just sweets but a great array of savoury finger foods and dips such as Darshana's mother and aunties used to make, things she's supposed to know how to do.

Caroline's school is near the city centre, where the redbrick terraces stop and the streets turn to uncleaned stone hedged-in with scratchy privet. The school is set among Victorian residences that used to be grand. The school itself is still grand, its boundary-wall castellated, its turrets wrapped in dusty leaves. It charges fees. The teachers travel in from nicer places. Ten per cent of the pupils live in the terraced streets of the inner city, the winners of bursaries. They wear the traditional clothing of their countries of origin, made up locally in the colours of the uniform.

Darshana pulls into the dropping-off point. Caroline takes hold of the rucksack on her knee and goes to undo her seatbelt.

Darshana half turns. 'You're ever so early.'

'S'alright.'

'Only I can't be late today, not with the inspectors coming in.'

'S'alright. Door's open, look. Common room'll be open.'

'Sorry.' Darshana's face reaches across to Caroline's, tilted sideways demandingly.

'I said it's alright.' Caroline obediently pecks Darshana's cheek. 'I could've come on the bus with the boys, you know.'

'No! You'd still have had some walking to do. Feeling like you do.'

'But I feel better,' says Caroline. 'It was just when I got up.'

'You've got your note,' says Darshana.

Caroline opens the door and reaches one foot down. 'Thanks for the lift.'

Darshana double-checks her watch against the little clock on the dashboard as Caroline drops down from the vehicle and hurries across the rain-swept gravel to the entrance steps. It is only seven thirty. Caroline will be the first pupil. Hopefully they won't notice and think there's something abnormal, some problem at home. Alongside the statistics for Oxbridge entrance, Caroline's school is very caring. They pay attention to the individual. It is, after all, what Joan and Colin are paying for. But it does mean that the staff poke their noses in if anything isn't normal.

Darshana feels exactly the same as Joan about education. She and Walter have gone private, too, with their boys.

She carries on doing little waves until Caroline disappears, then takes two strong painkillers from a blister-pack and swallows them. She checks her make-up in the mirror again. There's lipstick on her front teeth. Her eyeshadow is two messy green smears. She dashes a blunt lipstick around her mouth, rubs off some eyeshadow, then, making exasperated dabs into her compact, replaces what she has just removed.

Pulling the people-carrier out of the bay into the middle of the broad street, Darshana bounces away from the Belvedere Aske School for Girls, each jolt a thunder-clap behind her eyes. She leaves behind the formerly-grand Victorian terraces which used to have trees and wrought iron railings, drives northwards beyond the brick streets of back-to-backs towards the city's leafiest suburb and the clean lines of St Ninian's.

Just on half past seven, the caretaker arrives on foot at the gate of Braithwaite Primary School. Some days he's the first on the premises. Most days he finds Joan Blake's Vauxhall Astra in the car park. She's what he calls a proper teacher: plaid skirts with broad pleats, shoes like the ones the police wear on the beat, blazers the kids can respect – a bit military. Her heavy, business-like glasses make her face square and strong, which he likes in a woman. He likes her hair: short, fair, side-parted. You wouldn't say she over-titivated herself. He's never yet seen lipstick on her. He likes that, too. His wife never dolled herself up.

The caretaker stands in the porch of the main building, rattling through keys, trying to keep his cigarette going. He has heard that his wife is running a B&B in Filey with her matron-of-honour. If he saw his wife today she'd probably have turned grey, like him. Peering over the wall into the car-park, he sees Joan has beaten him again.

In a prefab classroom on breezeblock stilts in the playground Joan is already on her third task, mounting geography work about different American states on red, white and blue card. Next, she staple-guns the work all over a Stars and Stripes flag on the rear wall. When the display is complete she stands back and surveys everything, and feels satisfied.

Beside her desk is a cardboard box containing twenty-five folders, each bearing the label *Maths Resources for Key Stage 2. J Blake, Facilitator.* Joan is the only Braithwaite teacher who instructs other teachers within the local authority in her curriculum area. Her courses are for teachers who have no mathematics background, and she makes them simple and enjoyable. As it's Friday, today's attendees will be hopeful of being let off a bit early, and Joan will oblige. She needs to swing by the Sri Ganesh Sweet Home tonight and pick up Darshana's order. Tomorrow morning will be too hectic: Darshana will inevitably heap further tasks on her.

Joan moves on to a final job, taking a pile of hand-outs from her briefcase. If you pass them round the group there's always someone who ends up without, so she heaves the box of folders onto her desk, lifts them out, and begins inserting a hand-out into each.

Today's work for her class is already prepared and laid out in neat, labelled piles on the front table. The top sheet is a print-out of detailed lesson plans and notes on particular pupils. *It should be straightforward,* Joan has written, *apart from the two Davids.* Supply teachers can be late, often not arriving until after Joan has left to teach her course. If they arrive early enough, she likes to chat through the work. If one arrives in the next few minutes, Joan will be able to explain further. About who to watch for. The things you can't really write down.

Take David Sned, who cries when he arrives, blue-kneed with cold, cries when he gets told off, cries when he wees his pants and has to be taken away by the support assistant. He cries like leaky plumbing. His eyes, his nose, the pores of his skin seep fluid. He wipes it away with filthy hands, smearing in the grime.

David Sned stinks. There is no washing machine at his house. There are no clean underpants in drawers. There is no mother. David gets his own tea, and is given breakfast at school with the other pupils who, like him, arrive straight from bed.

Joan's approach is to give him time out. When he gets over the worst crying, she fetches a special flannel from the sink-corner, washes his face, and sits him in the library-corner with a computer game. At playtime she keeps him in and gives him two chocolate biscuits and lets him do helping jobs around the classroom. Sometimes she ruffles his hair.

Joan is the type to chuck chins, pinch cheeks and get them smiling. She teaches them in such a gentle manner that they don't even know they're doing work.

Supply teachers were an item on the last staff meeting's agenda: how they make a right pig's ear of things and leave the kids as high as kites.

'But it's not really their fault,' Joan had said. 'Look at our kids.'

'Supply teachers can be peculiar,' a support assistant had thrown in.

'Grubby, with a personality disorder and a twitch,' someone had agreed.

'It must be a difficult job,' Joan had said. 'They need a bit of help.'

'They're laughing all the way to the bank,' someone else had scoffed. 'I'm not helping them.'

Beatrice and Howard's black Polo is stuck at a junction while a truck backs out of a yard. The original cobbles, scabbed-over with tarmac, poke through here and there like raw knuckles. The pavement is cluttered with refuse: over-ripe left-overs from yesterday's stalls; last night's bottles, cans and condoms; a carpet of shattered glass around the skeleton of a bus-shelter.

The pre-rush-hour traffic starts moving again slowly. At last Howard turns left onto Mandela Boulevard, a dual carriageway with a central smear of turf leading into a council estate.

'Oh, God. Look at those tower blocks.' Beatrice sounds panicky. 'Jeezus, look how many windows are boarded up.'

'*Chill*, Beatrice. Just pretend you're in the Third World doing good.'

The school at the end of the road is a Victorian edifice, high-windowed like a dour, strict chapel. A grey fungus of prefabs has sprung up in what used to be the playground.

'Shit,' says Beatrice.

'You don't know. It might be good today. I'll pick you up as soon as I can. My school's over by three.'

Beatrice gives her fringe a last ruffle in the vanity mirror. She sees age-lines beneath her eyes.

Howard pecks her cheek. 'Least you're early.'

'I hope they notice.' Beatrice slams out of the car and hurries towards the entrance through the rain.

'Welcome to Braithwaite Primary School.' Below the lettering and the sunflower logo, the message is repeated in two other languages, hand-painted, scrawly. Beatrice presses the bell and looks over her shoulder at the bleak council blocks and the terraces beyond sloping drearily down the hill. She's got to do this; one day a week is really the minimum, in order to pay her way.

A child in a thin anorak and no socks dawdles past the porch into which the rain is blustering. Beatrice's watch says seven forty-three. There are three cars. At least the caretaker should be about. Beatrice presses the bell again, waits, presses it a third time.

After some minutes the child reappears like a stray animal, coat hanging open limply, drenched after a second aimless circuit.

One of the door's glass panes is boarded up. Through the other, a man in overalls finally appears, carrying a mop and bucket. He drops his fag-end into the latter and presses the lock release.

'Morning Miss!' He walks off. A heavy-duty vacuum cleaner starts up somewhere.

Beatrice looks at her watch: seven forty-nine.

The foyer is damp and poky and smells of cleaning fluid. The reception office through the hatch is unlit, deserted. The foyer's wooden panelling is like in all the old schools, standing to the height of a seven year-old, thick with a century of paint layers, scarred with staples and sellotape rippings. Some display boards stacked against the wall show photos from a trip to Alton Towers. 'Arran and Kamaljit have fun on the slide'.

Seven hours from now Howard will whisk her away from this dump. As it's Friday they'll eat somewhere a little more special, have a pint of draught Guinness in a pub, go to the Arts Centre, escape into a movie. Escape.

The machine-noise stops. Beatrice hears a slow drip patting into the carpet, then women's voices at the end of a narrow passage. She walks down it like an intruder, her shoulder fluffing up notices layered on a pinboard along the length of the wall. *Darren Stobart, 5D: Darren must not be allowed to drink pop at school due to hyperactivity. Doctor's note. Please take it off him as he goes and gets his own.* A glossy poster headed with police and local authority logos dangles by a single corner: *Resisting Religious Extremism. A Conference for Key Stage 2 Practitioners.*

She comes to the room in which the women are talking. The door opposite is the staffroom. It has a key-pad for tapping in a code, like they have in prisons. Beatrice wishes she'd clumped along noisily in her boots. She clears her throat and knocks.

'...if he was ever here, that is.' The door starts to open. 'He won't have them done in time for next year, never mind next term.' Beatrice sees a woman in a navy fitted suit. Her skirt has been worn to a shine, the nylony fabric sticking in the niche between her buttocks. Her shoulder-length yellow hair looks waxy, fixed into a tight upward roll by an adhesive hair product.

'Hi,' says Beatrice. 'I'm rather early; I'm the...'

The woman turns. The hair-roll continues up the sides of her face like gutter pipes. 'I'll let you into the staffroom.' Before the door swings closed Beatrice glimpses a room the size of a stock-cupboard, two PCs on a table and a wall of messy box-files and papers.

The woman is stabbing out digits. 'Nineteen fifty-nine, the year the Head was born.' A chunky gold bracelet clacks against her watch. 'There.' She keeps a foot against the unlocked door to stop it swinging shut until Beatrice puts her hand on it, then turns to leave.

'Is there someone I need to see? I don't know who I'm covering for yet.'

'Ed sorts out supply. Haven't a clue who you'll be in for. There's a few off. Joan Blake's got a course today so it could be her. Year six?'

'The agency said year six, yes. But I'm used to it changing–'

'Well Joan'll be in soon,' the woman interrupts. 'If she isn't in already. Normally beats all of us.' She smiles thinly, her tone even but acid-edged. 'She'll be coming in to start you off I expect.' Her plasticky patent shoes are already tapping down the passage. 'Ed'll sort you out.' She disappears.

The staffroom is gloomy. Its clock says ten to three. Her watch says seven fifty-eight. She hears a computer whirr into life in the room opposite, then an outbreak of cackling. Otherwise the school still seems to be deserted.

There is a waft of illicit nicotine. When Beatrice used to smoke she was never hooked, but the smell of it this morning is seductive. She feels an almost painful wave of nostalgia for a former life. It smells like mornings in Maria's house. It smells like home.

'Lovely school, St Ninian's,' Chaz at the agency said. 'A bit out.'

Howard's street atlas is open and resting on the wheel. Commuters from the outlying villages are already slithering down the fells on shiny lanes like slug-trails onto the main northern trunk-road, making the incoming traffic heavy. But Chaz's instructions lead Howard in the opposite direction, a relatively traffic-free cruise out of the city to the north. Red-brick terraces soon give way to modern avenues, crescents and cul-de-sacs of semi-detached housing with front lawns and garages. Some houses have lost their pebbledash in patches like balding pets, but home-owners in this area are evidently unenthusiastic about spending hard-earned money attending to structural details. Cheaply-constructed porches lean onto side-doors, cluttered with folded baby buggies, tomato plants, piles of trainers.

Howard pulls up at a crossing in front of some 1960s flat-fronted, boxy shops: E & H Robertson's post office; Butler, Webb and Spence, insurance brokers; Sheena, Coiffeuse, then turns down a crescent where the houses are suddenly more elegant, shielded by tall hedges and cherry trees. At the end is a church with a steeple. Spotting the iron gate and signboard of St Ninian's Church of England Primary School he slows to a crawl, turns smoothly onto the drive.

St Ninian's is modern: all glass and pale yellow brick, set in a freshly-mown green space sprinkled with daisies and encircled by ancient trees that curtain off the private gardens of large detached houses. Before, this must have been a meadow that extended to the rise of charcoal-grey moorland in the middle-distance. Now the land is a playing field with a netball court at its farthest reach.

The car-park is already quite full. Howard parks close to the building's entrance next to a people-carrier and reaches onto the back seat for his briefcase. A bottle-green estate car pulls in alongside him with pedantic caution. Howard gets out of his car and sees, over a low fence, a dovecote; rabbit hutches; some chickens in a run; a shed with a weather-vane; a vegetable plot.

Meanwhile the coat-hanger shoulders of a man in a dog-collar are edging out of the estate car until a black cassock emerges in full, unfurling to the ground without a crease. 'Good morning, good morning.' The clergyman holds out a hand. 'Welcome to St Ninian's. Are you with us for the day?'

Howard lodges his briefcase under his arm and shakes hands, putting on his professional, congenial face. It would be easier if he could put on make-up along with his clothes, like a woman; paint on a certain look. Split off his teacher-self from his real self.

With the outstretched arms of an angel the clergyman herds Howard to the entrance door. Behind them the peripatetic harp teacher's Morris Traveller is trundling through the gate. Howard listens politely to the clergyman's monologue: it's inspection day today; he's taking assembly; he's here every Friday; the school dates back to 1895 on its original site which is in the old part of the suburb; actually they like to think of it as a separate village but unfortunately it got roped into the metropolitan district, hey ho.

St Ninian's' foyer has sofas and concealed lighting like a hotel. Howard pauses to look at an impressive display of Zulu masks in papier mâché. The vicar calls a greeting to the secretary as he passes through the foyer to the head-teacher's office.

The secretary appears at the hatch. She has a beautiful silvery crew cut and an elegant, tailored look – a touch of the androgyny to which Howard is attracted, though overlaid, in this woman's case, with a certain inhibited conservatism of style, perhaps appropriate to her workplace, or perhaps innate to her personality. Her ears are adorned with neat pearls rather than the kind of drop ear-rings that Beatrice chooses to draw attention to the sensuality of a neck that is free of long hair. A hand-painted silk scarf is pinned in place over her shoulder with an intricate Celtic cross brooch. The precision of her apparel makes her look buttoned-up. She has Blu-tacked a flowery bookmark with a prayer on it to the hatch's sliding window, in which is propped her name badge: Lilian Peck.

Howard delivers his charming smile.

The secretary is surprised. Supply teachers are not normally early.

Yesterday, the Head had made her phone the agency to get somebody despite her reminders about the last one they sent, an elderly woman who turned up covered in cat hairs with something spilled down her jumper. A child had had to be disciplined for saying she was smelly.

The inspectors will understand, the Head had said. Everybody understands about supply. The important thing was for the deputies to be off-timetable for the day.

The secretary holds out a pen. 'Would you mind signing in, please?' She watches as he signs his name. 'American?'

Howard smiles again. 'Yes ma'am.'

The secretary notices the cleft in his chin, the Cliff Richard type, clean-cut. 'The men's toilet is down the corridor on the right. You can leave your jacket there if you'd like to; it's quite secure. That door at the end is the staffroom. Do help yourself to the coffee. You're asked to put twenty-five pence in the jar.'

'Thank you,' says Howard.

The secretary holds out a pack labelled Visiting Teachers' Information. 'Here's a timetable and the rules about giving rewards and sanctions. I suppose you know we've got an inspection today?'

'Yes,' says Howard, thinking that Chaz probably did say something.

Just then a woman in a loud, satiny sari rushes into the office and starts banging about in a filing-cabinet, riffling papers. She is feminine in an overdone way: plump-waisted; could be forty, maybe younger.

The secretary turns, looking slightly perplexed, and lays a hand of restraint on the filing-cabinet. 'Mrs Chatterjee-Fox – this is Mr Vogel who's covering for you.'

The woman looks round, pushing cherry-coloured finger-nails into her hair, her temples sheened with sweat. A red spot edged in glitter is glued to her forehead and eye shadow is smeared as far as her eyebrows, glossy and uneven. Her smile is a grimace, her teeth lipsticky.

'I'm still sorting out my class's work.' Her voice is as round and clear as a kids' TV presenter, but nervy. She slams shut the file-drawer and rushes out again to be waylaid in the foyer by the vicar as he reappears, beaming, from the door marked *John Forrester-Paton. Head Teacher.*

'*Missus* Chatterjee-Fox,' cries the vicar happily. 'We're *so* much looking forward to tomorrow. We've never celebrated Holi before.' He throws his arms wide. Darshana steps back.

The secretary comes to the rescue through the hatch. 'The coffee's percolating, Vicar. Should be ready in a minute.'

'*So* looking forward to seeing Walter,' says the vicar less certainly, appraising Darshana with an astute pastoral eye. 'Hasn't been golfing for *months*.' He thinks a discreet conversation with Darshana's husband might be enlightening.

The secretary asks the vicar to accompany Mr Vogel to the staffroom. Successfully distracted, he leads Howard proprietorially away. Mrs Chatterjee-Fox shoots into her office and slams the door.

Meanwhile, a dishevelled woman is staggering through the main entrance under the weight of an enormous canvas-wrapped harp. The secretary rushes to help her.

Lilian always goes fluttery with the harp teacher. Clarissa reminds her of the brainy head girl of her old school, on whom she had a crush. This reached its zenith in their final year, in the school play, in which the head girl played Romeo to Lilian's Juliet. The head girl went on to Cambridge and became a bluestocking. Lilian never heard from her again.

The harp thuds onto the mat. 'Glory be.' Clarissa straightens up with a hand in the small of her back. 'Somebody's parked in my space next to the vicar. I should put out a traffic cone.' She pushes back some frizzy strands that have become disengaged from her nest-like, matted bun. Her corduroy skirt is triangular and cardboardy, her shoes flat with oval buckles like the shoes worn by old-fashioned dolls. Lilian registers a faint whiff of pipe tobacco. She would not be surprised if Clarissa had a penknife and a cloth handkerchief in her pocket, always ready to improvise, like a girl guide. Clarissa is the type with whom you could have jolly good times in a tent.

'I say, Lilian,' Clarissa looks the secretary nakedly up and down, 'you're looking stunning for the inspectors. Top marks to *you*!' She moves closer, lowering her voice, though not enough. 'Are they here yet?'

'Yes!' Lilian is undergoing a slow blush, prickling with half-remembered emotions.

Clarissa attempts to lower her voice further, but owing to too much amateur dramatics can only achieve a forceful stage-whisper: 'What about Darshana?'

'She's in.'

Clarissa's jaw drops. 'Heavens.' She grasps the secretary's hand between hers; stares, unblinking, into her eyes. 'Is the anniversary do still on?'

Lilian feels like Juliet. 'Oh gosh, are you invited? Me too!'

Clarissa's nostrils expand. 'Wouldn't miss it! Always a marvellous spread. She's like Madhur Jaffrey you know.' She squeezes the secretary's fingers.

Lilian fleetingly imagines drawing Clarissa's hands up to her lips. 'She looks awful.' She extricates her fingers and adjusts the drape of her scarf. 'Definitely hung over. Again.'

Chapter 3

Howard is soon comfortably ensconced in St Ninian's staffroom drinking percolated decaff from a china coffee cup and eating chocolate biscuits. Women in cardigans and flat sandals waft gently in and out. There's a smell of newness from the dralon upholstery and something synthetically floral, the kind of air freshener that plugs into the electricity. The curtains look like a Liberty print.

Beatrice would have a good day here. A few days in this kind of place and she'd be in a better head-space.

The vicar comes and settles himself into a chair with his cup and saucer. He begins reeling off statistics of various ethnic minorities within the school.

'I'm fascinated by your multicultural society here,' says Howard.

'Oh, gosh,' says the vicar. 'Well done.'

By a quarter to nine, the Braithwaite staffroom is full of sighing females in sweatshirts and leggings dragging around with mugs of tea.

Beatrice is being ignored, until the door is slammed open by a big red hand. A man in shirtsleeves hurries in with a pink Post-it on his fingertips. His shirt is pulled taut over his stomach and harnessed in by a low-slung belt. A broad tie featuring cartoon characters is flapped over to one side of his chest.

'Bee-tricks,' he reads. 'Has she not come yet?' He looks straight over her head.

'Yes,' says Beatrice.

'Ah! Are you the…'

'Yes.'

'Did you not sign in with Fatima? She says she hasn't seen you.'

'I think I was here before she arrived.'

'Keen,' the man guffaws into the room.

Various women respond with smiles, or by rolling their eyes to heaven, or raising a single eyebrow.

'Keen,' he shouts again, grinning.

A woman with dyed black hair is pushing into the staffroom with an armful of books and a bulging shoulder bag. 'Morning all. Thank God it's Friday.'

The burly man moves aside, making a show of looking at his watch. 'This isn't keen, is it, Terri?'

Terri, in skin-tight black trousers, has the snappable body of an anorexic teenager, her narrow face sun-bed orange and vertically creased with black points painted at her eye-corners like a child's idea of an Egyptian. The v-neck of her pink skinny-rib top shows a tiny cleavage.

'Bog off, Ed,' she says good-humouredly, looking down on him from sling-back stilettos. 'Some of us have got a life.'

A bell rings, abrasive as an alarm-clock. People are at different stages of drink-making: squeezing out teabags, rummaging in the dented wall of lockers below the window for jars of powdered milk or sachets of instant hot chocolate. The kitchen area is a jumbled mess of dirty mugs. A scribbled note Blu-tacked to the fridge door says, *'Your mother dosen't work here. Do your own washing up!!! Yours, Fatima.'*

No-one reacts to the bell. Beatrice scans the walls again for any kind of timetable. She wants to know whether lesson plans have been left for her. Her stomach is tight.

'Do us a favour, Ed,' Terri calls over. Ed is evidently senior management, but Terri is older and not the type to be managed. 'I need to make a couple of calls relating to Chelsea Parker. We've got the Grandma coming in after school today, haven't we Chantelle?'

An overweight girl, early twenties, in leggings and a man's shirt, turns from the grimy kitchen area and pulls a face. 'Nightmare.'

'Only, Social Services kept putting me on hold yesterday and they haven't even confirmed they'll be at the meeting,' says Terri. She lets the books and papers in her arms tumble onto the nearest chair.

'Anything for you, my darling.' Ed breathes raspily. His fat fingers are nicotined on the insides. 'What do you want: register doing?'

'Ta, love,' says Terri. 'I'll do one for you some time.' Somebody makes a lewd noise.

Terri pulls out a packet of cigarettes from her back-pocket and heads out of the staffroom clutching a sheaf of documents. 'I'll do my phoning in my car.' She waves the packet and grins. 'For discretion.'

Chantelle is swilling out mugs under the cold tap. 'Have I to bring you a coffee out, love?'

'Chantelle, you're a star,' Terri calls back. The door closes.

'Don't get her used to being waited on, yer daft cow,' says Ed.

'Am just putting off going down to me classroom to the very last minute. Am saving me nerves,' says Chantelle. 'Little buggers.'

She catches Beatrice looking at her. 'Year ones,' she explains.

At last a second bell causes a slow-motion movement of staff out of the door, laden with bags, half-full mugs and sheaves of worksheets.

Another male, overweight like Ed, but dressed for PE, has been reading *The Sun* in a chair. At the bell he carefully puts the paper under his arm and heaves himself up, striped football shirt at full stretch, jogging pants gripped in under his hanging belly. As he files out with the women, Ed stays him with a hand. 'Frank – pub?'

'I'm doing reports at lunchtime, Ed,' Frank apologises. 'Don't want to ruin me weekend with them.'

'Frank's our technology man,' Ed bellows across to Beatrice, grinning at Frank. 'And you thought he was Mr Fit, the PE specialist!'

'This is me sideline,' says Frank, picking up the whistle round his neck. He gestures rudely with it at Ed: 'Up yours, Fatman,' and disappears through the door.

A young woman in a mini-skirt and hooded sweatshirt says, 'I'll be down there, Ed,' making a drinking action with her hand as she leaves.

'Friday's pub-lunch day,' Ed says to Beatrice as the staffroom quietens off. 'Come down with us. They've got a good menu.' He grabs his coffee mug. 'Follow me. You need to sign in.'

Braithwaite's office is cluttered with photos of Fatima's sister's children. Fatima looks sixteen. She's wearing a tubular grey kameez tunic like a drain-pipe. Her nylon shawl trails over her shoulders, down her back, and then over the furniture as she walks past. One end seems to have got wet and been squeezed out.

'Please write your details here.' She passes the visitor's book through the hatch to Beatrice, and says 'please' again.

Ed has been drawn into an argument with a scrawny, haggard woman in washed-out jogging bottoms who was prowling in the foyer. Her hair is like cold spaghetti, scrunched into an elastic band on top of her head. The woman's toddler, strapped into a buggy in the doorway, is watching with big, yellow-rimmed eyes.

'I want the *money!*' the woman repeats. She is brandishing a small parka at Ed's chest. Its sleeves have been ripped off. 'This is *your* premises, where it 'appened. Our Paul's staying at 'ome till you've paid for 'im a new coat. Seventeen ninety-nine. Av got nowt else to send 'im in.'

A figure is struggling backwards through the swing-doors into the foyer with a huge cardboard box and briefcase. Outside, the squally shower has become steady rain.

'Ah, Mrs Blake! I think this is a matter for you.' Ed slaps his big hand flat onto the glass of the swing door before it collides with Joan's box. 'We've got a problem with Paul in your class. I wonder if you could talk to his mum about it.' He quickly turns into a corridor marked 'To The Hall', gesturing to Beatrice to follow.

Joan's head jerks round, her heavy glasses wobbling on her face. 'I'm sorry Mr Lumb, I'm just off to the Teaching Centre; I shouldn't even be here.' She goggles at Beatrice. 'Are you the supply? I've been waiting in my classroom to go through it all. I like to go through it all when I leave cover-work, make sure you know what's what.'

'Well I've been in the staffroom since…'

Paul's mother is short. She hates how everyone's eyes meet above her level. 'Am not going anywhere til 'av got some cash in me 'and,' she cuts in, 'and our Paul's not coming back to this bloody place till it's bloody well sorted.'

'Can you just bear with us for a minute, Mrs Ackroyd…' Ed's voice can be felt as a tremor underfoot.

'Griffiths,' snarls the mother.

'Ackroyd is Paul's dad's name,' explains Joan, hovering, her look flitting from Beatrice to Ed to the snarling mother and back to Beatrice – a look of magnified, unblinking curiosity.

Another bell goes. There's the hum of children pouring out of classrooms.

'I just need to take Miss, er… down to year six so she can take Mrs Blake's register and then I'll get straight back to you, Mrs Griffiths. Just bear with us please.' Ed spots something happening outside, throws back the swing door with one striding leg and leans out: *'Get back* in that classroom Miss Batty's class. *Back.* Oy you – get in there. You haven't been dismissed. Wait for your register.'

'I've taken my own register,' says Joan, helpfully, shifting crablike with her box to the small counter in front of the hatch.

'Great.' Ed moves quickly, grabbing the year six register from the top of the pile of stuff under Joan's chin. 'You'd better get off, Joan.' He flings the register through to Fatima and barks, 'Have you got Terri's register?'

'It's down in the classroom,' says Fatima, unwrapping a cough sweet.

'This place!' says the mother in the background.

Ed can hear the ominous racket of kids already pouring into the hall for assembly. He dabs at his sweating bald patch with his tie and becomes aware of his pulse in the bulging veins of his temples.

'Bee-tricks, could you do me a big favour?' he says. 'Just pop through this door, go into that first prefab on the left, and take Miss Batty's register for me, then bring them into the hall.'

'I've left it all written out,' Joan smiles at Beatrice from the swing doors. 'It should be a doddle. Just watch Rajid, and don't let the two Davids sit together. I've written down who to watch out for.' She pushes against the glass with a square shoulder. 'Just ask Tania and Shabnam if you want anything. Lovely girls.'

Ed, the back of his shirt showing the outline of his vest in perspiration, is disappearing round a door marked 'Deputy Head Teacher'. The child in the pram commences a strange, inhuman whine. Paul Ackroyd's mother darts to the buggy and gives the handles a rough shake. *'Shut it,* Delaney.'

Ed re-emerges almost instantly, throwing over his shoulder 'Cheers, Carole. I owe you one.' He finds Beatrice still loitering.

'Go *now*, will you?' he barks, then looks embarrassed. 'Look, just bring them into the hall, love, then you can go down to 6B's room and sort yourself out while they're in assembly.'

Beatrice leaves mutely, wondering how long the assembly will be. Ed is saying, 'Mrs Griffiths: *if* you'll take a seat, Carole Coulson, the Deputy Head, will be out to see you in a moment. Oh *Bee-tricks*,' he shouts after her, 'Get one of them to show you where 6B is. Get Ramesh.'

The scrawny mother is snorting at Ed, 'Not the Head, then?' Her child is screaming for attention. The last thing Beatrice sees is the woman in the cheap navy suit, Carole Coulson, emerging from the Deputy Head's office, hard-faced.

When the door opens, a flurry of wind messes up Beatrice's hair. As she steps out into the prefab village, the rain hits her full-on. She still has no idea how much time she will have for a frantic skim through Mrs Blake's teaching materials before all hell will finally be let loose.

Mrs Batty's prefab is rocking with the disturbance within its hardboard walls. Beatrice sets her eyebrows into the angle of a stern frown.

An American.

Joan Blake feels spooked. Slamming her car boot shut she notices the supply teacher standing by the prefab steps, evidently getting psyched up to go in. Catching the young woman's eye, Joan gives her a thumbs-up, grins, winks, and hesitates. She wishes she didn't have to hurry off. It feels like fate, an American appearing out of nowhere. Especially one who looks like that: as good as, if not better than, Gillian Anderson in the *X-Files*. Definitely what you would call attractive.

The rain has turned heavy. Joan comes off the ring-road at the new church which holds discos with light-shows to evangelise the youth. It used to be a scouring mill. At night its neon cross flashes out across the bowl of the city.

Two women teachers, also heading for the Teaching Centre, are in the car directly behind Joan's. They have each applied fifteen minutes' worth of make-up for the occasion. They are discussing their divorces and miss the exit. Eventually they realise that they have driven too far.

'It's a sign,' says the one in the passenger seat, checking her lipstick.

'That we don't really want to be there,' says the driver, flurrying through the street plan.

'You never know; there might be some nice men.'

The driver laughs cynically, though by no means gives up hoping. 'I'm only doing this because my kids' school fees have gone up. Why would anyone do it, other than to get the increment?'

'Oh, totally,' says the passenger. 'I detest Maths, but you have to put your family first.'

Joan turns her Astra into a cobbled street with a vandalized graveyard featuring a leaning obelisk and a broken angel. Next door is Leadbetter Lane Teaching Centre. The words Board School and the date 1899 are engraved in the gable, and Boys and Girls above two bricked-up doors. The back-to-backs opposite are derelict. The pavement is smattered with broken glass, excrement and weeds. Behind the Teaching Centre are the arching steel poles of a new hypermarket with a purple wavy roof like a designer toaster.

Joan pulls into a space in the former playground, a long walk from the entrance, all the closer ones being occupied. The turn-out looks good. She is later than she wanted to be. The first session will begin at nine. The workshops later in the day are optional, but Session One is compulsory: *Using G-Tec Maths at KS2*. A repeat of the session she led in Manchester.

An intensely freckled woman in a Punjabi suit waves Joan over, holding out a cup of tea.

'You're alright for a few minutes yet,' says Melanie, as Joan crashes her rain-spattered box and briefcase onto a trestle table. 'We're expecting a couple more. There's time to get yourself sorted.'

Joan takes the teacup, fishing a very small comb from her blazer and slicking her wet fringe towards one ear.

There is a hum of voices. Around two dozen women and three men are clustered according to who previously worked together in the same school; who teacher-trained together; whose children are attending the Grammar School. Training days are good for catching up: who's leaving, who's new, who's had a breakdown.

'Morning, Bob,' says Joan.

Bob is tieless, dressed down for a non-teaching day. The top two buttons of his shirt are undone. His casual trousers, rubbed into small baubles round the groin, hang to an inch or two above his slip-ons.

'Thought you weren't coming and we could all go home,' he chortles. Teaching suits him down to the ground: weekends free to muck about in his shed; the same holidays as his lady-friend, who also teaches, as did his ex-wife before her. He often reflects on his good fortune at having a vocation in this line of work.

'I feel like I've already done a full day's work,' says Joan.

The whole room pauses to eavesdrop on the facilitator's conversation.

'I was in my classroom by half past seven,' Joan is saying, 'Setting up for the supply.'

Private responses to this are murmured within the groups. Those who also went to their schools before coming to the Teachers' Centre declare it. Others defend themselves:

'...three children to get up and out,' one woman huffs. 'Has Joan Blake got kids?'

'...unloaded and reloaded the dishwasher and made the beds,' says another.

'No doubt Joan Blake has one of those husbands who helps,' sniffs someone else.

Joan smacks the stack of folders onto the table. People are drifting into the seats, leaving the front row empty as a guard against being asked questions.

'She's good, apparently. Doesn't make you feel daft.'

'I've heard she makes it really simple.'

Joan is doing something technical down at the front with a projector connected to a laptop.

'Must be nice if teaching's your life,' someone murmurs.

'Personally I don't have the time to be careerist,' another woman responds, snidely. 'I couldn't go off running courses on top of my kids and everything, even if I wanted to. Which of course I don't.'

At a quarter past nine the two late-comers bluster in, shaking off their brollies, removing their macs to reveal very short suits. Within moments they have clocked the three male attendees, and feel disappointed.

Melanie ticks them off her list then calls out, 'Could we all...?'

People shift round in their seats to face the front, place their cups and saucers on the floor next to their handbags, search for pens.

From seats on the back row the two late-comers appraise Joan Blake: the skirt that doesn't match the blazer; old-fashioned honey tights; how she stands – feet turned outwards, looking planted; shoes that are not 'skirt shoes'; big, square glasses that emphasise her jaw.

'Work's everything for some people, isn't it?' whispers one.

'Some people are just not bothered about relationships,' nods her friend. 'Once they've got married and settled down.'

'Not full-blown ones,' the first woman agrees. 'The kind that comes first, before your job.'

Joan checks her watch. Ordinarily she would be starting literacy with her class. The kids will notice the supply teacher's accent. On Monday she can use circle-time to talk about America again.

She starts off her talk informally. For anyone who she hasn't met before, she is Joan Blake. As they can all read from the programme, she works at Braithwaite; she's been there eleven years; she's been the area Key Stage 2 Maths Co-ordinator for three years and since last May has been working on this G-Tech project as an advisor-stroke-trainer.

A mobile fanfares tinnily. 'Oh!' Joan reaches into her blazer. 'Forgot to switch it off. 'Scuse me.' She takes a couple of steps backwards, scrutinizing the caller I.D. and, not recognising it, turns towards the window to take the call.

'Mrs Blake? I'm your daughter's pastoral year-head, Monica Smith.'

Chapter 4

'I've got your note here, Mrs Blake.' Monica Smith says *Bleyk*; a more refined pronunciation than Joan gets at school.

'Oh yes.' Joan's response is cautious.

'Caroline tells us she feels unwell again with the symptoms you describe: headache, faintness; bit dizzy. Isn't that right Caroline?'

There is a whimper in the background.

'Obviously you're in school at the moment,' the pastoral year-head is saying, 'but we were wondering if there would be any possibility of Caroline being picked up at some stage?'

Joan checks her watch. Nine twenty. She addresses her own reflected face. 'Actually Mrs Smith, I'm in the middle of leading a G-Tech training session at the Teachers' Centre. There's no way I could come and collect her until lunchtime. You'd better try my husband.'

'Caroline says he's a policeman and he's at work.'

'He's on earlies. He might be able to come sooner than me. I'll give you his number.'

Bored teachers watch Joan slip a hand into her inside breast pocket like a man reaching for his wallet, slide out a small book, fiddle to open it with one hand, and thumb through a few pages. Clearly she isn't the flappable type. She reads out a number in a low voice, still half turned away to signify that the call is a private matter, but the conversation has been audible enough to know that it's a domestic difficulty.

'Look, if you get no joy with her dad can you get back to me after twelve-thirty and I'll come over in my lunch-break and drop her off at home.'

'I'll be teaching shortly, of course,' answers Monica. 'She's going to have to remain in sick-bay on her own.' Monica's voice goes distant. 'Will that be alright Caroline? We'll get admin to keep looking in.'

'Sorry, but I need to get off,' says Joan. 'Thanks very much indeed Mrs Smith, thanks a lot, thank you.' Joan switches off her mobile, slips it with her address book into her pocket and turns round. 'Sorry, folks. Didn't know I'd left that on. I'd like to get on please, if I may.'

The teachers sigh collectively, deflating further into their seats. At least, going by the aroma already drifting into the hall, the coffee at break time will be real, not instant.

Melanie is tiptoeing about at the back, positioning biscuits. Rain is seeping into the building, dripping audibly onto the upper side of new ceiling tiles, which are beginning to show stains. Across the street the rain filters through the collapsing roofs of boarded-up houses, sopping into blankets shaped into cocoons by the homeless. A small, wet cat mews in a doorway.

At lunchtime Joan heads straight for the exit.

'I'll save you a couple of samosas,' calls Melanie.

Joan gives her a thumbs up from the door – 'Meat ones please,' – then steps out into torrential rain.

Twenty minutes later Joan's Astra is in the picking-up area outside Belvedere Aske. Caroline, grey and quivery, has crawled onto the back seat. She is a bundle of sticks. Her gangly legs trail into the bottom of the car like a rag doll. The pleats of her too-short uniform are splayed like a paper fan over the goose-pimpled skin of her thighs.

Joan starts the indicator ticking. 'Wave at Mrs Smith, Caroline. I need to pull away so that she doesn't think anything's up, but I'm stopping again round the corner. I want to have this out.'

Caroline's skin is draped over her face-bones like uncooked pastry. Every day, new spots appear, bubbling and popping like a pan of porridge. She doesn't wave.

Joan pulls out of the lay-by, takes an arbitrary left at the junction and, after a further minute of ominously silent driving, parks behind an open van outside the Sri Ganesh Sweet Home.

A whistling young man is whisking a tray out of the back. Linen tea towels shroud the tray's contents. Standing in the shop doorway is an elderly man in a Nehru cap, a long, starched white shirt and billowing trousers. He gestures for the young man to hurry.

'Not here,' wails Caroline. 'There's loads of people...' She slides down into her mess of hair, pulling the travel rug over her head.

Joan stares into the back of the van. Pink sweets, yellow sweets, white sweets, segregated on trays. 'Why did you go to Darshana's last night?'

'I didn't feel well.'

'For goodness' sake, I'd only popped out to Asda. Your dad was only at the Cricket Club. What was the problem with giving one of us a ring?'

Caroline sees her mother's hands clenching and unclenching on the wheel. *I'll be over in just a few minutes, sweetheart,* Darshana had said. *We'll give you some aspirin. Soon have you tucked up.*

'There's nothing to do at home,' she whines.

'There's your revision to do, then bed, on weekdays, young lady. You've got your telly.'

'I do revision better with Baldev. We get loads done.'

'You were only there on Sunday,' Joan snaps.

'Why can't I do what I want?'

'I don't want you going there all the time.'

'Aunty Darsh doesn't mind. Neither do Baldev and Luke. We have a laugh. It's only you who's got a problem.'

'Aunty Darshana should never have given you that note. She signed it in my name.'

Caroline scowls at the back of her mother's head. 'You shouldn't let your fall-outs affect my friendships.'

Joan recognises the comment as one of Colin's, repeated verbatim. She hits out at the indicator. The wipers go onto top speed. 'Your Aunty Darsh and I don't... haven't got the things in common that we used to, that's all.'

'See. It's because you've fallen out.' Caroline is perked up for a moment by her sense of righteousness. 'If you deprive me of access to my second home I'll have to go and live there full-time.'

'Don't talk silly, Caroline.'

'It's true. The spare room has been made into my room.'

Luke has the biggest room because of his Hornby train set. Baldev has the smallest room because, for absolute contentment, he only requires space for his bed, his workstation and his pile of stinky socks. 'Happy as a pig in muck,' says Aunty Darshana, grinning. She sometimes picks up his dirty sports kit and just looks at it, as if it is cute baby booties.

Whenever you just want to get away, says Aunty Darsh. *Any time. You know that, don't you?* And, *this is your home too, you know, Caroline love.*

There are always waffles in the freezer, and in the spare room there's now a pink and white striped bathrobe from Laura Ashley.

That's for you, love, Aunty Darsh said last night. *I saw it and couldn't resist it.*

Joan grips the wheel in a strangle-hold. 'You've got your lovely room at home. We've done it out so nicely. Just what you wanted. There's your Ikea bed.'

Caroline's face is cold rice pudding. She feels nauseous. She feels faint. She didn't sleep last night. This morning she couldn't eat the rabbit-food muesli they eat at Aunty Darsh's house. Baldev and Luke chomped it down. Disgusting. Caroline went into the cupboards and found Darshana's diet crisp-bread instead. She put low fat marge on it. She put yoghurt on it. She pressed some currants onto it. Then she felt sick and put it in the bin.

Big tears begin spreading messily from the corners of her eyes. Her hair glues itself to her oaty cheeks and forehead. Her cheeks fold in on themselves, her shoulders curl, and she draws in her twig limbs like a fledgling. The engine noise is joined by another kind of hum. 'You don't want me, anyway,' she blubbers.

'This is late nights, this is,' bluffs Joan, trying to maintain a practical tone. Her daughter's emotional life is becoming ever more complicated and unmanageable. Joan is more comfortable dealing with little children. Especially other people's. 'This is staying up all night at Darshana's, mucking about with the boys.'

Caroline's phlegmy sobs gain force.

'This is GCSEs coming up.' Joan's tone wavers slightly. 'It's stress.'

'No issnot,' Caroline shudders out.

'You need a good night's sleep.'

'No ado-on't.'

'You need proper eating, not picking.' Joan's voice is louder than necessary, overly cheery. 'I could take you straight to Doctor Steed's. You might be a bit anaemic.'

'I need to go to Weatherhope.' Caroline's voice crackles with self-pity.

'Don't be awkward on purpose.'

'But I've left my stuff there,' she sobs.

'What stuff? Stuff you need for school?'

'Deodorant and stuff. My nightie.'

'I thought you meant *important* stuff.' Exasperated, Joan finally pulls out from behind the sweet van without looking properly. A Fiesta swerves round the Astra beeping its horn and a hugely fat skinhead leans out, thrusting his middle finger.

'Well that's all I need, that is,' Joan shouts. 'I've got a workshop to lead in twenty-five minutes, in this state.' She pulls round to the right, away from the ring-road, to an area where derelict shops with grilles over the windows stand in long lines like prison barracks.

Caroline has pulled the rug over her face again. Her voice comes out muffled. 'Alright then. Home.'

'Good.' Joan sets off northwards. 'I'll only be able to drop you off. Will you be alright?'

Caroline's wordless sobs jolt over the speed bumps. Eventually the crying assuages, and at last she pulls the travel rug off her head. Hair clings statically all over her face. She looks scrawny and savage, like an abandoned mongrel. 'But Dad's there with his Light Railway committee this afternoon,' she moans.

'You said you don't like it when there's no-one home,' Joan reminds her in a slowed-down voice.

'That was last night. It's alright otherwise.'

'You're being inconsistent now, Caroline.' Joan indicates right. Passing the mosque she turns onto the main road that carries commuters in from the north.

The Astra climbs steeply out of the city. Down below, the beck bleeds along a slime-coated channel between the walls of mills, frothing like a poisoned cauldron at the point where it descends into an underground tunnel. The former landfill site on the valley-bottom is nowadays covered by the vast hangar of a superstore, its roof the metallic blue of cleaning fluid. Up ahead, the skyline is scruffy with fifties tower blocks, communications masts and blackened churches.

After some minutes the pylon-straddled moor top comes into view, scattered with farms whose inhabitants probably have a reasonably scenic view from north-facing windows.

Joan's Astra passes rib after rib of cobbled streets, then a more modern semi-detached estate, at last reaching the detached housing along the upper valley. The houses are separated from each other by passages wide enough for bicycles to pass through. Each has a double-garage plus space for a third car on the drive. Unfortunately the recently-planted fast-growing trees provide an as-yet scanty shield from the twenty-four hour buzz of factories that have set up down below in the former woollen mills. On the plus side, living to the north of the city has had the advantage of allowing Joan and Darshana and the kids to make an easy escape most weekends.

Joan pulls up in front of the gate. She's been happy enough on this estate. She feels nostalgic for the sunshine on the patio before they built the shed that blocks it out, and the original green of the garage doors, although they do look rather classy in white.

'You've got your keys?'

Caroline scrabbles in her bag and finds them.

'I'll give you a ring in the afternoon break, make sure you're alright,' says Joan. 'Alright?'

Her daughter's face is closed-in, sullen.

Joan gets out of the car and opens the back door. 'What you need is proper meals.'

Caroline unfolds herself from the car and snatches her bag from the back, shoving into it her sensible school lace-ups and stray bits and pieces.

'Will you go to bed?'

'Dunno.'

Joan reaches over the gap between them and ruffles Caroline's bird's-nest. 'What you need is two paracetamol.'

Caroline shivers.

'I worry about you, you know.' Joan gazes over the roof of the house to where thick cloud is descending like a skullcap onto the moor top. 'I'm your Mum.'

'Tuh.' Caroline flings open the garden gate. 'Aunty Darsh says you never even wanted any kids.' Wobbling on her platforms, she clops off down the path.

Joan throws herself into the car, slamming the door furiously. She grabs her phone from her pocket to have it out right now; to disrupt Darshana's working day with some violent verbal pummelling. First she closes her eyes, taking deep, calming breaths.

She puts her phone away again, and leans down to the hollow in front of the hand-brake where litter collects, trapping a piece of card between her fingers. She brings it up to her lap. Caroline's school photo, aged fourteen. Joan picks at the flat circle of Blutack on the back with her nails until it is a small knob and positions the photo back on the dashboard.

She heads back into the city, her stomach turning over with hunger. She should have brought the samosas with her. That last session didn't elicit the round of applause she'd had in Manchester, but then some of the Manchester audience had travelled from Liverpool and north Wales. It was more of a conference. The Manchester crowd had often raised their hands, wanting further information, clarification. There had been discussion at the end. People had shaken Joan's hand as they left.

This morning they were only locals. Inevitably it was more informal. Not *over*-informal; people said the balance was right. Said they'd managed to get their heads round it. Said they'd be able to use the lesson-plans. But they didn't ask any questions.

Her eye wanders back to Caroline's photo. Two years ago her chin was pink and chubby. Darshana had just taken her for her first demi-wave.

Joan blinks hard and sniffs, and fumbles out a Mint Imperial.

Back at Leadbetter Lane the two women in suits have opted for Joan's afternoon session, 'Differentiation', and are already seated in the designated room looking at something in one of their handbags, happily aware that it isn't very long now until three o'clock. They will arrive home one or maybe two hours earlier than they would on a normal teaching day.

'Uff.' Joan collapses into a low chair, her skirt taut across her splayed knees, feet turned outwards. She holds a paper plate close under her chin. 'Hope you don't mind me eating, I just got back.' She bites into a second samosa. On the plate is an onion bhaji, a pile of yellow rice with red and green bits, a sausage roll and a plastic fork.

'It's been ever such a good buffet,' says a woman in a fisherman's smock with bulging pockets.

'How's your daughter?' calls one of the suited women.

'Oh, she's at that age,' Joan wuffles. Flakes of pastry drop into her lap. She puts down her plate for a moment to flick through a file. 'You can be looking at these.' She passes a pile of hand-outs to the nearest person.

A few minutes later Joan claps crumbs off her hands. 'Right, folks.' The workshop should have started eight minutes ago but luckily the whole programme is running late. Her optional session has attracted nine people, nearly a third of the day's participants. They know it will be relaxed and not too boring, and she won't make anyone feel stupid.

As she gets to her feet, her mobile, switched on at twelve-thirty to deal with Caroline, starts fanfaring.

'Damn. Forgot to switch it off again. Sorry folks. Talk amongst yourselves!' She reaches into her blazer pocket and steps out of the room. 'Hello?'

'Joan – '

'Darshana.' Joan jabs her toe at an ancient clump of chewing-gum. The impact wrenches the gum from the floorboard. It spins away.

'I've been trying to get hold of you for days.'

Joan's teeth are gritted. 'I've told you not to call me. We're not... it's not how it was any more. You know that.'

In the main hall, the two women clearing paper plates into a bin-liner look over.

Joan swings round to face the internal window and finds her group looking out at her.

'I know, I know.' Darshana's attempt to sound soothing comes out as a manic trill. 'I don't have a problem with that at all, Joan. Moving on and all that. A new stage of life. No problem whatsoever. All I want is the odd chat, for heavens' sake.'

'Not *now*,' snarls Joan, then collects herself, lowering her voice. 'I'm leading a day-course. You know I'm leading a day-course.'

'I wouldn't phone now if it were just anything. This is about Caroline.'

Joan's voice is serrated. 'I'm phoning you tonight about that.'

Darshana tuts in a girly way. 'There's no need to be...'

'Don't push it.' Joan stabs 'off,' squashing the button beneath both thumbs until the green light peters out.

The women in suits notice Joan's clenched face through the glass.

'Maybe she *does* have a relationship,' muses one. 'A proper one.'

Chapter 5

'Excellent school, St Ninian's,' is Howard's cheerful verdict, as Beatrice gets into the car. 'Great parental support. Lots of slips in the register telling you little messages phoned in by Mom.'

She slams the door hard. 'You always get the easy schools.'

'It's partly what you make of it.' He reverses out of the parking space, watchful for children.

Beatrice glowers. 'Apart from Shabnam and Tania, none of my kids today could write.'

'You're so much better than me at picking up the names.'

'Don't try to be encouraging.' Beatrice slumps in her seat to be less noticeable to a group of seaweed-haired boys hitting each other with their bags. 'I can't just enjoy the kids, like you do.'

'You like kids, really,' says Howard.

'I don't.' She shudders. 'Plus the teachers were hard as nails.'

'I don't think you're very fair.' Howard pulls out of the school gates and ups the speed of the wipers. 'They're realists, that's all. Schools like that, the best you can do for the kids is give them somewhere safe and warm to spend their day.'

The road out of the estate passes between high-rises, their run-down entrances hoovering up children.

'You wouldn't want this for your own kids,' says Beatrice.

'I wouldn't raise my kids in a place that has *weather* like this,' says Howard, 'let alone schools.' He accelerates. 'Hey. It's Friday. C'mon, let's drive to the top of the moor and look over the other side. Yorkshire's meant to be beautiful if you head north.'

It takes twenty-five minutes to escape from the city. The road dwindles until they end up on a narrow lane, an urban finger poking into rough, untamed terrain. Terraced cottages line the roadsides here like primitive fortifications, doorknobs threatening to clip the wing mirrors of passing vehicles. The last of the city finally twists out of sight behind the small, rough mountains of a former quarry that's gone back to wilderness.

Howard's car is trapped behind a school bus. The lane turns sharply and a smoggy view of the next valley appears. The moors open out all around, scrubby and unshaven-looking under a sallow sky. A sign announces Weatherhope. Howard pulls into a viewing point with park benches and a litter bin.

'Is this it?' asks Beatrice.

The village below has the unplanned shape of pots piled in a sink. A boxy red-brick mini-market has been plonked at the village's centre, and the floodlights of a petrol station's forecourt tower above everything.

Beatrice heaves a lugubrious sigh. 'The only nice thing about today was Mrs Blake.'

'Who?'

'The woman I covered for. She winked at me. As she was leaving. She gave me a great big wink.'

'She your type?'

Beatrice swipes at him half-heartedly. 'I'm just saying she was nice.'

Down at the foot of the hill the school bus is spilling out high-school kids, their ties loosened, talking and laughing. They let their coats flap open, inured to the climate. Some are just in their shirts and pullovers, or only a shirt, as though the local gene pool has predisposed them to immunity from the ravages of northern weather. As they filter off down paths and ginnels the first commuters are already drawing up, hurrying to their doorsteps in the driving rain.

'Let's go back,' says Howard.

Hailstones are sticking in Joan's hair and filling her cardboard box. It takes a lot of fumbling to get the car door open and sling the box and briefcase onto the back seat. The Astra gets going on the fourth try. She turns out of the gate into Leadbetter Lane, the last to leave the Teachers' Centre, and eventually pulls up outside the Sri Ganesh Sweet Home. Again. The son of the business is sent to help her load up the car with boxes of food, which are variously still warm or undergoing a slow absorption of aromatic grease into the cardboard. Finally Joan goes back into the shop and writes a cheque for Darshana's plentiful order. Her contribution. She has always been generous like that. Darshana takes it for granted these days.

It is dark when she finally gets home. She kicks the back door shut behind her and drops her box of training materials on the kitchen floor. 'Colin? Are you in?'

Colin comes ambling down the hall, still in his blue police shirt, his police tie loosened. 'T.G.I.F.' he says, contentedly.

'Huh?'

'Thank God It's Friday.'

Joan is energetically pulling off her lace-ups. 'How's our Caroline?'

'She was watching telly when I got home. She said she'd had to be brought home. She said she'd eaten some garlic bread.'

'We've got to make sure she eats, Colin. We should get in some Marks and Spencer's ready-meals.'

'She was blooming well eating my toffees when I came in.'

'So she hasn't been going faint again?'

'Not since I got home from work.'

Joan strides into the hall, yanking off her blazer, and calls up the stairs – 'Caroline?'

Colin comes and hovers in the hall doorway. 'She's at Darshana's.'

'What!'

Colin listens to the ensuing rant with a kind of obedient patience. He agrees about Darshana's drinking. He first noticed it two Christmases ago. It seems to have come on much more since then. All he knows is, Darshana has always been very good with Caroline. After all, Joan was never quite the mothering type. It's a shame that they've had this fall-out.

Joan slams into the kitchen where she dashes two heaped spoons of instant coffee into her favourite cup, flings more dried food into the bowl of Wesley the dachshund, who is tottering about amiably, wagging his tail, and eventually finds her way to her armchair opposite Colin's.

'It's the boys,' Colin continues reasonably. 'She goes to mess about with the lads. She's got her room there.'

'She's supposed to live here, not at Darshana's. I'm going to have to go over there first thing, bring her back here to get ready for the do, then drive her back. It's flipping ridiculous.'

'You'd be doing that anyway. Going in the morning. Darsh will want you to shift furniture.'

'And Darshana spends money on her. I'm not happy.'

'I don't know what your problem is, Joan. Let Caroline do what she wants.'

'…I'm not happy at all. *I'm* her Mum. She wouldn't even get a new pair of knickers if it was left to you.'

Colin looks hurt. 'It's not my place to see to her in that way. I'm her Dad. And let's face it, you were always perfectly happy to let Darshana see to all those girl's things until quite recently.'

Joan sighs, goes quiet for a moment. 'Thing is,' she leans down to fondle Wesley's ears, 'I'm not going to be seeing much of Darshana any more. Once we've got tomorrow's blinking party out of the way that I'm supposed to be doing everything for as usual.' She grimaces. 'It's not like it was. We've got other friends...' Her tone becomes determined again. 'So I don't want her put out.'

'Well Darshana's never complained to me. I don't think she sees a problem. She's very fond of our Caroline.'

'She's got her own kids.'

'I really don't see the problem,' Colin repeats mildly.

'You're blinking hopeless.'

Colin's TV-shaped glasses wobble. 'Don't start calling people hopeless. If we're talking about who's a good parent, *you* can't call anybody hopeless.'

'Shut up.'

In view of Beatrice's lack of earnings this week, she and Howard decide to go for a cheap meal after all. Some time after six they hurry under an umbrella from their bedsit in Henry Place to the Nawaz Curry House on Henry Rise, which is primarily a take-away but has a small seating area.

Nawaz likes his American customers; he has a brother in Detroit. 'Shocking weather,' he greets them, pleasantly. The seating area is functional: four square tables in a two-by-two formation. After the pubs close, when groups of loud white males pour into the streets, the place will fill up with buzz-cuts and tattoos. For now, it is quiet. Outside, an aimless gang of boys passes by now and again, roaming about as one animal.

Howard is soon sliding his finger down the menu leaflet. Beatrice, in her usual seat opposite the window, gazes out at the street. An obese girl walks past pushing a baby-buggy from which two sausage-legs dangle.

'Why the shudder?' says Howard.

'Look.'

Despite the weather the girl is wearing a pink sun-top, her breasts bulging sideways out of stained armholes. As her heels slap through a puddle something drops onto the wet pavement. She picks it up, a knitted hat, and reaches into the buggy, her trousers straining over the lumpen flesh bubbled along her knicker-line.

'Photo op,' says Howard.

'Don't,' Beatrice snaps.

Howard sighs. 'This town just doesn't do it for you, does it.'

Nawaz worked in an up-market Kashmiri restaurant in Fulham in his younger days. Now he pours bottled beer into Howard's glass, slips complimentary poppadum and pickles onto the table, says 'thankyouverymuch,' and retreats. He would like to emigrate; go to work with his brother.

'You're so good at separating out your career ambitions from everything else,' says Beatrice. 'You're not affected by where you live, or dumb jobs you have to take just to get money.'

'Can't we at least stick it out here till the summer?' Howard reaches for a poppadum. 'Let's be honest. If you weren't over here you'd only be smoking pot with Maria; hanging out.'

'I'd be back in my studio,' says Beatrice defensively.

'Precisely. You head straight back to her beat-up old place every time.'

'Maria's is home. I'd be able to be creative again.'

Howard leans forward. 'Beatrice, the whole point of being here is to be creative. That life – Maria's – it's just messing about with 'art' photography, which is okay for a hobby but it'll never make real money.'

'I sell my cards. I get by.'

'I'm the one who sells your real work.' Howard crushes his poppadum. It scatters on the greasy plastic table cloth. 'The travel stuff. The journalistic stuff.' He takes a piece and crunches on it. 'Think about it. Every single time you've submitted your photographs in support of my articles, they've been taken. I facilitate your main income.'

'Teaching's my main income.'

'I mean income from creativity.'

'I make enough money back home to exist at Maria's level.'

Howard throws out a laugh. 'Yeah, right. Along with those assorted drop-outs, refugees and losers.' He spoons mango chutney onto his side-plate. 'Anyway, I facilitate your teaching income, too. You leave it to me to set up these trips.'

'Sure I do.' Beatrice picks at the corner of her paper serviette. 'You love it. Organising.'

'What gets me is, you never actively *decide*. You never say – "let's go abroad again, Howard".' He shakes a blob of brinjal pickle from his spoon, his eyes never leaving her. 'But when I finally call you and tell you what I've set up, you agree to come along. So why *is* that, Beatrice, if everything's so cool at Maria's?'

Beatrice grins without humour. 'This joint's laid out like a classroom. Had you noticed?'

Howard reaches over for Beatrice's hand. 'We're good together.' He bobs his head into the line of her gaze.

'Your cuffs are so white, Howard, even though it's the end of a working day. That's so you. You're *so...*'

Howard swings back on his chair; takes a gulp of beer. 'I'm going for the tandoori chicken. You need to decide.'

Through the beaded curtain something lands in hot oil and sizzles.

'You decide.' Beatrice pushes her menu across the table at him. 'Like you said, I'm hopeless at deciding.'

'Friday night telly's gone really crap,' says Baldev. On *Eastenders* a school-girl is in a clinch with a middle-aged man under a bridge.

'She wouldn't,' comments Caroline. 'Not with an old, bald guy like that.' She stirs her leg, as though just to get comfortable, against Baldev's. The chicken skin of her thigh sparks on the fabric of his school trousers.

Baldev's leg twitches but he carries on staring at the TV. 'Do you realise my Mum must've started shagging my Dad when he was a fifty-three year-old man?' He screws up his face. 'It's like under-age sex, only over-age. It should be a crime.'

Caroline's hand creeps onto his thigh. 'That means Uncle Walter's – *seventy-one*. That *is* pretty gross, having a seventy-one year-old dad.'

'It's even worse for Luke.'

The bedroom door is thrown open. 'I heard you!' Luke stands legs apart in his muddy primary-school games kit, a football held above his head. 'What you saying about me?' He threatens to bring the ball down hard.

'Just saying you're a scrawny runt, so bog off.'

Caroline is giggling. 'Utterly *gross*.'

'What's utterly gross?' The football is quivering.

'We're just saying, Dad adopted you when he was an ancient sixty year-old man, which is why you're a weird little runt,' says Baldev.

'Bleargh.' Luke pretend-vomits all over them and heads off, slamming the door.

A voice comes up the stairs. 'Are you two revising?'

'They're snogging,' shouts Luke.

'We're doing our work,' Baldev bellows, nipping over to the door and quietly sliding the bolt.

'Don't torment them, Luke; not when they're working, love,' Darshana calls distantly.

'You shouldn't tease people about being adopted, though,' says Caroline to Baldev.

Baldev collapses back onto the bed beside her. 'Shouldn't be allowed, when you're ancient.'

On *Eastenders*, Chrissie flings a large glass of white wine across the bar into a man's face.

Behind the counter Nawaz selects a Richard Claydermann CD for his American guests and slots it into a chunky plastic machine. The 'play' button crunches. A piano lilts out a familiar theme from a washing powder advert.

Howard tips the last of the rice, the kind with raisins cooked into it, onto his plate. 'This place reminds me of that joint in Bangalore. Where I proposed and you said no.'

Two greasy fan-heaters fixed to the wall are vibrating like tin cans. Beyond is street noise, dogs and sirens and kerb-crawling vehicles.

'The tacky wallpaper helps.' Beatrice picks off a morsel of her hardly-touched naan bread. 'Though it didn't have this wonderful view.'

A bedraggled dog on the pavement is urinating against the plate glass by Howard's leg.

'Long time ago.'

'Seven years.'

'Tuh. I guess I thought it would be fun to go home with exotic wedding photos.'

'It was a bizarre time for you to propose, when you'd just had that run of 'encounters' in Mumbai.'

Irritation flickers on Howard's face. 'With guys it's not a relationship. It's a mere moment in time.' His eyes rove over his half-eaten dishes. 'I don't wanna *move in* with them.'

'That's a dig at me and Maria, right?'

'Not at all. I'm cool about her and you.'

'There's nothing to be 'cool' about. It's not like we're an item.'

His silence is cynical.

'Howard, that was *way* back.'

'Of course, marriage would've put Maria definitively in second place.' Howard glances at Beatrice's face, then back at his food. 'And you don't want that.'

She blanks this, but the thought of Maria gives her a pang. As Beatrice left, Maria had said, *This time I'm giving you space, honey. I'm not going to call you any more on these trips. You need to find out what you want. I'll leave it to you to call me.*

In the moment between two piano pieces there is the hiss of a pressure cooker.

'Anyway.' Howard prangs the remaining three okras with his fork. 'Water under the bridge. Proposing was a fun novelty.'

Beatrice's red lips are tightly closed.

The next track is an arrangement of the theme from *Love Story*. The door jangles. A man comes in for a take-away. Howard eats; Beatrice picks. Eventually the man leaves with a paper carrier-bag and Nawaz wipes the counter. The CD finishes.

Giving up on her main course, Beatrice orders gulab jammun. 'I've got this craving for something sweet.'

Nawaz appears swiftly at their table with the orange glob oozing syrup in its stainless steel dish, and leaves the bill. He gets good tips from the Americans.

Having finished his own meal, Howard eats a little of Beatrice's korma, washes it down with the Indian beer, then checks his watch. 'Hey, I need to call New York. Tomorrow's Saturday. Don't want to miss my chance – I'll do it outside.' He begins pulling his jacket from the back of the chair.

In the cold of the street, standing uselessly while Howard talks animatedly into his mobile about something important, Beatrice suddenly feels nauseous.

The party preparations are all in hand. Any outstanding tasks can be carried out by Joan in the morning. Darshana throws the remains of a vodka and orange into the back of her throat and leaves the kitchen with a clinking supermarket bag to replenish her sitting room's mini-fridge. Having done this, she fixes herself another drink and sinks down onto the sofa. Her sofa. Her special room. Her private space, where the kids don't come. Her phoning room.

She scrabbles for the remote among the velvet cushions, pulls it out and cocks it at the *Eastenders* credits. She flicks to a gardening programme. She flicks to a man frying something in a wok. She flicks back to the adverts. She lies back on the sofa, pulling her legs up onto the cushions, making her thighs, in pink jogging pants, go broad and thick. Her glass dangles in her hand, half-full.

The barn roof soars to a shadowy point beyond the warm moon-curve of concealed lighting. The roof beams look bleached, like the ribs of a fish. Darshana feels like Jonah inside the whale.

Jonah is a nice name for a boy. Baldev isn't normal enough. At school he mixes with Bens and Jasons. 'Baldev' was the request of her ailing mother. What else could she do, when they were all accusing her of worsening her mother's illness?

A week after they'd registered Baldev her mother was dead, and she could have had something English. If not Jonah, she might have chosen Hugh, or Rupert. Signposts to a good background.

Nice for a girl, too, Jonah. If she'd had a girl. Or Joan, obviously. That would have been nice.

The Fleece Inn is at the back of the Bengal Palace.

Howard drains his glass and looks into it, satisfied. Beatrice remains hunched behind an untouched Guinness. In the corner a man with a long-time-single look is pumping away at a slot machine.

Howard flips a beer-mat in a somersault and catches it. 'You have to be an anthropologist. This town, this northern culture is fascinating but you have to keep a distance. If you take photographs, you're putting the camera between it and you. That's your protection, see? You create a distance between it and you.'

Beatrice scowls.

'Hey. It's the weekend.' Howard chucks her chin. 'Your problem is, you let it get to you.'

Beatrice finally wraps her hands round her pint and sips the froth.

Howard grins. 'I covered for this weird deputy today. Mrs Chatterjee-Fox. Nineteen-seventies green eye-shadow. Going to seed.'

Beatrice grins back. 'That's not weird, you sexist pig.' For some reason the searching eyes of the teacher she covered for, Joan Blake, come into her mind.

'Okay, not *weird* as such, but –' he leans forward, putting on a scandalised face, 'she drank.'

'How d'you know?'

'See it a mile off. And she was obviously known for it: the vicar was being nice to her like she had a disability.'

Behind the bar, the bell is rung for last orders. Howard peers through the pub's curtains at the rain, then turns with raised eyebrows. 'Arts Centre?'

Beatrice nods and reaches for her jacket.

Chapter 6

Joan's Friday night routine involves a long soak in a Radox bath. Tonight it is also another way of putting off the phone-call to Darshana. The gentle hum of Colin's train-set next door is soporific. When she lies back with her eyes closed the American teacher appears before her. That sexy black suit. After bathing, she cuts her toenails, puts in a load of washing, makes cocoa, settles in her armchair with her weekend marking, and watches a serial.

It is eleven-thirty before, at last, she brings herself to reach for the landline. As she does so, it rings.

'Hello?'

'Joan, love. You didn't need to cut me off.'

'As you well know, Darshana, I was in the middle of leading a training day.'

'But children come first, Joan. *I'd* want to know if *my*–'

'Don't play games with me, Darsh. I knew about Caroline; I'd been phoned. The school phoned me. What's this about a note?'

'She needed a note. Obviously she needed a note, to say that she was unwell…'

'It was signed in my name.'

'Oh, you know I know your signature. It was just to make it look *bona fide*.'

'You pretended to be me. That's illegal, that is.'

'It might have looked like a funny carry-on if it'd been signed by me.'

'If I'd let on that I didn't know about that note Mrs Smith would definitely have thought there was a funny carry-on.'

'I was only thinking of Caroline's emotional well-being.'

'What d'you mean, her emotional well-being? What's that supposed to mean?'

'They can turn, Joan, at her age, when they have a funny home life. You see it time and time again.'

'What are you on about?'

'Caroline. They don't need funny set-ups.'

'Caroline hasn't got a funny set-up.'

'If you're not normal, Joan, people find out about it, and then your kids turn against you.'

Joan's breath catches.

'If she knew what sort of feelings you have,' Darshana rushes on, 'she wouldn't want any more shopping trips with you.'

The words penetrate, fast and smooth. 'Don't make threats,' says Joan very quietly.

Darshana swigs from her glass. 'I just thought it would look better if the note was from her Mum, not from somebody else. You don't want the school thinking she's got a funny carry-on,' she says again. 'They'll start thinking she's got problems. It'll look like she's in care or something. They might think her Dad's carrying on with another woman.'

'She shouldn't have been at your house to start with.' Joan's tone is icy.

'We don't send our children to private schools for them to be treated like a problem,' Darshana babbles on. 'She's got to look as though she's got a normal home.'

'She has got a normal home. She's got a normal home with her Mum and Dad. Half the pigging school comes from *divorced* homes. *That's* not normal.'

'Well, your household is still not as normal as my household, is it? We at least know what make-up is here, for example.'

'God, Darshana, I don't know what's normal about your set-up.'

'You might wish to note that Caroline wants to come *here*, when she's feeling poorly.'

'*I'm* her mother.'

'I got her all tucked up with a hot water bottle.'

'Will you *lay off* my child?'

'You're upsetting me now, Joan. We've practically brought them up together. Caroline's like a sister to my...'

'Is my daughter still up at this hour?'

Darshana can still hear Baldev's stereo. 'I think so. They were upstairs, revising.'

'Put her on, if she's awake. Please.'

'I don't like to stop them, when they're so keen. She feels she can revise better at ours.'

'Than where?'

'What d'you mean, love?'

'Better at yours than where?' Joan splutters, but Darshana's breaths have gone heavy with exertion as the sofa disgorges her onto her feet. 'I'll just go and get her. *Ca-ro-line! Your Mum!*'

''Lo.'

'Your Dad says you felt alright by teatime.'

'Yeh.'

'Are you alright?'

'Yeh.'

'Caroline, you're meant to be at home tonight.'

'I am!'

'You're at Darshana's.'

'I mean, I'm at my second home.'

'We've already had this discussion. We're already going to be spending most of tomorrow there.'

'I'm just seeing Baldev.'

'Are you revising?'

'Yeh.'

'When's your first exam?'

''Bout three weeks.'

'I can help you revise, you know. During the week. I've just stocked up on Wagonwheels.'

''Kay.'

'D'you think you'll be alright tomorrow?'

'Yeh.'

'If you don't feel well, you should just tell me. We'll take you to Doctor Steed. Never mind the party. Okay? Alright?'

''Kay.'

'I'll come and pick you up in the morning. I want you home for a bit, get some peace and quiet before the do.'

''Kay.'

'We could do something nice on Sunday. Spend some money. I'll take you to the Trafford Centre.'

Caroline suddenly arouses. 'You're just guilty.'

Joan is taken aback. 'Where did you get that from?'

'Tuh.'

'Because you're wrong, young lady. We spoil you rotten. You've got everything you need. You've got your lovely room. All I want in the world –'

'– I've got to go.'

When Caroline comes back up, Baldev is still lying on his bed in his school clothes, one hand under his head, the other aiming the remote at the TV. 'What did your Mum want so late?'

She flops beside him. 'Shove up.' Her uniform skirt rides up her legs. 'Just whining about me being here, as usual.'

They go back to staring at a talk-show and touching.

'She's taking me shopping again Sunday.'

'Guilty.'

'Yeh,' says Caroline. 'The one good thing about having parents on the brink of divorce.'

'Lofty and Dil at school get bought loads of stuff too,' says Baldev.

Lofty and Dilip have a special bond, having divorced parents. Baldev gets in on it to a degree, by claiming his parents' weirdness. *They lead separate lives,* he asserts. *They're as good as divorced.*

Caroline spreads out her hair on the pillow to look attractive.

'Lofty's got the worse deal, though,' says Baldev. 'His Dad got kicked out by his Mum for being a hippy, so his Dad doesn't feel guilty at all. His Mum has to pay his school fees, the lot. All he gets from his Dad is vegan seaweed on toast every other weekend, and weird presents made out of bits of wood.'

'Bummer.'

'I've invited them both for tomorrow, but Dilip isn't allowed to drink so he says what's the point.'

'Look at her. How can she get a job on telly when she's so fat?'

'Get her to get you an iPhone then, Sunday,' says Baldev.

'Might do.' She touches his chest. 'Is this shirt allowed at school?'

He fills his lungs, straining his shirt buttons. 'They say no jeans,' says Baldev, 'not no denim. I've got away with it all week.'

His reviled blazer is in a heap on the floor.

'Our sixth form's more lax,' says Caroline. 'They wear jeans non-stop.'

'Ours is too religious. That's my Mum's definition of posh. I wish she'd put me in a non-religious posh school like yours. She's not even religious herself. This party for Holi's a load of crap. It's not like we do any Hindu stuff. She's just looked it all up on the internet. Aunty Joan's more religious than my mother.'

'My Mum?' says Caroline. 'My Mum's not religious.'

'She believes in spirits.'

Caroline is taking off her green pullover, the tight neck scraping over her spots. '*Your* Mum acts totally guilty too, doesn't she?'

'Only with you,' says Baldev. 'She buys *you* stuff, not me.'

'It's coz she feels sorry for me, having a Mum like mine.'

'She's good, your Mum. She arranged all those holidays.'

69

'I don't call booking holidays and carrying the trays in cafés being a good mother. She even left it to Aunty Darsh to tell me about periods.'

I like Aunty Joan,' says Baldev. 'She likes cars, and she doesn't fuss.'

'Well, *I* like Uncle Walter. I don't care what you say about him. I like his posh voice.'

'He's a bloody write-off,' says Baldev. 'Doesn't even speak.'

'It's really hot in here.' Caroline undoes a couple more buttons of her blouse.

Baldev stares up at an advert for pension plans, his feet twitching. 'The only thing I can respect my Dad for is that he shagged my Mum before they got married. That's the only sign of being normal he's ever shown.'

'Did he *tell* you?'

'What — you mean, *speak* to me? Of course not. Mum was pregnant with me before they married, that's all. Like, nearly ready to drop one. That's why the wedding photos are only of their heads and shoulders.'

'Wow. Is that why they got married?'

'I reckon she trapped him. I think she wanted all this.' Baldev waves his arm at the wallpaper.

'Aunty Darsh says my Mum didn't even want to get married, let alone have me.'

'Don't believe everything my mother says,' says Baldev. 'She comes out with all sorts, does my Mum.'

'Humf.'

'Anyway,' he adds, 'nobody gets married if they don't want to.'

'I suppose not. Except Asians,' concedes Caroline.

'My Mum's from Surrey.'

'Tuh. I didn't mean Aunty Darsh, silly.' Caroline rolls onto her side and brings her face close to his. Inside her blouse her chest is blue-white and flat, rippled with ribs. She smells of salt and vinegar crisps with a hint of pencils.

'Are we getting under the duvet then?'

'Hang on.' Baldev rolls away, reaches an arm under the bed and pulls out a jam-jar of yellow liquid.

'What's that? Your wee?'

Baldev unscrews the top. 'Vodka and orange. Here.' He passes it over.

'Brill,' says Caroline.

'I've invited my other friend Russ too. He'll be coming over with Clarissa. They've only ever got sherry at his place.'

'That his girlfriend?'

'No, his mum. Nutter with a harp. Russ claims she's a lesbian, but he's always coming out with stuff like that. Trying to be cool. Personally I think she's part horse. Hey –' he grabs the jam-jar back from Caroline, chinks it on her forehead – 'Cheers!' – and knocks back the rest.

Chapter 7

The morning of the party is miraculously dry and almost spring-like. The snowdrops are still thriving, while crocus shoots are pushing through Walter's lawn. A light frost means no-one will be trailing mud in, and the smokers will at least not get wet when they are politely but firmly ejected.

When Darshana opens her front door and lays eyes on Wesley, she growls her disapproval.

Rather than growling back, Wesley remains aloof and apart, cocking his leg superciliously on one of her rose bushes.

Joan is marching up the drive with a stack of cardboard boxes of food. 'Had to bring him, he's off colour and Colin's working all day. Do you want these straight in the conservatory?'

'Kitchen.' Darshana's voice is a near-shriek. 'Don't bring him back this afternoon, he's incontinent.'

Wesley trots into the house on Jean's heels with a toss of his floppy ears.

'There's more in the car. Get Baldev to get up and help. It's nine-thirty. He's so *spoilt*.' Joan makes to stride across the hallway.

Darshana stays her with a hand, waving the crumpled tick-list. 'I forgot to tell you. Can you pop home and bring your four picnic chairs? I can put them in the conservatory with the eats, save bringing the big heavy ones through from the dining room. Oh and I'll need a load of wood bringing in and stacking up nicely in my sitting room.'

'Baldev can do that.'

'Baldev makes a mess and doesn't stack it aesthetically.'

'I've got other stuff to do this morning. Our Caroline needs to be taken home for a rest if she's to be fit for a party. We won't be back until you're actually starting.'

Darshana looks stricken. 'She can stay in bed here. You can just pop home and get her the clothes she wants.' Her voice rises. 'You've got to be here before people start arriving. I need you for that. You've got to serve the drinks.'

Wesley stands in front of Joan with a protective look in his eyes, though he is too close to the ground for anyone to note this.

Darshana ignores him anyway. 'There's more than fifty coming…'

Joan barges on to the kitchen, sets the boxes down and notices that her blazer sleeves are now impregnated with the smell and grease of mushroom bhajis. When Darshana comes up close behind her she flinches, feeling Darshana's small, tapered fingers touching the back of her neck, sliding up into her hair.

'Prick-tease.' It is muttered; a quiet observation to herself.

'That's vulgar.' Darshana briskly removes her hand. 'You haven't got a prick.' She stays close, one of her big denim-clad hips brushing Joan's thigh. 'I need you here.' Her plea is tinged with panic.

A shuffling noise attracts Wesley's attention and he goes to lick Walter's highly chewable slippers.

'Morning, Walter.'

He emits a vague pleasantry to Joan and waves a hand clutching spectacles to indicate that he is just on his way somewhere. Reaching his study door he pauses, turns back with what seems to be a sudden thought. 'Anything to do?'

'*Don't* wear that pullover this afternoon,' warns Darshana shrilly.

'Think it's all in hand, Walter,' Joan lets him off.

Walter acquiesces to Joan's assessment and disappears into his room.

'Okay.' Joan looks Darshana in the face. 'Compromise. We'll get back for two o'clock.'

Wesley peers up at Joan's compassionate expression and does a slow, loyal tail-wag.

Darshana is big-eyed and imploring, a look that he has himself perfected. 'But there's all the plastic sheeting to lay over the carpets,' she moans. 'And the champagne flutes to set out on the hall table. And you need to be here to help me greet people, you know how nervous I get.'

'No-one will show up before three.' Joan sighs. 'You set these things up and yet they stress you out so much. Come on – let's get cracking.'

'I'll get the kids up.' Darshana heads for the foot of the stairs.

'But I won't be doing this for you anymore,' Joan adds softly, although by now Darshana is out of earshot.

'*Bal-dev!*'

Wesley looks at Joan approvingly. A few drops of urine land on the hall carpet.

By midday a mellow hazy sun had taken away the frost. Now it has become the mildest, most pleasant afternoon of the year thus far.

'I said not to bring him back.'

Wesley stalks past Darshana on Joan's heels, and into the house. 'The folding chairs are in my boot,' Joan instructs. 'The boys can get them. Where's my daughter?'

Darshana's salwar kameez has a richly embroidered bodice, a myriad of bold colours and shiny pieces of mirror-glass incorporated into a paisley design on purple silk. The neck is low-cut and scalloped, the sheer chiffon scarf across her breasts failing to obscure her curves and the bulges around her bra's edges. While the outfit is tailored to fit skin-like to her upper body, the skirt and trousers fall demurely in many slinky folds. She looks like a queen of the East. She is in role.

In the ensuing hour Darshana faffs and prinks, drops two glasses, burst into tears, and gets put into an armchair with a vodka and orange by Baldev while Joan sets up the drinks reception table and surreptitiously downs a Foster's lager straight from the can. Wesley helpfully steers clear of Darshana so as not to wind her up further by his presence.

At ten past three the doorbell rings.

Darshana whisks into the hall. 'Oh God, we're starting.' Her scarf caresses Wesley's snout. 'Boys! The chairs – get the picnic chairs. Come on, come on,' she agitates Joan's arm – 'I'm not answering the door by myself.'

The scarf now has a glistening patch of drool at its end. Wesley patters after Joan to check out who is arriving. When the door opens a pair of ladies' dressy sandals and a long black frock-affair are what come over the threshold. Wesley has encountered the cleric and his wife before: last summer's garden party here, where he pooed on the lawn and a bit of it got onto this very same black robe. Wesley can still smell himself.

Other feet are stepping in. There starts to be a hubbub, accompanied by the subtle whine of sitar music from the kitchen CD player. Wesley flops under the hall table for the time being, his nose tickled pleasantly by food smells.

'Yes, of course he's here somewhere,' Darshana is trilling. 'If he's not still in his study he's in the garden. He does a lot in the garden does Walter. Ah! Walter, you're in demand.' She pats Walter's arm, smiling at him in the manner of a care assistant in a home for the aged. 'Has everyone got a glass of Cava? Did your children get one of these boxes of confetti? *Strictly* for use in the garden, kids. I'll come and explain it all...'

Wesley's mistress is doling out champagne flutes to new arrivals. A fizzy splat lands on her shoe. He licks it.

75

'Sorry Lilian, let me just top that up for you again,' comes Joan's voice, then Darshana's: 'Lilian, lovely that you could come! Oh, thank you so much, you really shouldn't have. The gift table's over there. Listen – can you rescue the vicar from my husband and take him through to the buffet? Lots of different kinds of bhaji and samosas and pakora and so on, I've labeled what they all are. Thanks, you're so good.'

Wesley follows the secretary's elegant boots and the black frock through to the conservatory where the aroma of greasy, meaty food has become compelling.

'Is that Darshana's son over there?' inquires Lilian of the vicar, steering him away from Walter.

'Yes, the younger one. Luke. The adopted one. I christened him, though we did it very sensitively. I used a text from the Brihadaranyaka Upanishad as a prayer. There's so much common ground between our religions, it's marvellous really. Terribly inspiring.'

'Isn't it. Isn't it. I've got Asians next door. Gosh, look at this wonderful array. Must try everything. It all looks delicious.' Lilian picks out the smallest morsel of pakora on the plate.

'Splendid,' yelps the vicar. 'Isn't Darshana amazing? Oops, this one's a bit slippery, lucky there's a dog about the place.'

Wesley snaffles the vicar's spillage.

'She's got two sons, hasn't she?' The secretary nibbles daintily at the pakora. 'I guess that must be the other one. Lovely to see some teenagers having a nice time together, not just sitting in front of a computer somewhere.'

'Yes, that's Baldev. Not quite seventeen yet but in the upper sixth already. Been a year ahead since primary school. Awfully clever. Due to start at uni a year early. They're jolly proud of him,' twitters the vicar.

'Well, but they got married fifteen years ago didn't they, as it's their crystal wedding? I've brought them a crystal

76

sugar bowl...' The secretary sounds doubtful. 'Although Baldev must have already... so they were living together, presumably.'

Wesley sees his owner's lace-up footwear approaching and wags his tail.

'Don't let my dog at the food, he's had an upset stomach.'

'I say, I think that's the Head arriving. Yes, it's the Head. Do excuse me.' The vicar sails off.

'*No more!*'

Lilian clutches her glass to herself and steps back, then sees that Joan is addressing the dachshund whose tail has been flicking annoyingly at the skirt of her suit. His mouth appears to be bursting with some batter-coated delicacy or other.

The secretary has become acquainted with Joan through once or twice-yearly encounters over the last decade or so, either at Darshana's regular parties or at staff Christmas 'do's or the St Ninian's annual concert, always Joan as Darshana's consort rather than Walter, which was invariably explained as being due to Walter's 'working on a paper'. The secretary finds Joan very capable, a person who takes charge and gets things done. Unfussy. Nice and reliable. She must be good for Darshana, in view of what Darshana's tendencies are.

Lilian shifts herself more neatly into the corner next to a profuse silk flower arrangement to make room for Joan, who has now finished serving the Cava. A strange coupling for a friendship though, she thinks again, noting Joan's shirtsleeves and casual trousers compared to Darshana's attire. Nothing apparently in common – after all, Joan works in one of those awful run-down schools: no P.T.A. to speak of, and no doubt filthy carpet tiles in the staffroom and a sink seething with germs. But some are cut out for that sort of school. They'd flounder if they had to deal with gifted children all day.

'I've trained her, her, her and him.' Joan points out some teacher-types lined up at the buffet. The contents of paper plates are being compared and appreciated. Milling through the house by this time are selected neighbours from Weatherhope's detached housing area, Walter's ex-colleagues from the university, Darshana's current and former teaching colleagues, and a handful of young children clutching the boxes they are not allowed to open indoors. The conservatory's outer door keeps opening and closing as individuals release themselves to the garden for a breather.

Lilian wrinkles her nose at a waft of incense from one of the sticks placed strategically around each room in balls of Blutack. Along the hall she catches sight of Baldev in the open-plan family room, where the teenage contingent is clustered round a hideous replica marble mantelpiece. 'By the way Joan, the vicar and I were getting a little confused. It seems Baldev was already around when Darshana and Walter married. This being their Crystal Wedding.'

'No, that's not right. Seventeen years they've been married. He'll be seventeen in a fortnight. He was well on the way, that's all. Par for the course these days.'

Lilian is puzzled. 'But crystal's the fifteenth wedding anniversary. I looked it up on the internet.'

'Oh, apparently there isn't one for seventeen so she just went for the nearest. She makes it up as she goes along, does Darshana.' Joan tuts and recklessly gulps the remains from her pint glass. 'He couldn't have got anybody else,' she adds, unnecessarily. 'Walter was fifty-four, you know, when she took him on.'

Wesley is standing companionably between his owner's planted feet, crunching on some strayed peanuts.
Lilian holds up her crystal flute to the light, looking a bit put out, thinking of her crystal gift. 'You've known her for all those years, then?'

'We teacher-trained together down in London – us two and Terri. Look, that's Terri over there: red stilettos; northern lass like me – have you met her?'

Lilian looks across at the leopard-skin-clad bottom. 'Erm.'

'No, you wouldn't have. She's at my school. More my friend than Darsh's. Doesn't normally come to these 'do's – I invited her. We both came back home, and Darsh made Walter retire early so she could follow me north. 'Scuse me.' Joan is reaching for another can. 'We've practically brought up our kids together.'

'She's got a lovely home.' The secretary's general gesture takes in the grand piano looming large in Darshana's sitting-room through the double doors, the antique occasional table with ornately turned legs, the reproduction Constable.

Joan is looking suddenly morose. 'Darsh could have had any man, looking like that. She could have married a normal man.'

'Oh!' Lilian is taken aback, though from what she has seen, Walter is indeed a bit odd. 'But there's a lot to be said for being connected to the world of academe. For we culture vultures, anyway!' She takes a sip of her Cava, noting Joan's newly replenished and swiftly emptying glass. She decides to do further research into this marital situation later. With Clarissa, perhaps, whose voice is coming in from the garden, right through the double glazing, audible over Darshana's Ravi Shankar CD.

Wesley has had enough of his owner's stern looks whenever she notices him snacking. He trots off along the hallway between the throngs and into the family room where he discovers Bombay Mix overflowing from a gangly teenager's fist onto the rug.

Baldev's two schoolmates, having arrived shortly beforehand, do not go straight through to the family room as instructed by Darshana until they have selected drinks in the kitchen to suit their respective images. Lofty, having opted for a double whisky in an appropriate tumbler and grabbed a handful of nibbles, has now pushed through the crowd to where Baldev is leaning on the marble fire-surround with Caroline. Instinctively, Caroline shifts her stance beside Baldev so that there is no unequivocal indication of what their relationship is, as she eyes Lofty, the tall one with the long curl flopping languidly down his cheek. Close on his heels is the more diminutive Russ with a can of Guinness, no glass.

Baldev does the introductions.

'Hi.' Caroline flicks her hair back. 'Your Mum teaches harp at our school.' Seeing Wesley she drops a whole mushroom bhaji that she's taken one little bite out of.

'Yeah, everybody knows Cla-*riss*-a.' Russ imitates his mother's loud horsey manner then slurps gloomily from his can. 'How could anybody not notice my mother with her bloody great harp and her phenomenally huge gob? She doesn't exactly blend in. I guess it's the same for you Bal, having a parent going around the place looking different.'

'Oh, that's only for work, those Indian clothes and saris and everything. She says it's what they expect, at St Ninian's. She isn't even doing Holi right. You're meant to chuck coloured paint over each other, not confetti. She's a hollow sham,' he sums up, grandly.

'Aunty Darsh isn't too bad really,' Caroline chips in. 'She's pretty normal to go shopping with. Blends in okay.'

'No she's not, she's weird,' maintains Baldev. 'She's shagged my Dad for a start. How weird is that. Plus she goes on living with him even though she can't stand him; that's weird too.'

'Well, as you know, Clarissa's a lesbian, but she goes on living with my father.'

'And what is your evidence for this remarkable assertion?' asks Lofty. Caroline looks at him interestedly. He is so posh and polite.

'Girl on girl porn movies,' says Russ. 'Found 'em in her desk. I can lend them out if you want.'

'Maybe she got them to turn your Dad on,' suggests Caroline.

'And she smokes a pipe.' He motions at the window with his Guinness. Out in the garden Clarissa is hunched with Terri on a decorative wrought iron bench – mock-French – in deep discussion beneath a pall of cigarette and pipe smoke and a flutter of confetti released by some squealing children. 'She just *is* a lesbian. She's pretty repulsive by heterosexual standards, don't you think?'

Lofty swirls his whisky, unable to refute this. 'Who's the tarty old bird in the leggings?'

'She's a very nice lady,' says Caroline. 'Really old friend of my mum's. Heart of gold.'

'Tart with a heart,' suggests Lofty.

'Nothing wrong with looking like that. I think she keeps herself nice, for her age.'

'Sorry. Cheap stereotyping. I really didn't mean to sound judgmental. Truly.' Lofty sweeps back his long curl.

'No problem,' says Caroline softly.

Wesley trots off between feet to a relatively private alcove in which an earnest conversation is underway. He sniffs appreciatively at the familiar black frock.

'…And the divorce made her mother turn particularly nasty. I never met the woman, but Darshana lived under mental torture until she died.' Walter's tone is empathetically doleful.

The vicar pats him on the shoulder.

'So Darshana's got no contact at all with her family these days.' Walter bends down creakily to hand Wesley a Quality Street from a bowl. 'You see, there are all these reasons for her unhappiness and that's why she has... her behaviour.'

The vicar pulls a thin, sad smile. 'And might I ask what the situation is with the gentleman she divorced?'

'I believe he took up residence in Australia. Certainly there's no contact. He was terribly bad for her. Hmm. Not that I'm...' Walter tails off and looks out at the crocuses.

Wesley snaffles a crinkle-cut crisp, then decides to do the decent thing by Darshana after all. He retreats outdoors to pee.

After watering an ornamental fern Wesley goes to where Terri is beckoning him from a bench.

'I knew I'd seen you before,' she is saying to Clarissa. 'It's your pipe that's reminded me. You've been to the Todmorden disco. In the cricket club.'

Clarissa snorts wildly. 'Heavens! Do you go there?'

'The women-only one. I've been going there all my adult life. I do the rota for the bar.'

Clarissa slaps her thigh. 'I haven't been for years and years. I'm married now.' She takes a first puff, tossing away the match, the pipe's bowl clasped in her big talon hand.

'Lot of it about,' Terri says. 'Personally I'm a gold star dyke. I've kept up standards.'

'Least I've only done it once, and frankly I treat him more as a lodger. One that covers the mortgage and utilities. So anyway, do tell: how did Darshana's number two come about? The Walter story?'

'She used to work in the college refectory while we were students. On the evening meals. And she got to know this professor, i.e. Walter, because he came in every single night. So once she was pregnant, what she did was go and sit in the refectory, waiting for him to come in.'

Clarissa is rapt. 'While she was still married to number one?'

'When she'd just walked out on number one.'

'Gosh, really? She knows how to get her man.'

Terri sniffs. 'It's the wrong people, though, isn't it? She goes the wrong way. But I'm saying nothing. Here, Wesley.' She puts her paper plate down on the path.

Wesley sets about lapping up the spicy raita sauce and all the other remnants.

'So Darshana ensnared a professor.'

'I don't know about ensnared,' says Terri. 'She just asked him to look after her in return for cooking his tea etcetera. It was obvious he couldn't cook his own.'

'Jolly decent of him to take her on when she had a little one.'

'Easily manipulated, bless 'im,' humphs Terri. 'He's not quite normal, Walter. Joan's convinced he's got a syndrome. He can't relate well, person-to-person. There's no sex. Luke the second son's adopted. Hey, Wesley – no need to eat the plate.'

The descent of dusk turns the garden damp and miserable. Both ends of Darshana's floaty scarf have finished up bedraggled. One gets chopped into by a slamming car door as she over-fusses – the worse for vodka – at the final departures. Joan is packing the picnic chairs back into her boot with a hang-dog look, in the grim knowledge that she has drunk too much to drive home.

When the last guests have left, the teenagers swoop on the remaining alcohol and sneak bottles up to Baldev's room. Soon, four bodies are lined up side by side, four pairs of legs sprawling over the edge of the bed across the bobbly rug, listening to Lofty's Dad's vintage Bob Marley. Caroline is sandwiched between Baldev and Lofty while Russ is slightly estranged from the group, cuddling a pillow and a bottle of Pils. The respectful silent homage to the music is mainly induced by the mixture of drinks that has made keeping their eyes closed to stop the room spinning the most sensible course of action.

Between two tracks, they hear the distant hum of a vacuum cleaner, then Darshana's sudden shriek.

'Wonder what that's about,' says Caroline.

The next track starts up, quietly enough to hear shouting between Darshana and Joan but not to catch the words. When the refrain commences Luke, a jack-in-the-box figure, bursts through the door shouting, 'Wesley's barfed under the piano!'

'What's materialistic about objecting to dog sick on my Persian carpet?'

Joan is rubbing her arm above the elbow where the Shiva Nataraj flailed into her. 'This can't go on any more.'

Darshana lets the statue drop to the sofa. An involuntary sob gurgles out of her.

'A rug's only a *thing*, Darshana. Life isn't all about *things*. I'm getting my priorities straight. No going back this time. Life's about being true to yourself.'

'But you like your things. You like your house and all your bits and pieces in it. Your nice patio and Colin. It's hard getting everything. If you give it all up, what have you got?'

'Your true self, Darsh.'

'Don't be ridiculous.' Darshana is rushing into the kitchen for a bucket and gloves, with Joan following on. 'What would you do without your husband doing your washing and ironing and keeping on top of that garden?'

Joan takes over the task, roughly pulling a bucket from below the sink and setting it under the tap. 'My husband's not a thing. He's always been a friend.'

Darshana snaps on pink Marigold gloves then swiftly picks a half-glass of something left on a shelf and knocks it back in one. 'I don't know why you can't just *leave things as they are*. Everyone's perfectly happily living a perfectly normal life —'

84

Joan spurts in cleaning fluid. 'Who's happy? I haven't been happy. You're not happy.'

'All I've done is exactly what everyone else does. And so have you.' Darshana snatches the bucket and cloth and totters unsteadily down the hallway in her high heels, slopping suds onto the plastic sheeting. 'What's different about me and you? Nothing. We're married with kids and a house. You haven't done it any better than me.'

'But me and Colin have been compatible. Not like you and Walter. 'We're both *Star Trek* fans. We both wanted a detached house with a garage.'

'See? *You're* materialistic.' Darshana, on her knees, scoops at the mess with the cloth and flings it into the bucket along with one end of her scarf.

Joan, brought up short, ponders the accusation. 'Actually you're right,' she concedes. 'That was very materialistic of me. Or is pragmatic the word?'

Darshana gives Joan a big triumphant smile. 'See. We're the same.' She squeezes out the cloth with an emphatic twist. 'So, let's just keep things as they are.'

Joan has remained in the doorway where Wesley has taken up position beside her. 'I'm going to live as the person I really am. I'm really doing it this time. And it seems that means I'll be by myself. Which I've decided will be okay after all.'

'But we've GOT EVERYTHING!'

'Not me. C'mon, Wes.' They leave Darshana kneeling under the piano and stride out into the night. As she walks away Joan phones for a taxi, at the same time gingerly nursing her bruise. Wesley barfs a further pile of vomit onto the drive, feels better for it and scampers after her.

Chapter 8

Sunday afternoon already. Beatrice so looks forward to weekends these days – but then they pass emptily. Howard's self-discipline heightens her sense of inertia. Her incapacity to plan ahead, even look ahead, has become a sore point. Maria would call this a crisis. *You gotta decide which life you want, girl,* she would say.

After his usual Sunday gym-and-swim Howard spends the rest of the day at his laptop. The day is dulling off, the first streetlights flickering on, when he finally stretches in his armchair. 'How's this for an opening?'

Beatrice lifts her head out of *Tilly Trotter.*

'This city of immigrants looks set to become a city of emigrants as decent, law-abiding folks move out, leaving the drunks and the junkies to their violence and vomit. As I write, relations between the colorful, assertive downtown neighborhoods and the grey depression of the suburban 'social housing' areas are on a knife-edge...'

Howard grins at her.

'You're like someone watching insects under a magnifying-glass,' says Beatrice. 'Can't you write in a more sympathetic way?'

'I'm not writing for *The Reader's Digest.*' Howard scans down his screen.

Beatrice flips to the cover of her novel where grimy children shuffle shoeless along a track against a backdrop of belching chimneys. 'Sometimes it feels like Catherine Cookson's world is all around me.'

Howard laughs absently, rattling off another line.

'You're a scavenging rat, you know that? Feeding on the debris of people's lives.'

'This city's a creative opportunity,' says Howard. 'If you were to produce pictures to illustrate what I'm saying...'

'I'm not happy being a predator. I don't like the tone you take in your writing. You're inhumane.'

Howard clicks on *save*. 'You're missing some great breaks. I could sell for you in Toronto, New York, London...'

'You're not listening. I don't approve of exploitative photography. It's a moral stance.'

Howard rolls his eyes. 'Images made for art's sake aren't necessarily more pure. Let's get real, here. Not only do they make no money, they also don't change anything. Whereas images that appear in the news media can really have an impact.'

'Philistine.'

'Gimme a break, Beatrice. We're both creative people. It just so happens my way of being creative is the one that sells.' He shifts about with his mouse, moves a line of text. 'My perspective translates into money. Don't knock it.'

'Excuse the cliché, but money isn't everything.'

Howard gives a cynical laugh. 'This discussion is entirely hypothetical anyway, isn't it?' He does a final save of the document and goes into his email account to send off his piece. 'You're not even doing art stuff anymore, let alone pictures to support my articles. You've given up. All you're doing is teaching.'

Beatrice feels slapped. Right on cue the phone rings. With the usual sinking feeling she greets Chaz. He sounds frazzled. 'Sunday night comes round so *quickly*,' he groans. 'Big stress this week. Plenty of work for you two, you'll be pleased to hear.'

'Good,' says Beatrice flatly. She ought to put in a four-day week to get back in the black by the end of this month. Payments for the digital camera – a spontaneous buy when they first came north, when she was still feeling good – have become a burden.

'First of all, Monday,' says Chaz. 'Could I ask you, Beatrice, as a special favour, to cover a year one? A teacher's called in sick but the other year one teacher's setting work.'

'I don't do year ones, Chaz..'

'I know, but they're desperate.'

'I'm not trained for it.'

'I can't knock off tonight until I've sorted this one out,' Chaz wheedles. 'I just thought, since you were already at Braithwaite on Friday, it'd be the devil you know...'

'I really don't...' Joan Blake's wink comes into Beatrice's mind. She hesitates. 'Okay, Chaz. Seeing as it's Braithwaite.'

Arriving at Braithwaite the next morning, Beatrice sees that the scruffy girl is doing circuits of the building like on Friday, as though she might have been there all weekend, going round and round. Today her unfastened anorak has a tear down the front from which grey wadding is bulging.

Beatrice looks away, hums, looks at her watch, rings the bell once more. It is nine minutes past eight. There are two cars, but no sign of anybody. She wonders whether one of the cars is Joan Blake's. She thinks of going to look for Joan in her prefab then blushes, feeling that that would look foolish.

Eventually the smoking caretaker lets Beatrice in. He spots the hovering child and signals with his head that she should come too. 'I've been told to let her in,' he tells Beatrice. The child walks by under Beatrice's nose, stinking of cigarettes, unwashed body, and urine, and takes up a position on the doormat, looking uninterested.

'Wait here for Miss,' the caretaker shouts at her as if she were deaf. 'Case for the social,' he says to Beatrice, his cigarette waggling. He moves off.

The girl has an unattractive little face, its features all squashed together in the middle.

'Okay?' says Beatrice.

The ugly child, standing vacantly on the mat, doesn't seem to hear.

'Which teacher in particular do you have to wait for?'

The girl gets out a plastic top from a drinks bottle and starts fiddling with it.

Beatrice checks her watch. Eight fifteen, is that the time? She turns briskly and marches off to search for Chantelle's room.

She suspects there'll be no work set after all; that she'll end up pulling Howard's emergency worksheets out of her briefcase, searching for the photocopier, finding it has a secret code to prevent people like her from using it. The secretary will be late and there'll be no-one to ask. The children will start arriving; meanwhile the photocopier, which someone will finally have given her access to, will run out of paper, or it will jam.

In Chantelle's classroom, a timetable has been laid on the desk with a note.

Literacy hour: do shared reading from the giant book sitting in carpet corner, look at capitals and full stops. Lots of oral practice of sentences. Get them to follow model at end of story inserting own adjectives. Get them to write a sentence in their literacy books in their neatest writing. Let them draw a picture. Pack up 15 mins before playtime, hand out milk and biscuits (don't ask any kids to do it, it will go everywhere). Make them sit cross-legged on the carpet for milk or they'll spill it. After break: repeat same with my class (I take Chantelle's class and repeat numeracy). Watch twins Shane and Dane.

Afternoon: PE in hall, no bother, do catching and throwing and piggy-in-the-middle. Afternoon playtime is 2.30. You're on duty. Take whistle for lining them up at end. Science for 40 mins then end with story, Enid Blyton, The Wishing Tree. They're halfway through it. Am only next door if you need anything. Claire Scott.

Repeating a lesson with another class means twice as many names to remember.

'Are you alright with everything?'

The woman, who must be Claire, is wearing the same kind of hooded sweatshirt as on Friday, only blue, with another mini-skirt and clumpy black DM boots with pink laces. Her legs, in black opaque tights, look muscular. Her hair is very short, sporty. She's twenty-five at the most. She doesn't introduce herself.

'This looks great,' says Beatrice brightly. 'What about the Science?'

'Oh, I don't know what she's doing with them,' says Claire. 'Look where they're at in their books. Just make something up; I always do. Do food.'

Behind Claire, the girl in the anorak is lurking in the doorway.

'I've brought Chelsea through,' Claire says, beckoning to the child. 'She's in Miss Baxendale's class, aren't you love?' Claire lowers her voice to Beatrice, 'When Miss Baxendale shows up. She's off with her period.'

The child is drifting into the classroom between tables, looking sidelong at Beatrice.

'Chelsea, this is Miss...' says Claire loudly.

'Kirby.'

'I said to take your coat off and hang it up, didn't I, Chelsea?' says Claire.

The child ignores her.

'Get a book please, Chelsea, and sit in the carpet corner.' Claire is moving towards the connecting door between the rooms. 'Any problems, I'm just next door,' she calls back to Beatrice. 'I'm not normally in this early. Catching up on marking. This is keen, this is!' She disappears.

Beatrice moves the timetable and note to one side and scrabbles through the mountain of papers, PE shorts, plastic folders and exercise books. She uncovers some whiteboard markers and the dinner-money pot. She searches the classroom for the literacy books, rummages around for scrap paper, discovers the crayon tray, searches for, but fails to find, the science books. Through the window she can see a handful of children already pressed into a corner, some without coats, sheltering under an inadequate overhang from the worst of the downpour, their hair pasted down, their skin scruffy and grey. In the middle of the playground four tiny Asian boys are squabbling like starlings, while two white boys and one with an afro and a wide, gentle face are standing in a huddle, doing something with cards.

Beatrice rubs her hands over her face.

On the drainer in the sink-corner are two rows of plastic cups with names felt-tipped on their sides, each half-filled with earth and sprouting a small, green shoot. Chelsea is using a measuring jug to fill each cup to the brim with water.

'Thank you for watering, Chelsea, but I didn't actually ask you to do that, did I?'

Chelsea begins, instead, pouring water into one end of a length of rubber tubing, the other end of which is hanging over the edge of the sink.

'Don't.' Beatrice dives and flicks the tubing into the sink after a spout of water has already splashed into some jars of powder paint.

Chelsea grunts. Her features are dug out deeply, like a potato etched with a pen-knife.

Beatrice hovers behind her inadequately, thinking how Joan is the type who would feel warm towards this child and would be able to get her to do things. 'Would you like to sit down somewhere else now please, Chelsea, and get a book out, please?'

The child ignores her.

Beatrice turns Chelsea by the shoulders, pulling her away from the sink. The anorak feels crispy. Beneath it is a dirty cardigan. The jug in the child's hand tips up, pouring onto Beatrice's shoulder.

'A book, please.' Beatrice stands up, brushing at her jacket.

91

The knob-face doesn't twitch or blink.

'Or a game; I don't mind.'

'Miss Baxendale lets me play 'int sink.' The child's voice is rough, gravelly, like a smoker's.

'Well I'm not Miss Baxendale.'

The little girl shrugs. 'Well, fuck you then.'

Claire bobs her head through from next door. 'Ah, there you are, Chelsea love. You can go up to the hall now. They've started giving the breakfasts out.'

'Miss Scott, Chelsea's not being a very nice little girl this morning.' The water stain on Beatrice's shoulder is spreading. 'What do we do when they say fuck?'

The morning meanders on nightmarishly.

During shared reading Kyle suddenly climbs onto the table wearing a policeman's helmet from the play-house, going 'Ner ner, ner ner, ner ner'.

Beatrice falters, looking to the support assistant.

Jean defends her inactivity with – 'I'm here to do Benetton.' From his position between Jean's feet he gives Beatrice a fully-engaged grin while peacefully picking his nose. Not the kind of autistic behaviour requiring Jean's constant undivided attention. Kyle wriggles and screams as Beatrice tries to lift him to the floor, then he cleverly raises his arms, slips downwards, landing like a cat, and within a second is under the table, siren going full blast.

Claire's head appears round the door to see what the noise is. Beatrice thinks of the staffroom talk later, how her hopelessness will become the gossip; how Joan, being nice, might defend her, but on the other hand might be appalled. Claire is advising Beatrice to send two nice girls for Mrs Coulson who will come and take Kyle away. The chosen girls set off sweetly, hand in hand.

The carpet corner is now seething with children stretching their legs, picking fights, pulling resources out of cupboards. Jean is still perched on her child-sized chair, keeping one hand on Benetton who is reading a Ladybird book in his own little world.

The two girls don't return.

'That Kelly,' Jean tuts. 'She'll be up to summat.'

Beatrice asks Jean's advice on two more nice girls. Fozia and Sanna set off for Mrs Coulson's room holding hands.

The number of children has dwindled to less than a dozen. A quarter of the class was already absent when Beatrice took the register: two in Pakistan, one in Tenerife, one in hospital, one at her dad's this week, and then a few others either sick, or dead, or something.

When Mrs Coulson marches in trailing Fozia and Sanna behind her, there are children playing in the sink, in the play-house, on the tables and under them. Clearing her throat, Mrs Coulson terrifies them into silence.

Beatrice reddens, and fluffs, 'I was just about to introduce the writing work. I was just waiting until Kyle was removed.'

Mrs Coulson ignores her. 'Found *this* young man in the toilets.' She gives a rough push to a snotty boy with a skinhead haircut. 'Connor can sit at the naughty table and do something extremely boring until breaktime, Miss – er…'

'She's American,' Fozia calls out, chewing the end of her plait.

Mrs Coulson's nose is profiled against the window, pointing nastily at the class. Her spring of hair turns sharply. She uses the same voice with Beatrice as with the children. 'Who is it you want rid of?'

At last Mrs Coulson takes Kyle by the elbow, slaps his police helmet down on a cupboard and propels him out of the room.

Claire's class, after morning playtime, is almost as bad as Chantelle's, with another support assistant, purse-lipped among the slow-learners, watching.

Chapter 9

The staffroom chair that Beatrice sinks into at lunchtime is so low that her bottom almost touches the floor. Her cup of tea slops onto the carpet tiles. She slides it onto the coffee-table, feeling a fool. The table is heaped with bulletins, newspapers, children's work, a few executive toys which can be ordered by filling in a form on a clipboard.

Terri is hovering by the electric kettle. 'How've you got on with the little ones this morning?'

Beatrice avoids her eye. 'Okay.' She reaches into her briefcase and draws out her paperback.

Terri shudders. 'They're clingy when they're five and six.'

The staffroom is quiet other than a few support assistants at one end, eating school dinners on red plastic trays. Beatrice eavesdrops on them harrumphing about their hours of work, their hourly rate, their benefit payments, the payments they get from their children's fathers. The teachers' conversations tend to be about their kids' school fees, their exes' parental contributions, their exotic holidays. Sometimes a staffroom unites in discussing the head-teacher. The head earns a lot of money and what does he or she do for the money? The head comes up with all sorts of crap for school assemblies, totally out of touch, unbelievable. Can you believe he said that?

Claire comes in holding a paper bag from a baker's shop. 'Where is everybody?'

Terri is picking at the corner of a long, pink finger-nail. 'Pub. Can't afford it, me.' The kettle clicks off and she turns to make a cup of tea. A cigarette packet in her skin-tight pocket is moulded to the curve of her buttock.

'Everything alright, that last session?' Claire asks Beatrice through a mouthful of something.

Beatrice shrinks. 'The Pakistani boys said Kamal was calling their mothers bad names in their language so they all went and thumped him.'

'Aw,' Claire laughs indulgently. 'They do that.'

Terri turns with a full cup. 'Is that your Kamal again?'

'"eadbanger.' Claire shakes her head. 'Total nutcase. One of nine.'

'They have to be like that at home,' says Terri. 'It's the only way they get attention.'

The door is thrust open by a cardboard box. Beatrice feels a lurch.

Joan Blake's blazer is navy blue polyester, bus-conductorish. Her tartan skirt has a furry nap like a cheap travel rug. She strides to the teachers' end and dumps the box on a stack of newspapers. 'It's like a grave in here.'

Beatrice notes with shock that Joan has attempted to apply lipstick. It looks slightly drag-queenish.

'Beatrice!' Joan pronounces an extra half-syllable on Bea. 'How ya doin?'

'That's a nice name,' says Terri, sitting down. 'Not very American. Joan wants to live in America, don't you, Joan?'

'Who the hell would want to live there?' says Claire.

'They wouldn't have her.' Terri points at Claire. 'They'd arrest her for communism or something. Don't blame you for coming over here.'

Joan sits down facing Beatrice square-on. 'My class loved you calling them 'honey'. Never hear the last of it.'

Beatrice picks up a waft of something like pine needles. 'I really appreciated the lesson plans you left. They were really detailed.'

Claire jumps up, dusting crumbs from her hands. 'Well, I can't waste me time in here any longer.'

'Oh,' says Beatrice. 'Only, I still don't know what to do with them for Science. What do you mean about 'food'?'

Claire seems slightly irritated. 'Look, just get them to draw what they had for dinner and label it. Tell you what,

95

we'll give them an extra-long afternoon playtime, then you'll only have fifteen minutes to fill anyway, and you can just read them a story until the bell goes.'

Terri nods agreement over her tea. That's what she'd do.

'Okay?' says Claire, then without waiting for an answer, throws 'Ciao' over her shoulder and scoots off.

Terri gets up. 'Just going for me lunch.' She flashes her packet of cigarettes at Beatrice and Joan, and teeters off.

Joan is eating a salad-spread sandwich made with white sliced. 'So whereabouts are you from, exactly?'

'Vermont.'

'Because I'm looking into emigrating to the States,' says Joan. 'Or Canada. I don't mind. I'm easy. I've got an agency looking into it.'

'Is that so?' Beatrice raises her eyebrows encouragingly while peeling her banana.

'I've had to give them all my details and say what sort of school I'm looking for, which states I'd like to move to and suchlike, and they're doing all the sorting out.'

'Really?'

'They sort out the legal side too. That's why it's so expensive.'

'Why does it need to be expensive?'

'The lawyers. You know what lawyers are like in America. Oh, but they do a good job, I don't mean that. They do your green card for you and whatnot.' Joan starts on another sandwich, peeled from its mate in the cling-film. 'I'm looking upon it as an investment.'

She pauses until Beatrice asks, 'How much is it?'

'You expect to pay them near enough three thousand pounds. I've already paid out fifteen hundred. They're very good. They phone now and then just to give you an update. Or I phone them, when I want them to do a search. They've got an overview of all the jobs.' Joan pulls at the stretchy bread with her teeth. 'It's all on their computer.'

Beatrice places her paperback face down on the chair. 'Why don't you just go there if you want to live there?'

'Oh! I wouldn't know where to start. They sort it all out for you. They can even help sort out your accommodation. They'll literally organise a car to pick you up at the airport. It's all included.'

'It sounds like a lot of money.'

'It's for professionals though, isn't it? Professionals don't have the time to do all this, you see. I mean look at me. I'm in here for seven-thirty some days. I don't get home till five. Call it six. Weekends I'm doing my prep. Not all weekends but a lot of weekends. I mean when are you supposed to do all your applying for jobs, etcetera? And it's a different system there anyway.' Joan smiles cheerily. 'As you know!'

'I'm sure you could turn up and start applying for posts, just like other teachers.' Beatrice gets up to drop her banana skin into the bin, aware of Joan watching her.

'That's a very nice suit,' says Joan. 'I like the pinstripe. I like jackets. I'm a big blazer person myself.' She peels the top from a bottle of cherry drinking yoghurt. 'No, I want to do it properly,' she goes on. 'Get all the legal side sorted out. Because I might be there for ever.'

Beatrice sits down again. 'So you don't have any children to worry about.'

'Oh, Caroline's a very independent young lady,' breezes Joan.

Beatrice stops polishing her apple.

Joan looks gratified. 'I've just got the one daughter. She's fifteen. Nearly sixteen. Exam year. Oh, I don't need to worry about her. Doesn't need her Mum. She's always been *very* independent.'

'So, she wouldn't want to come with you?'

'No no no.' Joan looks away vaguely. 'No-o. She's got her friends. She'll be fine here. Absolutely fine.'

'I suppose it'll be nice for her to come for vacations. Once you're out there.'

'Come whenever she wants. No problem at all.'

Beatrice bites into her apple.

'No problem at all, once I get set up,' says Joan after a big gulp of yoghurt.

The distant screams of the playground give Beatrice, temporarily, a sense of calm, as when the mayhem of family life faintly heard through the wall of the bedsit serves to enhance her own peace.

'So have you got a job to go back to?' Joan asks.

'No. I'm not a teacher in the U.S. I qualified, but gave up after one semester in a school. I only teach when I'm travelling.'

'Means to an end,' Joan suggests.

'It's a good way of getting round the world,' says Beatrice.

Joan considers this for a moment. 'I'm obviously a bit unadventurous compared to you. You can be a bit more spontaneous, anyway, being young.'

'I'm thirty-seven,' says Beatrice.

'Are you?' Joan blinks with shock. 'Well, I like to have everything sorted out, everything just-so, before I take the plunge,' she says defensively. 'But I'm adventurous in my way. More than this lot in here.' She points her thumb over her shoulder at the staffroom as though it were full of staff.

The clock above the door shows it to be already Monday evening. According to Beatrice's watch it's another six minutes to the afternoon bell.

Joan notices. 'Can I make you a coffee?' She is jumping up, holding out a hand to stay Beatrice where she is.

Beatrice watches Joan as she takes a jar of freeze-dried from her locker, noting how smooth and young her face is, how her glasses are too square and heavy. Her lace-ups, the way she stands, would be fine if she were in trousers. She's not overweight; just broad; strong.

'Strong, please.'

'Oh, I make it strong.' Joan's back is turned. 'I know Americans drink it strong. We don't know how to make it here. My coffee makes their hair stand on end in here.' She flicks her thumb over her shoulder again. 'Milk? Sugar?'

Beatrice pushes her paperback back into her briefcase while Joan sets down the coffees on the mess of the table, pulls her chair forward and perches on its edge.

The coffee is bitter but drinkable. 'Good coffee.'

'Good.' Joan grins.

'Vermont's beautiful, you know,' says Beatrice.

'I've been advised not to go that far north. I wouldn't be in the right balance. I'd be better somewhere in the Midwest. It's to do with my stars. There are certain places, like, ley-lines, all around the planet, which will work positively for me. My advisor has them all mapped out. I see her once a fortnight. She's very good.' Joan smiles at Beatrice's single raised eyebrow. 'Don't you believe in things like that?'

Beatrice shrugs, turning her palms upwards in a gesture that says nothing. 'What kind of advisor is she?'

'She reads cards.' Joan clasps her hands round her knees. 'She's told me all sorts of things about myself. She's from Wales originally, but she's actually got Cherokee blood in her. She's a Red Indian.'

Beatrice nods, non-committal.

'I'm very interested in Red Indian spirituality,' Joan goes on. 'My advisor can see what your totem is. Normally it's hovering somewhere around you, and a seer can spot it. Mine's a snowy owl.'

'It's interesting that you've hooked into Native American spirituality when it's such a different culture from – from here,' says Beatrice. 'I mean, most people are Anglican or whatever.'

'I've always liked Red Indians. I mean Native Americans. Ever since I was a child. That's why I've got this pull. It's my natural home. There's something for me there. I don't know what it is yet; I have to go and find out.'

Beatrice surreptitiously checks her watch then hurriedly fishes out her timetable.

Joan is still sipping coffee, unheeding of the time. 'We're not all just boring teachers, are we?' she asks, smiling.

'God, no,' says Beatrice. 'Like I said I'm really not a teacher at all back home. I only did the training. Actually I'm a photographer.'

'A photographer?'

Beatrice feels peeled by Joan's naked way of looking. 'An art photographer. I'm an artist.'

Joan looks stunned. 'But — that's amazing. I'm an artist too.'

A bell rings. The support assistants say 'Ey up.' The catalogue they've been perusing flops closed.

Joan's look is hungry. 'Will you be back in Braithwaite?'

Beatrice stalls. 'I never know; it's up to the agency.'

'I'd like to show you my art,' says Joan urgently, as the hum of children builds up in the corridor. 'Look, I could take you out for a drink sometime. You could tell me a bit about the teaching over there.'

The clumsy suggestion of going out on a date, if that's what it was, makes Beatrice fluster, embarrassed. The invitation is left hanging in the air as the noise of stampede intensifies and she looks around nervously with her empty cup.

'Allow me.' Joan sweeps the cup from her and deposits it in the sink below Fatima's flapping note about the washing-up, then makes three big strides to the door and holds it open like a gentleman.

When Beatrice ducks under Joan's arm she catches, again, her warm, woody scent.

By the end of the day, Chantelle's class are rioting, apart from Benetton sitting at the feet of dull-eyed, unsurprised

Jean. When the bell goes, Connor, Kyle, Kelly and little Mohammad shoot out of the door. Beatrice lines the rest of the class up, after a fashion, and walks them to the cloakroom, then slips back, leaving Claire and the support assistants to help put on coats and deal with mums and lost shoes.

It takes twenty minutes to clear everything away. Finally Beatrice closes the windows, picks up a last scrunched drawing from the floor and bins it, hoping that by now Howard will be waiting in the car-park. She makes a last round of the tables, collecting stray crayons in one hand and pencils in the other and throwing them into the trays balanced on Chantelle's paper-mountain. After scanning the classroom one more time she picks up her briefcase and marches to the door, then stops. Putting her briefcase down again she gets out her pencil case and takes out her Tippex.

The display board at the back of the classroom has been bugging her all day. It is mostly vacant. Its faded yellow sugar-paper shows brighter squares where work used to be pinned. At the top, a dis-attached strip of the numbers one to ten is swinging out like a palm branch. At one end of the board three magazine pin-ups of pop stars are lined up crookedly. Above these, on a strip of grey card, a teacher's clear and careful hand has written in luminous green highlighter pen *Our Favourite's*.

Beatrice goes up to it and, feeling catty, paints out the misplaced apostrophe, then hurries away from the wall in case someone comes. But as the Tippex quickly dries and becomes indelible she starts to go hot and cold with fear at the ill-feeling towards her that this might unleash. She scrabbles through the desk drawers, turns over piles of paper, but is unable to find a green highlighter pen to undo her work. Almost panicking, she turns out the lights and runs down the empty corridor to the exit.

Wind howls through the car park. In the distance, a green double-decker bus is dodging through the council estate that spreads like a maze from the school gate. On the hill, white clouds above the two high-rise blocks have transformed them into cooling towers. The estate could be a vast power station like the ones you see from the M1, except that this one is overrun by scuttering insects disappearing into crevices.

A gust of hailstones hits Beatrice full in the face. She hurries along the line of cars to Howard's, her jacket flapping, her hair getting scuffed and messed.

'Phew.' She crashes into her seat, slams the door, wipes her face with the palms of her hands.

Howard is concentrating on reversing out of the space. 'Had a good day?' He straightens up and heads down the short drive.

'I'm gonna get me a double G and T and sit in the tub,' Beatrice groans, lying back in the seat.

A woman in a blazer, humping a briefcase and an armful of files, strides out in front of Howard's bumper. He brakes to let the woman cross to her car. When she looks into the windscreen, mouthing thank you, he sees heavy, mannish glasses. Recognising Beatrice, the woman grins, then stares at Howard.

'She's the one who winked,' says Beatrice, pulling a little smile back at Joan.

Howard extends his fingers from the wheel to give a tiny wave. 'She does look like a dyke.'

'I think she's married.'

'You like them older like that.' He puts his hand on Beatrice's leg. She looks woodenly at his pristine cuffs, his beautiful nails.

'She's a nice person.'

When Howard removes his hand to change gear, she crosses her legs, out of reach.

Chapter 10

It's an ordinary Thursday. A mist is descending from the hills like a damp blanket smothering everything. Colin's shift finished a bit too late to make it to Caroline's school production, so he's at home alone, making himself an evening cup of tea.

Joan's decision to leave him, announced last night, will not really change anything, except that she'll take Wesley. No more dog bowls to wash up. He catches sight of himself in the window's reflection. He checks his neat side parting and smooths down his moustache, then reaches for the dangling toggle. Joan chose the kitchen blind the year they moved in. It must be fourteen years old but it's still alright. He goes round the house, pulling closed the curtains, which are all fourteen years old except for his daughter's bedroom curtains. He notices he is the first on Moorland View to be closing the curtains against the miserable night.

Bedroom three is his den, where he connects with fellow railway enthusiasts on the net. On the wall is a print of a train steaming across the Ribblehead Viaduct with Whernside rising beyond, and on the desk, a clutter of photographs of Caroline. He picks up the one where she is standing on Morecambe promenade, caught in a hug between her Aunty Darshana and his wife, who is now to be his 'ex'. Some of his colleagues have a problem with pictures of their exes. Colin doesn't have a problem. Why should it be a problem? They are still friends. He pulls his curtains shut.

Later he does himself boil-in-the-bag chicken, taking his meal through to the lounge to catch the snooker.

*

Another Friday dawns. Beatrice wakes first, hearing a thunder of feet on stairs through the wall, a woman's voice calling *Abu! Abu!* She used to feel relatively good when she woke up on a Friday – a day of teachers' camaraderie up and down the land, all of them uttering Thank God It's Friday. Today she remembers, with a sinking feeling, her appointment after school.

Howard is curled into a ball, his satiny back like a radiator turned on low. A further week has passed with him romping, unscathed, through chaotic days in run-down schools then immersing himself each night in writing, phoning, networking. When Howard is working Beatrice skirts unobtrusively around his space. Whole evenings have passed without a word of conversation. Their separateness extends to their shared bed, where they lie like two islands, falling asleep without touching. They have always been oddly formal in the realm of physical intimacy. Desultory sex occasionally ensues if Howard, needing help late at night to switch off from his work, gets her to share a bottle of wine.

Her artwork and her camera have remained under the bed. She has continued to bury herself, instead, in the squalor of Catherine Cookson's industrial north.

When the alarm goes off Howard turns over without opening his eyes.

'Go and make coffee,' she says. Her leg slinks inadvertently against his silk pyjamas. She withdraws it, remembers the brief quiet sex-act last night in the dark; remembers too when she first noticed, soon after they got together, the pleasure Howard took in slipping into silk, ironed to perfection.

Howard jumps abruptly out of bed and drags on his dressing-gown. He shivers, and for a few seconds jogs hard on the spot. 'This climate is invigorating,' he puffs cheerfully, his bare feet punching the carpet. She spies on him pulling on clean cotton socks and disappearing into the chilly kitchenette, hears him put the kettle on then curse. He comes back for his wallet, shakes it for coins, raids Beatrice's purse for fifty pences. The meter ticks and whirrs like an old-time robot as the coins chink in. The kettle sighs. The fan heater by the bed starts up. Through the wall a radio jabbers then switches to tabla drums and the nasal whine of a woman singing.

Howard returns with two mugs of coffee. 'C'mon, get up. This is a working day.'

She remains under the duvet. 'Give me one good reason.'

'Look, you should stop being depressed,' says Howard, helpfully. 'The trick is to know your aims, Beatrice. Know what you want, then go for it.'

Beatrice pokes out her head. Last night's empty wine bottle is standing precariously on the bedside table's accumulated mess. 'Your positive attitude, Howard, in a dump like this, borders on the deranged.'

He checks his watch. 'You need to get moving.'

Beatrice ducks back under the duvet, sliding out of sight. 'I don't want to start the day.'

Unexpectedly she feels a hand resting on the outside of her cocoon.

'Look – it'll be okay.' Howard's voice is gentle, encouraging. 'It's Friday. We'll do something fun tonight.'

In one movement Beatrice flings herself out of bed and across the room. The bathroom door slams and the bath taps go full on.

'Take it easy,' he calls.

A few minutes later the phone rings. She hears Howard's amenable laugh. When he gets off the phone he comes to the bathroom door but doesn't enter.

'They've changed our placements,' He calls. 'We're both going to Braithwaite.'

The niggle of her doctor's appointment after school is over-ridden by a frisson at the thought of Joan Blake; of being the subject of her eagerness again. Then she groans, foam sliding from her elbows like wet snow as she covers her face. 'Oh God. The apostrophe.'

The bathroom has a watery echo. 'I can't hear you. May I open the door?'

Beatrice slumps flat in the bath until her breasts and pubic hair are hidden under bubbles. The door opens a couple of discreet inches.

'What if that Chantelle character lynches me? Did you already tell the agency I'd do it?' She is revisited, even as she is wailing, by a whiff of pine; Joan's woody smell like an old-fashioned aftershave. She wants to go there.

'Yes,' Howard says, placatingly. 'Someone called Chantelle's off sick. I'm doing her year one. You're down to cover a maths specialist so all the work'll be set; she'll even be there to supervise a little.'

Beatrice feels a further flutter. 'That's Joan. The winker. The one in the parking lot.'

'Oh *that* school.'

'Howard, you've taken me to Braithwaite twice already. I was there a week ago. And the Friday before.'

'You know how it is. They all merge into one.' He waits. 'It'll be no sweat. Whadaya say?'

'Okay, okay.' She pushes the door closed and climbs out of the bath. 'I'll do it.'

They arrive at Braithwaite early.

'It took me ten minutes to get into this place last time,' says Beatrice as they walk from the car to the entrance. 'We'll probably be in the porch for a while with a smelly little girl.'

Chelsea is not in the porch.

'No sign of her the last few days,' says the caretaker, when he eventually lets them in.

Beatrice points out Chantelle's room for Howard. 'I hope Claire next door has sorted out some work for you.'

'No problem,' he breezes. 'They're only year ones. I can wing it.'

'If you get straightened out in time I'll see you back in the staffroom for a coffee before the bell,' says Beatrice. 'It's Friday morning; there should be a staff briefing.'

She heads off towards Joan's prefab.

When Beatrice enters the classroom, Joan springs immediately from her chair. 'I'm glad you've come early.'

Joan's blouse is an ocean of shiny turquoise with pearl buttons and lace-edged collar, bunched into the waistband of an ugly pleated polyester skirt, worse than last week's. The outfit ages her by twenty years.

She hurries over to Beatrice. 'I'll show you it now, while it's quiet. I've been carrying it around in my boot ever since you were last in.'

Beatrice looks blank.

'My art.' She waves back at her desk. 'You can be looking at today's work. I've laid it all out. Everything's there.' Then she runs out, jangling her car-keys.

Two minutes later she returns with a king-sized pizza box, opens the top and lifts out the contents like treasure. Each sheet of cartridge paper is carefully separated with white tissue. She begins laying them out on the desks.

Beatrice moves closer and sees coloured pencil drawings. Candyfloss pastels swirl and fuse in whimsical skies with the perfection of computerised imagery. There's a unicorn and a swan; a turreted castle on a hill; an eagle in flight; a portrait of a weathered Native American woman staring wisely off the page within an intricate frame of Celtic knots. Woven into the fibres of the knots are peacocks, tigers, squirrels, the eyes of an owl. Another shows a churning sea and a mermaid, a dove, a rainbow; another a profile of a Cherokee chief with a Celtic pattern woven into his headdress.

'One day, I'll leave all this behind,' says Joan, waving distractedly at the classroom.

Beatrice crouches closer. 'They're – incredibly skilled.'

Joan's expression is dreamy. 'They're not in any order.'

She points to a howling wolf on an overhanging rock; a fairy-tale castle swathed in mist. As her arm reaches, Beatrice catches a waft of something fresh and open-airish; a reminder of woodland walks. 'That's my favourite,' says Joan.

Beatrice's fingers hover over the detail. 'You're very talented. The animal and bird drawings are superb.'

'This is my spirituality,' says Joan. 'Are you a believer?'

'I went around with Hari Krishnas when I was a student.'

'It's not for everybody,' says Joan, surveying her work. 'But I do it for me.' She leans across, lovingly straightening a picture.

'They're so –' Beatrice casts around for an appropriate comment – 'meditational. It's all so... so positive. Peace and wisdom and the beauty of nature.'

Fronds of hair have dropped over Joan's glasses. 'My art will help me to escape.' Her gaze is far away. 'At the moment I'm in the wrong life.'

Beatrice feels a prickle at the back of her neck.

Joan looks at her, distantly. 'Do you ever feel that?'

At eight forty-seven Howard finds Beatrice in the heaving staffroom. 'You should bring your camera in here,' he whispers enthusiastically. 'The poverty of these kids lends itself to some intensely poignant photo opportunities.'

'Christ, Howard.'

The teachers who haven't managed to get a chair have formed a ring of folded arms and tapping feet, waiting for what is going to be a very-last-minute staff briefing.

At last Carole, narrow-eyed, brittle-haired, bangs through the door. 'Right everyone, listen up: Community Cohesion Agenda for Ofsted – I need those forms in.'

'Jeezus,' murmurs Howard.

In the middle of the lunchbreak the staffroom is quiet. Joan's bulk causes a whoosh in the chair next to Beatrice.

'How's it gone with my lot this morning?'

The distinctive scent again: pine woods, mixed with perspiration.

'Oh... not too bad,' says Beatrice lamely. She thinks of big David pummelling little David in the face. The grubby feel of their sleeves in her grasp. The unfamiliar screaming – her own – then Frank Lumb's floor-shaking bellow when he stormed in from the year fours.

'They're alright, my lot,' says Joan happily. 'Some headbangers, but you always get that with boys.' She rummages into a boxful of plastic folders labelled *G-Tech Short Courses: Lesson Plan 1*, and retrieves a flattened packet of sandwiches. 'My lessons with the visitors went down well. Even though Barry Fenton escaped from Frank Lumb's class and harassed us through the window.'

'You give off a very positive aura,' says Beatrice.

Joan flusters with the clingfilm, turning pink.

Beatrice blushes. 'No, really. I mean, people must get inspired by you.' She rushes to the bin with her apple core. 'Can I get you a coffee?'

'That would be very kind indeed,' says Joan.

Beatrice retrieves a jar from her briefcase and returns to the kitchen area, feeling awkward, scrutinised. Joan's look is greedy. Beatrice puts her shoulders back, resting her weight on one foot, as though in front of a camera. When she throws a smile over her shoulder, Joan snaps it up like a dog biscuit.

The staffroom is empty except for some support assistants eating from red trays at the far end, the two who are always left out when anything is planned; the two whose sweatshirts are embroidered with sequins. Each day they sit in the same corner, tutting and sighing.

'Where is everybody?' Joan calls over.

'Pub,' the women say in unison.

'It's Claire's birthday,' says Beatrice. She pours boiling water into two cups, uses milk from a bottle marked 'gerroff me milk!' and brings over the drinks, setting them on some newspapers next to Joan.

The scent, again. Like forests.

'They all took off to have their lunch there,' says Beatrice, 'but I didn't feel like it.' Joan's look is so inquisitive that Beatrice screens herself behind her coffee mug. 'Bit of peace and quiet,' she adds.

'So where's your boyfriend?' asks Joan, unravelling cling film from a second pair of sandwiches.

'Oh – gone with them. He likes that sort of thing. He was having a bit of a joke with Frank Lumb. And he's not my boyfriend.' The last part is blurted out. Joan reacts with an intake of breath. Beatrice instinctively looks over her shoulder in case anyone else is listening. 'We've just got this travelling relationship. We're buddies.'

Joan's attention becomes more intense. 'I'm –' she says, then stops herself from saying 'married.' She dwells for a long moment on her sandwiches; on carefully peeling the one – white and gluey – from the other like an operation on Siamese twins. She looks up with a new topic. 'I see you're into healthy eating.'

'I gotta say this, the British eat some real trashy bread.'

'I know. I saw your face looking at this,' Joan waves her sandwich, 'and I thought, she's disgusted, she is. We all eat white sliced, as a rule. Well, I do. Most people do. Whereas you eat bagels and all sorts, don't you?'

'I like the curries here.'

'You need to tell me all about your life,' says Joan. 'Over there, I mean. In case I *do* decide to emigrate. Coz I don't

110

know where I'm going yet. Haven't a clue, really. Last time I saw my advisor she was a bit vague.' Joan's teeth pull at the stretching bread and she collects a piece of processed cheese from her lap.

When she isn't staring, thinks Beatrice, she has incredibly gentle eyes.

'So. Have you been to the Bombay Garden?'

'Um,' says Beatrice.

'You've *got* to go to the Bombay Garden. It's Egon Ronay recommended. I'll take you.'

'Oh!'

'Take you out. Show you one of the sights. You can't come here without going to the Bombay Garden.'

'I'd really like that,' says Beatrice. She is reminded of Fenella in Cambridge who took her and Howard to her weekend cottage, and of Barnie and Nelson down in Brixton who invited them to celebrate Christmas, Jamaican-style. There has been too little warmth on this northern leg of their trip.

'Super.' Joan whips an old lottery ticket from her breast pocket and writes her name, number and mobile on it. As an afterthought, she turns the card over and writes her address, pressing hard to make it legible over the printed matter. 'Here. You can call me. In fact you can call me any time you like. Any problems or anything. I'm normally available. My mobile will be on.' Then something occurs to her. 'I'm probably moving soon. You'd better just use my mobile number.' She averts any inquiry about this by adding quickly, 'So how about Friday, a week today, then?'

'Friday's good for me,' says Beatrice, thinking that Howard can go for a drink with the grotesque Frank Lumb and then write up another typical Yorkshire character. 'I'd better give you my mobile number too,' she adds.

Joan snaps up the card that Beatrice offers. 'Who are you being this afternoon?' she beams.

'I'm covering for Carole in the I.T. area.'

'Doddle. No problem whatsoever,' says Joan happily. 'The I.T. area's in year six, just outside where I'll be working. Any bother, you send them in to me. I'll pop out and check on you.'

'Thanks.'

'Are you in next week?'

'Maybe. I think so. Ed'll still be off. We might both be in if Chantelle's still off.'

'Excellent.' Joan screws up her clingfilm and throws it into the swing-bin. 'So can you bring in your art, then?'

'Oh.' Beatrice goes red. 'I... it's all work-in-progress at the moment.'

'I don't mind!' says Joan. 'I'll still get an impression. What subject do you do, anyway?'

Beatrice flusters; imagines the images that she might be working on if she were motivated. 'It's all about... here. This place.'

Joan's eyes go big and serious. 'That's fantastic. Nobody does any art about things round here. About how it is. Do you mean the town, or here? The kids?'

'I guess a major theme is the kids,' Beatrice bluffs. 'How they live. Trying to capture their perspective.'

'That's so important. About time someone took notice of how these kids have to live. That's wonderful.'

The bell goes for afternoon registration.

'It's amazing to think of people in other cultures getting an insight into life in this neck of the woods,' enthuses Joan. 'I mean, when they go to exhibitions.'

'Erm. It's a little premature to be able to say...'

But Joan is exuding admiration. 'We're so lucky to have you here.'

The support assistants get up creakily with their emptied trays, straightening their skirts. Just as they are leaving the staffroom door opens and a boisterous crowd stumbles in, larking about, with Howard grinning in the middle. Not for the first time it strikes Beatrice that Howard can be *too* gregarious, sapping the energy of a group until it's all fountaining out of himself.

Joan catches Beatrice's eye, nods in his direction. 'Popular.'

As Howard drives them homewards Beatrice fingers Joan's lottery ticket in her pocket, lost in thought until, reaching the Henrys, she jolts to attention.

'I'm going for a new prescription for the pill. Let me out here, would you?'

'Sure.' Howard pulls in outside the surgery. 'Um. Was that not okay, with the condom? I thought you'd decided to stop taking…'

'I didn't exactly decide, I just forgot it all the time. Don't worry. My decision.'

'Should I wait?'

'No. I'll walk back.'

The waiting room of the clinic on Henry Avenue is packed with mothers and children, airless, pungent, intimate, like an armpit. Beatrice squeezes into a corner next to a girl with a nose-ring. The baby on the girl's knee has bluish feet. A pair of Muslim teenagers in black headscarves swish in, pulling on the hands of a toddler in a tinselly dress. They are greeted by other women with covered heads; women holding onto children in satin garments. The chatter is unintelligible, like radio noise.

It's a long wait. Eric's Fisheries next door opens for teatime and the smell of chips starts wafting through the swing doors. Beatrice, rummaging aimlessly in her briefcase, rediscovers a handful of homemade greetings cards from last week. Some kids in Joan's class made them secretly during reading time. You Are Our Favourite Teacher, they have written. The Best Teacher In The World.

They didn't all manage to remember her name.

The best drawing is the black-suited figure with the wide smile in red felt-tip, waving an American flag.

A nurse calls out 'Beatrice Kirby?'

The pregnancy test is on the spot; no need to send off urine in a bottle and wait three days for a verdict. When Beatrice confirms that she is able to pay, a private termination can be offered immediately, the required signatures of two doctors being a formality.

Beatrice goes ahead and books. She'll decide later. It is arranged for three weeks on Saturday.

Arriving home, Beatrice showers and dresses in clean jeans and a black hooded sweatshirt; boyish. 'You always commandeer the best armchair,' she grumbles.

Howard is already settled in his makeshift workstation, his laptop on his knees, a spider's web of cable and phone lines spilling over the chair-arms and snaking off across the carpet.

'We could stay home tonight for once,' says Beatrice. 'I don't mind. We could get a take-out delivered later.' She sets about organising a workstation for herself on the bed, setting up her printer, plugging in cables, sorting out an extension lead. Eventually her laptop, in the middle of the duvet, is blinking like a comfortable cat. She reaches her folio out from under the bed and turns through the few images she made in the first weeks of northern life.

At last she glances up, feeling looked at. 'Forget it, Howard. I'm not illustrating your articles. I have something to say.'

Part Two:
Learning Difficulties

Chapter 11

Joan cannot start her weekend happily until every last bit of her marking is up to date and her prep for Monday morning is sitting neatly on her desk. When she finally leaves Braithwaite it is already turned six.

The days are, at last, getting longer. It is still light, though gloomy, as Joan makes her way to her new home. She crosses town easily, the snarl-up of commuters having already dispersed. The ring-road circles the bowl of the city, passing above the pink roof of the shopping precinct, along a dark stretch between old factories, then down a steep lane beside the grand dome of the mosque. After a week, Joan is still noticing new things on her new commute – the back-to-back streets rimming the basin of the valley like scum on a sink; the spent-firework look of redundant mill chimneys down in the bottom.

She's renting from a policeman. Colin sorted it out. It all happened so fast, it was meant to be. After a further drive uphill, Joan comes to the blue-grey suburb, her new neighbourhood; a villagey cluster of wet slate and cobbles which would originally have been an isolated hamlet of weavers' cottages. The square – once a market for sheep – is now a car-park bordered by shabby shops: Crabtree's General Store, Watson's Butcher, Sylvia Coiffeuse, The Packhorse. Next door to the well-lit Spar, the dim and peeling Co-operative battles on.

Joan turns off into an alley alongside a converted church, its stained glass windows protected with grilles like riot-shields. The former parish noticeboard has been stripped and varnished and now reads, in silver lettering, Laycock and Small, Architects and Surveyors.

The alley passes between the graveyard and a scrap-metal dealer. After a tower of crumpled car skeletons

Joan takes another right and slows to a crawl. It feels familiar already, like coming home: the stony track, the dry stone wall, the small field, that dirt-matted pony tethered to a stake, the metal gate, the home-made sign hanging on string: *Badger's Dell, no.s 1-4. Private Property.*

Through the gate is a gloomy woodland, and a stream that is said to disappear in summer but which is currently gushing with melted snow from the fells. It runs directly to the west of Joan's bungalow, confirming for her that this was the right place, for the time being.

She puts in a CD. Gregorian chant set against an electronic beat rises eerily as the car rattles over a cattle grid into freshly churned mud. The male voices soar. Joan turns up the volume, fills herself with the sound. A flimsy bungalow comes momentarily into view between the trees. Parked out front is a red and white pick-up. Along the track, a number two is nailed to a pole, and a similar bungalow appears; this one with brown boards nailed over its windows, a chimney emitting a trickle of smoke, and a drive overgrown with brambles. The track crosses the stream over a concrete bridge, only half-built. Waterlogged bags of cement are slumped in a pile at one end. A thicket of rhododendrons almost obscures the third bungalow, though in the curve of its drive, clearly visible, are three semi-dismantled vintage cars. A dog barks somewhere, and a man with a mane of dreadlocks bobs out from under an early Ford and waves a friendly spanner, his face a small white patch in all the fuzz.

Joan's dwelling is at the end of the track. Its farm gate, painted white, is open. Its drive is laid with ornamental gravel, lawn shorn in neat stripes. The bungalow appears to be constructed from board the colour and texture of mud. Its uncurtained picture windows give it the look of a caravan. The room on the left has a fringed lightshade in pale pink; the room on the right, a wooden light fitting with red silk shades. On the moor, a few dirty sheep are mooching about. The horizon is staked out with black telegraph poles joined as though with a fine pen-line like dot-to-dots. Joan pulls in and switches off the engine. When the music stops a howling wind takes over.

She was attracted by the privacy of the trees, and of course the view: when commuter traffic isn't lined up on the distant lane, it could almost be a postcard of the Yorkshire Dales, except for the scavenging gulls circling overhead. The woodland hides the tip that falls away discreetly towards the council estate. The man next door says it's unusual, except in mid-summer, for the wind to carry over its fishy smell.

Joan pulls a box of paperwork from the back seat, hooks her briefcase over her arm and hurries to the porch attached like Lego to the front of the property. The porch contains a parade of shoes ending in wellingtons and a line of margarine tubs sprouting daffodil bulbs. Wesley is pressed against the frosted glass of the inner door. When Joan opens the door he barks and fusses.

The answerphone is beeping. She puts it onto silent mode, changes coats and goes out with Wesley, but after a short walk down the track he has done his business and marches her firmly back. Joan hangs up her dog-walking coat and leaves the opened umbrella behind the settee next to the divan, her bed when Caroline stays.

She starts the evening by giving the living room a hoover. It's part of her routine. Dachshunds don't particularly shed, but Joan finds it meditational. The carpet is smooth nylon; red and gold autumn leaves.

Eventually she pushes the hoover back under the sideboard and puts on a Diana Ross CD. Beside the stereo is a willow-pattern drinks tray with three brands of whisky, a bottle of Gordon's, a Christmassy box of Bailey's Irish Cream with a dangling gift tag, and two cut glass tumblers. She pours herself a medium Jack Daniels and sits on the settee with the glass, fondling Wesley as he twitches his tail to 'Touch Me In The Morning'. At the end of the album she goes to the kitchenette and returns with a mug of coffee. She sits down next to the landline with a heavy sigh. There are five answering machine messages. She presses play.

'Message one,' says the machine.

'Hello, Joan? It's me. I'll call later.'

Joan presses delete.

'Message two.'

'It's me again. Catch you later.'

Joan presses delete.

'Message three.'

There's a pause; then, 'It's time you were home from work. Are you there, Joan? Pick up, if you're there.' Breathing. Waiting.

Joan deletes message three.

'Message four.'

'I know you don't want –'

Joan stabs at the button.

'Message five,' says the machine.

'Joan –'

Stab. 'Cut it out, Darshana!' Coffee spills down Joan's blouse. She changes into a sweatshirt. Back on the settee she pulls out a crystal on a string around her neck and holds it, fondling Wesley, calming down. Finally she reaches for the phone and calls her former home. She listens to Colin's recorded voice. After the tone she says, 'You're never in. When is my daughter going to phone me back? By the way Colin, I've picked up some *World of Steam* magazines second-hand.' She pauses. 'I'll try again.'

On Saturday morning Beatrice wakes up shortly after nine to hear Howard making calls already. 'This is a phenomenal city,' he is saying. 'It's like two different cities. I'm gonna call the piece *Contrasts and Contradictions.* You'll like it.'

She always thought that she would be able to somehow feel a pregnancy, but there's nothing. She stares up at the cheap curtains sticking out in cardboardy folds. Above the window, grass is growing in the gutter. Occasionally great clods of muck, disturbed by pigeons, drop onto the pavement, but the main effects of the blockage are the hollow, unstoppable beats of a drip, and the mushrooming of mould at the top of the wallpaper.

Beatrice kneels up in bed and looks out at the sky, draped over the city like a wet tea towel. Henry Place is littered with cars, some of them taxis whose long aerials are decorated at their tips with little bits of lace from Asian weddings. Glittery ornaments hang from mirrors. Outside the shop, a scattering of little boys is playing in the street with a cricket bat and ball, twittering and shrieking in Urdu. She gets up, pulling a sweater over her nightie, and takes her digital camera from the bedside table. The boys are too far away to get a good focus. She wonders about investing in a good telephoto lens.

Howard is seated like an emperor in his armchair, mobile in hand, laptop open on his knee, coffee cups and papers strewn around.

Beatrice goes to stand in front of the fire, holding her hands out to it. 'So, what did Marcus say, anyway?'

'Pretty exciting stuff. There might – *might* – be a regular column in this for me. He's acting as my agent. We've agreed on his cut if he pulls it off.' He consumes a chocolate chip cookie whole. 'Like, I could be the next Alistair Cooke, only in reverse. Marcus suggested a *Letter from the U.K.*, but I convinced him it'd be better to do a *Letter from the North of England.* This is a region that people don't know about. A whole different ball game. Far more exotic than London.'

'Wow,' says Beatrice. It comes out too flat.

Howard looks at her, uncertainly. 'It's really happening for me.'

'No, I think it's great, all these things taking off. Are you going to get back to Fenella's father about that Sunday supplement opportunity?'

'Max. Yeah, that was one of my calls.' Howard lowers his laptop to the floor. 'He definitely wants the feature; it's only a matter of when. Plus there's the Toronto commission. And of course there's the ongoing contribution to the *Wayfarers* magazine. Okay so it's not high-powered but it's a regular thing.'

He extricates himself from his makeshift work-station and moves towards the kitchen, putting a hand on Beatrice's shoulder on the way. 'They could all be *your* opportunities, too, don't forget.' He gives her shoulder a squeeze and goes to make coffee.

At lunchtime Howard brings through a saucepan of *penne rigate* tossed in pesto and places it on the hearth. 'Quick and easy,' he says.

Beatrice is cross-legged on the bed, concentrating on her monitor. 'Thanks,' she says, vaguely.

'You seem to be working hard.' He shares the pasta between two dinner plates on the rug and passes one up to Beatrice.

'You know that weekend when we first came north when I took loads of pictures?' She holds out a sheaf of printouts. 'Look. They're great shots.'

Howard forks in a mouthful of pasta then takes the printouts. He leafs through the street scenes: flapping laundry; beaten-up cars and playing children; the broken windows of the former chapel down Henry Place on a snowy day; a crowd of Muslim mourners gathered for a funeral, all in white, surging about on the cobbles.

He sees that the latter image is currently on Beatrice's monitor and that she has turned the mourners from colour to monochrome. The shrouded figures are now stark; jagged as ice.

Beatrice ups the contrast further then draws a box around a child peeping between the adults; half a face, looking at the camera. One eye, staring. A small hand, clutching at the cloth of someone's thigh. Beatrice enlarges the boxed area to fill the screen. The shadowy ground between the mourners' feet breaks up, turning speckly. Cobbles burst volcanically through tarmac. The centre of the child's cheek pales to pure white and her eye is a black hole. Finally Beatrice leans back and looks at the screen through narrowed eyes while pranging the pasta with her fork.

'I see you're back onto "art" images,' says Howard.

Beatrice stiffens. 'That's because I'm an artist.'

'Hey. I've always said you're an artist, Beatrice. Don't get me wrong.'

Beatrice stares into the child's eye. 'I'm doing what I want, in the way that I want. This is me.'

'Terrific. Honest.'

Beatrice clicks on Save then picks up her plate of food. 'You know, I've got contacts I've never really used. I'm visualising my work in the arts space where Maria worked in Toronto.'

'That's wonderful.' Howard wanders into the kitchen, eating. 'I'm so glad you're getting some ambition.'

Beatrice is drawn back to the screen. She scoops pasta between clicking on Special Effects, then Soft Focus. 'My issue is the kids,' she calls. 'Their stunted existence in this no-hope city and this miserable climate. They're so limited. You know what I think? People here are constrained by the place. Like mice running round in a wheel. They can't see beyond that oppressive horizon they're all so proud of. They talk about those moors, those 'dales,' like they're paradise, or something.'

Howard appears in the kitchen doorway, waving the cafétière. 'You just covered a whole bunch of issues. You need to be more specific.'

'I'm not asking for your approval.'

'I'm *so-rry.*'

When he returns to the living room he's carrying a tray. 'I'm not disagreeing with you, Beatrice.' He kneels, pours milk into the two cups. 'I won't be raising *my* kids in a dump like this.'

Behind the bungalow a sleet-shower is hurtling across the fell. Joan is trying out a cinnamon bagel, toasted, when the phone rings.

'Hello Joan? It's me.'

'Colin.'

'Which issues of *World of Steam* are they?'

'I've no idea, Colin. They're all in a bag. I've been trying to get you since Thursday.'

'I swapped shifts with one of me mates.'

'And Caroline never answers.'

'She does text messages. She thinks all the calls on this phone'll be the lads from Light Railway.'

'I want to know how she's been.'

'She seems alright. She seems fine. Why?'

'She seemed a bit tired last weekend. What did she say about Sunday, by the way?'

'What about it?'

'Shopping therapy. I took her to the Trafford Centre. Didn't she mention it?'

'I didn't really see her after you dropped her back home,' says Colin. 'Well, we watched an *Avengers* video and had a bit of tea, but we didn't really say anything.'

'That's great, that is. She got that iPhone she's been after.'

'That's a bit dear for an ordinary shopping trip,' says Colin mildly. 'No wonder she didn't show me it. She knows that should be birthday or Christmas.'

'It's a necessity, her old mobile's knackered. Anyway she got two new tops and a skirt as well. And new sports kit for school.'

'Well that's all clothes, isn't it? She doesn't show her dad clothes. She can show those to Darshana.'

Joan slams a lid on a pan. 'What have I said?'

Colin sighs. 'She likes messing about with Luke and Baldev. It's company for her.'

'I'm not happy, Colin. I'm not happy at all.'

'But she's doing what you wanted. She's keeping it to weekends.'

'Well, that doesn't apply any more, does it. She should be coming here for weekends now.'

'You shouldn't let your fall-outs with Darshana affect our Caroline.'

'It's not about me and Darshana. I just don't want Darshana put out, that's all.'

'But Joan, that's where Caroline wants to be.'

'Well it's got to stop.'

Joan ends the call and immediately redials Darshana's number, only to get Caroline, who informs her that Darshana is at Sainsbury's. Joan tries not to moan at Caroline, but fails.

'I've told you. It's too quiet, where you live,' says Caroline. 'It'd be boring.'

'There's your nice room. There's your own computer and your own telly.'

'That's *your* room. It's full of your clothes. You got a place with one bedroom coz you don't want me there.'

'Don't start, Caroline. Your dad wanted you to stay at Moorland View with him, near your school, where all your mates are. We've *said* this. It's all been gone over.'

Chapter 12

The lifeguard is perched at the top of his ladder reading the *Mail on Sunday*. Sundays are the worst shift. Too many kids. At the deep end some Bangladeshi boys, skinny as whippets, are jumping in on top of each other, curled into tight bombs. Their shrieks are deafening.

Close to where Howard is floating on his back, Beatrice is treading water, her small head as smooth as an otter's, her lips bluish. 'I'm getting out.'

Howard spouts water like a sperm whale. 'I'm going through to the gym after this,' he reminds her.

'Whatever. I want to get back to work. I'll see you back home,' she calls, wading towards the steps.

'Alrighty,' Howard calls back.

'I'm not feeling too great,' she adds.

He doesn't hear; waves, backstroking smoothly away.

The plate-glass is steamed over from the inside as though a grey blanket has been thrown over the building. Beatrice pulls the belt of her mac tight against the seeping chill, turning herself into an hourglass. Stepping out of the exit she puts up her new, sturdy umbrella.

She descends the steep street towards the dual carriageway, a cage around the city's southern perimeter. The broad, fast road flattened slums, splitting an area of redbrick streets down the middle, the rows of terraces stopping abruptly where the bulldozers sliced through. The terrace-ends are now thickly graphitised. The back yards have sheds that used to house toilets and new gates where wheelie-bins stand like sentries. Beatrice read in a newspaper that the population on either side is ghettoised: one side from the Indian subcontinent, the other side white. An issue of local concern. Something for Howard to write about.

Beatrice walks through the white side. There are no people about, only dogs and cats. Most of the windows have net curtains – grey and sagging, rigged across the window on bits of string, or bleached and frothy, arching over perky artificial flower arrangements. Windows with no nets offer glimpses of football matches on TV screens. Some houses have white plastic doors with ornate knockers. Others are flaky and scarred, house numbers daubed messily across their panels. Beatrice catches whiffs of Sunday roasts, Yorkshire puddings, dogs, cigarettes. She thinks of the leafy terrace where they stayed in Cambridge, its picturesque back yards with French garden furniture and clusters of plant-pots. She heads for a bridge spanning the dual carriageway and spirals up the walkway built for prams and the elderly.

The city spreads out to the north like rubble. A church with an imposing steeple stands isolated in a wasteland of burnt-out cars and broken bricks, its noticeboard bearing a luminous orange poster with the kind of lettering used by shops when the sales are on. *Jesus is the Answer. Now, what's the question?* In the middle of the bridge the wind gusts under Beatrice's umbrella, spattering her face with rain. She would go for her camera and come straight back here to capture those streets, this wasteland under the grey blanket of the sky, if she didn't feel so nauseous.

At around teatime, as every Sunday, the phone rings.

'Chaz!' Howard snaps shut the laptop on which he has been rattling away since returning from the gym, and lazes back in his armchair.

'We're snowed under, here,' says Chaz. 'I hope you're both available for work this week.'

'No problem.'

'So could both of you do Braithwaite tomorrow?'

'Fine,' says Howard. 'The devil you know, eh?'

'Oh. Did you have some problems there last week?'

Howard laughs. 'Absolutely not. Braithwaite wasn't a problem, was it, Beatrice? No worse than anywhere. The place could do with a new roof, mind.'

'Marvellous. They can use you for another couple of days. I know you like being placed together.'

'It's Sunday,' whispers Caroline. 'I keep thinking it's Saturday. This weekend's just, like, *gone*. Seventeen days to my first exam. If you count orals.'

Baldev reaches out of bed and yanks down the window blind. Under the duvet he is wearing nothing except his watch. 'It's ten to seven,' he whispers. 'What time did you say your dad's picking you up?'

'After his shift. Nine-ish.'

'We'd better do some work,' says Baldev. 'I need to do some Latin for tomorrow.' He hops out onto the rug and pulls on his underpants with his back turned. They scuffle into their clothes. Caroline picks up tissues from the floor by the bed and disappears to the loo, passing Luke's room, where the TV is on loud. When she returns, Baldev is sitting on the duvet with files spread out.

'You don't need to go to your room. I'll have the bed; you can have the desk,' he says.

'Good.' Caroline plonks herself down. 'We'll still get quite a lot done before my dad comes.'

'I think I'll work all through the night tonight.'

'We could've both worked all night if my dad hadn't got so strict about me having to be home. It's only because Mum's been ranting on at him.' Caroline pulls an elastic band from her wrist onto a fistful of hair.

'My mother would've loved that. She'd wind Aunty Joan up with it: *oh, she studies all night long when she's at ours.* She's such a freak, the way she tries to score points.'

'I sometimes work all night at my dad's,' asserts Caroline.

128

'Weirdos. The way they keep falling out, then the next minute, they're on the phone again.' Baldev drags his school bag onto the bed and starts rummaging.

'But it's stopped. The phoning. They used to phone each other every single night. Nine o'clock news, pick up the phone. But it's stopped.'

'That's weird, too.' Baldev picks out a file. 'And the way your mum goes ballistic about you being here.'

Caroline swivels on the office chair and makes herself open her French folder. 'Did it ever strike you that the weirdness started last time we stayed in Morecambe?'

Baldev yawns, scribbles something. 'Dunno. Maybe.'

Caroline procrastinates, re-doing her ponytail. 'It's definitely since then.'

Baldev grunts. Luke's TV, turned up too loud, thrums through the wall. Walter's clock chimes distantly.

'Mum expects me to go and revise at hers – in her little chalet thing. Can you believe it?' She sharpens a pencil into the bin. Then another. Longer curls of sharpenings drop into the bin as she tries to beat her record. Eventually a whole pencil's worth collects.

She chucks away the remaining stub, turns to her verbs, and starts unbending a paper clip. 'Do you think they still do it, your mum and dad?'

Baldev looks up. 'Christ, no. No way.'

'Just coz they've got twin beds doesn't mean they don't do it.'

'He never sleeps with Mum. He sleeps in his study on the "spare bed". In the mornings it's smelly and steamed up in there. He doesn't even use the upstairs bathroom.'

Caroline turns her chair and stretches her long bare stick-legs to rest on the duvet. 'That was probably my mum and dad's problem. Not fancying each other any more.' She tickles Baldev's knee with her toes.

He shifts his leg. 'You should get down to work.'

*

Darshana is putting flamboyant red ticks in exercise books without paying attention. When she can't bring herself to do any more, she uses her red pen in the TV Guide to jigsaw together the evening's viewing. Seeing the time, she goes to the kitchen and pulls out a pizza from the freezer for the boys and Caroline and makes herself a baguette sandwich. She carries her sandwich and a bottle of tonic to her room and settles in for the night.

Through the French windows the sun is golden on the lawn, the willow silhouetted against yellow sky. Beyond the garden the shoulder of the fell is scattered with sheep. If she hiked, she could walk from the back hedge right to the National Park without going through a built-up area. If it weren't for the motorway. Which is better than Joan's ridiculous new residence. Apparently if you walk a few yards beyond the trees behind the bungalow – the prefab – you're looking down onto the council tip. Joan has always needed advising on aesthetic things. Look where she ends up when she doesn't ask for help.

The late film ends in tragedy. Darshana switches off the TV, wipes her eyes, picks up her glass again, lies back into the enveloping sofa and blinks. The baby grand needs dusting. The house has settled into silence. They must all have gone to bed. Her eye comes to rest on her ceramic-handled telephone. She decides to have one last try. The phone is on the bureau next to Walter's Chesterfield. Old-fashioned piece of junk. She totters over, crashes onto it and redials. She is startled by an instant 'Hello?'

'Joan, love.'

'Flipping heck. It's quarter past midnight on a Sunday night, Darshana.'

'I was trying to call you all afternoon.'

'You've left thirteen messages.'

'Well, can't you pick it up, when you hear it's me?'

'You block up my answerphone. Where are the boys? Do they know you're pissed?'

'They're fine. Absolutely *fine*. There's no problem, Joan. Can't we have a conversation?'

'You're an alky. Where's Walter?'

'Ashleep. I jus'... I jus'...'

'It's over, Darshana. We don't do this any more.'

'Please. I jus' want us to go on like before.'

'Don't phone me again.'

The phone goes dead. Darshana crashes the receiver into its cradle, stands, lunges at the mantelpiece and grabs Shiva. Lurching to the cupboard she pushes the tawdry statue into it, right to the back, with all the other rubbish.

On Monday morning Walter's alarm goes off as usual at six a.m. He has continued to get up early despite being retired. Darshana's alarm will go off at six forty-five. Since he withdrew his alarm clock and himself, Darshana has made the upstairs bedroom hers. His hand reaches from under the blankets and pats about for his bifocals, his bottle of pills, his little plastic clock. He sits up before his eyes can close again.

A dull light is already penetrating the heavy paisley curtains. The study is dense with breathed air, body-odour, the musk of books. Walter blinks around at the hulk of his ancient computer, the German pendulum clock with its ponderous tick, the threadbare carpet inherited from his grandmother, the walnut wardrobe, the skinny pipes of his legs laid on the narrow bed. He throws back the crumpled counterpane and stands up, feeling his lungs unfold like paper bags, feeling the strings and pulleys in his back re-arranging themselves in a new balance. His knees tremble as he steps into his slippers, his waist creaking as he reaches for the curtains.

Without his glasses the dry-stone wall over the back hedge is a line of soft pearls strung out to the brow of the fell. The sky is thick and milky. A blackbird is picking at the contents of the birdbath. Walter's face goes misty. In all the years in Weatherhope, the view has rarely been so gentle. On moving in, he had the windows replaced to protect his new family from the gusting wind and rain, though their home continues to sigh with mysterious draught insurgencies and smell pleasingly of stone.

He shuffles into his shower room, sits on the toilet and listens. It is his time. Sometimes he wanders through the sleeping house, noticing all the things that have nothing to do with him. It used to be yoghurty finger marks on the curtains, matchbox cars under the furniture, small brightly coloured items of clothing. Nowadays it is football kit in the hall, dirty plates in the sink.

Sometimes, in the early hours, he puts his head into the barn itself – nowadays, Darshana's private sitting room – and looks up into the gnarled and beautiful rafters. His eye then inevitably catches on the piano that nobody plays, the tacky ceramic telephone, that wedding photograph. Darshana's style of décor has always been anathema to him: peachy roundness everywhere – frilly covers, everything plumped-up. And yet he remains convinced that getting married was a good thing. Marriage made him normal, made him feel less watched.

Of course, it was a huge adjustment. There were the months of mess and smells after the birth of Baldev, and when Luke came along, a phase of bed-wetting in the middle of the night. The most difficult to deal with was the unpleasant clogging of the bathroom with women's things: tampon boxes in the cabinet nudging his shaving equipment into a corner, tights dangling on his head in the bath, talcum powder on the bath mat, an ear-ring in the soap-dish, the sickly smell of female urine.

Not long into their marriage – their new life in Weatherhope – he had the shower room installed next to his study. 'It will take the pressure off the bathrooms,' he had explained. 'A house must adapt itself to growing children.' Darshana had been all for the idea. It would add to the value of the house.

Yes, taking everything into consideration, he has to acknowledge the advantages of being a married man. For one thing he eats better. Furthermore, while he was still working, relationships with his colleagues were improved since they were able to find more to chat about with him. He was no longer vulnerable to their questioning looks – bachelors are practically assumed to be paedophiles.

An hour or so from now, normal teenagers will dash through the house, half in, half out of their school blazers, pieces of toast gripped between their teeth. At weekends he hears stereos raging in bedrooms, and sometimes Caroline, or even complete strangers, thunder past him on the stairs. Occasionally he corrects his boys' manners, or reads something aloud from the paper, which they ignore. These days, when they walk by him in his armchair with his pipe and the *Yorkshire Post* they have taken to patting his bald head impudently. They are, to all intents and purposes, a normal family.

Walter's shower room is empty of toiletries apart from a bar of plain white soap. Walter smells of the soap. The shower room smells of Walter. His journals are stacked against the radiator. This morning, like every morning, sees him sitting on the toilet turning through an old *Spectator*. The blackbird in the garden is singing. He picks his nose and reads, feeling more normal than he ever did in his younger days. He prefers putting up with a few things to living alone. If he didn't have a wife and family, what would he be?

It is seven-twenty. The frost is being smudged gently out of the garden by a pale, unobtrusive sun, and Walter is standing on the landing between two closed doors.

The boys had better be woken.

He clears his throat. 'Boys!'

There is no response.

He knocks on the nearest door, 'Lu-uke,' then on the next, 'Baldev.'

Silence.

Walter briskly opens Baldev's door. 'Time to get up, please.' He does the same with Luke's.

'Where's Mum?' Luke yawns, coming out in bare feet.

'Good morning, Luke. Unfortunately your mother has a migraine. Now, could you get your brother out of bed for me please? I'll see what we can find for breakfast.'

'Just toast, Dad.' Baldev lopes out of his room, gangly and naked except for underpants printed with a cartoon strip. The flesh of his torso is smooth, perfect and beautiful. 'We just eat toast.' The bathroom door slams against Walter's staring eyes.

At seven-forty-five Walter knocks on Darshana's bedroom door with a cup of tea.

'God…'

Walter pushes the door open. The light inside is pinkish. Darshana has an arm crooked over her face. Her other hand is clasped to her forehead. 'Oh my God.'

'Tea,' ventures Walter. He reaches out to place it on her bedside table, keeping well back. Darshana doesn't like to be seen without make-up. He has always endeavoured to reassure her that looks don't matter to him, apart from clothes being cleanish.

'My head,' says Darshana.

'Can I get you something?'

'Are the boys up?' Darshana sits up too quickly. 'God, I'm going to throw up.' She drops out of the side of the bed and stumbles, doubled-over, into the en-suite.

'Sorry.' Walter backs out like a servant, pulling the door closed, not wishing to hear the noise of vomiting.

'Where are the boys?' Darshana calls out, her head in the washbasin.

Walter opens the bedroom door a crack again, dithery, uncomfortable. 'They've gone for their bus.' A whiff of vomit comes through. 'It's seven forty-five, Darshana. Would you like me to phone in sick for you?'

Darshana catches sight of herself in the bathroom mirror. Matted hair, eyes embedded in spongy folds, the mildewy texture of her cheeks. She looks seventy. She looks like the wife of a Walter. 'I have to go in,' she calls through walls to wherever her husband is cowering. 'I've got a pile of reports to collate. I have to go in.'

'You know you can't go in when you're like this. I'll phone in,' Walter calls back.

Her forehead screws up with pain. She hates that Walter is kind. 'Alright, but tell them I'll be there tomorrow.'

'I'll say migraine again, shall I? You phone them later if you feel you can go in tomorrow.'

'I'm going in tomorrow, Walter. I'll be fine.' She feels hot, stifled. She goes through to the bedroom, starts fiddling with the window lock.

Walter hesitates outside the bedroom door. 'It's more convincing to say you don't know yet about tomorrow. You can't be sure with migraines.'

The window opens and cool air from the fells swills over Darshana's cheeks. 'I've got to go in tomorrow. I've got meetings tomorrow.'

'What I mean is, you don't want them to suspect it's just a hang-over,' says Walter.

Darshana rests her elbows on the sill. The garden looks forlorn, elderly – the willow dripping sadly, the lawn a scalp showing through thin hair, the rose borders spindly and frail.

She leans out and retches.

Chapter 13

Braithwaite School has been under a dark cloud for what seems like weeks. Sudden stormy rainfalls have been lashing in from the moors, keeping the playground permanently flooded. There is tension in the air, claustrophobia, like being crowded onto an ark.

Carole's hair is a coiled spring. 'In the absence of Mr Bottomley I'm Acting Head today. Ed's off with stress.'

There are murmurs of 'No!' A man has been lost overboard.

'Mr Bottomley's apparently out all week, on some head teachers' course.' Carole quivers with contempt. 'Therefore we'll be having supply in all week to cover some of my lessons. Plus, as you know, Chantelle's still off.' Her intonation indicates an opinion. 'And obviously there's Ed's timetable to be covered.'

'*And* Mrs Khazim,' calls out a dowdy woman with a grown-out perm. 'How long's this going to go on, me having to teach the year-two classes all together? I'm getting sick of this, Carole.' The woman folds her arms.

'Can you bear with us one more day, Thelma?' Carole's tone signifies *do it, Thelma, or die*. 'We thought Mrs Khazim was going to be in, finally, after the official period of mourning, but she was on the answerphone with a head cold.' The ailment is pronounced as though it were a bad case of chipped nail-varnish.

'Don't forget my demonstration lessons this morning,' Joan pipes up happily.

Howard catches Beatrice's eye and twitches his lips, but Beatrice finds Joan heart-warming, not comical.

'Plus Joan's doing Maths training for G-Tech,' adds Carole. 'As we all know.' Two deep, powder-clogged age-lines form brackets around the mean slit of her smile.

'Speaking of which, there'll be Joan's visiting teachers in the school, so if you see any strange faces, *don't* ask Fatima to phone the police.' Finally, Carole nods over at Howard and Beatrice. 'We're going to try and cover all this with just the two supplies.'

'Ill-mannered witch,' whispers Howard.

'We'll see how we go,' Carole finishes.

Beatrice throws a cursory smile in the direction of Terri's blatant stare, realising that Howard's whispering looks couply and at odds with her claim to singlehood. She draws away from him, turning her head to study the National Lottery chart. A bell goes. Beatrice's stomach lurches, and the staffroom begins to stir at the rattle and hum of children tumbling in.

Howard leaves quickly to return to Chantelle's room where, he says, there's chaos, due to her having been away most of last week. He is first out. The staffroom door swings closed after him.

'He's keen, for a supply,' says Frank Lumb, whose normal voice equates with anyone else's shout.

A few looks are shot at Beatrice; a couple of smirks exchanged just beyond her vision. Terri covers her mouth theatrically, making big eyes at Frank and darting a long pointed fingernail in Beatrice's direction. Beatrice turns her back, picks up her briefcase and Joan's lesson plans and walks out.

'Is that Baldev?'

'Speaking.'

'It's me.'

Baldev feels a surge. 'Where are you?'

'Home, of course,' says Caroline. 'Just thought I'd let you know she took me to Leeds this time. It's quite good for shops on a Sunday. All the main ones are open. I got loads of new stuff. Like, disco wear, make-up and stuff.'

'Guilty,' comes Baldev's habitual verdict.

'You should get your mum to take you shopping.'

'Huh. You know my mum's always pissed at weekends.' He can hear the trill of a computer game. He visualises Caroline's pink computer and pink mouse on the glass top of her desk. 'Aunty Joan and Uncle Colin spend loads on you. You're dead lucky.'

'But you get *piles* of dosh from Uncle Walter at Christmas and birthdays.'

'I'd still rather have your dad, any day. At least policemen are normal.'

'My Dad listens to recordings of steam engines, Baldev. Anyway, listen, can I come over?'

'To revise?'

'*Course* to revise. It's bloody boring here.'

'Is Uncle Colin there? Coz my mum can't come and get you. She took another sickie today. And I've just seen her with a glass, so she can't...'

'No prob. You know what my dad's like. I just have to ask. He might let me stay over too. We're not pandering to Mum all the time. What's up with Aunty Darsh, then?'

'Your mum upset her again last night,' says Baldev.

'Have they started the phoning thing again?'

'Not that I've noticed. I don't think so. I think maybe Aunty Joan's giving up on my mum coz of going to America,' Baldev muses. 'Coz like, there's no point staying friends with people over here.' He checks his watch. 'Are you coming, then?'

'D'you want to watch holiday videos?'

'Not really.' Baldev wants Caroline under the quilt first, then Latin after.

'Oh, go on. The Butlins one – you are *so cute*.'

Baldev bites a nail. 'Okay, after we've revised a bit. Just *come over*.'

'Sand in the beds, sand in the sandwiches...'

A surge is rippling up Baldev's body from his groin. 'Are you getting Uncle Colin to bring you, then?'

'Yeh. I'll just get my stuff. I'll see you in a little while. 'Bout eight.'

'Love ya.' His voice crackles stupidly.

'Yeh.'

On Tuesday lunchtime, Terri straddles the wooden arm of Beatrice's chair, pointing to Beatrice's breasts and then at her own nipple. 'Snap!'

Beatrice looks down uncertainly at her pinstriped jacket; her white Lycra vest with the scoop neck which flattens her breasts to look boyish, adolescent. 'Ah,' she says, realising that Terri's vest is the same one, except that it is purple and stretched over a bra that squeezes her breasts into plums.

'Hobbs,' says Terri, as though uncovering a huge area of common ground. She wriggles her bottom on the chair arm, settling down to eat the tiny pot of yoghurt which she loudly declares to be 'lunch'.

Beatrice leans slightly away.

'Don't mind me. We're like this in Yorkshire; not stuck up, like down south.' Terri winks at Frank Lumb.

'What's teaching like in America, then, compared to here?' bellows Frank. 'Better pay?'

'It's easier. Where I come from, at least.'

The handful of teachers lounging about with sandwiches glance up, mildly interested.

'There aren't the social problems. The children are well-behaved.'

'Doddle, then.' Claire is tipping a sachet of Chocolate Break into a mug. 'Money for old rope, that is. Think I'll emigrate.'

Frank takes a bite of a large teacake. 'Coz you had a bit of trouble controlling the lads in Joan's class yesterday, didn't you?' Bits of salad shoot out of his mouth onto his shirt.

'Aw, leave Bee-tricks alone.' Terri throws an arm round Beatrice's shoulders and presses her drawn, bronzed cheek to Beatrice's in a best-friends way. 'She's come from better than this.'

'That's not hard,' somebody says with a sandwich-filled mouth.

Claire waves her mug as though it were a lager can. 'You're invading Bee-tricks's space, Terri, you big lezzer.'

Terri swings to her stilettoed feet. 'Ooh, yes, darlin'.' She wiggles towards the kitchen area making kissing noises at Claire, fingering Frank's hair as she passes behind his immense back.

'Where's your friend, then?' Claire asks Beatrice.

'You mean *Howie*,' Terri calls over. 'He's a laugh.'

'So *are* you a couple, or what? Did you meet over here, or…'

'God, you nosy cow, Claire,' one of the support assistants says from the corner.

Claire grins. 'I just like to know these things. Coz you seem to say different things. Like, yesterday in the pub he was saying 'partner' all the time.'

'I think he's helping with the Book Club down in year six,' Beatrice sidetracks.

'Is that *keen*, or what?' bellows Frank Lumb. 'Really keen for a supply,' he grins, chewing. 'Only kidding.'

Beatrice engrosses herself in a teaching union's newspaper, an article about league tables.

Mrs Khazim, newly returned this morning, is snuffling into a cloth hanky in her special seat by the radiator. A gloomy cardigan sags to knee-length over her sari. On her lap is a meticulous meal of rice and chicken, which she brought to school in Tupperware, transferred to a china dinner-plate and microwaved.

Don't worry; she's always in a bad temper, Fatima had whispered to Howard and Beatrice this morning, after

140

Mrs Khazim had barged past. She's a spinster but call her Mrs, like the kids do. Not Miss, it upsets her.

'And where is Joan?' Mrs Khazim asks imperiously.

'I've seen her car,' offers a support assistant.

'Fatima says she got called away,' says Claire. 'Family matter. Meant to be back in this aft.' Her voice lowers. 'That's why Carole's spitting venom. She had to be down in year six for two periods this morning.'

'But Joan hasn't got a family.' Mrs Khazim looks stern, as though Joan is truanting.

'She's got one lass,' Frank Lumb corrects her.

Claire lets her jaw drop. 'God. I knew she'd been married but I thought that was just a cover.'

'My wife's brother married a lesbian,' says Frank. 'Well, she swings both ways. They're still together. He's got some sort of arrangement with her and her girlfriend. Alright for some.'

The support assistants begin listing, between themselves, all the gays that they know of among their friends and neighbours; mostly, wayward sons.

A yellow dribble has appeared down Mrs Khazim's sari. Now she loses a clod of rice from her quivering fork. 'We shouldn't be running around after our children when we're employed to do a professional job.'

The bell for second lunch sitting makes Beatrice jump and glance again at the afternoon's timetable on her knee. Covering for Ed. Information Technology.

'The problem with today's teachers is lack of commitment,' chunters Mrs Khazim.

Within minutes of the final bell Braithwaite's car park is an ants' nest of zipping vehicles. The children stream along the pavements beside the jam of teachers' cars, making rude noises and gestures or smiling and waving, excited to spot their teacher outside of school; even one minute outside.

Beatrice, slouching in the passenger seat, notices a slight ripple of flesh above her trousers and wonders whether it relates to her condition. Her hair is glued to her scalp with perspiration, a by-product of trying to manage the uneasy mix of humanity gathered in one class: the vulnerable, the stunted, the hardened pre-adolescent criminal types. Her fingertips are blue from the white-board, from fevered rubbings-out done with her hand instead of hunting for the rag. She scrutinises slivers of coloured crayon embedded in her palms.

'I feel begrimed.'

Once off the estate, the ring road unrolls across a wasteland caged in by temporary fencing. A hoarding marked Development Opportunity is leaning on its side where it fell in the wind. Shopping trolleys and traffic cones are embedded in the mud. A mattress, its middle ripped out, lolls over a fly-tipped fridge-freezer.

'Did you hear that Joan Blake was called away to a family crisis?' asks Beatrice.

'Sure did. I was called in to take her class for P.E. along with Ed's but they wouldn't co-operate. One David smashed the other David's watch into little pieces against the wall. I had to send for Carole. It was mayhem.'

'I got off lightly,' says Beatrice. 'I just let my year fours play computer games. Wonder what Joan's problem was?'

Howard shrugs. 'She'd showed up by the time we left.'

'Might get the story tomorrow.'

'Dunno. They say she's a private person. *A bit funny.*' Howard imitates the accent. He turns off the ring road into the Henrys. 'Apparently when she does hang out she has one too many. Frank showed me a photo on his mobile of Joan and Terri at the Christmas party,' he slows to turn into Henry Place, 'in the john.'

'Doing what?'

Howard grins. 'Terri was sitting on Joan's knee while Joan was peeing. Wild, huh?'

'Jeez, that is *so tacky*.'

'On school premises,' Howard adds.

'Howard, are we prudes?'

'Actually I think so. Hell, once you've all pissed in front of each other there are no more taboos and everyone can just get on. Yeah. I think we're uptight snobs.' He pulls into the space in front of the bedsit.

'Will this go into a 'Letter from the North of England'?'

'You bet.'

It hasn't rained all day. Some shrouded women are gliding swannishly along the pavement of Henry Place, scuttled after by duckling-headed children. An elderly bearded man in an embroidered hat approaches, peering at Arabic script on a newspaper held close to his eyes.

Beatrice gets out of the car and slams the door. The man with the newspaper pauses, hawks, spits, walks on. The spittle lands by Beatrice's heel. She turns to look at the man's retreating back.

Howard skips round from the driver's side and steps up to the peeling entrance with the key.

Beatrice doesn't move. 'Did you see that?'

'What?'

She points to the glob on the pavement and nods down the street after the man. 'Was that on purpose?'

Howard tuts. 'You've got a persecution complex.' He goes into the hallway, trampling over weeks of junk mail.

She follows Howard in. 'Your problem is, you always think everything's just fine. Everybody. Everything. Maybe I'm more tuned in than you.'

Once indoors Howard hangs his jacket on a gentleman's outfitters' wooden coathanger, loosens his tie and crashes onto the settee. 'I'll call Chaz to confirm we'll be at Braithwaite a third day.' He picks up the phone.

Beatrice makes tea, still in her suit, wrinkling her nose against the kitchen's rancid smell. She detests the mishmash of broken drawers, the encrusted pans hanging from hooks, the wall-cupboards from which doors are missing, the bacteria-ridden fridge. She lays a tray with Art Deco teacups picked up for a pound in a charity shop and a rosebud plate, on which she places supermarket *petit fours*. When the tea is made she carries the tray through, sets it down on the rug at Howard's feet, and sits cross-legged on the floor.

Howard has finished phoning. 'They only need one of us at Braithwaite tomorrow.'

'Why? Ed won't be back. Chantelle won't be back.'

'Chantelle's back. Chaz said the year one isn't available for me tomorrow.'

'Shit. That means I'm there with Chantelle. She'll lynch me.'

'I knew you'd say that, so I told Chaz I'd prefer to stay at Braithwaite myself because I committed to a lunchtime ball practice with the boys – hope that sounded convincing.'

'Howard!' Beatrice reaches up, pecks his cheek. 'I rely on you.' She yawns and stretches, holding her stockinged feet to the fire.

Howard sips his Earl Grey. 'So you're at St Ninian's tomorrow. Covering for the alcoholic deputy.'

'The snobbish school?'

'Church of England. Polite, articulate kids, spotless staff kitchen, filter coffee. You'll love it.'

Beatrice takes a *petit four*. 'I guess that's as good as it gets.'

Chapter 14

At the sound of the entrance buzzer the secretary looks up from checking the milk order and spots, at the top of the car-park, Clarissa's Morris Traveller shuffling itself in between two cars, the hump of her harp visible in the back. Meanwhile a slender, stylish woman is waiting at the door. The secretary releases the lock and Beatrice enters the foyer.

'Welcome to St Ninian's.' A long, creamy hand reaches through the hatch. 'I'm Lilian Peck.'

'Beatrice Kirby. Glad to meet you.'

Lilian Peck's voice sounds like the Queen's. Beatrice shakes the hand. There is a smell of polish, like in a museum. In a glass case in the foyer is a spotlit display of elaborate gothic castles constructed in clay.

The secretary sees Beatrice looking. 'Our Land of Gondal project. We had the inspectors in last week.'

'Seems a lovely school.'

The secretary's smile is superior. 'Oh, it's a very good school.' She hands the visitors' book through the hatch. 'If you'd like to sign there, I'll show you to the staffroom in a moment. It's one of our deputies who's off today.' She suddenly cranes her neck over Beatrice's shoulder. Beatrice turns to see a harp on legs approaching.

'This is Clarissa, our harp teacher. She's Royal Academy. She only does private schools really; we've got her through sheer parental demand.' Lilian emerges from her office to hold open the door. 'She can play anything, you know. Mor-ning!' she calls out girlishly. 'Clarissa, you're as strong as an ox.'

The harp wobbles up the steps, then Clarissa, dishevelled, heaves her instrument through the door and lands it triumphantly on the mat. 'Phew!'

The secretary brushes fussily at Clarissa's shoulders.

'Dusty thing. Let me bring you a cup of coffee.'

Clarissa whinnies.

The secretary leads Beatrice to the staff suite, pointing out the cloakroom and catering facilities. 'If you'd just like to take a seat, Mrs Forboyes will come and sort you out. *Do* help yourself to the refreshments.'

The secretary loves her Wednesday morning gossips in the front office with Clarissa during Mr Forrester-Paton's assembly.

'She's off again.'

Clarissa lowers her coffee-cup. 'Doesn't surprise me in the slightest. It'll be the usual.'

The secretary swivels closer on her chair. 'I'm sure you're right. I mean, off Monday, in yesterday, then off again today – what sort of a migraine's that?'

'How did she look?' A spindly arm reaches for the secretary's knee.

The secretary feels a frisson. 'Shocking. White as a sheet; blood-shot eyes.'

Clarissa tuts. 'Dreadful.'

The secretary slides cattishly from under Clarissa's hand and opens the first register on the pile. 'I don't know how it's going to end.' She starts inserting today's notices.

'We all know each other's business of course in Weatherhope.' Clarissa fumbles under her skirt, pulling up pop-socks. 'Her eldest son refers *quite* openly to his mother being under the influence; finds it *totally* normal – just inconvenient that she can't drive him about.'

'What about her husband?'

Clarissa splays her thin fingers. 'The poor man. Though I'm sure he's part of the problem. They can *never* have been suited. Complete enigma, the whole thing.'

The door opens. The singing has already started in the hall. 'Morning Clarissa.' Mrs Forboyes brings Beatrice into the office and hands Lilian a spiral-bound resource book. 'I've just shown Miss Kirby the literacy materials in Darshana's classroom for period one. Could you copy twenty of this in time for period two?'

'Leave it with me.'

The three women's heads then come together while Beatrice loiters, ignored like a child.

'Is it the same thing, with Darshana?'

Clarissa tipples an imaginary glass. 'The usual.'

'Clarissa hears it from the village,' adds the secretary.

'It's so difficult.' Clarissa wrings her hands. 'We all do so much together as a village community. All our church activities. It'd be awfully good for her to get out more... but it's all Christian, you see. One can't draw them in in the same way.'

The women cluck agreement and sigh, then Mrs Forboyes turns to Beatrice and uses a louder voice. 'I'll take you into assembly and stand you on the end of Darshana's line so that you can lead them back to their classroom. They've already had their register taken. Is there anything else you'd like to know?'

'Nothing at all. I really appreciate all your assistance.'

Beatrice gives Mrs Forboyes a charming smile. The vibrations of child-noise in this school induce a pleasant frisson rather than a clenching of the stomach, and Darshana's classroom looks orderly and plentiful.

'Beatrice is from Vermont.' Mrs Forboyes' expression is warm. 'Lovely suit, by the way.'

The secretary feels Beatrice's cuff. 'Yes – I've been admiring it too.'

On Wednesday evening Darshana goes to borrow Baldev's ointment. She finds him sitting in the eerie light of his computer with the curtains drawn, engrossed in the periodic table. He has changed out of his school clothes into a drooping vest, baggy shorts and an old leather waistcoat raided from Walter's wardrobe. In what seems like only weeks, his shoulders have turned knobbly and narrow and he has shot upwards, his child's body stretched into a long reed.

'Thanks Mum,' he says, vaguely, not turning when she knocks.

'Oh! I'm awful,' she says, ashamed of her lapse in mothering instinct. 'I'll bring you a coffee, love. In a minute.' She slips in, takes the little tube from his dresser and creeps backwards.

Baldev turns round. 'Mum.'

She pauses in the doorway.

Baldev scowls his mother up and down. 'Are you alright, Mum?'

She feels embarrassed, knowing she looks frumpy and rotund in her towelling bathrobe with the long threads pulled out of it here and there, and last Christmas's slippers whose fluffy tops are dampened-down and grubby. She looks down at the satin bow of her nightie trailing limply from her neck. She put on her face this morning but hasn't checked it all day.

Baldev stops at her eyes, looking suspicious.

'I've had such a head all day,' says Darshana.

'Have you been drinking whisky?'

'I always have a small whisky after my tea.' She tightens the belt of her robe. 'As you well know.'

'You used to only do this at weekends.'

Darshana doesn't acknowledge his meaning. 'I'm back at work tomorrow. I just needed another day.'

Baldev swivels back to his keyboard and taps a few times, hunched, head down, sullen. 'Only, there's a cricket thing on Friday night over in Hebden Bridge and it's sort of your turn for lifts. The village team, not a school fixture,' he adds. 'They all know about Dad's eyesight,

Mum.' His voice is low. 'It's getting a bit embarrassing, thinking of reasons why you can't take a car-load now and then.'

Darshana slouches against the door, feeling a weight pressing down on her neck and across her shoulders, as it has all day, like a yoke. 'Hebden Bridge is a long way for the youth club to be going.'

'I wish I'd passed my test,' Baldev growls.

'Fine. No problem. I'll take you there, darling. You and whoever. I can't bring you home as well though. Is that fair?'

'As long as you'll be alright,' he says, grimly.

Walter's ancient clock is distantly chiming nine.

'Joan? Joan, it's me.'

'*You…*'

'Look.' Darshana's voice catches. 'I know you don't want to hear from me, but I think you should know…' She has a sudden memory block. 'About Caroline.'

'Caroline.' Joan's voice is a tightrope stretched to snapping point. 'I'm trying not to blame you for this, but it's very hard.'

Darshana reaches up from the sofa and sets her glass with extreme care on the piano. Joan is so tense on the phone nowadays. 'Joan, love. I –'

'Did you have any idea at all what's been going on?'

'– I just wanted to tell you about Caroline…'

'Or have you been legless in your sitting room every night, letting them get on with it?'

'They work ha – hic – *hard* when they're together. They're going to do so well. Make us both proud.'

Joan makes no sound. Darshana senses something serious is afoot. 'Joan?' She uprights herself, tries to sound more sensible. 'Joan? What's the matter?'

There is a small, powerless sigh, spent of everything. 'I've been to hell and back since yesterday.'

'What I was going to say is,' Darshana blurts, remembering, 'Caroline's using our Baldev's ointment for her spots. It's ever so good, only it's a prescription ointment, otherwise I'd get her some. I was going to suggest you could take her in and get a prescription. It's called – hang on; let's have a look–' She reaches for Baldev's acne cream on the piano.

'We were at Doctor Steed's most of yesterday.' Joan cuts in savagely. 'I was called out of school because Caroline fainted again. Steed's good. He was very direct. He asked her if she could be pregnant and she said she didn't know. He did a test and it was positive.'

Darshana goes rigid as a stick. Among the dried flowers in the dead grate of the fireplace, a spider has crocheted a cobweb between an ear of corn and a blue daisy. The tube of ointment is being squeezed out of shape in her hand.

'Are you in a fit state to take this in, Darshana? She's nine weeks pregnant. Her and Baldev.'

'But...'

'But nothing! She's got her GCSEs next week.'

The receiver vibrates in Darshana's hand.

'It's alright for your Baldev. It's alright for the boy. No problem. *No problem whatsoever.*'

'What... what shall we do?'

Joan chokes. 'It's not your problem, is it?'

'We'll all rally round,' says Darshana, 'If she decides to keep it...'

'We're *not working class,*' Joan spits. 'She's *fifteen*. She wants to do her GCSEs and carry on. She doesn't want a bloody *baby.*'

'She's not there, is she?' Darshana frets, hearing Joan's yells echoing around the prefab.

Joan quietens down. 'She's at her dad's. He's being very good.'

'Colin never over-reacts,' says Darshana.

150

'He never really reacts,' agrees Joan.

'She'll need counselling,' says Darshana.

'She's horrified by the whole thing,' says Joan. 'She's having an abortion in Doncaster a week on Saturday. She just wants it to go away and so do I. She's only got orals the following week so she should be alright.'

'What about the father?'

'Colin? He'll drive her down on the Saturday and I'll pick her up on the Sunday. They spring back, apparently. She just has to wear sanitary towels for a few days.'

'Baldev, I mean.'

Baldev – for crying out loud, Darshana. They didn't even know they'd had proper sex. There's no "father" about it. They're kids. He's got his A-levels.'

'Yes but... does he know?'

'Of course he doesn't know. *We* only knew yesterday.'

'Well, who's going to tell him?'

'Caroline doesn't want him to know. She says she's embarrassed. She wants it all to be kept secret. She just wants to get it over with and do her exams.'

'It's got to be her decision,' says Darshana. She sees Walter holding his new grandchild in the awkward crook of his arm looking helpless, like he did with his sons, bottle-feeding in the manner of someone dripping a pipette into a test-tube. 'There could be options...'

'Caroline was quite clear with Doctor Steed, Darshana. She knows what she wants, and this most definitely isn't it, at this moment in her life. *Never in a million years.*'

'That's you, though, saying that.' Darshana cringes, and holds the phone a little further from her ear, but goes on, 'We know what you were like, when you found out you were pregnant.' Darshana can hear stark, empty space; how the very daylight, shot in through Joan's prefab's barren windows, is exploding on the walls.

Chapter 15

By midweek, the track through Badger's Dell is deep in mud. Returning from his evening walk, Wesley meets his sworn enemy and ends up on his back legs, half throttled, eyes bulging, as Joan pulls on his collar. Buster the Rottweiler puppy is being similarly restrained by Derek from number three.

'Nasty weather for the middle of May,' says Derek. Stray dreadlocks snake out around the neck of his nylon hood, which is stuffed solid with hair.

'Rotten,' says Joan, as they haul their animals past each other. She opens her mouth to add more but Derek doesn't notice and walks away down the track, his anorak dissolving into the darkness. Rain patters down Joan's neck. She scoops Wesley's business into a plastic bag and they return to the bungalow.

After Wesley's paws have been sponged off in the porch he flops happily in front of the fire. Joan hangs up her dripping raincoat, stands her wellingtons on newspaper and goes to sit by him. She switches on the TV as Big Ben is chiming ten o'clock. She switches the TV off again and lets down the window blinds. The constant rain-noise drumming on the roof is calming, like the evening chirping of crickets on *The Waltons*.

She picks up Caroline's school photos from the mantelpiece, one by one, youngest to oldest. In the last three you can see the acne on her chin. Joan's shoulders sink. Her eyes slide to the Jack Daniels on the sideboard. She goes over, fingers the tumbler. Wesley is snoring.

She reaches under the candlewick on the single bed for her pyjamas, undresses and puts them on, laying her day clothes over the back of the settee. She doesn't sleep in the big bed in the other room any more, wanting

Caroline to feel that it's more 'hers'. She takes today's underwear through to the laundry basket then goes into the kitchenette to put on the kettle, and waits for it to boil, gazing at her 'X-Files' calendar. Gillian Anderson in leathers. Picking up a green crayon, Joan counts ten days hence and writes 'Doncaster' across Saturday and Sunday. The space for the coming Friday is filled with 'Beatrice' and a mobile number. A green arrow wiggling up the calendar's margin leads to BOOK TABLE.

She leaves the kitchenette taking the calendar and a mug of Ovaltine, her mules slapping on the hall's lino, and settles into her armchair by the fire, in front of the long gallery of her daughter's face. Her hand reaches down the side of the cushion for the phone.

Beatrice is on the bed peering intently at her monitor.

'I like reaching Wednesday evening. Broken the back of the week.'

Howard murmurs agreement, his fingers rattling over his keyboard.

'So how was Braithwaite today?'

'Uff. The usual. Frank Lumb says Ed's exploring early retirement on mental health grounds.' He deletes a whole line then rattles on.

'I'm packing up for tonight,' yawns Beatrice. She makes two mugs of tea then curls up at the end of the settee with her latest Catherine Cookson.

At half past eleven, the phone rings.

'Hello? Hello? Can I speak to Beatrice Kirby please?'

'This is Beatrice Kirby. Is there an emergency?'

'Oh! God, is that the time? Look I'm ever so sorry, I hadn't even looked at my watch. It's okay, no problem, I'll phone you tomorrow. I thought it was about ten-ish. Sorry about that. Bye - '

'Joan? Is that Joan?'

'Sorry. Did I wake you up?'

'No! No, it's really okay. I'm just reading in front of the fire. Haven't gone to bed yet.'

'Sorry, anyway. I'm just phoning about Friday.' Joan does her nervous laugh, like the tossing of a small thought into the trash.

'Are you okay?' asks Beatrice.

Howard, tapping away in his armchair, glances up, inquisitive.

Beatrice shrugs at him, turning one hand palm-up.

'I guess so. It's been a helluva day, but I'm okay.'

Beatrice hears an American accent. Maybe it's to be friendly. Maybe it's not even conscious. Maybe Joan's in a late-night fantasy where she's already in the States.

There's an awkward pause. Beatrice puts on a bright, conversational voice. 'I'm still fine for Friday.'

'Super. That's great. That's why I'm phoning. I was about to phone and book us a table and then I thought – better double-check with Beatrice that she's still alright.' Joan does one of her laughs but for no reason. She doesn't seem her usual self. There's another pause.

'I wasn't in Braithwaite today,' Beatrice says, inanely.

'No,' Joan rushes in, relieved. 'Your friend was. I didn't speak to him.'

Beatrice traces Tilly Trotter's bonnet on the book in her lap. 'I was in St. Ninian's, if you know where that is.'

'St Ninian's.' The line sizzles with new animation. 'You weren't, were you? That's a co-incidence.'

Beatrice tucks her bare feet inside her nightshirt. The corner of the settee has been eroded into a bowl-shape, and she nestles in more deeply. 'Why co-incidence?'

'I have a very good friend there,' says Joan. 'Well, we *were* good friends. Best friends from college. We go back a long way. I don't actually see much of her any more.' A small pause. 'We've moved on.'

Howard, already in his silk pyjamas, lifts his laptop from his knee to the floor and stands up.

'Would I have met her?' asks Beatrice, as Howard taps his watch and indicates that he's going to bed.

'Darshana. Darshana Chatterjee-Fox? Quite short, very feminine?'

Beatrice becomes more interested. 'That's who I was covering for.'

'She was off, then?' Joan sounds crisp.

'Migraine,' says Beatrice.

'Migraine?'

'You sound cynical.'

'No. No-o. She gets terrible migraines,' says Joan. 'We go back a very long way.'

Beatrice fishes again, her curiosity aroused. 'Howard's met her, though. Actually he has an *opinion* about her.'

Joan is hooked. 'Oh yes?'

'He thinks she's an alcoholic.'

'Pshsh.' The nervous laugh again. 'I don't think so. She's senior management.'

'Is she married?'

'To Walter. He was a professor of something to do with scrolls. He's much older.' Joan abruptly changes the subject. 'They don't know they're born at St Ninian's. They've got selection.'

'They've certainly collected together some smart kids.'

'So, will you be in with us again at all?' Joan's voice sounds slightly pleading.

'We never know for sure until the night before.'

'So I might see you, or I might not,' says Joan. 'Before Friday.'

A few butterflies stir in Beatrice's stomach. Like in high school. Like dating. 'So we'd better arrange now how we're going to meet up.'

Howard returns from the kitchen with his habitual hot water bottle, despite it being May.

'I don't drive in this country,' Beatrice adds.

'I'll come and pick you up, then.' Joan sounds delighted to take charge. 'No problem whatsoever. Pick you up and drop you back off. So where are you?'

'Do you know the Henrys?'

'You don't live there, do you?'

'47c, Henry Place. Top bell.' She watches Howard slip the hot water bottle into the bed and get in.

'I'll have to show you some nicer places,' says Joan.

Beatrice begins patrolling the bedsit, flicking electrical switches. 'Shall we say, around seven?'

The line is zinging with Joan's enthusiasm. 'No prob.'

'I really need to go to bed now,' says Beatrice. Howard is already a mole beneath the duvet.

'Sure thing,' says Joan.

'So I'll see you Friday.'

'Seven o'clock. I'll ring the bell.'

'So. *Ciao,*' says Beatrice.

'*Ciao* for now.'

Beatrice goes to brush her teeth and finally bounces into the bed. 'That's my date!'

Howard is turned away. 'I'm very happy for you.'

'*God,* Howard. Did I ever object to your recreational encounters?'

'I've never objected to Maria, have I? But when we're away together, I thought the deal was, it's just us.'

'Who made that decision? And what about the next time you slip away discreetly to some English gentlemen's public convenience? Who's making the rules, here?'

'Don't get tacky, Beatrice. The point is, I don't *date.* It's not the same. *You're* the person with whom I choose to go places; spend my time with. Whenever I met someone recreationally – which I don't do any more, in case you haven't noticed – we didn't even exchange names. It was completely irrelevant to you and me.'

'So is Joan, Howard. Stop being a jerk.'

Beatrice yanks on the quilt and turns back-to-back. Howard's shoulder blades point sharply at her through the silk. She curls away in the bed into her own island.

It is approaching midnight. Around this time, Baldev is normally brought another coffee and an orange Club biscuit by his mother as she heads for bed. When Caroline is here, his mother brings two cups and two Club biscuits on a tray. Sometimes Baldev and Caroline are under the duvet when they hear her coming up the stairs. They will still be scurrying into their clothes as she is pressing on the door with her elbow, holding the tray, finding the bolt on.

'We've been keeping Luke out, Mum,' Baldev will call, hopping about to get his legs in his trousers. 'He's been a nuisance.'

'Coffee.' Darshana is by his shoulder, carefully placing a cup and saucer on his mouse-pad.

'Thanks, Mum.' Swivelling round from the periodic table he smells the whisky as his mother pushes his ointment back among the debris on his chest of drawers. Then he smells the Club biscuit, melting in its wrapper where it touches on the cup. Later he'll carefully lick clean the paper. Never waste good chocolate.

Luke is snoring asthmatically next door. His mother has stopped in the middle of the room, just standing there. Normally she doesn't stay and chat at this time of night. Normally she's slurring her words by now. But tonight she says, 'You and Caroline. You've got a relationship, haven't you?'

'So what?'

His mother's face is shadowy. 'She's going to have a baby, Baldev.'

When he swings round to face his computer, the periodic table is still there, unblinking, unchanged. His coffee is steaming blandly in its prissy saucer as though everything's ordinary and usual. The heat of it is melting the chocolate. It will run off the biscuit and spread into the wrapper, where, if not licked off, it will cool during the night hours and re-solidify, deformed. Eventually the periodic table will blink and disappear and the screen-saver will begin swirling its oily bubbles, purple and blue. Any moment now, Dad's grandfather clock at the foot of the stairs will strike once for a quarter to the hour, which will be four minutes later than the correct time. It is approximately eleven minutes to midnight, and there are thirteen days to go until his first A-level exam. It will be Chemistry, paper one. After the exams are all finished, there will be Lofty's barbecue, and the cricket finals, and the French trip, and…

His mother is slipping out of the door as though she'd done nothing more than kiss him goodnight.

'Wait.' Baldev lurches out of his office chair, all knobbly joints, like a puppet. No-one has ever considered him a grown-up, a real person. You can't then turn round and suddenly throw it in someone's face: *be an adult*.

A father.

His face screws up. He kicks out at the waste paper basket. It rolls across the floor and bits of discarded paper go everywhere. His life is over, scrunched into a little ball of rubbish. The whole future, lost from the screen at one click. Deleted.

'Mum!'

She hesitates at the door, turns.

He falls back onto his chair. It skates against the desk.

'What's going to happen?' he blubbers.

When he was growing up, when he cried out loud like this, when tears came in uncontrollable floods and he rubbed his fists into his eyes, his mother would take him on her knee and say things, and it would be alright.

He feels her crouching next to his chair. He feels the grotesqueness of his own knee that his mother is

158

nevertheless stroking. He looks down on her, a blur of pink towelling, and knows that that stage is over. Now that she's smaller than him she can't do anything.

'She's got to have an abortion, Mum. She's *got* to. It was an accident. I don't want it.'

The pink blur tugs a man-sized tissue out of the box on the bedside table and passes it up to him. 'It's a shock.' She waggles his knee as though his team had just lost a match.

He stares at her. 'I don't –' He puts his two hands over his face. 'It's a mistake.'

'Well, when you've got used to it, it might be alright.'

Baldev's arms fling out, his hands landing with force on Darshana's shoulders. '*No.*' He wants to shake her, but she's his mum. 'Don't be so *stupid.*'

Down on the carpet his mother sighs, holding onto his knee to keep her balance. 'You're sure, then.'

'We didn't even *do* anything.' His voice squeaks and cracks. 'Not properly.' He scrapes savagely at his face with the tissue.

His mother stands unsteadily, knees clicking in an ordinary, everyday way. 'You know, you might feel differently tomorrow...' her voice trails off.

A tremor starts somewhere inside, building up until every bit of him, to his fingernails, is shaking. He thinks he might vomit. 'She's *got* to get rid of it, Mum. Tell Aunty Joan I don't want it. She mustn't have it. I don't want *anything* to do with it.'

His mother's voice is a whisper. 'You could all live here.'

Chapter 16

Chaz calls, flustered, early on Thursday morning. 'Beatrice! Can you do a day in Sunnydale School? It's literally round the corner from where you live. Everyone's off with the flu. They're desperate.'

Beatrice takes in her new zoom lens, acquired in a sale. In spite of its dour Victorian exterior, the school is chaotic, vibrant and homely. She introduces herself as an artist who is supply-teaching in order to gather photographic images around local schools for her current project. She is welcomed with smiles and a cup of sweet, milky tea flavoured with cardamom, and taken into the central hall where women in saris and salwar kameez are milling about, waist-deep in children. Beyond the tall, high windows, the sky is as grey as ever, but indoors the colours are festive. Parents linger, chatting, in corners, with children running up to show them a drawing or a page in a book. The day has a spontaneous, haphazard feel: activities begin with a clap of the hands rather than a bell. The timetable seems infinitely flexible. The clamour would not be out of place in a fairground.

Between task-setting, Beatrice takes portraits of cross-legged little girls, their kohl-pencilled eyes huge and solemn, eating cold rice with their fingers from plates. She zooms in on stick-drawings over their shoulders. She snaps the boy with his leg in plaster saying his prayers standing on his mat surrounded by upturned bottoms.

She arrives back at Henry Place a full hour before Howard and plugs her camera into her laptop to pore over the fruits of the day. After showering and changing, she spends the rest of the evening cutting, enlarging, re-sizing, adjusting colour balances, re-touching faces. Her folio of finished work is thickening. Meanwhile Howard ensconces himself in his work-station. He has taken up

160

smoking again, rolling his own cigarettes, his collar unbuttoned, a pen tucked behind his ear.

Sunnydale asks for her again for Friday. She carries on snapping: two teachers laughing in their shared language while re-pinning their headscarves, old Dr Singh sipping camomile tea at his desk, a moon-faced child offering up a segment of tangerine. By the end of Friday afternoon, after the first day of May sun, the puddles in Sunnydale's playground have completely dried up and exotic fabrics are dancing on washing-lines down the back alleys.

'Come again,' everyone says. Beatrice is given a paper plate of Indian sweets to take home.

When Howard gets in from Braithwaite she gives him the phone message from Max, Fenella's father, asking for a thousand words of copy. It's a tight deadline. Howard sends Frank Lumb a text to say he won't be able to make it to the bowling alley. 'This is it,' he says, re-pocketing his mobile. 'This is real money. It's the big-time.'

Beatrice is slipping her newest print-outs into her folio when, bang on seven, the doorbell rings. Feeling butterflies, like college days, she takes a last look in the mirror then catches up her long-stringed purse and flings it over her shoulder.

Howard is concentrating hard on his monitor. He doesn't react when Beatrice pecks his cheek. 'Later!' She skips away down the stairs.

Joan is standing on the doorstep, firm in steel-toed black lace-ups, one thumb stuck jauntily in her trouser-belt, the other jangling car-keys. Her blazer has shiny gold buttons and a decorative shield on the breast pocket. A pale linen shirt draws a crisp, clean line around her neck. Her hair is spiked with wax.

Beatrice feels a flutter. 'You look good.'

'You look super,' Joan blurts. 'Your hair.' She turns red, looks down the street. 'I like the way you gel it.

Good stuff, that. Can't do a thing with mine.' She tosses out her little laugh.

'Your hair looks terrific.' Beatrice feels foolish, shyly tucks a tendril behind her ear. A light breeze is lifting a polystyrene carton along the pavement.

'Let's be off, then.' Joan holds open the passenger door of her car, then sprints round into the driver's seat. 'I'll see to that for you.' She leans across Beatrice's chest, pulling strenuously at the seat belt while holding it at a certain angle. 'You've got to have the knack.' Her breath smells faintly of peppermint.

The belt continues to jam. Joan flushes from the effort, her nose close to Beatrice's vest. Looking over the frames of Joan's spectacles, Beatrice notices surprisingly long lashes, and that her eyes are pale blue, like her shirt.

'Sorted!' Joan flops back into her seat red-faced and wipes her forehead. 'Let's go.'

Summer is coming. The sky feels opened-out, pale and huge. In the new light the bottom of the valley reminds Beatrice of backpacking in Europe: a place she visited with Howard in Berlin, an art installation of wildly-graphitised metal junk piled into towers or dug into the soil to form dungeons. The industrial landscape below looks similar, like discarded tin cans heaped in piles.

The restaurant is beyond the ring road on the main route to the Dales, on a road of blackened mansions with ornate, dilapidated conservatories. A few have been spruced up into offices, sandblasted back to yellow.

'These were the mill-owners' houses,' says Joan. 'It used to be posh. My mother's great-grandfather lived in one of them but the money didn't come down. They've mostly been broken up into flats now.'

'They're beautiful,' says Beatrice.

'Who'd want a big house here, though, when you can have a barn conversion in a nice village?'

Beatrice is feeling more relaxed. She is aware of the scent that can only be aftershave. Joan's concentration on the road allows Beatrice to surreptitiously glance at Joan's profile, the strong line of her cheek, how she controls the pedals, manoeuvres the gear-stick.

Joan nods at a turreted manor set among trees. 'Aske family. Owned Belvedere Mill. My daughter's a day-girl.'

Beatrice sees the signboard under a tree: Belvedere Aske High School for Girls. The road follows a long, high wall, beyond which are playing fields.

'We all put our girls there,' says Joan. 'Carole's girl, Ed's girl. Treena, the support assistant's girl, has started there since her husband's done well in mobile phones.'

'It must set you back a bit,' says Beatrice.

'Cheaper than some. And they get several into Oxbridge every year, they're very good.'

The road starts to climb. Beatrice sees, at the top of the hill, some glitzy shop fronts. 'Do you have great ambitions for your daughter?'

'She can do anything she wants, can my daughter.' Joan changes gear with a clenched fist. 'Anything whatsoever. We're not pushy, me and her father.' She misses the gear and thrusts violently. 'We just don't want her to throw herself away, that's all.'

They come to the first premises of the row. The restaurant looks recently renovated, its frontage hung with brass lamps, its entrance a Roman arch. A sign in swirly italics reads 'The Bombay Garden'.

Joan darts in front of Beatrice to hold the door. An inner door is opened by a waiter in a white three-piece suit and bow tie.

Once inside, Joan steps smartly to the fore. 'Table for two, name of Blake, please.'

The carpet is green, springy as turf, and patterned with the restaurant's logo, a stylised red rose. At dimly lit tables middle-aged women in spangled tops smile and clink glasses with square, grey men. Joan helps Beatrice into her seat before the waiter has a chance. Instead he flicks a cigarette lighter at the single red candle. The upholstery is plush and full of static. The cutlery is Thai bronze. The menus have maroon tassles. Candlelight plays on the unlit chandelier-style wall-lamp. Its plastic beads glitter dully.

'Fancy place,' grins Beatrice.

Joan grins. 'It's good, isn't it. I thought you'd like it.' She starts perusing the wine list.

Beatrice stretches her legs under the table and lounges back, feeling the unknotting of her neck and shoulders, feeling moved to spontaneously observe, 'Know what? You changed my life.'

Joan flushes intensely. 'Don't be daft.'

'No, really. You made me realise that I want to go on with my art.'

'Pshsh.' Joan carries on slipping her finger down the list, bashful, pink with pleasure. 'Will Chianti be alright for you?' She doesn't wait for an answer but waves down a waiter and orders a bottle.

'I'd like Perrier too, please,' Beatrice says to the waiter.

'And a bottle of Perrier, please,' Joan interprets.

The waiter glides away.

'The last couple of weeks have been great for me,' Beatrice continues. 'You've influenced me a lot. Your enthusiasm for your art triggered something in me.'

'Well, I've always loved my art,' says Joan, happily. I might be a fully fledged artist myself one day.'

'When you showed me your drawings I knew I wanted to be doing that too. I mean, making images that say something deep, something spiritual.'

'I've got more at home,' says Joan. 'I've got a whole sideboard full.'

'Have you ever exhibited?'

'No. No-o no. Nothing like that. Never dreamed of it. I've just shown them to friends. Of course my advisor – the lady I go to – she claims my art will take off if I move to the States.' Joan pulls a face. 'If I'm to believe her.'

Maria would find Joan creative, courageous, unduly modest. Howard would dismiss her as deluded and ridiculous. Beatrice smiles encouragingly across the table.

'Hey, you could even come back tonight and see my stuff if you like.' Seeing Beatrice's hesitation Joan immediately dismisses her own suggestion: 'Ha! *Come and see my etchings*, as the saying goes. It's alright, honestly. I didn't mean to put you on the spot.'

The waiter sails up to Joan's elbow with the wine and Perrier and a plate of complementary poppadum. Without looking at the menu Joan asks for Set Meal Number One. Beatrice opts for king prawns in a hot, spicy sauce with fresh coriander prepared in the traditional Kashmiri way. She takes no account of the price. She is in the mood for living a little. The waiter inclines his head and sails away again without a word.

'You're very welcome to come round some other time,' says Joan. 'You'd like my place.'

'Didn't you mention that you were moving?'

'That's right. I'm off the beaten track now. Good as living in the National Park, where I live. You can see out of my back for miles.'

'You're so enthusiastic,' says Beatrice. 'A great person for children to be around.'

'Pshsh.' Joan goes pink again, snapping a poppadum and placing a large fragment on Beatrice's plate.

'And kind,' adds Beatrice. 'I've seen you.'

Joan hides her face with a hand. 'Oh flipping heck, I'm just a normal teacher.'

'The kids adore you, Joan.'

'Pshsh.' Joan pours them each a glass of Chianti.

Beatrice savours the spices in the air: subtly sweet, more cardamom than chilli. Feeling Joan's leg wedging her own against the table makes her fluster – 'The thing about going back to your place: you've got family. I wouldn't want to disturb them. It'd be quite late.'

'Ah. Well, that wouldn't be a problem, coz...' Joan stops, sighs hugely, sits back, clasps her hands behind her head and stares up at the ceiling. 'I've had a helluva week.' It's almost a whisper.

There's a long pause. Beatrice's eye wanders over Joan's unfastened blazer, the blue shirt straining out of a man's broad belt, its rugged brass buckle. She moves her leg against Joan's. 'You don't have to talk about it if you don't want to.'

Joan jolts upright, her leg springing away. 'God – I thought you were the table leg. Sorry.' A deep flush spreads to her hairline.

Beatrice takes long swigs of wine and water, then opens up a neutral topic. 'So what's wrong with Ed?'

'Can't cope,' says Joan, looking relieved. 'Stress.'

'And where's Brian Bottomley most of the time? The support assistants told Howard the Head has a time-share in Tenerife that he uses during school terms. Is that true?'

'Oh, Brian's an alky, basically,' says Joan dismissively.

The waiter delivers a cluster of steaming silver dishes and stainless steel pots of sauces.

'My guess is Carole will be sick next. She's doing three jobs: Ed's, the Head's and her own. I feel sorry for her.'

Beatrice recalls Carole's eyes, like arrow-slits in battlements; how her thin lips twisted around Joan's special status.

'Poor Carole,' Joan goes on. 'The worst thing is having to get all the staff absences covered. Must be a nightmare. I'm only off for the G-Tech courses, but that's bad enough. Well, apart from last Tuesday.'

Beatrice raises an inquiring eyebrow.

'That was my daughter fainting at school.' Joan spears a mushroom bhaji. 'She's at that age. But otherwise I'd never be off unexpectedly. That's when it can be really touch-and-go. The sudden sickies. We were lucky to get you and Howard when Chantelle and Mrs Khazim were both off. Poor old Mrs Khazim. She's got no life.' Joan peers at and pokes into each dish. 'She's not off half as much as Chantelle though.'

Beatrice pauses from forking mango chutney onto her sideplate. 'I have something of a problem with Chantelle.'

Joan looks surprised. 'She's a nice lass, our Chantelle. We were lucky to get a Newly-Qualified Teacher. You can't get them these days. They're spoilt for choice. They all go somewhere nice, down south.'

'It's not Chantelle's fault. It's my problem. When I taught her class, I corrected an apostrophe on her wall-display. I'm terrified of meeting her since I did that.'

Joan looks blank.

'It was patronising of me.'

'Well, but she's dyslexic is Chantelle. I don't expect she'll have noticed. If she did, she wouldn't say anything. What would she say? She's twenty-three.'

'I'm just scared of unpleasant confrontations. I'm not confident in a staffroom at the best of times.'

'Not confident? I'm flabbergasted. You're good. You're a professional.' She tops up Beatrice's glass, shaking her head, amazed. 'I mean, what could Chantelle say, anyway?'

'Uff. You know. She's that type.' She stops, embarrassed. 'I found it easier down in Cambridge. Teaching, I mean.'

'Well, *obviously*,' says Joan. 'Who wouldn't?'

'Everyone was so... polite.'

'Don't know they're born,' says Joan. Then, 'Ha! Scared of meeting Chantelle.' She rips off a piece of stuffed paratha. The coconut filling tumbles out and drops off the table. 'If she did notice what you'd done, she'd be mortified. Honestly. We already had tears in the staffroom when the dyslexia came out. That was one of the support assistants trying to show how clever she was. They get above themselves, sometimes.'

The restaurant is filling up, mainly with older couples. Two women with black patent handbags are having their chairs shovelled under their bottoms by husbands in suits and ties. A waiter is delivering champagne in a chiller to an elderly man with a young, skimpily clad escort.

Beatrice wipes her hands on her napkin. 'I guess your colleague Terri would like it here. This glitzy kinda place.' She moves to top up both glasses.

Joan puts a hand over her own. 'I'm driving. The rest's yours.'

Beatrice empties her glass in one, and happiness wells in her: Sunnydale School being such fun, the weather being sunny, being out on the town on a date. She smiles ecstatically. Again, her leg applies light pressure to Joan's. Joan fleetingly looks like a creature sensing a predator, then seems to take a deep breath and grins shyly.

Beatrice reaches over and fondles the soft, sculpted peak of Joan's untouched napkin. 'So tell me some more about your art.'

Later they pause outside the restaurant to look at the orb of a full moon hanging above the city. The air is muggy like a summer's night, pungent with the scents of fast food and urine and roses. Beatrice is unsteady on her feet.

Joan grins. 'That was three quarters of a bottle you had.'

'I need to hold onto you.'

'My pleasure.'

Joan had insisted on paying. Once in the car Beatrice repeats, 'Really you shouldn't have.'

Joan reaches over to deal with her seatbelt again. Beatrice smells her woody scent. The blue shirt pulls out of Joan's waistband revealing the unsightly top of her nylon tights, but above that, a glimpse of firm flesh.

'You've got lovely eyes.'

Joan jerks back instantly into her seat.

Beatrice, confused, fastens her seatbelt by herself.

Joan's face is puce. 'Phew. Hot in here.' She turns the key, revs the engine loudly and takes off for the Henrys.

Beatrice looks away from Joan, out of the window, her hands resolutely in her lap, and resigns herself to crawling, shortly, into her own bed; to warming herself against Howard's turned back. She makes innocuous conversation about life in Vermont, describing her studio in a friend's home.

Talking about her art buoys up her mood again. 'I'm in a really creative space right now. I've started building an exciting folio here. Ready for summer when I go back.'

Joan flinches. 'You guys are definitely leaving, then.'

'Not Howard. He needs to be in the UK. Things are really taking off for him here. But all my opportunities are in Vermont. For exhibitions and stuff. I'll just need to network a little. It'll be an exciting time for me.'

Joan thrusts the gear stick. 'I want that for me.'

'Well, hey, you should come over. Start your new life!'

Joan shoots her a startled look. 'What do you mean?'

'Just come. My friend has a big house that lots of people share...' Beatrice's enthusiasm falters, as a chilling feeling of responsibility creeps in.

'Wow...' Joan accelerates. 'Brilliant. I'm going to just do it.' She grins at Beatrice, then laughs out loud. 'Wow!' For the rest of the journey she fires urgent questions – the price of food, the seasons, the price of rents, which airport to fly to. Until they reach the first of the Henrys, Joan is in a whirl of planning.

At the junction of the ring road and Henry Avenue the Asian shops are in darkness, having long since packed up their vegetable stands and fixed the night-time window-grilles. Cabbage leaves strew the pavements. Odd boxes skid about. But there are still a lot of people around. Joan's headlights reflect on the white skin of men's forearms and girls' bare legs. There's a buzz in the air. The straggly groups could almost be called a crowd, pouring down into the Henrys.

'It looks like the football, but it's nearly midnight,' says Joan. The Astra overtakes a substantial, boisterous gang and turns right at the bottom of the hill into Henry Grove. The sky instantly brightens with the glow of a bonfire. Flashing police lights add to the festive atmosphere.

'Trouble,' says Joan.

Entry into Henry Place is blocked by police vehicles clustered like feeding animals. Silhouetted in the first floor windows of the corner shop are excited children, leaning out to watch, waving their arms like insects. The shop's ground floor has been barricaded with hardboard and an old cart. At the far end of the street is a raging fire – the skeleton of a vehicle pushed onto its side. Along the terrace, lights are on in upstairs windows while the ground floors have a battened-down look.

'What's going on?' says Beatrice.

Joan winds down her window to talk to a policeman in riot gear. He pushes up his visor with a knuckly glove. Meanwhile Beatrice takes her mobile out of her little purse. 'Hey – I'm on the end of the street. Are you okay?'

'Beatrice!' Howard's voice is adrenalin-fuelled. 'I'm okay. Are you okay?'

'We're fine. There's a roadblock. Can you see it?'

'I can see it. There's been a fight. I think it's the Muslims and the whites. I dunno. Maybe it's the Hindus. Anyhow, the whites came pouring down the street and

170

drove the Asians back. I gotta find out the ins and outs of this thing. I'm writing this up, Beatrice. It's terrific.'

Joan is winding up the window again. 'I'll take you home. We can't get in here tonight. They're expecting more trouble. They're using tear-gas. We have to get back on the ring road and keep away till they give the all-clear.'

The Chianti surges in Beatrice's stomach. 'Home to yours?'

Large, dark vans have suddenly spilled out hordes of clones in riot gear. They begin to link themselves into chains, swing across streets. The radio of a nearby police vehicle is chattering, and the siren of an approaching fire engine, its way blocked by the crowds, is deafening.

'I gotta go, Howard,' Beatrice shouts breathlessly.

'S'okay, I hear you.' He sounds amused.

'We've been told to move on; we're going back to Joan's. Listen, I'll phone you when we get there, okay?'

'I'll see you in the morning,' says Howard, calmly. 'When it's all over.'

'Talk later.' Beatrice puts her mobile away and checks that her window is fully closed. Seeing the human chains – how they are unwinding themselves, glinting with metal – gives her goose bumps.

'Don't worry,' says Joan, reversing slowly. She turns the car to leave Henry Grove from the other end. 'You don't get this where I live.'

There is a roar behind them, like a home team winning the game. All around, small groups are emerging, the men's oil-black hair shimmering in the streetlights as they hurry in the direction of Henry Place.

Joan touches Beatrice's knee. Her hand lingers. 'What you need is a Jack Daniels.'

Chapter 17

Beatrice is on the phone to Howard in Joan's living room. Howard would enjoy the retro furnishings, the bits of ornamental kitsch about which he could make witty comments. The settee looks like something out of a Clark Gable movie: three lace-edged antimacassars draped over its back, matching protective sleeves hooked over its arms. Behind it, a single divan with an old-fashioned candlewick bedspread is pushed against the wall. The fireplace is finished in a grainy wood veneer, its focal point a plastic sculpture of logs back-lit with a red bulb. Across the mantelpiece a procession of school photographs shows a thin-faced, cheerful little girl transmuting into a glum teenager.

Joan is clinking things in a back room somewhere.

Beatrice cups her voice into her mobile. 'I'm in some kind of trailer park. It was too dark to see much.' She looks over her shoulder then hisses, 'This place is made of hardboard, Howard.'

'Guess you two'll be cozying up for warmth, then?'

'Yeah, along with her husband and daughter.' The lie is automatic.

'Okay, okay. Only kidding.'

Joan comes into the living room minus her blazer, carrying two ice-cube-filled tumblers. 'That Howard?' She moves over to the spindly-legged sideboard.

Beatrice nods, ending the call with, 'Promise me you won't go outside, okay? I'll see you tomorrow.' She switches off her mobile, returns it to her bag and sits on the settee. Slipping off her shoes she holds out her feet to the glowing electric bars.

Joan brings over the tumblers of whisky.

Beatrice stares at the triangle of freckled skin where a further shirt button has been undone. 'Howard's been hanging out of the window and thetear-gas has turned his face red,' she babbles. 'He says the rest of the media is at the end of the road, but not *on* it, like him.'

With one hand Joan pulls out the smallest of a nest of side-tables and plonks it down, an action which affords a fleeting view of the space between her shirt and her breasts. 'Good for this reporting job he does, then.'

'Oh, this is *great* for Howard,' Beatrice flusters. 'He's just been on the phone with a contact in New York, and he's just had a call from our friend Fenella's father in London to do a weekend supplement piece...'

Joan slaps a coaster onto the side-table and sets down one of the whiskies. 'You could do with this. You're looking a bit flushed.' She gives the dachshund a push. 'Hup, Wesley.'

The dog clambers off the settee and lies along the hearth. Joan beats a cushion and takes his place.

Beatrice takes a swig of the whisky. 'Yeah. I've sort of got butterflies. Those riot police. Anyway this guy Max, he says any copy Howard can get to him overnight, he'll see what he can do.'

Joan is pulling the cushion about, trying to get it right.

Beatrice feels her pulse racing. She puts down her glass. 'Did I tell you he's gotten a commission from a U.S. daily?'

'No.' Joan throws an arm over the back of the settee and draws up one leg. Her foot, in tan-coloured tights, is blunt and stumpy. Her big toe-nail has made a ladder.

'He's going to do, like, a Letter from the North of England,' – the fabric of Joan's trousers is pulled taut across her thigh – 'As a regular column,' says Beatrice distractedly.

Joan gives the cushion another beating, rolls it up and jams it behind her neck. 'Don't mind me.' She emits a big yawn. 'Sorry.'

'I'm boring you.'

'You're not. It's just, it's all Howard.'

'Sorry. I get excited for him when he gets good breaks. I guess I want him to get where he wants to be.' For a moment Beatrice thinks of next Sunday, of Howard bringing her home from the clinic in his car, how he will make her a cup of cocoa, tuck her up in bed. She feels a surge of affection. At the same time her eye has wandered back to the open neck of Joan's shirt. 'Why didn't you tell me before that you'd left your husband?'

Joan inspects her glass. 'I didn't know you well enough.'

Beatrice gulps whisky then reaches out, touches Joan's cheek. 'You remind me of Maria, my ex-girlfriend.'

Joan jumps. Wesley sits bolt upright.

'Joan,' Beatrice retracts her hand but remains leaning forward. 'I'd like to straighten something out. I'm not great at knowing what I want, but I do know I've never wanted heterosexual monogamy. With Howard, it's... it's a working relationship.' Suddenly it is clear to her how things now stand between herself and Howard, and it is how she wants it to be.

'You told me that already.'

But now it's true, thinks Beatrice. 'Howard and I support each other creatively, that's all.' She clasps her hands, looks Joan full in the face. 'The fact is I've always had various ongoing relationships. I mean, simultaneously sometimes. With guys and girls.'

'I knew from the start you were that way,' whispers Joan.

'Pardon me?'

174

'Not everyone would see it. Even with your short hair. But I saw it. I mean, you're not butch.' Joan leans back. 'It's alright. I don't personally have a problem with it.'

'Problem with what?'

'*Gay girls*. No problem whatsoever,' she says cheerily.

'Joan, you're not homophobic or anything, are you?'

'Me?' Joan folds her arms and crosses her legs. 'I'm live-and-let-live, me. No problem with it at all.' She springs up and removes herself to the sideboard. 'As a matter of fact I can be attractive to women as well as men.' She is opening a second whisky bottle. 'A lass fancied me when I was at teacher-training college.'

'Was that your St Ninian's friend? Darshana?'

'We need more ice-cubes.' Joan hurries off into the kitchen and calls back, 'Darshana? Ha! She's as feminine as it gets.' After some clinking she reappears. 'We go back a long way, me and Darsh, but she's never been...'

Beatrice drains her glass and holds it out. 'That's too bad.'

'What?'

'For you, I mean. If that's what you wanted.'

Joan looks wary. 'I meant I've had *other* girls after me.'

'I must say it's hard to imagine a woman in a sari getting off with another woman,' Beatrice concedes.

Joan refills Beatrice's glass. 'Things just happened. It wasn't me, going out looking for it.'

'*What* happened?'

'Pshsh.' Joan returns the bottle to the sideboard.

When she comes back Beatrice pats the floor beside her. 'Sit here.'

Joan settles herself instead in her armchair and looks at the ceiling. 'Pshsh.'

The moon is high and pale, the sky the black of deep night. It is still hours before dawn but long after the last home-going rioter will have found his front door or some

175

other place to collapse in a stupor. Foxes are feasting in dustbins and Badger's Dell is haunted by a solitary owl.

The photos along Joan's mantelpiece are in disarray where empty glasses have been pushed in.

'But then what did she do but follow me north,' Joan is saying. 'I don't normally tell people all this. You're getting it out of me, you are.'

Beatrice is stretched out on the rug, sleepy and mellow. She is reminded of the end of one of Fenella's parties. She rubs Wesley under his ear with her toes.

'Jeezus, Joan, you should have stayed in London.'

'No no no. That was my misspent youth. A phase. Stuff you only do at college. I couldn't have gone on having those carry-ons, one after the other. They were always going to end in tears. As Darshana always said, you can't have a normal set-up if you go down that path.' She holds up her empty tumbler, scowls at her reflected spectacles. 'I didn't want to finish up on my own.'

'So you left London to put that kind of relationship behind you.'

'Well, no. I left London because I married Colin; because he'd got a job up here with the police.' Joan gets up from the rug. 'Pass me your glass.' She bumbles unsteadily to the sideboard and divides the last of the Bailey's Irish Cream between the two tumblers. 'At least I left marriage late. It was two and a half years before I got married. I was one of the last in our year. Apart from Terri, obviously. She never did want a bloke. Darshana was already getting married for the second time.' Returning to the settee she sets Beatrice's tumbler on a coaster. 'I thought I'd better give it a go. Plus my grandma wanted a wedding.'

'Those are not good reasons for marrying.'

'Better than some people's.' Joan flops down next to Beatrice. 'Darshana went straight to number two without a gap. It's hard, watching your friend muck up her life.'

'What happened to number one?'

'She married our college counsellor but he used to smack her about.' Joan knocks back the liqueur in one. 'She brings that side out in people.'

'God.' Beatrice pours drink slowly down her gullet.

'You don't know what she can be like,' says Joan darkly, then – 'I'd have looked after her, if she'd come to me. After the first bloke. She certainly couldn't go home.'

'Why not? Not that I ever would. Not to my parents.'

'Oh, Darsh's mother already thought she was a slut for going off to college and wearing miniskirts.' A pensive moment passes in which Joan nudges Wesley repetitively with one foot. 'I used to hope she'd come out. Out of that difficult family situation, I mean,' she quickly clarifies. 'With me helping her. But she never has.'

The horizon beyond the uncurtained window is beginning to lighten, the way water seeps up blotting paper. The clock on the bedside table shows five to four. Beatrice comes into the bedroom in borrowed pyjamas. Joan, in a striped nightshirt, is going through a drawer.

'Just getting my underwear for morning.'

Beatrice goes to look out of the window. Beyond the bungalow's thin walls a soothing patter of rain has begun. She turns. 'So for more than fifteen years you haven't had any girlfriends?'

Joan rummages, back turned. 'I didn't want my daughter upsetting.'

'Why would she have been upset? Is she anti-gay?'

Joan stops, clutching a vest. 'I've always believed, when you've got a child, you've got to be normal, or they get picked on.' She turns round with a fistful of underwear. 'We're starting to get on better.' Her voice cracks. 'It's brilliant. It's only just happened. She knows she needs me.' She looks at Beatrice, bright-eyed. 'I don't want anything to drive her away again.'

Beatrice's hand passes over her stomach. Still firm and flat. 'I've chosen to be an artist, not a mother.'

'I don't regret having Caroline,' says Joan defensively.

'Will she be coming to the States with you?'

'I haven't asked her. I should.'

Beatrice goes to where Joan is standing. 'That divan in the living room looks awful narrow. You needn't sleep through there.'

Joan drops the bundle of underwear and touches Beatrice's sleeve. 'It's too warm a night for winceyette.' She undoes Beatrice's buttons, slips the pyjama top off Beatrice's shoulders. It drops to the carpet. Kneeling, she unties the chord at Beatrice's waist. The trousers drop to the floor. Her hands slide over Beatrice's skin.

Beatrice reaches down Joan's back to pull up her shirt. 'No. Later.'

It is still overcast at midday when Joan's Astra leaves Badger's Dell. Approaching the Henrys the humidity increases as though the inner city is a stickier place.

Beatrice thinks of the piece Howard wrote about how the various neighbourhoods can seem to have different climates. It's one he read out to her, pleased with himself.

'Driving from estate to estate, from this to that suburb, the classes, races and cultures change as though one were moving between countries or from one climate to another, or even time-travelling between centuries.'

She found it pretentious.

Joan stops at the end of Henry Place and Beatrice gets out of the car. The humidity sticks to her face. A police cordon, a fluttering strip of red and white tape like the winners' line on sports day, is tied across the street between two lamp-posts.

'I'll be fine. I'll call you.' Beatrice waves Joan off then approaches the cordon.

There's a sense of occasion. It feels like the site of a rock festival after the crowds have gone home, resi-dual adrenalin suspended in the air. The pavement is scattered with half-burned rubber and dusted with ash blown along from the carcasses of vehicles. The smouldering remnant of the fire takes her back to Guy Fawkes Night in Barny and Nelson's garden in Brixton. She sees the postman hurrying through his round, looking important. She is reminded of New Year's Day in Hong Kong, exploring the downtown alleys with Howard, scuffing through the debris of firecrackers. A smell of the Far East.

Caroline staggers from the people-carrier to her mother's Lego porch with a rucksack, a hold-all of books and her big winter coat. She bangs into the porch and presses the bell long and hard, making Wesley bark and frisk in the living room. 'Mum!'

Behind her, Darshana looks at her watch. 'She can't still be in bed. Not at one in the afternoon. That's not like your mum.'

Caroline goes to check round the corner of the bungalow. 'Car's gone. Prob'ly at Asda.' Scrabbling one-handedly she manages to unlock and slam open the door. She barges straight through to her bedroom with Wesley wagging companionably around her legs.

'Tuh, She's been in my bed again.'

The duvet is mountained at the foot of the bed. Her washed-out Betty Boop dressing gown is in a heap on the rug along with Joan's towelling bathrobe and striped pyjamas. In addition, the striped nightshirt that she picked out for her mother last birthday under Darshana's supervision is strewn across the pillows.

Caroline drops her baggage and instinctively closes her bedroom door. 'No, don't come in, Aunty Darsh. I can manage. I'll be done in two seconds.'

The bungalow is still, but there's a sense of recent activity, like an echo. Darshana tiptoes around the living room. The hotchpotch of run-down furniture reminds her of another life — their student flat. An ancient settee, a polished sideboard, a nest of cheap veneer side-tables. She notices two coffee-mugs on the carpet and several empty glasses on the mantelpiece. Caroline's photographs are strewn about messily on their backs, knocked off their cardboard feet. One side-table stands crookedly on the edge of the hearthrug. On the sideboard are two empty whisky bottles.

'This isn't like your mum,' Darshana murmurs, 'this mess.'

In the bathroom the shower curtain is beaded with droplets. Two flannels are slopped over the side of the bath. Three burgundy towels darkened with damp patches are draped over the towel rail.

Caroline is yanking drawers open and closed, pulling out clothes she might need in the coming week including a stack of clean knickers, ironed and folded. Pushing her nose into them she smells the iron and her mum's fabric conditioner. She stuffs her big warm coat into the wardrobe, extracting instead a denim jacket and a red Gortex hip-length jacket which she folds haphazardly into the rucksack, pushing her knickers in on top.

In the kitchenette Darshana finds an opened pack of cinammon bagels on the work-top. Beside it, two crumb-strewn sideplates; two buttery knives.

'Shall I put the kettle on?' she calls, shakily.

'What's the point, if Mum's not here? I'll be ready in a minute. I'd rather have a cup of coffee back at dad's.'

On the wall above the electric kettle is the calendar that Caroline bought for her mother when Darshana took her Christmas shopping in Leeds. Darshana doesn't watch that series on TV. Caroline insisted that her mum was a fan: 'I know my own mum.'

'I love you, Caroline,' Darshana had responded, adding quickly, 'Shopping with you. Baldev and Luke sulk and moan all over Leeds unless they're in a sports shop.'

There are only a few notes on the May to June page. A couple of the squares are marked *G-Tech Course*. Next weekend has a line of green crayon across Saturday and Sunday, and the word *Doncaster*. An arrow in the same crayon joins the words BOOK TABLE – scrawled large in the margin – to yesterday's square, in which is written *Beatrice* and a phone number.

When Caroline enters the kitchenette wielding the phone-pad Darshana jumps, crumples a scrap of paper into her pocket, pretends to be staring out of the window. Caroline thinks she looks stressed. She was already being odd, jumpy, on the drive over. 'Have you got a pen, Aunty Darsh?'

With a brave smile, Darshana offers a green crayon.

Dear Mum, Gruss dich! Salut! Just popped in to pick up my stuff for the week, mainly to get my science that I forgot. I am revising today at Dad's. Did he tell you he's gone to that steam rally? Aunty Darsh happened to phone and offered to bring me over. Sorry you weren't in. Thanx for my knickers etc. Don't move my bag of books, I need them at the weekend. See you, au revoir, bis dann, lotsaluv, Caroline xxx
P.S. Hope that wasn't you rioting!
P.P.S. THANK-YOU for keeping my bed warm!!!! Not.

Caroline whirls through the living room, props the pad in an obvious place, picks up her rucksack and steps out into the porch. 'Come on, Aunty Darsh. We should go.'

Chapter 18

Henry Place is deserted apart from a few children craning their necks on a doorstep as their father fixes a large board over the bay window.

Beatrice approaches the cordon, anticipating finding Howard, unshaven and in his shirtsleeves, busily e-mailing all over the place. He probably won't have been to bed yet. He'll look up when she walks in and grin from ear to ear. She'll make him coffee.

The cordon is being guarded by a lone policeman, hands behind his back, looking as fair and reliable as a dry-stone wall. He is too fresh-faced to have been on duty last night.

'Is it safe?' Beatrice peers over his shoulder.

'Do you live here?'

'Yes. I tried to get home last night but I couldn't. My friend spent the night down there.'

'If he stayed indoors he'll have been alright,' says the policeman. 'There was no torching. Not on this street. Nafeez up towards the ring-road, that got torched.'

A few cars are still parked at the near end of the street, apparently unscathed. Beatrice scans along and spots Howard's car. 'How many vehicles were burned?'

'Just the three down here. Two cars and a transit van. If you don't mind my asking, are you with the American gentleman who's got a bedsit down on the left?'

Beatrice starts. 'Is he alright?'

'He interviewed Mr Ahmed this morning. I just thought there can't be many people in these parts with your accent. You don't have this in America, do you?'

The sweep of the policeman's arm takes in not only the smashed-up corner shop but also the dirty cityscape, the distant grey rise of the fells, the rain-cloud squatted on the horizon. 'We don't have it where I come from either,' he adds. 'It's not normal, this, you know, in England.'

Beatrice smiles at him reassuringly. 'We did spend some time in Cambridge.'

A ray of sun breaks through the cloud at last, sparkling on the star-shapes of smashed windows. The owner of the corner shop and three or four young Pakistani men are hammering an assortment of boards and old doors over the two main windows, their trainers crunching on glass. A few houses down, a shabby front door opens and a boy in jeans and gelled hair, looking the worse-for-wear, gets pushed out with a shopping bag. Behind the door, female voices jabber. He looks back dumbly. The door closes in his face. When he walks into the street Beatrice sees his bandaged arm and the face of a Pakistani cricketer on his teeshirt. The youth approaches the corner shop, dull-eyed.

'I'm surprised they're open for business,' Beatrice comments.

'They're not getting the glaziers in yet. They're convinced there'll be more trouble.'

'Is that what the police think?'

'All I know is, I've been drafted in from Sheffield.' The policeman eases peaceably up and down on his toes.

'I wonder whether they're doing samosas.'

'They're good; they keep bringing me cups of tea.'

Beatrice treads carefully over the glass and into the shop, where Mrs Ahmed is gesticulating at the closed-faced youth, pointing at his bandage, mopping her eyes with her shawl, the corners of her mouth pulled down cartoonishly. She turns to her new customer, rattling on, unintelligible, her small, quick hands thrown in the air in an international gesture of despair. The young man's eyes are hooded, his glances sidelong.

Beatrice asks for four vegetable samosas. After snacking with Howard, she will come back to the shop and ask Mr Ahmed for permission to photograph the broken glass and Mrs Ahmed's troubled face behind the counter. She pays her money, takes the brown paper bag and heads with crunching steps for number forty-seven.

The cardboard air-freshener hanging from Darshana's rear view mirror was a present from Joan. It is in the shape of a bouquet. Darshana appreciates anything floral. Flowers lift my mood, she would always tell Joan.

The circuitous route by which she is returning Caroline to Colin's avoids the stretch of ring road that is full of police. Not that they've blocked it off; in fact, on the journey to Joan's, she and Caroline travelled along that stretch without any problem. But the longer the route, the more chance Caroline will have to open up.

A rain-shower is still smudging the line between the moor and the sky, but the forecast says there will be sun. Later Darshana will put Baldev's cricket whites from last night's match through a boil-wash and hang things outside to dry for the first time this year.

Caroline has re-tuned the radio from Classic FM to something loud, and turned up the bass. She is gazing out of the window, pounding her fists on her knees to the beat, acting unconcerned, answering Darshana's probing questions with curt, superficial responses. All she will talk about is her French and German orals next week, trotting out sentences in one language or the other as though that were the only thing in her head.

'You're *sure* you don't want to come back to ours for a spot of lunch?'

Caroline shoots Darshana a slightly irritated look. 'No. I mean, thanks, but I've just told you how busy I am. Don't keep asking me, Aunty Darsh.'

'Are you planning on seeing Baldev tonight?'

Caroline looks out of the side window. 'No.'

'Oh?'

'I already said, Aunty Darshana.'

'Not even tomorrow, though, when you've done all your revision?'

Caroline sighs. 'This weekend's my most important revising weekend. I need to be at dad's. On my own.'

'You've got all of next week; you've got a study week.'

Caroline jams her hair behind her ears. 'You sound like you're trying to put me off revising.'

'Actually, I just want to find out how you are,' says Darshana, as Caroline takes up a new rhythm on her knees. 'Because I know what you're thinking of doing next weekend and I just want you to know…'

Caroline's fists freeze mid-air. 'Oh my god. Baldev doesn't know, does he?'

Seeing Caroline's face, Darshana says, 'No. No, he doesn't know.' She switches off the radio and indicates right, deciding to follow the hopper-bus because it goes all around the houses. 'I thought we should have a talk about it.' Her little sideways glances tug at Caroline, trying to hook into her. 'You've got options, you know. I just want to be sure you've really been through it thoroughly with your mum.'

'I told her not to tell anyone,' snaps Caroline.

'You know what me and your mum are like.' Darshana's voice is bright. 'We go back a very long way. We tell each other everything.'

'You've fallen out, though, haven't you? She has her answerphone on permanently to stop you harassing her.'

'We haven't fallen out. Not really. It's just stress. Your mum's got a lot on, with the maths co-ordination and everything. We're alright underneath.'

Caroline sees Darshana's cheek twitching. 'I thought *you* were the one with stress, Aunty Darsh. I thought that was why you have a drink.'

The cheek turns pink. 'It's not a crime, Caroline, having a drink.'

'You've never been sober enough to give Baldev a driving lesson.' Caroline says, daringly.

'Tuh. That's all boys think about.'

'True.' Caroline reflects that Baldev never thinks about his mother and her problems. He moans incessantly about his parents but never tries to understand them. Selfish git.

'Anyway, that's not what we're talking about at the moment.' Darshana's voice wobbles. 'Your mother *had* to tell me about you.' Suddenly she is fierce. 'After all, I've been a mother to you too, as *you well know*.'

Caroline's neck prickles, seeing how Darshana's hands are locked on the steering wheel, her rings digging into the skin, fingers turning blue with the pressure.

'Have you thought of keeping it?' Darshana's voice is a stretched hair. If you pull they snap, recoil, then split.

'No I bloody haven't. It's just a *stupid, stupid* accident, Auntie Darshana. There's nothing to talk about. I'm doing my GCSEs and A-levels and going to university.'

The car swerves into the grass verge then centres again. 'You could still do that.'

'Forget it, Darshana!' shouts Caroline, then adds, lamely, 'Sorry.'

'It's alright, Caroline. You're upset.'

'My mum supports me in this, Auntie Darsh. It's not actually such a big deal. It's the right thing. I just want to put it behind me as soon as possible. Okay?'

The people carrier is at last approaching the mini-roundabout at the end of Moorland View. Darshana's face is turning blotchy. Caroline un-clicks her seatbelt and reaches for her rucksack on the back seat. 'You can let me out here. No need to come down Moorland View, you can carry on round the roundabout.'

The vehicle jerks to a halt. 'It's your mother who's making you do this.'

Caroline tuts with annoyance. 'It's *my* decision, Darshana.'

Darshana's eyes have that glazed look, like when you play Nintendo for too long without realising. 'This is what she wanted to do with you, you know.'

Caroline yanks on the door handle and backs out of the car with her baggage. 'You've said that before,' she spits. She slams the door.

Darshana's face is lost behind the windscreen in the reflection of an overhanging tree.

Suddenly Darshana is frantically winding down the window. Her manicured nails appear over the glass pane. 'You could come and live with us, you know!'

Caroline realises she is standing in a massive dog-turd. The smell is sickening.

Darshana rewinds, accelerates and is gone.

Baldev stays in bed even later than usual for a Saturday. Eventually he pulls the string hanging by his bed. The blind shoots up. Outside it is bright. Inside, there's condensation on the glass, and something like mildew blooming inside his head.

Last night was an embarrassment. His mother was comatose in her sitting room when it was time to give him, Lofty, Russ and Dil a lift to the cricket match. Russell's mother had to give up on her choir practice to take them. She was unbearably charitable about it. Three of them had to cram into the back seat of Clarissa's Morris, having removed the stupid harp. Naturally he slagged off his mother all the way, ending by saying he didn't give a fuck, which made Clarissa, who had until then pretended not to be listening, go '*Bal*dev!'.

They all agree that it's hard for Russ having a Christian as a mother. But even Russ concedes these days that

Clarissa isn't as big a problem as Darshana. Russ and the others don't even know the half of it. It's no longer just embarrassments. Baldev is living in fear. In collusion with Caroline, his mother is about to mess up his life.

After the match Lofty's dad came all the way from that field where he lives to bring them home in his vintage Ford. Russ and Dil got dropped off first. When it was just two of them in the back, Lofty asked, 'You alright, Bal?'

In the rear-view mirror, Derek winked knowingly from between his dreads. 'Women problems.'

The bedsit smells faintly of burnt-out car.

'Brunch, sweetie.' Beatrice lays the bag of samosas on the coffee table and goes to kiss Howard on the forehead. He's on the phone and waves a pen at her. It's Max or somebody. Beatrice makes coffee.

Howard comes through to the kitchen, his hands rammed into his hair. 'I'm about ready to sleep. That was some night.'

Beatrice hands him a mug of instant coffee. 'So how was it?'

Howard is already wandering out, rubbing his eyes. 'Actually I need to go to bed immediately. I'm setting my alarm. Have to call New York at midday their time.'

Beatrice is disappointed. 'Fine. I'll go out with my camera and get some pictures. We can catch up later.'

Howard goes into the living room and flings himself on the bed. 'You won't believe how much work I'm getting out of this,' he calls. 'They say this city's been a tinder box for years.' He yawns and turns into the pillow.

Beatrice comes through, cupping her drink, and stands near the settee. 'Was that more London work?'

'Hmm? Oh, no. That was just Fenella.'

When Joan sees the note she instantly calls Caroline's mobile.

'Hi Mum.'

'What were you doing with Darshana? Why did she come here?'

'Don't snap. Anyone'd think I'd done something wrong.'

'Sorry,' says her mother quickly. 'I didn't mean to be...'

'Don't worry, I'm at Dad's. I've been revising all day.'

'That's my girl.' Her mother hesitates; becomes awkward, almost shy. 'I am proud of you, you know.'

Caroline fiddles with her dad's police handcuffs on the coffee-table. 'Don't worry about Aunty Darsh, Mum. She didn't make me change my mind.'

Her mother catches her breath. 'I'm sorry I told her, Caroline. She phoned when I was fuming.'

'It's nothing to do with her, Mum.'

'Good.' She hears her mother heave a huge sigh. 'So why did you see her today?'

'She phoned to ask how I was. I should have guessed that she knew. Then she offered to bring me to yours to get some clothes I've been wanting. It's not the most convenient thing, you know, living in two houses.'

'Sorry.'

'Mum, I want to stay at yours for a few days after Sunday.'

'Super.' Caroline can almost hear her mother's face cracking into a smile. 'She didn't upset you then, your Auntie Darsh?'

'I told her it was none of her business.'

'It's because she had such a lot to do with you, growing up,' says her mother.

'Sometimes you're kind about people when you shouldn't be,' says Caroline.

'She's not a... a happy person, your Aunty Darshana.'

189

Caroline thinks of Darshana's white knuckles on the wheel. 'She's just a mess.'

'Well, but it's your Uncle Walter.'

'I like Uncle Walter. He can't help being a professor. I don't like them not being nice to him.'

'It's been very difficult for her,' says her mother.

'You've fallen out with her though. Haven't you?'

'You're right. It's... it's over.'

Caroline's hand, clutching the phone, turns sweaty. This feels like talking in sleeping bags on someone's bedroom floor after a school disco. Really talking. The kind you do in the dark, when no one can see your red face, where you confess things. Her mother is saying stuff without really coming out with it, but at least she's trying.

'I'd feel a bit uncomfortable at Aunty Darsh's house after this,' Caroline reassures her.

'I need to keep my distance,' her mother goes on. 'I'm not prepared to live like that – like her – any more. I've come to realise, you have to take your life by the reins and... and be true to yourself.' Her mother's voice goes crumbly. She clears her throat. 'This is your first really big decision, Caroline. I couldn't bear to see you derailed.'

The garage door clanks. 'Dad's back.'

'Remind him there's a railway documentary – BBC 2.'

Later, Caroline will tell him that Joan nearly came out with everything, but not quite, and he'll remind her how difficult it must be for her mother. Although he's nerdy and he wears satin ties, the great thing about her dad has always been, he gives an honest answer.

Chapter 19

On Monday Beatrice returns to Sunnydale School. They call her The Artist. They ask her to stay until the end of the week. The days are mostly spent making masks and costumes for the Celebrating Diversity Festival. In the evenings she and Howard sit in front of their laptops, absorbed in their projects, speaking only occasionally. There never seems to be a suitable opening to mention the termination. Bringing it up out of the blue might make it seem more important, as though it were an issue.

By the end of Thursday afternoon the classroom under Beatrice's care is strewn with unmarked books. The contents of the stock-cupboard have spread everywhere. Pencils crunch underfoot and the sink is piled with unwashed paint palettes. The children prance about in their costumes. Beatrice has taken hundreds of photos, promising copies. The headmistress is delighted.

Later, at home and settled into a foam bath, her mobile rings.

'I'd like to move you to St Ninian's tomorrow,' says Chaz. 'Nice school.'

'I know. I've been there before.'

'Yes,' says Chaz. 'They've asked specifically for you.'

'For me? But Howard's been there too.'

'It's you they want.'

'But I'm having fun at Sunnydale,' says Beatrice.

'Sunnydale just phoned. The year three teacher's back from Pakistan; she'll be back in tomorrow.'

'Darn.' Beatrice slips down in the bath.

'I know. You've learned the names, ywhen to have the milk, what the procedure is for collecting the dinner money.' Chaz clucks. 'That's the way it goes. At least we can still offer you a full working week.'

The bath-foam is turning thin and grey. There are a couple more laptop payments to go. And there's the termination fee. Beatrice sighs. 'Okay, I'll do it.'

'Terrific.'

'Will I be covering for the deputy again? Mrs Chatterjee-Fox?'

'No, it's a year four. The deputy asked for you.'

'But I haven't met her.' Goose bumps prickle on Beatrice's shoulders.

'Your reputation obviously goes before you,' breezes Chaz. 'And you're unavailable next Monday and Tuesday?'

'Yes that's right.' She dismisses the goose bumps, pulls out the plug with her foot.

'Well, let us know if you have a change of plan; we're desperate at the moment. Have a nice weekend, Beatrice.'

'Huh.' She thinks of the clinic. 'Thanks Chaz. Ditto.'

At teatime on Thursday, after an abortive attempt to interest Baldev in the six-form post-exam cricket trip to Headingley, Lofty phones his father.

'Baldev's kind of losing it, Dad.'

'Who's Baldev?'

'You gave him a lift home from Hebden last Friday!'

'Keep your hair on, son. I just forget names.'

Lofty thinks his dad is brain damaged from the dope.

'Why don't you bring him over?' suggests Derek.

'When? Now?'

'Bring the man to me, son. I'll cook.'

Baldev thinks there's a distinct possibility of getting stoned, so agrees to meet Lofty in town in order to get a bus out to his dad's. They get off the number three at the converted church. Baldev immediately lights a cigarette, inexpertly, and coughs. He has a crumpled, discarded look; his skin is dull and flaking.

On the walk to Badger's Dell he slows up. 'I think this is where my Aunty Joan lives.'

'Past the scrap-yard?'

'Funny little bungalows in the trees? Caroline described it.' The rain on Baldev's face tastes metallic.

'It's cool,' says Lofty. 'Come on, we're getting wet.'

'Only, Caroline might be there.' Baldev's voice cracks. In the scrap-yard the wind is knocking things about.

Lofty stops. 'You've split up, haven't you?'

Baldev kicks a screwed-up drinks can. 'I don't want to bump into her.'

'My dad has nothing to do with the neighbours. He's a recluse. You can't even see the other bungalows.'

Howard puts on Radio 4 for the six o-clock news. They half-listen to a discussion programme. Howard microwaves a pizza and brings it through, divided on two plates. Beatrice works on her images, altering colour balances, trying different effects, while eating and listening. The radio discussion meanders around the subject of urban lifestyles, how to balance the professional and the personal.

Abruptly Beatrice switches off the radio. 'Howard, what do you want? I mean, ten years from now. Say twenty. Where do you want to be? What will have happened to you?'

'Ah.' He lowers his copy of *Time* magazine, stretches out his legs, looks philosophical. 'I think I'm with you. The whole settling down subject.' He heaves an exaggerated sigh. 'Where will it be, that elusive place where we'll finally come to rest?'

'No. That's not it.'

'No, wait,' says Howard. 'I know, it's your body clock ticking. God, I don't envy you, being a woman.'

'I'm serious. Just tell me, Howard. Twenty years from now, how will you feel if you don't have children?'

'Twenty years? Hmm. Rather disappointed, probably. Rather empty.'

Beatrice sits forward on the settee. 'So how do you plan to make it happen? And when?'

'You're totally, totally right. We need to think about this. I'm being the thoughtless male. I confess I want to put my career first right now. Damn it – things are moving. It feels pretty exciting.' Howard drags a hand through his long forelock, a gesture that makes the little girls at Braithwaite flutter and giggle. 'But I *do* want a family to happen.' His expression shifts. Now he's misty-eyed. 'Yes, children. Definitely. And that means a home to raise them in. And commitment, obviously. Not necessarily marriage,' he says quickly. 'Just, whatever.'

'Wait,' says Beatrice. 'Just wait, before you go off into fantasies. Because the fact is, I absolutely don't want children at all.' She switches the radio back on. A play is just beginning: Oxford accents; the sound of tea pouring into cups. She'll tell him the main thing later.

Derek knows he's good at vibes, at feelings. He's also in tune with vintage engines, plus he's a great vegan cook. His gifts are not recognised but it's society's loss.

He peers through the hatch from the kitchenette into the deep red gloom of his living space. The boys are sitting on bits of foam salvaged from skips and wrapped in fringed shawls. Lofty is tapping away – allegedly answering exam questions from past papers – on a piece of hi-tech equipment supplied by Derek's ex-wife. The screen of Baldev's laptop is a psychedelic swirl of purple bubbles and Baldev is staring into space. Material goods make kids lose sight of what really matters. It's not their fault. Derek blames the parents.

When he eventually carries through two steaming plates of rice and dahl, Lofty is going on about university offers, making Baldev scowl ferociously into his tea. While the boys eat, Derek rolls a long spliff for dessert.

Later, as the moor outside the window turns hunch-backed against the sunset, Derek begins strumming on his guitar. 'You've got the brains,' he says to Baldev. 'You've got the technology. You've got to dream, man.' He passes Baldev the joint. 'Look at Lofty. He's going to plant a forest. He's going to live communally in Wales and learn to lay a hedge.'

'After university,' says Lofty evasively.

'He's not into possessions.' Derek smiles fondly at his son. 'In spite of his mother.'

'Obviously I'll need to keep my laptop in the commune.' Lofty rests his hand on it like a sleeping pet. 'But you can rig up a battery to a bicycle and create enough electric power to run a computer.'

'Thanks to me, Lofty hasn't been brainwashed by your school's propaganda,' says Derek.

Baldev exhales blue smoke, bats ash from the end of the joint.

'That's because ever since he started there,' Derek goes on, 'I've been taking him away at weekends to spend quality time with real people.'

'In all fairness, real people don't live in teepees, Dad.'

'Real people don't stand on other people's heads to get rich in the capitalist system,' retorts Derek.

Baldev is sprawled on his back, watching the motion of a bead-and-feather mobile dangling from the light fitting. 'We're not in control,' he says into the gloom.

'These exams are really getting to you,' says Lofty. 'Bal's a brain-box, Dad. He's a year ahead.'

'Woa,' says Derek.

'So what,' says Baldev.

'You should be going for it,' says Lofty.

'Go for it, man,' says Derek.

Baldev takes another long, slow drag. 'We've all got a pre-destined fate, so there's no point.'

'You've got to believe in your*self*,' says Derek. 'Not *fate*.'

Baldev snorts. 'You don't get it, Derek.' A long structure of ash drops, unheeded, onto his chest. 'Nobody does.'

By the eleven o-clock news bulletin the floor of the bedsit is covered with printouts: temples, mosques, grimy back-to-backs, and always, children. Beatrice isn't sure whether there's an atmosphere between her and Howard. He hasn't uttered a word since the meal. Switching off her printer, all done for tonight, she watches him via the dressing table mirror, sitting at his laptop; the way he stares into space then gets an idea and rattles on.

She decides that he's being normal and that this is as good a moment as any. 'You've identified as a writer all along, haven't you,' she says. 'It's been the whole point of travelling, for you. You've always known your focus.'

His eyes narrow, scanning text. 'I've been getting on with my life, if that's what you mean.' Tap tap tap.

'I feel like I'm getting on with mine, at last,' she says to his reflection.

'That's great, Beatrice.' He glances up. 'Listen, I didn't mean to put you on the defensive like that about the children issue. Maybe when you finally know where you're going we'll be able to review it.'

'I know where I'm going.'

'Well, good. That's terrific. So maybe we should find time to really talk about this.'

'Actually Howard, since we're on the subject, there's something I haven't mentioned. I'm booked in for a termination.'

Howard's fingers go still. The bars of the electric fire buzz faintly. Beatrice unplugs the memory-stick

196

containing her back-ups, drops it into her briefcase's zip compartment for safekeeping.

'Are you saying you're pregnant?'

'Technically.' She begins collecting printouts. 'I always thought it would feel like something, but it doesn't.'

Howard's nest of equipment stirs and slips as he reclines, very slowly, until his head comes to rest in the wing of the chair. 'When...?'

'Saturday.'

'Saturday! As in, the day after tomorrow?'

'It's no big deal. They say if I take it easy, I can be back at work by Wednesday.' She smiles at him reassuringly, but he is staring at the ceiling. 'Which is just as well because it'll cost nearly eight hundred bucks.'

'Pounds,' says Howard.

'I mean pounds.' She grimaces. 'I hoped I was going to get my camera paid off in the next couple of weeks.'

Outside a lone male voice, singing drunkenly, approaches along the street and then passes by.

'So,' Howard addresses Beatrice via the mirror. 'What can I say?'

She stops him. 'It's okay, Howard, you don't need to say anything. I finally know what I want. I'm getting my act together at last.' Her voice is bright, but hearing her own words, how they fall through the silence like dead weights, makes her end on an uncertain note.

*

At seven thirty on Friday morning, as on every morning barring those with torrential rain, Derek is standing in his garden to eat his muesli. Fine drizzle settles like dew on his beard. He stares rapturously into the trees, beyond which the refuse tip slopes steeply downwards, and above which the fell is a watery blur. The hype around the Yorkshire Dales National Park fools some people into leaving the city. They head over the hills, leaving the grit

197

and the dark splendour in search of dry-stone-wall gentleness. Unreal, man. Bourgeois and precious. They've succumbed to the widespread prejudice against good, honest smut. They can't see what's under their noses.

As usual at around this time of the morning, Derek hears Joan Blake leaving for work, her Astra chuntering down the track. Other than this, nothing disturbs his peace. Taking a last deep breath of the clammy air, he bumbles indoors with his muesli bowl and sets about frying tofu and mushrooms for the boys' breakfast.

It was around eleven last night when Lofty and Baldev, stoned, crawled into their sleeping bags on the living room floor amidst the paraphernalia of their laptop lives, and Derek retired to his futon. Now, he hears them beginning to stir from sleep.

When Baldev comes through in his underpants, spindly and golden, Derek gives him an affable slap on the shoulder. 'Morning, Mahatma. What time's school?'

Baldev checks his empty wrist. 'Dunno, my watch is in my shoe. Prob'ly around now.' He goes to the threshold of the back door and stretches like a cockerel. 'S'okay. It's our last day before home study starts. Kind of like a leaving day. We won't be doing much.' He steps out into the long grass, barefoot. 'It's really private here, isn't it?'

'It's a hermitage,' agrees Derek.

By the time Baldev ducks back into the house, his expression has regressed to last night's scowl.

'Hey man, it's a beautiful day,' says Derek. 'Be happy.'

When Howard drops Beatrice off at St Ninian's, the car park is already full. Howard is being taciturn.

'Hey. It's Friday!' Beatrice gives his cheek her usual peck and gets out of the car.

She is asked to wait in the staffroom for Mrs Chatterjee-Fox whose remit it is, as deputy-head, to supervise supply staff. Beatrice smells the familiar aroma with its hints of polish, museums, filter coffee, talcum powder. The staffroom's curtains would suit a chintzy tearoom. She browses the notice board: a poster about refugees, a pristine pamphlet – 'Equality, Diversity and Community Cohesion Framework', an envelope collecting for famine victims, another for used postage stamps to send off to fight AIDS.

Most of the staff have melted away into their classrooms apart from two women in pencil skirts working on the staffroom computers, prim as poodles, their handbags under their chairs, and a man in brogues with a dry sniff reading *The Guardian*, his legs crossed girlishly at the knee. Behind the newspaper he'll be wearing a checked brushed-cotton shirt, a tweed jacket, a knitted tie with a blunt end; the kind who chips in when *Brain of Britain* is on the radio; a man with a car-hoover.

Beatrice feels peacefully invisible until the staffroom door opens.

'*Lovely…*' A tall, black-frocked clergyman, as lean as a furled umbrella, enters. Seeing Beatrice he extends a long arm. 'Welcome, welcome…'

The Guardian quivers.

'Have you helped yourself to a spot of this excellent coffee?' asks the vicar. 'Our Lilian does us proud.' He makes a gesture like sowing seed encompassing the china teacups, the small, neat biscuits on silver trays, the chrome percolator, the white, lace-edged cloth. To Beatrice it looks like a holy communion.

The vicar's eyes are arched windows. 'I take it you're waiting for our Mrs Chatterjee-Fox?'

'I guess I am,' says Beatrice. 'I think she's the person responsible for me.'

The clock says twenty minutes to nine. One of the prim women is now snatching sheets from the printer as they emerge, puncturing them with sharp cracks of the staple. The tweedy man checks his watch then folds his newspaper neatly. His facial hair is meticulously clipped. He looks like a squirrel. He rises in the manner of someone about to make a speech. 'I'd better take you down,' he says to Beatrice with gravity. 'You're covering my class, actually. I'm off-timetable all day with meetings. I don't think we had better leave things to Mrs Chatterjee-Fox any longer.' His moustache twitches.

'She has a long drive to work, of course,' says the vicar sadly.

The man's eyes are beads. 'I'll go and retrieve my lesson-notes from her desk.'

Just then the staffroom door opens and a woman in a yellow and pink sari swishes in. She is pretty but unkempt, like scattered sugar. The edges of her beautiful mouth are blurred with raspberry lipstick. Her sari, bunched in a creased mess at the shoulder, is slipping untidily down her arm. The shoulder strap of her briefcase trails on the ground.

'Aha.' The vicar's smile is wide but his forehead is chiselled.

'Traffic,' she says. A hairpin tinkles to the floor.

The squirrely man gives her a look.

'Again,' she adds. 'Absolutely snarled up. My village is almost in the National Park, you know.'

Beatrice notices that her accent is BBCish, like the *Woman's Hour* presenter.

'Perhaps I should take this lady down myself at this stage, Mrs Chatterjee-Fox,' sniffs the squirrely man.

Darshana turns a dead stare on Beatrice.

Beatrice is struck by her hair, a black twist heavy enough to rope a ship to the dock. The French roll has slipped down the back of Darshana's head and is already partially coiled on her shoulder, the tail of it curling down her breast. Her olive forehead is coated with perspiration like oil brushed on pastry. Dark circles bloom from her armpits into her close-fitting blouse. Her deep-set eyes are sheltered behind half-closed lids. Her sari, gaudy and sunny, contrasts with her brooding presence. In the stretched-out, wordless moment, Beatrice starts to hold out her hand.

'Mrs Chatterjee-*Fox*.' The vicar once again extends an arm. '*Do* sit down for a moment and allow me to serve you with a cup of coffee. *So* stressful, driving in traffic. You need to collect your thoughts…'

'Yes.' Darshana turns away, and Beatrice tucks a non-existent strand behind her ear.

The squirrely man invites Beatrice to follow him through the staff suite. Passing the reception office the secretary appears, catches his eye, nods towards the staffroom and pulls a face. The man twitches his mouth.

At last, the morning drizzle clears and the sun breaks through. After a protracted breakfast, Baldev and Lofty tidy away their laptops into smart cases and push these into their school bags between files and filthy socks.

Derek loads his Rottweiler onto the front seat of the vintage Ford. He works out from the position of the sun that he's going to be late for his Job Centre appointment.

The two lanky boys fold down into the back, wedged in by all their stuff, and the vehicle coughs its way onto the main road.

'Come again whenever you want,' Derek calls over his shoulder.

'Yeh.' Lofty pokes Baldev encouragingly. 'It's been good, hasn't it?'

Baldev is scrunched up in his seat, his face as creased and rumpled as his uniform.

Lofty gives up. He checks the time on his iPod. 'I think we'll be there for mid-morning break. I've never been this late for school before.'

'So what?' sneers Baldev, his chin inside his collar. 'What are they going to do? This is the end.'

Chapter 20

A message comes down to year four in the hands of a child.

Dear Ms Kirby, would you mind popping into my office for a word during breaktime? Thanks! Darshana Chatterjee-Fox.

After seeing the children out to the playground Beatrice takes a short cut to the staff suite through the assembly hall. Clarissa Woolf is rocking back and forth playing something Irish on her harp, watched by two spectacled little girls with mini-harps. The pomegranate on which the vicar's assembly was centred is still on the lectern.

In the staff corridor Darshana rushes up behind Beatrice rattling keys, a trail of children following behind like disciples, carrying her books. Her hair has been re-rolled into a smooth shell on the back of her head, her lips redefined, and her eye sockets deepened with brown eye shadow, but her armpits are giving off a heavy floral perfume behind which is a strong tang of sweat.

Darshana pushes open her office door with one foot and ushers the children through, addressing them with the grotesque cheeriness of a kids' TV presenter: 'Thank you Melissa, just put that on the floor in the corner over there for me please. Thank you, darling. You too Duncan, just pop it there. Lovely. Perfect.' She lets her briefcase drop to the floor. 'Thank you very much, all my helpers. Not now, Jessica, sweetie, I'll see about that after break.' She places her hands on two of the children, manipulating their heads to face the door, shooing the whole bunch out of her office. 'Out to play now please.' Without looking at Beatrice directly she says with a sunny smile, 'Do sit down.'

The door closes itself.

Darshana seats herself on the opposite side of her cluttered desk. Amongst the papers and child-made paperweights is a large framed photograph of two boys in school uniform. The older one, around sixteen or seventeen, looks like Darshana. The younger boy is white and freckly. Slotted into the bottom corner is a passport-sized photo of Joan's daughter.

Darshana starts rummaging in her briefcase, calling from below the desk, 'How's it going in year four?'

'They're adorable,' says Beatrice.

'Just let me know if you need anything.' She sits up, begins tidying pens into pots. 'We want visiting teachers to feel at home.' She opens a drawer, shuts it again.

'Thank-you.' Beatrice feels the pull of caffeine as the aroma of a fresh brew filters in from the staffroom.

Darshana slams closed the drawer of a filing cabinet. 'You can send for me if you need any assistance, in any way.' She picks up her keys, moves them to another place on the desk. 'Actually –' a nervous titter twitches through her. 'Actually, there's something else I wanted to mention that's not *actually* to do with this school.' A grin contorts her mouth. Beatrice sees red lipstick on her incisors.

'I understand you've been working at Braithwaite.' Darshana's eyes are needles. 'Where my best friend Joan works.'

'Hey, that's right. Joan Blake, you mean?'

'Yes! *Such* a small world, isn't it?' Darshana's fingernails skitter about on her papers. 'Especially among teachers. *Amazing*, really.' One of her high heels clicks repeatedly, metallically, against a chair leg.

There is too long a pause.

Beatrice tries nodding encouragingly. 'So Joan's a friend of yours.'

Darshana swivels away from Beatrice, looks sideways at her, then away again. 'I'm talking personally now,' she says to the bookcase.

Beatrice leans back, crossing her legs loosely, and smiles. 'Alright.'

'This is very strictly between you and me, now. Very strictly. Because Joan's a very good friend of mine.' Darshana swivels back sharply and leans across the desk. 'We go back a long way.'

Beatrice feels her shirt sticking to her skin. 'Okay.'

Darshana is looking through her to something beyond. 'I hope you don't mind my saying this. I'm only thinking of Joan. *And* yourself, of course.'

'I'm rather mystified at the moment,' says Beatrice, determined to seem at ease.

'I don't know how to say this without embarrassing you. That's not my intention; I don't want anything unpleasant to come of this.'

'Hey, don't worry about it,' says Beatrice. 'Best to get it off your chest. I'm okay with that.'

'I understand... I understand that you and Joan have got quite *friendly*...'

Beatrice nods. 'Sure.'

'I think you should know something of Joan's *history*.' Darshana is fiddling with her rings, looking everywhere except at Beatrice, 'Regarding *friends*. *Special* friends.'

The staffroom door is opening and closing. The hubbub through the wall sounds attractively normal: clinking cups, idle chitchat over nibbled biscuits, the aromas of coffee and cleanliness.

'I'm listening.'

The room smells sour. Darshana lowers her voice further. 'I think it's better if you know what she can be like. With her... her *special* friends.'

'Well, I dunno how special I am. We've talked a lot.'

204

'I think you know what I'm saying.' Darshana's heel is like a hammer beating lightly on glass. 'I think you ought to know that she can be violent.'

'Pardon me?'

Darshana's hands are trembling. She removes them from view. 'People have got close to her on a number of occasions in the past and it's ended in violent scenes. I mean physical violence.'

In her pocket Beatrice has begun flicking a retracting pen in, out, in, out, in time with Darshana's heel.

Darshana's eyes are shifting across the room's smooth surfaces. 'People she gets... *especially* friendly with.'

'Women, you mean?'

The heel misses a beat. 'I'm talking about *colleagues*. Please understand that I'm only saying this to protect you. *And* her. Because there's the risk of talk.'

'I don't really get this. I mean, *why* would she get violent?'

'Drink,' says Darshana. 'Not that I'm saying she's got an alcohol problem.'

'So let's get this straight. Joan has got close to a number of... *colleagues*, and then beaten them up?'

'I'm not saying that. Nothing like that. I just... don't want her to be involved in any of the kind of upsets that she's been through in the past. She needs saving from herself.'

'Mrs Chatterjee-Fox: what's your intention in telling me this?'

A snake's hiss. 'Don't see her again.'

A bell goes. Darshana springs up and flusters over some sheaves of worksheets. 'I mean, not outside school,' she rushes on, 'otherwise I'll worry about you both.'

There's a child's timid knock. Darshana spins, yanks open the door. '*Do* go and get yourself a coffee, Beatrice.'

At twenty past three on Friday afternoon, the secretary is straightening out her office ready for Monday. Re-sticking the prayer card to the hatch, she sees a child approaching, his eyes brimming.

The secretary takes pride in knowing every child in the school by name, unlike Mr Forrester-Paton, who knows hardly any names at all and who sometimes mistakes girls for boys and vice versa. The tearful child is one of three Rameshes. He's year four Ramesh. Darshana's class.

'What's the matter, Ramesh?'

A tear spills over. 'Mrs Chatterjee-Fox won't come out of the library corner, Miss.'

Behind Ramesh are the two Charlottes, holding hands, doing down-turned mouths like the pictures in their reading books.

'It's because she's crying,' says Charlotte Green.

'My Mum cried when Belle died on *Home and Away*,' whimpers Charlotte Cherry.

The secretary hurries to the Head's office, knocks, and pops her head round the door. 'Excuse me.'

Mr Forrester-Paton and Martin the vicar are facing each other over the tea tray.

'I'm afraid it's Darshana,' says the secretary.

'Ah. Oh.' Mr Forrester-Paton lowers his cup.

'I'm afraid she's having an upset.'

Mr Forrester-Paton looks apprehensive. 'Is it hormonal trouble?'

The secretary purses up.

The Head goes pink.

The vicar is already leaving his seat. 'I think this is a pastoral matter.'

'Absolutely, absolutely,' Mr Forrester-Paton splutters gratefully. 'Most kind of you, Martin.'

'My pleasure.' The vicar makes for the door. 'Perhaps I could bring her to your office for a one-to-one chat?'

'Certainly, certainly. I'll be only too happy to make myself scarce.'

The vicar's smile is broad enough to insert a collection plate. 'It's alright, I know the way.' He waves a hand.

'You need to go too,' says the secretary firmly. 'They'll need telling to put up their chairs and pick up everything off the floor, then they'll need dismissing.'

The Head looks like a cornered rabbit. 'Of course.'

'Immediately. Or they'll be left on their own.' The secretary propels the Head out of his office. 'Ramesh! Charlotte and Charlotte! Could you please show Mr Forrester-Paton the way to your classroom? Thank-you.'

Shortly after three-thirty Beatrice emerges from the main entrance of St Ninian's. Howard is waiting in the car park. He watches her approach, her long legs striding through throngs of mothers and children.

She crashes into the passenger seat, slams the door and leans across to peck his cheek. 'Thanks for picking me up, sweetie. How's your afternoon at home been?'

He switches on the engine. 'Met the two deadlines.'

'Great. Worth taking the time off, then.' She fastens her seatbelt.

'I can afford to.' He pulls out of the parking space. One thing she hasn't clarified is the abortion fee. He guesses she will have a fifty-fifty split in mind.

'Isn't it great? Soon you'll be able to afford not to teach at all.' Beatrice yawns, stretches. 'It's so great to get to the weekend.'

'I can't believe you just said that.'

'Uff. What I mean is, least on Sunday I'll still have two days off to look forward to,' she says brightly.

He drives through the suburb with care, on the alert for straying children. A mother hurries her little boy across the road in front of him. She smiles and waves thanks. She's carrying a baby in a harness on her chest, its tiny head cupped in one hand.

'My day's been *weird*,' says Beatrice.

Howard doesn't react. The sun is shining and he is struck by the avenue's feminine touches: daisies in the verges, whitewashed houses with wysteria or clematis – family houses where thirty-something mothers in summer dresses and sandals are leading children down garden paths like Easter chicks. A Sikh woman in a sari, holding the hands of twin boys with white topknots, is gliding into a drive with lions on the gateposts.

'You're not gonna believe this,' says Beatrice. 'I've been *warned off* seeing Joan. What do you make of that?'

'Really.'

'I thought you'd be riveted. Darshana told me all this stuff about Joan becoming violent when she's had a drink.' Beatrice guffaws.

Howard doesn't respond.

On leaving the suburb, the shelter of trees ends and a sudden rough wind blows in through Beatrice's window. She hurriedly winds it closed. 'So. What else did you do this afternoon?'

'Dealt with stuff. Made calls.' Howard feels his neck and shoulders pulled into taut knots, the way he gets when he spends too long in front of the computer. In the past, the remedy was always to lie on his bed and guide Beatrice's massaging fingers to the right places.

Beatrice's hand settles companionably on his thigh.

'Want to know what I think?'

'Tell me,' he says woodenly.

'I think Darshana's a snob.'

'Sounds like jealousy to me. Maybe you've stolen her lover.' He changes gear, jerking Beatrice's hand away.

Beatrice pushes his leg. 'Darshana's totally straight – totally a man's woman. Joan's told me a lot. And she does come across as very het. Her sari and everything.'

'Whereas Joan comes across as a total dyke, which is why you find her hot.'

Beatrice ignores his remark. 'I'm sure Darshana's worry is about gossip. She doesn't want herself to be tainted by how her best friend behaves when drunk.'

Howard is uninterested, staring straight ahead. They leave the ring road, begin the long descent. At the bottom of the hill stands the roofless shell that was Nafeez, like a cardboard box with the top open.

Beatrice pushes his knee again. 'So how was your morning in Braithwaite? Any new gossip there?'

Howard turns into Henry Place. 'Some.'

'Tell me!'

He throws Beatrice a humourless grin. 'Joan Blake's left her husband.'

Later, when Beatrice pads out of the bathroom in her robe and slippers, she finds Howard watching her, his laptop switched off and on the floor beside his armchair.

'May in the North of England,' she shudders, pulling her robe tight. Howard's mood is unfamiliar, unidentifiable. Her bath provided an escape from the long, blank, wordless gaps.

Howard notices the single wet curl spiralling from the white towel knotted round Beatrice's head; how graceful she is; how feline. He flicks on a second bar of the fire. 'I made coffee.'

'Thanks, sweetie.' Beatrice begins scrabbling under the bed for something.

'We'd better talk about... tomorrow,' he says.

'Sure.' Beatrice grins over her shoulder. 'It only just occurred to me, I need to pack.' She pulls out a small leather hold-all, fetches one set of fresh underwear and one pair of socks from the chest of drawers and puts them into the bag, then throws in a couple of pots; a deodorant stick; a jar of hair gel.

'Come and drink your coffee,' he says.

She leaves the bag and flops down near him with a tube of hand lotion. A thought comes to her and she suddenly springs up again. 'Cheque book.' She gives him a rueful grin, goes to the bedside cabinet, takes her cheque book from the drawer, drops it in her bag and returns to the settee. Her feet reach across to rest on his armchair. She takes a sip from her mug and eyes him. 'Good coffee.'

He looks at her small, pale, perfect feet. 'You seem very relaxed about... all this.'

Beatrice shrugs the subject away. 'So what exactly *were* your deadlines today, anyway?'

'Well: the first Letter from the North of England has gone off to New York...'

'*Tadah*. That's terrific.'

'And I got that piece emailed off to Max. And I did a little piece for the travel mag.'

'Very productive,' says Beatrice.

'And I got another call from Fenella. About her dad's sixtieth birthday. He's throwing a big party at his club.'

'Wow. Are we invited?' Beatrice's hands are sliding over themselves, slippery and uncatchable, coating each other in a lotion that smells of satsumas.

'It's tomorrow night.'

'Darn. I could've made a different termination appointment if we'd known earlier.'

Howard winces, hearing Fenella's voice again calling Beatrice hard-faced. 'Thing is, it's going to be the *total* media scene. Like, everyone I could possibly desire to meet is gonna be there. Fenella's done the inviting. You should hear —'

'Howard, I don't want you to miss this. This will be great for you.'

'There's a guy from the *Telegraph* interested in the spread I did for the magazine. Max says —'

'Listen,' Beatrice interjects, 'I can take the bus to Doncaster. You don't need to deliver me there.'

She is smiling at him. She seems to be delighted for him. He says, 'Look, I'll ask if he's interested in your photographs. I'll do what I can to swing something for you.'

Beatrice taps his chest lightly. 'Don't worry about me; I'm working on my exhibition.'

'And anyway,' says Howard, 'I *can* take you to Doncaster tomorrow, don't worry about that. I can take you on my way. What time do they want you there?'

'Mid-day. Listen, you've got to go for this.' She smiles.

He used to love how she smiled. He says, 'Would it be okay to take you a little earlier?'

'Sure that'll be okay.' Her long hand is on his knee. 'I'm gonna load up with magazines and stuff. I'll find a corner to sit in.'

He goes to roll a cigarette, tapping his pockets for his tobacco pouch, then remembers it's empty. He craves that first drag. 'Thing is – I'm not planning... I won't be back in time to pick you up on Sunday.'

Outside it is still bright and sunny. Kids are playing noisily in the dried-up, teatime street. Someone thunders up the stairs of the house next door. Howard's watch beeps the hour.

'Are you sure? They said four-ish would be alright. When will you be back?'

'Not... in time to pick you up.'

When Beatrice's face is completely still she looks her age, maybe even older. She could be already forty. At the same time she looks like a child.

'There's more coffee.' He disappears into the kitchen.

At around nine in the evening, Beatrice returns from a brisk circular walk she took to the corner shop. She is armed with two samosas, three glossies and a little box of chocolates; a treat for Sunday night, after the event.

She puts them in the fridge. The note says Howard has gone for a curry. Beatrice eats her samosas straight from the bag. She is in bed with the small lamp on, reading, when Howard walks in. She lowers her book.

He stands in the middle of the room. 'Lot of cops around.' He starts fussing with his small rucksack on the back of the door. 'I'll just…'

Beatrice goes to the bathroom.

When she comes back, Howard is wedging his laptop into the top of his stuffed bag. 'That's me packed too. Cup of tea?'

'No. I'm going to sleep.'

Later she wakes from a doze. Howard is in the bed with his back turned.

'So it's going ahead,' he says.

The alarm clock ticks loud then soft, loud then soft. Sometimes it seems to miss a beat, like an irregular heart.

'I didn't know you'd feel like this,' says Beatrice.

'I always wanted to be a father.'

'You never told me.'

'You never asked.'

Part Three:
The Excellence Challenge

Chapter 21

The filter coffee smells over-stewed. Beatrice opts instead for a mug of strong brown tea. The woman serving drinks looks robust, the sleeves of her shiny overall rolled up over strong forearms. The women and girls shuffling past are swaddled in unflattering, man-sized bathrobes or tatty quilted dressing gowns, comfort-clothing that ordinarily they would never wear in public.

'Help yourself to two biscuits.' Cheerfully brisk, the woman passes on from Beatrice to the next in line.

The lounge is high ceilinged and ornately corniced in accordance with the house's original status as a mill-owner's elegant residence. When Howard swished to a stop on the gravel, Beatrice exclaimed, 'Wow. A mansion.' The way he was sitting prevented her from kissing him goodbye. She managed to land a light peck on his cheek. 'Have a good party.'

'Goodbye, Beatrice.'

The girl behind Beatrice has a GCSE revision guide under her arm, the subject of which is hidden by her dressing gown. She is so typically adolescent as to look familiar: gawky-limbed, awkward, her lank hair curtaining off all but her chin which is bubbled with acne.

With her tea, two rich-tea biscuits and a magazine clenched under one elbow, Beatrice pads self-consciously in her socks to an unoccupied sofa. The king-sized sanitary towel is warm and gluey between her legs. Its bulkiness turns them all into invalids.

The last few women are shuffling along the refreshments counter. Most are now seated on one of the pink sofas arranged around low Formica tables dotted with pot-plants, and are sipping their drinks, not looking at each other. A doll-like blonde girl in Winnie-the-Pooh pyjamas, pink-cheeked, too young to have breasts, is stretched along an entire sofa with her head in *Cosmopolitan*, chomping contentedly on chocolate digestives from her own private packet. The room has an echo that inhibits talk. Beyond the mullioned windows, shifting branches of oak trees hide the clinic from the view of other houses on the suburban lane. There is a distant peal of Sunday bells.

This is the first coming together. On arrival yesterday they were taken to individual rooms. Beatrice spent several hours immersed in magazines, banned from consuming food or water, before being wheeled to the theatre on a trolley.

Two women in their late thirties have chosen to sit on sturdy wooden chairs at a large central table. They are not for curling gingerly into a sofa like everyone else, giving in to painkiller-induced wooziness. When they start talking, everyone listens, staring into their magazines.

'I've already got four, you see,' says the one in the huge brown tee-shirt. Excess flesh, bagged up in tartan jogging-bottoms, wobbles on her knees.

The other woman cradles her mug of tea, elbows on the table, her wiry shoulder-length hair streaked with grey, her belly cascading in rolls like tractor-tyres. 'Well, my own daughter's expecting and she's still at 'ome, so it's 'er turn, in't it?'

'I'm already a grandma,' says the first. 'Our Blair will be ten next month.'

Beatrice feels the dragging again in her womb, the pain that made her yowl and throw up before the painkillers got to work.

'…so I don't think it's right,' the brown tee-shirt woman is saying.

'Tell me about it,' says the other. 'I've had to get a bank loan to pay for this. Bloody disgusting.'

*

The lounge is emptying. It feels more like a hotel foyer now that everyone is dressed and waiting for their lifts.

Now, if they catch each other's eyes, they half-smile.

Taxi for Kirby,' calls the receptionist.

Beatrice fingers away lipstick from her mouth corners, drops her mirror into her hold-all and stands up. The sanitary towel feels as obtrusive as a diaper under her trousers. She tugs at the back of her jacket, wishing it were longer. She should have brought a skirt.

Pulled in on the gravel are three or four cars. A man in a suit springs out of his Rover to look after the woman who was wearing a slinky negligee earlier. He catches up her vanity case, puts it in the boot and eases the woman into the car with a guiding arm.

Beatrice throws her bag onto the taxi's back seat. The driver is dressed from head to toe in snow-white cotton with a home-knit waistcoat on top. On the dashboard is a hologram sticker, a colourful pattern of Arabic script.

'Long way for me go,' he says.

Beatrice eases herself gently into the back seat alongside her bag to avoid having to make conversation for a whole hour. It is going to cost almost a day's pay to get home. The back of the driver's neck is a concertina of wrinkles. He is looking at her in the rear-view mirror. She wonders whether he knows what this clinic is for.

''Av got family up your way,' he says pleasantly. He turns the ignition key. An exotic sound-track fills the car. The taxi is pulled in behind a Vauxhall Astra. Beatrice sees the acned teenager pushing her rucksack into the car. It tumbles over the headrest onto the back seat. The girl says something to the driver and jumps in. Meanwhile the taxi driver indicates and deftly slides his vehicle out. As the taxi passes alongside the Astra, Beatrice, reaching for her seatbelt, finds herself looking Joan in the eye.

*

Joan's daughter gives the passenger door a good slam.

Beatrice stares forward, rigid in her seat, as the taxi crunches away, turns left and heads northwards.

''Ope there's no rioting when we get up there,' the driver calls happily over the music.

'Look at this traffic,' says Joan. Even on a Sunday, the main northern road out of Doncaster is thick with cars.

Caroline is twiddling the radio. She gives up and checks out the CDs in the glove compartment.

'Was the food alright?' asks Joan.

'I didn't really eat it.'

'Are you alright?'

'Yeh.'

'So. Wednesday's your French oral.'

'Yeh. And Friday's my German, and that's everything this week.' Caroline inserts *Barry Manilow's Greatest Hits*.

Joan lets her jaw drop. 'I thought Barry Manilow was naff. I thought I showed you up with this one.'

'I like 'Copa Cabana'. The rest of it makes me puke, obviously.'

'Will you be able to eat Marks and Spencer's pizza and some chips?'

Caroline is reclining the seat. 'Dunno yet.' She settles back, eyes closed.

'Or something else. I'll make you what you want.' Joan glances across. 'You look washed-out.'

'I always look like this.'

'You're so tall. I told you that assistant in *Virgin Megastores* thought you were at university, didn't I.'

Caroline opens her eyes and looks at her. 'I'm alright, you know, Mum. Don't worry.'

Her mother reaches over and gives her bony knee a quick squeeze.

'Are you still going to America, Mum?'

'Yes, love.'

218

'Doncaster looks quite posh,' says Caroline.

'You'll end up somewhere really nice, one day. Aim for the stars. Aim for somewhere sunny.' Her mother darts a look, and suddenly blurts, 'You can come with me if you want, you know.'

'I do quite fancy Disneyland.'

'Otherwise, I'll miss you.'

'To be perfectly honest, Mum, I'd rather do my A-levels here. Stay on at Belvedere Aske. Could I just come for holidays?'

Joan grins, cuffs her daughter gently on the chin, laughs. They head along more familiar roads, between liquorice walls and derelict fields.

'D'you know what?' says Caroline. 'I've got a, like, Christmassy feeling. Or... or like, being pushed on the swings when I was little. Do you remember when I'd be in bed and you and Dad would read me a story, doing the different voices?' She slips off her shoes and draws her legs up on the seat, loving the smell of her mother's car, of mud and paper; loving how the back seat is always overflowing with a mess of junk.

Towards the end of the journey the Astra is lashed at by a rain shower.

Joan sighs. 'Look at this. Nearly June.'

With a shake of maracas, *Copa Cabana* kicks off.

'Actually,' says Caroline, 'I think I could eat a *small* piece of pizza.'

Before arriving home, Beatrice asks the driver to stop by a cashpoint. She withdraws seventy pounds to cover the fare. When the taxi turns into Henry Place there is an amiable-looking policeman on the corner. The sun has come out again after the shower, and children are playing hopscotch on the pavement. The taxi driver takes the wad of notes and heads off to visit his relatives, to be served a home-cooked meal in a terraced house somewhere in the city. It has been a good day for him.

Beatrice takes a bath and puts on a voluminous nightdress, the first time she has worn it, a birthday gift sent through the post by an aunt. It makes her feel swaddled. She takes the chocolates from the fridge and puts them with her magazines and her book by the bed, then goes round switching things off: the cooker, the fire, the sockets. She stops at her mobile phone on the mantelpiece, touches it, but leaves it switched off.

She decides against listening to the radio as she'd have to get out of bed again to turn it off, then she changes her mind, removes Howard's extension lead from his armchair and trails it around the furniture until it reaches the bed. If he comes home late tonight and wants to work he can use his laptop on batteries. Hell, he can wait until tomorrow. She brings over the radio and plugs it in.

It is only seven-thirty. She is restless, not yet tired, and is also irritated with herself for having this feeling of waiting. He is, after all, a free agent. They have always come and gone as they pleased. Her laptop catches her eye. Shrugging away any further thoughts of him, she decides to work.

The clinic had felt like a retreat. All she could do on Saturday was read and think. A magazine article seized her imagination – a picture of the wartime King and Queen visiting somewhere surrounded by poor-looking children waving Union Jacks. Only the boys' shorts and caps betrayed the date. She finds the picture in her magazine and clips it out.

Another article was about some British author who killed himself. The piece included his sepia wedding photo, the bride as gauzy as a fairy, her bouquet huge, red roses and fern trailing down elegantly to the floor.

Beatrice scans in the two pictures, eats a chocolate, clips her nails, moisturises, then plays around with a work-in-progress, the portrait photograph of the policeman. She graphitises his helmet and duplicates it to create a Warhol-style grid in rainbow colours. The policeman's eyes peer out from each image, piercing blue, then canary yellow, then scarlet, then green. It's clichéd. She takes it back to the original image and tries something else.

Eventually she goes to retrieve her folio from under the bed. As she kneels down she holds onto the thick wad of towel through her nightdress, sandwiched inside her tightest knickers, to stop it shifting out of position.

Her folio is satisfyingly thick. Twenty-eight finished images. One day soon she will improve the basic website she set up for herself as a student and assemble her latest images in a new gallery. She will reactivate her contacts, network with old art-school friends again, get Maria and the rest of them to help her.

The painkillers are wearing off. She gets up slowly, changing her mind about working late. In the bathroom, doubled over, she takes two aspirin and brings the rest of the blister pack and a glass of water to her bedside. She pulls back the duvet, then looks over again at her mobile on the mantelpiece. Better to leave it off than switch it on but not receive a call. She eases herself into the bed and pulls the quilt over her ears.

On Tuesday morning a cheque arrives in the post for four hundred pounds. No note.

It is late afternoon when Beatrice finally shuts down her laptop. The last two days have been highly productive. She has completed a triptych. The first image is of the old chapel down Henry Place, cleverly restored using Photoshop tools to what she thinks its original appearance would have been. She has removed the latter-day blue signboard with its Arabic lettering and painted in the broken windows so that the carpet rolls that are

221

stored inside nowadays are hidden from view. On the chapel steps are the 1940s children clipped from the magazine, the boys' caps tangerine, pink and lime, the girls' frocks banana yellow or turquoise, and in their hair, straggles of luminous ribbon. In the archway stand the gauzy bride and her groom, still in sepia except for the roses of the bride's bouquet, which drip, scarlet, down the front of her gown.

In the second image the chapel door is open, but there is only darkness inside. In the foreground the shrouded Muslim mourners are milling about. The Arabic signboard is now in place but the windows are still intact. To the side of the archway, the policeman from the end of Henry Place is standing guard.

The third image is of the policeman's helmet turned upside down like a bucket and filled with the rolls of carpet, which are stuck with orange stars denoting special offers per square yard. Around the helmet, digitally manipulated to fit the curve of its brim, is the slur of Arabic script from the chapel's latter-day signboard.

Beatrice slips the three images into her folio and pulls the swathes of nightdress over her head and wraps herself in her bathrobe. She runs a bath and returns to the living room for her phone. She places it, her Filofax and a pen, and a gin and tonic on the toilet seat, and lowers herself into the water. There is salt in the bath. *It's soothing*, the nurse advised in a hand-patting voice. Eventually she reaches for her mobile.

'Hello Chaz. It's Beatrice Kirby, just calling to see if you have any work for me for the rest of this week.'

'Beatrice! We've been trying to call you both. We're snowed under. Braithwaite's desperate. They want Howard – where's he got to?'

'I'm calling about work for *me*, Chaz.'

'Sorry. I'm sorry, Beatrice. We've missed you. One of our most reliable teachers.'

'I've been ill.'

'I'm sorry to hear that. Teachers' hazard, that. You end up picking up everything going. Look, do you mind my inquiring about Howard's availability?'

'He's still in London. I've no idea.' Howard took at least seven shirts to London. She counted on Monday evening, going through his drawers.

'London. Ah. Well Braithwaite's asking for three teachers and we haven't even placed one there yet. Would you be able to do that for us?'

'Who's off? Is it the maths specialist? Joan Blake?'

'Let's see... nope. There's a Section Eleven teacher off, Mrs Khazim, plus both deputy-heads are off with stress.'

'What – Carole too?'

'Mrs Coulson, it says here.'

'It'll be hell Chaz, with the deputies off. There'll be anarchy.'

'As a matter of fact –' Chaz turns salesman-like, 'we've put Braithwaite on our Priority Schools list, which is an acknowledgement of the special demands of the school, so we are able to offer an enhancement on your daily rate to the tune of an extra twenty pounds.'

'Ah.'

'And as with all our priority placements we're able to offer an extra incentive for every full week completed, to the tune of twenty-five pounds. That means a potential one hundred and twenty-five pounds extra for each full week at Braithwaite on top of your basic pay.'

'So if I start tomorrow, that will be Wednesday through Tuesday.'

'Ordinarily we're counting a full week as Monday to Friday, but we can call this a special case.'

'If I wasn't desperate for money I wouldn't do this.'

'Great. I'll let them know. I'm sure it'll be fine, Beatrice. Brian Bottomley, the Head, will still be there.'

'He's an alcoholic, apparently.'
'It's not really a good idea to repeat rumours like that.'
'Sorry Chaz.'
'Phone us tomorrow; let us know how it went.'
'Sure. Thanks.'
'Cheers, Beatrice.'

The last of the bath water shrieks down the plughole. In the living room Beatrice tries on one of her few skirts, a narrow wrap-around in beige linen. The looseness around her legs is a novelty. She looks at herself in the mirror. Summery, but still smart. She imagines Joan's reaction when she sees her in a skirt.

She puts on a hardly-worn pretty lace bra and touches her lips with a pale pencil she once bought to go to a wedding. Tomorrow she will wear those feminine earrings. She pictures Joan's face.

For now she pulls on a hooded sweatshirt with the skirt and irons a white blouse for morning.

The bus-map is behind a candleholder on the mantelpiece. Beatrice extracts the street-plan from under a settee cushion, locates Braithwaite, spreads the bus-map on the hearthrug and starts plotting her route. When her mobile rings she is drinking camomile tea. It splashes over her skirt.

'Shit.' She grabs the phone. 'Lo?'
'It's me.'
'Hello Joan.'
'I just wondered whether you're alright. I've tried phoning loads of times.'
'I'm fine. Thanks for asking. Is… is your daughter alright?'
'Oh, she's right as rain. Very resilient, my daughter.'
'You've had a lot to deal with then, recently.'
'So've you.'

In the background Beatrice can hear a breathy Celtic ballad. She pulls her wet skirt off her leg, hoping camomile doesn't stain. 'I'll be seeing you tomorrow.'

'Thank God for that,' says Joan. 'It's a mess at school.'

'I heard Carole's off.'

'It's just how I said it would be. Dropping like flies.'

'I nearly didn't take the work, but I thought, if you're there, that's *something*,' says Beatrice.

Joan hesitates, then – 'Are you being looked after?'

'Yes,' Beatrice fibs.

'—because Howard hasn't been in this week, so I thought, it must be that he's at home, looking after you.'

'Actually he's in London,' Beatrice confesses.

'London? You mean you're on your own?'

'Yes.'

'So you're *not* being looked after.' Joan makes noises. 'I did wonder, seeing you get into that taxi. Does Howard even know?'

'It's okay. I told you. We're not really an item.'

'I could have given you a lift home.'

Beatrice laughs, and hears it sounding like Joan's laugh. A little ironic. British.

'You'll need a lift tomorrow, then. I'll come and pick you up.'

'Oh, but...'

'No problem whatsoever. Caroline's at her dad's tonight coz he's taking her in for her French oral tomorrow. I can be at yours around ten to eight.'

'That would be really helpful,' Beatrice concedes. 'Otherwise it's three buses.'

'Look, are you really alright? Do you want me to come over now?'

'Honestly I'm fine. Just like your daughter.'

'If he'd known I'm sure he'd have looked after you, you know.' Joan sounds slightly scolding, in a kind way. 'He's the type. He's a nice chap.'

225

By nine Beatrice is in bed. Her book is open but resting on the duvet. Despite having already brushed her teeth she eats the last chocolate. She imagines Chantelle, wobbling with secret hatred, giving her evil looks. She thinks of the money. She thinks of Joan.

The phone rings. Beatrice gets out of bed and goes to the mantelpiece. 'Hel-*lo?*'

There's only breathing.

'Hello? Hi!'

The line goes dead.

Beatrice hammers out Howard's number. His recorded voice is as charming as ever. 'Please leave me a message.'

'You miscalculated slightly.' She gulps, races on. 'You omitted to include fifty per cent of the fare for my taxi all the way home from Doncaster. That'll be another thirty-five bucks. I mean, *pounds.*' She slams the phone down on the bed, picks it up, presses the end-of-call button then slams it down again, harder. It bounces and comes to rest on Howard's pillow.

Chapter 22

The next morning Henry Place is bathed in sunshine. Beatrice skips from the house to the waiting car. She feels Joan staring at her skirt. Climbing in, she sees that Joan is wearing the trousers and blazer she wore to the Bombay Garden. She touches Joan's leg. 'New school image?'

'I'm being me. I like the skirt,' she adds, and blushes.

On the way, Beatrice describes her triptych and hears of Joan's weekend plumbing feats. It feels more than companionable. It feels intimate.

In Braithwaite's car park a couple of barelegged children are already skittering about, kicking each other's shins. As Beatrice steps out of the Astra her skirt flaps in the wind and she has to hold it down, feeling girlish.

A Mini appears out of nowhere and zips into the next parking space. Terri springs out in hoop earrings the size of saucers. 'Hi, girlfriends,' she calls in an American accent. Her top's plunging neckline offers a glimpse of red bra. She's wearing a suede mini-skirt and flat Indian sandals with little bells on the straps. Without heels she is tiny, teenaged in all but her face.

Her grin broadens, seeing Joan in trousers. 'Well. Very butch-femme.'

Joan turns tomato-red. 'You're keen,' she growls, looking at her watch.

'So are *you.*'

Walking to the entrance Terri scans the car park. 'Bottomley not here yet. This is killing him, this is. Actually having to come in. He was sweating like a pig yesterday.'

'He doesn't know who anybody is,' says Joan. 'I think Fatima's in charge of this place at the moment.'

Terri nudges Beatrice. 'Do you know who you're standing in for today?'

Joan takes Beatrice's arm. 'I'll get Brian to let you do Mrs Khazim's timetable. She hasn't got her own class. All she does is group work, improving language skills. Doddle. You could just do the register for Carole's or Ed's class.'

The staffroom has a lingering atmosphere of clandestine cigarettes, sheepishness and reluctance. The long coffee table between the two rows of seats is a sewer of tossed-away plastic food-wrappings, newspapers and junk. A bumper-sized air-freshener aerosol is wedged among the debris like a sky-scraper rising out of slums. The sink is piled with pots. Fatima's note about doing your own washing-up is mottled with splashes.

'I'll get t' kettle on,' says Terri.

'Excellent.' Joan puts some stuff down in the corner, picks up some more stuff and heads back out. 'I'm just taking this down to my room. Don't worry,' she says to Beatrice. 'Today'll be fine.' She marches off.

The electric kettle sighs. Terri picks out the cleanest three mugs and rinses them again under the tap.

Beatrice leans against the lockers, accidentally detaching the list of who's paid up for the lottery. 'Is Chantelle normally an early bird?' she asks lightly.

Terri laughs. 'Not likely.' She turns, drying a mug on a grubby teatowel. 'You're looking very… pretty. You're not normally a skirt person.'

'Well, it's meant to be summer.'

'So you and Joan have got quite – *friendly*, then.'

'We went for a curry the other week,' Beatrice says, evasively. 'It's hard to get to know people when you're a supply.'

228

The kettle is boiling. Terri extracts three teabags from a box buried under pots, slings one in each of the mugs and pours on water. 'Have you been warned off, yet?'

'What do you mean?'

Terri turns, a mug in each hand. 'Have you been phoned, yet? By Joan's *best friend?*'

Beatrice maintains a blank look.

'Maybe it won't come to that.'

'What?' says Beatrice.

Joan strides in.

Terri holds out a mug of tea, black, to Beatrice. 'No-one's paid the milkman, again.'

It is break-time before Beatrice encounters Chantelle. She finds her in one of the staffroom's sunken chairs, blotchy-cheeked, swollen-eyed, a mushed-up length of toilet-paper dangling mucoid from her fist. Seated on either side of her are a policeman and a policewoman. Beyond the staffroom window Beatrice sees the familiar orange and yellow stripes of a police van and two more officers chatting. She hovers just inside the staffroom door, waiting for someone else, for an explanation.

Staff members slam in one by one. All stop, stare. The start of break-time turns into a long, tense pause like the eternal moment after a road accident; everyone shuffling, whispering, tiptoeing to the kettle.

Eventually the Head barges in, pushes through the crowded room to the window and turns to face everyone. Someone wedges their foot in the staffroom door for the benefit of those still pressing in from the corridor.

Brian Bottomley's sleeves are still rolled up from the strenuous task, first thing, of dividing up and dispersing classes among the available teachers. A tide of sweat is seeping up his shirt from his trouser waistband. He clasps his scarlet face, pulling the flesh downwards until his expression is grotesquely mournful. 'We've just been informed,' he booms, 'of the murder of little Chelsea in Chantelle's year one.' He lowers his head for a moment, his ham-hands clamping together to no effect, a prayer that won't be wrung out.

Someone discreetly closes the fridge door again, finding no milk. People who have already made themselves drinks set them down on the nearest surface out of respect. 'Who did it?' somebody asks, ineffectually.

'We've already had *The Echo* on the phone,' he booms on. 'I need to ask you all to keep stum if approached by any members of the press. The Local Authority will liaise with them on our behalf. Our priority is to keep things low-key for the sake of the children.' He absently pats his chest, fishing out a pack of cheap, strong cigarettes, then hurriedly puts them away again. 'I hope we'll all be able to co-operate with the police while they make their inquiries. Over to you, sir.'

He nods at the policeman and descends onto a chair. It makes a splitting noise. Everyone sinks onto chairs or less comfortable perches, some kneeling bravely on the dirty carpet. Two crouching support assistants paw Chantelle's fat knees empathetically.

The neat, efficient policewoman stands up and proceeds to give further details: the date and time, the house on the estate, the physical abuse evident on the child's body. She describes the age and appearance of the prime suspect – the mother's partner, who is understood to be the child's father, who has not yet been tracked down, and asks whether anybody knows anything that might help the investigation in any way.
The staffroom remains hushed.

Joan is standing by the window. The police van's lights flash in her glasses. 'What are we going to do with the children?' she asks, sensibly.

'Close the school,' offers a small, hopeful voice.

Claire calls out, 'Let's get them all into the hall for a sing-song.'

The Head points at her: 'Superb idea. Well done, at the back.'

'They'll be full of all this by the time they come in from break,' a support assistant points out.

'High as kites.'

'It'll be murder,' agrees the girl who does the late readers.

The support team unites in an intake of breath. Beatrice notices Frank Lumb catching the eye of Terri, who makes a tiny strangled noise. The late-readers' girl has curled in on herself, the tips of her ears on fire.

'I think we'd better have an extended playtime until we've got ourselves sorted,' the Head bellows. 'I need to get Local Authority advice, so can I ask you all to pull together as a team and wait for further announcements.'

Beatrice has thrown open the staffroom window to disperse the steam and is washing every mug and teaspoon in a hygienically foaming sink. In the assembly hall, the music specialist has completed the full cycle of her piano repertoire and returned to the beginning. The form teachers have had to remain in the hall to subdue their classes with constant, frowning looks, whereas most of the support assistants are with Chantelle in the computer room, where she was led by the hand like a child that's wet itself.

The two older assistants are helping Beatrice to tidy the staffroom. One of them takes a break from pulling the chairs into new positions to unbutton her cardigan. 'Joan Blake looks different. Don't you think, Joyce?'

Her friend pauses from drying up with the dirty towel. 'It's that suit. She should get a perm.' She pats her curls. 'It'd soften her.'

The cardigan woman surveys her work. The chairs are now in clusters, like in a café. She nods towards next-door. 'Personally I don't call that 'teamwork'.'

'I like to do some tidying at a time like this, not just sit,' Joyce agrees. 'It's called pulling together.'

'Everyone mucking in,' adds cardigan woman.

Joyce comes to Beatrice's elbow. 'That's England for you. We all join together in a crisis. Do they do that in America?' Her tone signifies that she knows the answer.

'I wouldn't know,' says Beatrice.

Brenda brings two more dirty cups to Beatrice at the sink. 'We used to share privies, you know, around here. You won't know what a privy is, will you?' Brenda keeps her superior knowledge to herself and goes to sort out a tipped-up cactus on a shelf.

The door opens and closes quietly, letting in the faint sound of a relentless piano and children singing. Terri slips in with an unlit cigarette already in her mouth, goes straight to the open window and lights it. 'I saw him once,' she declares. 'The father. With Chelsea, in that café at the back of the indoor market.' She puts her head out and exhales.

The support assistants and Beatrice stop what they are doing and look at her.

'It looked like it was his access day. I remember him ordering her an ice cream and a milkshake without asking what she wanted. My mother was with me and she was going – look at that. That's not a tea.' Terri takes another drag then does a long, shaky exhalation. 'Poor little thing – she got ice cream all the way up to her elbows and was trying to mop it off herself with napkins then licking the napkins and the table, trying to control it. All he did was look at his watch the whole time – no eye-contact, no talking. The worst was, seeing her reach for his hand when they left – automatic – coz he's her dad.' She flicks ash onto the carpet and grinds it in with her sandal.

'Fucking useless. Part of them's missing. Something in the brain that never developed.'

Joyce frowns.

'I read that,' says Terri defiantly. 'Throw-backs. Unevolved beasts. Brain-dead mongrels.' She stabs her cigarette onto a newly washed plate. 'The question is, why do women shag them?'

Joyce tuts and tidies some magazines.

'And there are so *many*. Look at this estate. Look at this country. God, I hate them.'

Brenda is looking nervous. She finishes drying a mug and inspects it uncertainly. The World's Greatest Dad. 'We didn't used to have all these murders and whatnot,' she says to Beatrice, apologetic. 'This was a good estate. Not the kind of people who'd do that to a child.'

Beatrice turns back to the sink, rinses the last two cups then pulls the plug.

Brenda joins Terri at the window and looks out at the playground sadly. With a shiver she re-buttons her cardigan. 'Still tights weather and it's nearly June.'

Beatrice is still in the staffroom at lunchtime, watering the cactus, wondering whether she'll get full pay for less than a full day, when at last Joan reappears.

'I'll take you home.'

Children are streaming up the school drive, excited about their half-day off. The girls are linked in long lines, squeezing out tears at each other. The boys are shouting and throwing their bags in the air.

As Beatrice is getting into the Astra the door of the Mini slams and the horn pips. Terri waves then shoots backwards.

'You lied to me.'

Joan stops in the act of belting herself in. 'What?'

'You said you hadn't had any relationships with women since London.'

'Ah.' Joan clicks the belt into its socket. 'The Terri thing didn't even last a month though. It was nothing.'

She checks over her shoulder for straggling children then backs out.

'I'm really not comfortable with being lied to,' says Beatrice.

'It was because you knew her. The only time I ever fib is if it's to protect someone else's personal secrets. You can ruin lives.' Joan turns out of the school gate.

'Why didn't it work out?'

'Pshsh. There was a bit of jealousy. Look down there: that's Moor Park Close where the body was found.'

'Jealousy?'

'Erm... it was just, Terri couldn't cope with me and Darshana being best friends.'

They reach the ring road. Soon they are passing the bulldozed wasteland that has become an illegal dump, from whence a panoramic view of the valley opens out.

Joan breaks the silence. 'I did try to pull back from Darsh, but we'd got this tradition of phoning each other at nine o' clock, and Darsh just carried on doing it.'

Down below, the city-centre's tower blocks, multi-storey car park and town hall clock could almost be a child's model made of cereal packets.

'But we've stopped that now.'

Even on a bright day the bedsit on Henry Place doesn't get sun. Beatrice drops her briefcase and stands on the hearthrug in the chilly room. I'll pick you up, same time tomorrow, Joan had said as she drove off. She flicks on the fire, then the radio, feeling lonely. Another day she'll invite Joan in.

As arranged, Colin is waiting outside Belvedere Aske after Caroline's French oral. On the way to Joan's, where

Caroline needs to pick up her hay-fever tablets, he springs a surprise. Caroline looks unenthusiastic.

'I thought it'd be a treat, to celebrate your first exam,' says Colin. 'You like Pizza Hut.'

'Thanks, Dad. Only I thought, since I'm having to go over to Mum's, I might as well stay there and revise for a couple of days coz it's *really, really* quiet.' She fluffs up Colin's bits of hair. 'Can we do it on Friday instead?'

Colin is amenable. It means he can spend this evening catching up with *World of Steam*.

The afternoon sun on Joan's bungalow makes it look holidayish.

Colin leaves the engine running. 'Got your key?'

'Got it.' Caroline kisses her father on the cheek and jumps out. 'Thanks for the lift. See you Friday, then.'

'Alright, sweetheart.' He watches Caroline until he sees her enter the inner door, then conducts a three-point turn on Joan's ornamental gravel and drives home.

When her mother arrives back, Caroline has just boiled the kettle. Joan flings her blazer on a hook and launches into the latest disaster at Braithwaite.

Caroline hands her a cup of coffee. 'This is the worst yet, Mum. I don't know how you can work there.'

Joan crashes into an armchair. 'You need your fees paying, and they need their education.'

'Well I think you should get a nicer job. Somewhere nice. The Yorkshire Dales,' says Caroline.

The ornamental clock emits three tinny strikes.

'If America doesn't work out,' she adds.

Her mother slips off her shoes and puts her feet on the chair-arm.

'Ugh. Gross.' Caroline puts two fingers in her mouth and makes a puking noise.

'What?' Joan grins.

'Tights under trousers. *Don't*. You are *so* uncool.'

Caroline spends the afternoon in her pink room staring at pages of biology notes until, at around teatime, Wesley barks to go out.

'I'll see to him, Mum.'

The bungalow's large front lawn slopes down to the thick beech hedge that divides her mother's property from Derek's. Caroline wanders after the dog into the sunshine, nursing a fourth coffee.

Someone is barbecuing.

Approaching the hedge Caroline hears the crackle of fat. Wesley, encouraged by her interest, dives into the foliage. A familiar-sounding voice calls, 'Hey, dawg.'

Derek's voice says, 'That's Joan's dog.'

'Sorry,' Caroline calls out.

Derek comes into partial view, peering through the hedge's scrawny lower part. 'He's never come through the hedge before.'

'Sorry; it's prob'ly the smell of meat,' says Caroline.

Someone is leaning past Derek to get a better view. A face appears with a distinctive long fair curl hanging over one eye. 'Hi Caroline. Is this where you live?'

'No – I'm just here revising.' She waves a hand behind her at the bungalow. 'It's good. It's *really really* quiet.'

'So am I,' says Lofty. 'Revising.'

'Shall I come round and get him?'

'Would you like a burger?' Lofty asks. 'My dad's a vegan. He thinks it's disgusting.'

'Okay. I'll just go tell my Mum.'

Chapter 23

Baldev doesn't join one of the huddles of blazered boys when he leaves the examination room. No point discussing it if you've done crap. He takes an earlier bus that beats the Friday rush hour and is home in time to catch the end of some live cricket. He hears Luke arrive home from school, then shortly after, his mother.

She doesn't shout up the stairs about pizza or anything, and anyway he doesn't feel hungry. A gardening programme comes on. He can't be bothered to switch channels.

Suddenly, surprising even himself, he leaps off his bed and destroys his chemistry file, transforming the thick wad of A4 sheets into a confetti mountain in the middle of his bedroom. A few puffs and blows and the whole room would whirl with the shreds, like one of those snowstorm ornaments.

He returns to watching the gardening thing. A back yard is transformed into a Mediterranean paradise. For the millionth time, he pulls out his mobile, stares at it, keys Caroline's number in his head. *Hi Caroline – I hear you're pregnant.*

He knows his Mum; what she's like. He knows she's looking round for baby buggies, and a cot to match Caroline's bedroom. It's like he's not allowed an opinion.

Joan turns off the ignition.

'I thought you'd never ask.'

'Because I'd like to show you my artwork.' Beatrice leads the way into number forty-seven Henry Place, picking up a letter in the hall. 'Sorry about the trash.'

Joan follows her up the poky stairs.

'*Tadah.*' Beatrice presents the forlorn bedsit. She has bunched the net curtains to one side to maximise natural light, but the room is dim. She flicks on the top bar of the fire, although outside it is a warmish day.

Joan touches the threadbare back of the settee. 'It's like student days, this. Like London.' She notices that Beatrice is fingering the letter.

'Take a seat, Joan.' Beatrice slots the letter behind a candlestick as though it doesn't matter. 'Relax. Put some music on if you like. I'll make coffee.' She goes into the kitchen.

'Thank God It's Friday,' Joan calls out.

Beatrice is setting up the percolator. 'What a week it's been,' she calls back. She sets a tray with milk and sugar and her stylish junk-shop china.

Joan pops her head through. 'I'll just go find your loo.'

'The door next to the entrance door,' says Beatrice.

When she hears the bathroom door close she goes and gets the letter. Inside is a cheque for thirty-five pounds, and a note.

I'll be up on Saturday to get the rest of my stuff. Don't worry, I won't be staying over. I'll continue to go halves on the bedsit until the end of your term (when you'll move on?). I feel that is only fair. I'm not paying accommodation at the moment (Fenella's cottage). Things are really happening for me now. We can talk on Saturday if you want…

'What does he say?'

Beatrice jumps and breaks off reading. 'He's coming on Saturday to get his stuff. Tomorrow.' She fumbles the note and the cheque back into the envelope and returns it to the shelf. 'I don't want to be here.'

Joan breaks into a delighted smile. 'I'll take you out!' She goes to lift the tea tray. 'I'll take you up into the Dales. We can do some teashops. You won't believe how nice it is up there. Tell you what: come back with me now. Our Caroline's going out with her dad tonight. We can make a good start then, tomorrow.'

'Actually I wanted to do some printing this evening. Finish something. And there's a call I need to make.'

'No problem.' Joan chops a teaspoon around in the sugar bowl.

'Could I – could I stay tomorrow night?'

Joan perks up. 'Excellent! Makes a weekend of it, that does. Super. I'll come and get you about nine tomorrow morning, then.'

Beatrice grins. 'Great.'

Joan takes the tray through and sets it on the hearthrug. She looks vaguely around at the dingy room. 'You haven't got a good impression of the north, have you?'

Beatrice shrugs and pours the coffee, adding sugar to Joan's cup. Then she sits at Joan's feet, sipping her drink, contemplative. Outside an ice-cream van tinkles by.

'Men,' says Joan, commiserating.

Beatrice catches her faint scent, like trees and bracken.

'Oh, he's okay. He wanted children, that's all.'

'So *that* was the problem.'

'It was all very abstract in his mind, though. He hadn't really thought it through.' Beatrice drapes an arm over Joan's knee. 'I know I don't want children, Joan.'

A hand touches Beatrice's neck. 'I was like you. I suppose I just gave in.'

Later, Beatrice whispers, 'I still haven't shown you my art.'

They slip out of the bed and go around collecting up and putting on their scattered clothing, bumping into each other, laughing, touching, moving apart again.

Beatrice pulls the duvet and pillows off the bed, smooths the mattress's white sheet then spreads the contents of her folio over it.

'Wow. Out of my league, this,' says Joan. 'Did you go to art college?'

'It's different from what you do, that's all. We've got different skills.' Beatrice places her hands on Joan's shoulders. 'Listen. You should set up your own website to promote your work. That's what I'm doing. It's a great way of putting your pictures out into the world. Especially to reach the U.S. I reckon that's where your best chance is of finding a market.'

Joan's eyes go dreamy. 'You make me feel like a real artist.'

'We have to turn our fantasies into reality,' says Beatrice.

'That's so American.'

'It's a rule of life I learned from my friend Maria. Look – I'll be able to help you out with some connections when I get back to Vermont.'

Joan snaps alert. 'You'll still be here till the end of term, won't you?'

'Sure. I need the money. But I'll be leaving pretty soon after that. What is there for me here?'

After Joan leaves, Beatrice sets up her laptop and calls up her latest piece. The backdrop is a Mediterranean sky with cotton-wool clouds. Superimposed on this is a Muslim boy kneeling on a prayer mat, eating a Twix. It's meant to look like a magic carpet.

Her mobile rings. She goes to the mantelpiece and picks it up, but the reception must be bad, or something.

'If you can hear me, I can't hear you.' She hangs up. She checks her watch, does a mental calculation of USA time, and makes a call to a saved number.

*

240

Darshana switches off her mobile. Americans do what they bloody well like. What a very nice life, doing *exactly* what you want. The phone skids from her hand across the piano and comes to rest against the wedding photo.

She looks at it grimly. Walter has hardly changed. When she first noticed him in the refectory he didn't look much different from his young male students with whom he would sometimes sit, their heads together, fingers pattering over Semitic texts while eating their bread and soup. Like his students he still had a full head of hair, despite being in his fifties; still had that skinny, under-fed look of young men who have only recently started to live separately from their mothers.

Darshana saw how he was with them. The eye contact. The hand contact. The thigh contact. She observed it all from behind the serving counter, like a study of animals, like her paperback copy of *The Naked Ape*. When she went over with coffee refills, she would see how Walter trembled; the tremor in his leg under the table.

Yes, he looked nearly the same before their wedding as after, except that before it, he was so much more pathetic.

The grandfather clock chimes distantly. Nine o'clock. Darshana fixes herself a third vodka and orange.

Maria's laugh ripples through Beatrice. 'It's been months,' she exclaims.

Beatrice spreads herself ecstatically along the settee, imagining Maria's elbows resting on her scrubbed kitchen table where, on a rush mat, there'll be a steaming teapot, its herbal aroma mingling with spices and doggy smells. 'I thought this'd be a good time to catch you. It's just turned nine here. I'm done for the week.'

'It's a beautiful afternoon, here,' says Maria.

'It's already dusk, here. In fact it never seems to get light in this part of the world. Not bright light.'

241

'So you're still in the north?'

'Yeah.'

'I can't believe you've stayed in that place. You were so miserable, that last call. I was worried about you.'

'I guess I was depressed for a while, but now I think there was a reason for it all.'

'Like what?'

'It's given me a kick in the pants, Maria. Seeing these kids. How they live. The poverty; the racial tensions...'

'It's not like you to be *political*.'

'It's just the contrasts that get me. North and south. Rich and poor. The clash of different universes. It throws up lots of creative stimuli.'

'So have the sparks been rekindled in that area?'

'I've been working on a new collection, if that's what you mean.'

'Fantastic.'

'I'd like to get this stuff enlarged and mounted on huge boards. I'm dreaming of an exhibition, Maria. I don't just mean Burlington. I want New York. I want to really go for it.'

'Well, it's about time! What's Howard's take on all this?'

'Howard's living with a woman named Fenella.'

'Hey. What's up?'

'It's over with Howard.'

'It never even started with Howard.' Maria sounds satisfied. There's a note of vindication. 'You did always say it was more like best friends.'

Maria's warmth envelops Beatrice like a comforter. She feels tucked up, cared for. '*You're* my best friend, Maria.'

'Your *boy* best friend, is what you said. You've had a great time together. All the travelling. Did you ever want it to be more?'

'You know I never wanted it to be more. I liked it being very – very *surface*. We had fun. We liked the same movies. We *looked* good together. I enjoyed that.'

'It was never anything to do with love,' says Maria comfortably.

'You're right. He wasn't capable of that. I put up with a lot, you know. His gay guys. Lots of women wouldn't have gone along with that. I was always cool about that.'

'I always said you were wrong to tolerate that,' says Maria.

'The trouble was he had a rule for himself and a different one for me,' says Beatrice. 'He never really accepted my relationship with you, you know. Not deep down.'

'Ha. *Deep down*. There is no deep down, with him. Howard is a very surface person, Beatrice. He may be a very nice, charming person but what you see is what you get. There's nothing underneath.'

'No passion.'

'Exactly.'

'But in a sense that's what made it work. It was – uncomplicated.' Beatrice pauses.

'Honey.' Maria's concern enfolds her. 'Are you alright?'

'I'm fine.'

'Fact is, you need a man like you need a hole in the head, Beatrice. I guess we all need to discover that for ourselves.'

'Really, I'm fine. I guess Fenella burst the bubble.'

'Honey, it's time for you to come *home*.' The word is drawled, seductive.

Beatrice visualises the crooked room under the roof, the hand-sewn quilts of Maria's musky bed. 'I know. I've decided what I really want, at last.'

'Your art?'

'My art,' confirms Beatrice, 'but also my home…'

Maria's laugh pours over Beatrice like chocolate. 'You've said enough, gorgeous.'

Beatrice stretches and picks at a shredded patch on the upholstery with her nail, like the cat in the settee's former life. 'I just have to work another few weeks, pay off some stuff.'

'And then?'

'Maria, you pull decisions out of me like a midwife.'

'Honey, is there anything or any*body* to keep you there?'

Beatrice lets Maria wait.

'Aha.' Maria sighs.

'She's a little eccentric,' says Beatrice. 'You ever heard of a teacher living in a trailer-park?'

'You're *such* a snob,' says Maria.

'But she's interesting. She's a nice person.'

Maria's voice is warm liquid. 'Beatrice, I don't mind what you get up to or with whom, but I'm expecting you home in August, okay? I'm going to be fifty. You gotta be here for that, girl.'

Beatrice ends the call, feeling loved. Replacing her phone next to the candlestick the envelope catches her eye again. She hesitates, takes out the contents. Pocketing the folded cheque she scans the rest of Howard's note.

...We can talk on Saturday if you want, but I can tell you some things now. First, I was always there to help you make decisions, knowing how hard you find that. So your decisiveness about something that wasn't even for you to decide (not alone, anyway) came as a painful irony. Second, I always told myself your lack of passion was a kind of self-containedness. I respected that about you, until I was forced to confront the reality that there were no emotions going on underneath after all. Third, you always had double standards about my bisexuality vis-à-vis your own. I don't know why I tolerated that about you for so long. And fourthly, your

dishonesty in all this has come as a great shock. So much deception and denial. I realise that I don't know who you are.

I think you will agree that a shared enjoyment of travel, clothes and cuisine does not constitute a relationship of any depth; a relationship of trust. I was fooling myself.

Maybe one day we can be friends again.

Next to Howard's signature is the usual smiley face.
Beatrice manically folds the note in half then in half again, smaller and smaller, folding and folding until it is a tight, cubic parcel. She goes into the kitchen and jabs the knob of paper into the bin, where it sops up the wet coffee grounds, turning black.

Darshana starts, hearing the door of her sitting room click open. She has no idea of the time. She looks over the back of the sofa and sees Baldev's scowling face.

'Mum?'

She lowers her glass to the floor. It teeters on the edge of the thick rug then tips over. A puddle of vodka appears on the stone flags. 'Oh dear. Never mind, it's like water. It'll dry up on its own.'

Baldev comes over and stares, appalled. 'You haven't worn that outside, have you?'

'What, dear?' She moves her feet and pats the velvet for him to sit down, but he remains hovering at the end of the sofa, fixated on the enormous boulders of her thighs in cream tights, how they bulge out from the hem of her skirt.

She looks down at herself, at the mini-skirt from college days, and blushes. 'It's just something I found in the back of the cupboard. It's only for relaxing in. Round the house. It's just that it rides up, when I sit like this.'

'Mum. What's going to happen when Caroline...'

'Sit by me, Baldev, love.' Darshana picks up the tipped-over glass from the floor and drinks the last dreg.

Baldev goes instead to sit on the piano stool, straddling it, his legs splayed like a boat's oars. His elbows thump onto the piano lid and his chin drops down between his fists. 'She hasn't phoned me.'

Darshana stares hard at Baldev to keep him in focus. 'You should have come down earlier, love. I'm too done-in now. You know what I'm like by Friday.'

'Yeah,' Baldev sneers.

'Stressed.' She absently trails her fingers in the pool of vodka and brings them to her lips.

Baldev's face crumples. 'You're in this together. You're all just getting on with it, never mind me.'

'I haven't spoken to Caroline but I know she's decided the right way. It's almost a mother-daughter telepathy between us.'

Baldev springs up. 'It's *not* the right way, Mum,' he shouts. 'It's not like a new kitten or something.' He towers over her. 'It's not right for *me*.' He swings down to Darshana's level.

She cringes.

He grabs her shoulders, shakes her. 'You're ruining my life!'

She puts her hands over her head.

Baldev gives the sofa a kick that reverberates in Darshana's stomach, and runs from the room.

Walter is in his pyjamas, writing, when he hears rustling in the kitchen. He sets aside his notes and shuffles out to look. Darshana is rummaging in the supermarket bags that she left dumped in front of the fridge when she got in from school.

'Goodnight,' says Walter.

She stands upright, holding a bottle of vodka and a bottle of tonic. She looks unsteady. Her blouse is done up wrongly. He recognises with a creeping horror the yellow skirt, the one she used to wear in the refectory. He finds women's legs too fleshy and powerful. They can clench round you, swallow you up, like something that's just been born getting sucked back in again.

She glares at him.

'I'm sorry. I saw those bags earlier but I forgot to unpack them. I'll do it now.' He sidles along the breakfast bar as though it offered protection. Seeing how Darshana is swaying, he points to the vodka. 'That wouldn't seem to be a good idea.'

'I saved you from yourself,' she slurs.

'I don't want to get into a philosophical discussion.' He looks at the floor to avoid her legs. A crinkle-cut oven-chip is smeared on the slate tiles.

Some time ago Walter laid the drink problem before the vicar, at the third hole. But the vicar treads too carefully around people of other faiths. He said he didn't want to interfere with Darshana's spirituality. A kind of protectiveness inhibited Walter from explaining that Darshana doesn't actually believe in anything.

He scrapes up the chip with his fingers. 'The forecast's nice for the weekend. I thought we might sit in the garden tomorrow.'

'Look what I've given you,' says Darshana.

'I'll hose down the patio.'

'A normal family.'

'Yes. I'm sorry,' says Walter.

'Sorry! Ha. Sorry.'

'You gave me so many things.'

'*I'm sorry. Lessall sit in the garden,* he says.'

'I'm sorry you drink, I mean.'

'Why sh'd you be sorry? I'm the one who sh'd be sorry.'

'I don't know why you do it.'

'He doesn't know why I do it.' Darshana leaves the kitchen, tripping over a shopping bag.

'Sorry,' says Walter.

Chapter 24

The next morning, when Baldev surfaces from sleep, his room looks wrong: full of sun, happy, too bright. As he wakes memory floods in: a tidal wave, obliterating the whole day, the whole weekend, his entire life. He pulls the duvet over his head and escapes into sleep for another hour.

He is woken by agitated knocking.

'Baldev.'

His father's voice is high-pitched and reedy.

'Baldev.'

He can't even do a good shout. 'Fuck off, will you?'

Baldev turns to the wall, slamming his pillow over his head. He has learned to skate dangerously close to his father's hearing level. It's a game. Sometimes he says stuff right in front of his Dad but with his lips turned away. If Luke is there he will stop, scared, looking from Baldev to his father, waiting to see whether it was heard.

So what if his father heard? All he'd do is stand stock still and turn purple, the pressure cooker act: the hissing and spurting; hands vibrating but remaining stiffly by his sides, incapable of giving a good smack.

His dad never hits out, never does anything normal.

The knocking is insistent. 'Baldev.'

His Dad is too scared to just come in, in case he sees Baldev undressed, which embarrasses him.

Weirdo.

'It's after eleven, Baldev. I think I'm within my rights to enter your room if you refuse to open the door.'

Wimp.

'Your brother's gone to the football practice and I need urgent assistance.'

'Just *fuck off.*' Baldev flings a pillow at the door. It opens to reveal his father, blank-faced, the garden hose in neat loops over his arm.

'The garden tap won't turn off.'

'Get Mum.'

'I can't rouse your mother.'

'Get a plumber, Dad.' Baldev stares up at the ceiling, his hands behind his head. 'You know you're crap at dealing with stuff like that yourself.'

Walter's eyes are drawn to Baldev's brown ten pence nipples. 'Crap is not a word we use in this house,' he says automatically.

Baldev twitches the duvet up over his chest. 'Fuckin 'ell,' he says quietly to the ceiling.

Walter's face is twitching. 'The patio's going to flood and then it'll come into the house. I've put a bucket under it but it will be full by now. I need you to attach this end of the hose-pipe to the tap whilst I take the other end round the side of the house to the drain.'

'*Stupid,*' breathes Baldev at the ceiling. Loudly, irritably, he says, 'Why can't you just do that yourself?'

'The hose pipe won't stay on the tap,' says Walter, looking quivery, not coping. 'You need to come, Baldev. There's a lot of water.'

'For fuck's sake,' Baldev says to the wall. 'Look, put the hose-pipe down the drain then walk round with the other end of it to the tap. Do it that way.'

'I need your help, Baldev.'

Baldev realises the pressure cooker is on the boil. His father is turning deep red from the neck upwards. His breathing is quick and forced.

'Don't smile at me like that,' Walter splutters. 'Sons help their fathers.'

Baldev rests his head on one hand and stares, willing his father to actually *do* something for once; something

249

that other dads do. He wouldn't even mind getting thumped. It would be worth it. His dad – a normal man.

'I don't like it,' shrills Walter. 'I don't like it.' His hands are quivering. The rolls of hose cascade from his arm onto the landing carpet but he doesn't seem to notice. He is beside himself.

Baldev, repulsed, sits up slowly. The duvet falls away, revealing his briefs, and Walter's eyes turn glassy, ricocheting around the room, dodging his son.

Baldev shudders. '*Weirdo*.'

'Get out of my house.' Walter's shriek is a whistling kettle. 'Get out. Get out of my house, boy.'

'It's my house,' says Baldev, calmly. 'You're my dad, sadly, and this, therefore, is my house, where I unfortunately have to live with a weirdo like you because you happen to be my dad.'

Walter's throat clicks and ticks. 'I'm not your dad.' His neck gobbles like a turkey's. 'You're not my son. I'm not your father.'

Hairs prickle erect on the back of Baldev's neck. 'What you on about, Dad?'

'Don't call me Dad. You're somebody else's. You're not my son. No son of mine would treat anyone as you treat me. Now, get out of my house.'

Baldev leaps up, shocked, and starts dragging on clothes in confusion, stuffing his bare feet into trainers.

Walter takes a step into the room. He looks like a burning fuse. The air sizzles.

Baldev springs onto the bed for safety and spreads his hands in appeal. 'Okay, I'll stop swearing, Dad.'

Walter is vibrating like a washing machine on spin. 'I took her and you on.' For the first time his hands, rigid at his sides, have a volatile, dangerous look. 'I'm starting to wonder why. She's even stopped cooking. And *you* – I don't like you. You're not a son to me. You're not a good boy. Not like Luke.'

Baldev snatches his rucksack from the back of the chair and grabs a sweatshirt. He can feel tears coming up, just like the other night. He skirts round the edges of his room as though his father, in the centre of it, were an uncaged animal. Leaping over the loops of hose on the landing he clatters down the stairs and out of the house.

Caroline's pasty-white skin needs maximum protection from the sun. She has no choice but to set up her dad's 1970s psychedelic umbrella with its grubby, woolly fringe. She spends Saturday morning memorising a model German essay that uses all the tenses, flicking occasional ants from her spread-out papers.

Freitag Abend war ich im Pizza Hut.

She sat next to Lofty, opposite her dad.

'Lofty's got a place at Durham University,' she told her dad over the garlic-bread starter. 'It's only two and a half hours on the train.'

Lofty was interested in her dad's police work. He called her dad Colin. They talked like two blokes.

Caroline stretches out her legs on Colin's short-cropped lawn. The neighbours have brought their old mother out of a home for the day and parked her in a deck chair in their garden. Her monologue carries over the fence like a droning lawn mower.

Caroline feels it would be more fruitful, academically speaking, to be at her mother's this weekend, since Lofty will be revising for his German A-level through the hedge and she could ask him things.

When, around lunchtime, her dad gets called in for an emergency shift, it all works out nicely.

The bus-shelter opposite Weatherhope's mini-market was vandalised a long time ago. It no longer has side panels but still provides a roof. The heat wave predicted for June has arrived and Baldev is perched inside the shelter, avoiding the full blaze of the midday sun.

He doesn't know about Saturday bus times, or even whether they run at all. The timetable has been destroyed with felt tip graffiti. If a bus comes, he might get on it. He has not yet managed to think about where to go. His head is buzzing. When the image of his vibrating dad revisits him he flushes, but is not able to name the emotion. At the same time he is suffering a repeated tightening of his stomach each time he notices the shape and weight of his mobile phone in his trouser pocket. His mobile has started to torment him, like a phantom of Caroline, passive but ever-present. If he were to press a few buttons, she would speak.

He doesn't know what to do. He longs for the retreat of his Mp3 Player but it's in his bedroom recharging. The mini-market is busy. Baldev recognises most of the people going in and out and feels conspicuous, yet too indecisive to move. Presently a younger kid from his school walks past the bus shelter and calls, bravely, 'Yo.'

Baldev scowls, looks at his wrist, pretending irritation with a late bus. But he is not wearing his watch. He slouches further, drops his head back and gawps despairingly at the aluminium ceiling. He doesn't know which is worse: his dad not being his dad, or the fact of imminently becoming a dad.

A good half hour goes by. Maybe even an hour. He successfully avoids catching the eye of any acquaintances. He even has his eyes closed for some of the time, immersed in his dilemmas. After a very long time, a bus finally goes by in the wrong direction. It occurs to Baldev that he could easily walk down to Russell's, just out of the bottom end of the village. But the thought of Russell's mother puts him off. Lofty's dad's place would be a good refuge, if it were not for the frightening possibility, with Aunty Joan next door, of bumping into Caroline.

He notices that a vehicle has pulled up a few metres beyond the bus shelter. It reverses in a short spurt. The driver leans over to the passenger window. Baldev sits up a little, expecting to be asked directions, but then recoils, seeing the dog collar.

Too late. The window is down and the vicar of his mother's school is calling him by name. 'Would you like to get in, Baldev? For a chat?'

Baldev stares at him, appalled. The vicar clearly knows something.

'I'm on my way to see your father. I gather you two've had a little row. He phoned, terribly upset about it.'

'To be honest I've got an arrangement to meet someone. Sorry.'

'I'm here to help.' The vicar's eyebrows arch to an extreme degree. 'If you'd like to talk anything through?'

The vicar couldn't possibly know about Caroline, too. Could he? Baldev shudders.

'We all say things we don't mean, sometimes,' says the vicar.

Baldev squirms. 'Look. Sorry. I am expected somewhere.'

The vicar puts up his hands and smiles apologetically and suddenly looks human, his cheeks crinkling kindly. 'Alright. Not now. I'll go and see what Walter needs. Seems there's been a flood.' He reaches to press the window's rewind button, pauses. 'He loves you like his own son, Baldev. Always has.'

A city centre bus toots loudly, pulling in behind. The vicar drives off and Baldev, feeling knocked for six, waves at the bus-driver to wait and starts rummaging in his rucksack for his wallet. Not finding it, he frantically turns out his jeans pockets and realises he has no money on him at all. The bus takes off up the hill without him, and Baldev begins plodding dully after it, in the direction of the city, away from Weatherhope.

Chapter 25

The teashop has a prime view of the shimmering cliffs of Malham Cove. The surrounding meadows are dotted with buttercups and blanket-stitched with grey walls, while up on the high fells, sheep stroll about freely on the untamed land. On days like this the National Park looks even better than its calendar.

The teashop's garden is bordered by a stream that trickles down from the tarn. Ducks have clambered up the bank to beg for titbits from the outdoor tables, full with Saturday trippers. There is a smell of egg sandwiches and brewed tea, the homely chink of crockery.

'I'm not sure I can move in with you,' says Beatrice.

'I only mean, until the end of term. No strings, obviously. It makes sense, doesn't it?'

'It's not that it doesn't make sense,' says Beatrice. 'It's not like I want to stay in that shitty bedsit.'

A waitress is shuffling tea for two onto their table, simultaneously removing the previous customers' debris.

'This is called a cream tea,' says Joan. The waitress sets down a large plate with four scones, a bowl of fresh cream, and sachets of butter and strawberry jam.

'Part of me would really like to move in with you,' says Beatrice.

'So what's the problem?'

Beatrice waits for the waitress to move away. 'It's still the lying.'

Joan pours out tea, wordless, sheepish, clanking around with the stainless steel teapot, topping it up with the extra pot of boiling water then giving the teabags a rigorous stir and squeeze.

'I never know whether I can believe you,' says Beatrice. 'I'm not comfortable with that. I believe total honesty is important in a... a friendship.'

Joan scrutinises her teaspoon, avoiding looking Beatrice in the eye. 'I've tried to be straight with you. I've told you just about everything. More or less.'

The sun emerges from the edge of a cottony cloud and is suddenly scorching. Beatrice places her straw hat back on her head. Her features turn dappled. A young man at the next table in a white vest, shoulders bronzed and bulging, hair razed to bristle, narrows his eyes in Beatrice's direction while his little son stabs at his wife with a truck.

'But you didn't tell me Terri was a lesbian.'

The man immediately shoots a look at Joan, then back at Beatrice. A corner of his mouth twitches up.

Joan gives him a withering look and turns her shoulder. 'I told you why that was. Here, you haven't had a scone.'

'I think you should be open, Joan.'

'I am. I've started to be. I've decided.' Her teaspoon clatters into her saucer. 'Except with Caroline.'

Beatrice claps her hand to her forehead. 'For Chrissake, Joan. She's the *first* person you should be open with.'

'We've got a very good relationship now. She's off Darshana and onto me. It's great. I can't risk spoiling it.'

'Kids aren't dumb. I bet you she knows.'

'Knows what?'

'That you like women.'

'I've been terrified of that.' Joan spreads her scone with jam. 'Darshana used to threaten to tell Caroline things about me.'

'So why hasn't she, then? If you two have really fallen out?'

255

Joan pauses to consider, her spoon in the cream. 'Because Darshana hasn't accepted that it's over. Our friendship, I mean.' She jerks a dollop onto her scone. 'I must admit, I'm still living with this niggling worry that she'll phone Caroline one day and say stuff.'

'Joan, it's the twenty-first century. Tell Caroline yourself.'

The family at the next table gets up to leave. The man presses the crotch of his jeans against Beatrice's back and feels her bra-strap with his hand. 'Oh, sorry love.'

Joan and Beatrice journey back to the city on narrow lanes that take them up and down the dales, wending through low, gentle villages then climbing to sudden, dramatic panoramas.

'I could happily run off and live up here, if it wasn't for the kids,' says Joan.

Beatrice looks puzzled. 'Who – Caroline?'

'No. I mean my class.'

High above Weatherhope, the ice-cream van at the viewing point on the main route into the city is busy. The litterbins are overflowing and humming with wasps. All afternoon, tourists have been pulling in and out of the lay-by to take photos of Weatherhope's stone-roofed dwellings, mini-market and petrol station piled in a jumble at the bottom of the dale.

Baldev has spent the afternoon undisturbed, seated on one of the park benches with his back to the world, gazing, unseeing, across the dale.

The vicar would have had answers for everything. The vicar would have wanted to take him home for a big reconciliation scene with Walter.

Thoughts of facing his dad make Baldev periodically clasp his hands to his reddening cheeks with the emotion that he still cannot own up to. Going home does not feel like an option for a very long time, if ever.

As for the other issue: a vicar would tell you, presumably, to marry the girl. Or at least, live together and share the parenting.

In the course of the afternoon the issues of being homeless and being a father churn around each other in his gut until they throw up a desperate fantasy. If Caroline can be put off moving in with his mother at Weatherhope (which should not be too hard, he thinks, looking down at the dump of it), she'll get set up in a place by the Council. Probably in the city centre: one of those tower blocks, handy for everywhere...

He imagines a living room with surround-sound, a plasma TV screen on the wall, leather sofas. It would be a home. At least for when he's not away at uni. Obviously he would muck in with the nappy changing whenever he was around.

Before he has time to think – to chicken out – he whips out his phone and calls Caroline's number. His pulse begins thumping painfully in his ears, and words stumble over themselves in his head. But her mobile is switched off. And anyway, as keeps happening, a baby is now rampaging through his fantasy, screaming and bawling and messing up his high-tech high-rise apartment with dirty nappies and sick. Baldev's head droops down to his knees and he weeps. One thing has, at least, become clear: nothing can possibly be resolved until he speaks to Caroline.

The heat subsides to a pleasant, balmy temperature. The ice-cream van finally shuts up shop and pulls away. Baldev's grinding stomach clarifies the most pressing concern: the need for a bed – and food – for the night. It looks as though his best bet is, after all, Russell. Maybe Russ can let him into the den above the garage without

Clarissa even knowing. He sets off down the hill, back into Weatherhope.

At last, Joan's Astra turns off the rutted and, lately, dusty track through Badger's Dell, and parks beside her neat lawn.

'I didn't leave that window open,' says Joan, and then, 'The door's not locked. It must be Caroline.'

Her daughter is lying on her stomach in front of the TV eating crisps, kicking her bare feet in the air.

'I thought you were at your dad's for the rest of the weekend.'

Caroline looks round, hearing her Mum sound a bit put out. 'He dropped me off coz he was called back on duty. They're expecting more riots because of the weather.'

'But you could've stayed on your own, couldn't you? For one night?'

'You're always saying this is home.' Caroline's tone is reproachful.

'It *is* home. Don't get me wrong Caroline…'

A woman is standing a little behind Joan, trailing a new-looking straw hat. Caroline stares, big-eyed and stunned (a look she's practised in front of the mirror), recognising her from the clinic. The woman is pretty in a boyish way, even in a skirt. The type to get a perfect tan. She's created a good effect on her fringe with gel.

'…only, I've got someone from work staying over,' her mother is saying.

The woman says in an American accent, 'Hey, don't worry. You can drop me off back home. That'll be fine.'

'No.' Her mother looks kind of desperate. 'No. Not with the riots.'

Caroline switches off the TV to be polite and sits up. 'Are you a teacher?'

'Yeah. I'm Beatrice.' She comes forward and reaches to shake hands. 'We've... er, seen each other before.'

'Funny place to meet,' grins Caroline.

Beatrice smiles. 'Not a good conversation-starter.'

'I thought everybody else there was a housewife. Apart from that girl with blonde hair.'

Joan touches Beatrice's arm. 'Look, we'll manage. You can sleep there.' She points to the single bed behind the settee. 'No problem at all.'

Realising the implication, Caroline says, 'No way. I'm not sharing my bed with you, Mum. I won't sleep a wink. I'll sleep in here.'

'Let's just share the bed, Joan,' says Beatrice drily. She drops her hat and lands on the settee, looking at home.

Joan turns pink. 'I'll get us some cold drinks.' She hurries out.

'That was such a great day,' Beatrice calls after her. 'It's really beautiful up there. Thank you.'

Caroline follows her mother into the kitchenette. 'I thought Lofty was going to be next door, revising,' she confesses. 'But Derek says he's not coming till first thing tomorrow.'

'I see.' Her Mum gives her one of those knowing smiles mums give their daughters on TV. 'So long as you don't distract each other.'

Caroline chews on her little cross. 'You didn't tell me about her.'

'What? Beatrice? Oh, she'd never been to the Dales so I offered to drive her round. We've been to Grassington, Malham, Burnsall – where else did we go…'

'Did you know she was at the clinic?' whispers Caroline.

'Yes. Isn't it a small world?' She bends into the fridge.

'I don't want to be *in the way*.'

Her mum straightens up, red in the face. 'You're not in the way. This is where you live.'

259

'She's nice, isn't she?'

'Caroline.' Her mother leans on the worktop, holding the ice-cube tray. 'I'm going to be totally honest with you.' She begins snapping the tray in and out, bouncing the ice-cubes in their sockets.

'She's nice, but –' Caroline's voice drops to a whisper again – 'I wouldn't trust her. She obviously swings both ways.'

'Uh?' The ice-cubes halt.

Caroline takes the ice-cubes from her mother and starts sharing them between the tumblers. 'Better than Aunty Darsh, though.'

Joan is looking stunned. 'Your Aunty Darsh has got problems,' she says in a faint voice. 'It's not her fault.'

'You're not going to get back with her, though. Are you?'

'No.'

'That's a relief. Personally I don't want anything else to do with that family.'

She notices that her mother's chin is quivering, that she is blinking and frowning, like watching a sad film and trying not to fill up. For a moment Joan looks like a child.

Caroline pats her. '*Honestly*, Mum.'

'We do love you, your dad and me.'

'I know. Anyway I like having gay genes. Means I'm not just boring and conventional.'

Chapter 26

On Saturday teatime Russell takes a break from his revision to listen to the six o'clock news. After that he phones Lofty for a post-mortem on last night's cricket fixture. 'My mum's a bit fanatical about me revising,' he apologises yet again. 'I'm having to give up my commitments. How did it go?'

'It wasn't just you who didn't show.' Lofty sounds morose. 'Bal didn't turn up either. We should've slaughtered them. It was only Wyke.'

'That's bad,' says Russ.

'Bloody useless. He could've at least texted; we could've tried to get another man.'

'Is this still about Caroline dumping him?'

'I don't blame her, if he's the kind who can just leave us in the lurch,' says Lofty. 'She's better off without him. She deserves someone more mature.'

Russell doesn't register Lofty's smug tone. 'So what happened, last night? I mean, no Bal means no bowler.'

'They crucified us. My dad wishes he'd never cooked Baldev his tea.'

Following the phone call Russell procrastinates for a further few minutes, foraging in the kitchen for yet another snack. In the moment when the crumpets leap out of the toaster, he spots Baldev plodding down the long private road from Weatherhope proper. Arriving in the yard he stops and stands there, looking as though he might kick one of the chickens to kingdom come.

The two of them retreat with the whole packet of crumpets to the snooker room above the garage where Russ goes to escape from his mother's harp. Russ notes that Baldev appears to have been crying. After urgently devouring three crumpets, his friend throws himself on his back on the camp bed and says his dad isn't his dad and that he's homeless.

With Baldev in such a bad way, Russell doesn't bring up the cricket match. It doesn't surprise Russell that the issue of being dumped by Caroline gets no mention at all. Pretty insignificant, compared to this other thing.

But Russell doesn't really know how to help, and eventually he says, 'Look, I've got to revise. You can stay in here and watch TV if you want. You can stay the night if you want.'

'What about your mum?'

'She's out playing in a concert.'

'Don't tell her I'm here, okay?'

'Alright,' Russell shrugs, but feels slightly nervous. He ought to tell her, really. In case of fire, or whatever.

As the evening unfolds, he pops back now and then to check on Baldev and deliver another can of Coke from the fridge, or a sandwich. It feels like when he was a little kid, when he found a baby bird and put it in a box and dropped food in. Each time, he finds Baldev lying on the camp-bed, doing nothing.

At around ten Russell returns again to the snooker room, and is perched on the end of the camp-bed with his friend, watching a video of *The Simpsons*, when over the TV noise he hears the familiar engine bleating down the track. His mother's Morris chunters into the garage, the balls on the snooker table rolling about with the vibration.

Clarissa switches off the engine. 'Russell, are you up there?'

Russ heads off down the stairs.

'Could you lift the harp into the house for me, darling?' His mother is sweating heavily, clawing at the clasp of the cameo choker round her stringy neck, her bun frayed out like a derelict nest. Although it is not

262

velvet weather she has been performing in a navy-blue velvet evening gown. The bra-part of the low-cut dress lies flat and empty, scrunched into little folds like something deflated. The sight of his mother's scrawny, freckled chest always makes Russell feel sick.

Once indoors, with the back door closed, he lets on to his mother about Baldev staying the night.

'That's perfectly alright, darling,' she says vaguely. Russell hovers by the Aga while Clarissa, hot and dishevelled, drags a bottle of sparkling water out of the fridge. The bowl of her pipe, hidden in a pocket in the dress's folds, clunks against the breakfast bar as she clambers onto a stool.

'He's a bit upset,' Russell adds, thinking, the whole village will probably know everything soon, anyway, at which point his mother would ask him accusingly, Did you know?

She looks over her glass at him, gulping. 'Oh yes? What's he upset about, darling?'

He might as well tell her. She'll drag it out of him eventually, anyway, like everything.

'Bal's dad isn't his dad. They had this big row, and his dad just said it.'

Clarissa's excitement is quickly overlaid by concern. 'Do Darshana and Walter know where he is?'

Russell is already beating a guilty retreat. Looking at it another way, his mother is very caring; she'll try and do something to help. 'Search me.' He scoots off.

'Hello? Hello? Is that Walter?'

'This is Professor Fox speaking.' Walter's presence at the end of the line has no more substance than a small moth settled on the receiver.

'Clarissa Woolf here. I'm sorry to disturb you so late, but I just thought I'd let you know your son is here.' A meaningful pause. 'With us.'

'Ah.'

Silence.

Clarissa doesn't know how Darshana has coped this long with Walter. At the last Weatherhope Carol Service he was wearing his slippers. 'I thought I'd better let you know, since it's after ten.'

'Thank-you,' he says thinly.

'Could I perhaps have a word with Darshana?' Clarissa waits. It's as though he's been given something to puzzle out. She thinks he's degenerated in the last couple of years.

After some seconds he says, 'Just a moment, please.' There is a curious noise like a dog sloshing out of a river, then normal footfalls mounting a staircase. Somewhere in Darshana's opulent barn-conversion is an impressive, if somewhat slow-running, clock. Clarissa counts ten bongs. Apparently the antiques are Walter's and the colour schemes are Darshana's. The Chatterjee-Foxes' cleaner is Clarissa's cleaner. The cleaner feels sorry for the boys.

More than a minute later Walter speaks into the phone again. 'I'm afraid Mrs Chatterjee-Fox is indisposed.'

Just that.

'Well, does she know where Baldev is? I don't want her to worry, that's all.' Clarissa imagines him tucking the information about his son's whereabouts into a dusty mental file between other lost snippets.

'We've had a bit of trouble,' says Walter.

'Oh dear, I'm so sorry to hear that.' She switches to her Samaritans voice and settles on the bedroom steps. 'Is it a private matter?'

'A flood. All through downstairs. All the carpets.'

'Oh goodness.' Clarissa thinks of her Axminster. 'And how do you feel about that?'

'Darshana says it's ruined.'

'Oh goodness. You must be feeling pretty awful about that.'

'Everything,' says Walter. 'She says everything's ruined.'

'Terrible,' Clarissa empathises. 'And what about Luke? Where's Luke?'

'Luke has retrieved all his belongings and carried them upstairs to his room. Which is where he is now.'

'Please tell Darshana, if she thinks there's anything I could possibly do to help, she should call me. Sounds as though she'll need time off work, Walter. Especially with antiques.'

'Poor Luke,' says Walter.

'Well, poor *all* of you.'

'It was the outside tap.'

'The outside tap.' Clarissa is mystified. 'Terrible. Awful. *Do* tell Darshana I'm here to help.'

'I'll tell her.' Walter's voice is blank, unreadable. 'When she comes to.'

At the end of the call Clarissa starts to redial again directly, hesitates, then goes instead to get rid of her big dress. She comes back down in her nightclothes to make Ovaltine. Her husband, returned from his nightcap at the pub, is seated at the kitchen table with the *Financial Times*.

'Did you hear anything about a catastrophe at Walter's and Darshana's?'

'Mmm.' Her husband reads on.

'We've got Baldev in our garage.' Clarissa sets a mug of milk turning in the microwave and waits, leaning on the Aga. 'I don't imagine St Ninian's will be seeing Darshana for a while.' Restlessly she picks up her cross-stitch from the dresser and begins to sew, then looks up, anguished. 'It's so difficult. One doesn't want to interfere.'

Her husband wordlessly turns a page.

'Don't mock, Peter. One has a duty to help one's neighbours.' She stabs with her needle. 'On the other hand, I'm already in my pyjamas.'

Peter looks up, then back at his paper. 'Do what you think Jesus would do.'

Clarissa's cross-stitch frame clatters back onto the dresser. 'Yes, yes, we all know you haven't got a shred of spiritual life. Just go away if you can't be helpful.'

The microwave pings.

Peter folds up his newspaper and tucks it under his arm. 'I'm going to my room. Goodnight.'

Carrying her Ovaltine to the sitting room, Clarissa manages to pass the telephone without looking at it. Later, on her way back to the kitchen with her empty mug, she stops.

'Doh-oh.' She picks it up and dials. 'Hello – have I got the vicarage? Martin? Clarissa here. I'm sorry to trouble you so late. It's about Walter and Darshana. Oh – you were there this afternoon? Look, if there's anything I can do to help...'

The winking clock on the Woolfs' video recorder shows three a.m. The snooker-room is stifling although the window-blind is up and the window thrown open. A distant streetlight twinkles through the trees, and a creamy strip on the horizon denotes dawn.

Baldev is still awake, zinging with the caffeine of half a dozen cans of Coke, going over and over everything. His mobile is hot in his hand. There's no question of texting. He can't think of anything he could text that would not come across as utterly superficial. He sits up, and for the fifth or maybe sixth time tries calling Caroline's number. Still switched off. An owl hoots.

In a sudden burst of desperation he keys in her home number, with some mad hope that Uncle Colin will be out on nights and Caroline will be home, maybe watching the movie channel, or revising through the night, or something.

'Colin Blake.'

'Um.' Baldev feels sick with embarrassment. Maybe Uncle Colin is intending to take him to court to get him to pay paternity something-or-other. 'Is Caroline there, please?'

'It's three o'clock in the morning, Baldev.' Uncle Colin sounds gently puzzled without being cross.

'Sorry. I was revising. I just wanted to...' Baldev tails off, unable to think of one single credible reason for the call. He curls up inside.

'You're lucky. I've just walked in from my shift.' Uncle Colin's tone is as peaceable as always. Maybe he doesn't know about the baby yet.

'Caroline's gone to her mother's for the weekend,' says the placid voice. 'Have you got that number? Don't use it now, though.' The word of advice is measured, policeman-like.

Baldev jots down the number and ends the call with a lame apology. He flings himself back on the camp bed and lies there, sleepless, deciding.

Chapter 27

In Joan's judgement of what a dachshund's constitution can handle, there are very few nights of the year when it is warm enough for Wesley to be left outside. But last night saw him bedded down in his outdoor kennel. By breakfast-time on Sunday the kennel's roof is already warm to the touch. Wesley's nose, poked out of the front, twitches in a patch of sun.

In the living room the plain blinds glow white like slide-projector screens. On waking, Caroline puts her head under the pillow out of the glare. Her frothy nightie from Auntie Darsh is in a twist around her waist. The green candlewick bedspread is flung over the back of the settee, and the sheet is on the carpet, kicked off in the middle of the night when the bungalow was stifling.

Hearing a car's engine she sits bolt upright. I'll be there first thing, Lofty had said. Mum can only bring me if it's before she goes to church. Caroline pulls her nightdress stickily over her head, shrugs on her Betty Boop dressing gown and pads into the hall, where a beam of sun is strobing a path from the doorway of the kitchenette. The door of the bedroom is firmly closed.

She tiptoes into the bathroom and tries to shower quietly. Last night she sorted out what she needed from her wardrobe. She's glad she thought ahead. Her clothes are hanging on the bathroom door. She puts on the short, stretchy sundress. Ice-cream pink. Shoestring shoulder straps. The bodice is double thickness so it doesn't look indecent. She pulls on a little pair of knickers. Wearing only two items of clothing feels free-and-easy. She wriggles her toes into flip-flops and wants to skip.

The jar of really good hair-gel is on the bathroom shelf. If it were in Beatrice's sponge bag Caroline wouldn't touch it. She takes the tiniest blob and does a small experiment, separating the feathery growth at her hairline into fronds and curling them artistically down her forehead. That done, she pulls the rest of her hair into a ponytail with a pink scrunchy.

Clarissa gets up in time to attend the early communion at Weatherhope Parish Church, since she will miss the family service due to helping the Chatterjee-Foxes with their clean-up operation. Leaving the church she pops into the mini-market and picks up a new pair of rubber gloves. Her intention is to return home first to see whether Baldev can be counselled into coming with her.

It is still only nine. Russell has not yet surfaced. Clarissa goes out to the garage, climbs the stairs and puts her head around the door of the snooker room, but Baldev and his rucksack have disappeared.

Caroline is raiding the freezer compartment when her mother comes out in a dressing gown, bare-foot, tousle-haired, yawning like a lion.

Caroline jumps guiltily. 'I thought I'd take these bagels over to Lofty's for breakfast. I've put the kettle on for you.'

'S'okay, I'm going to set up the coffee machine,' says Joan.

'I thought we could get off to an early start,' Caroline explains. 'Revising.'

'You're not in the way, you know, Caroline.'

'So I can go, then?' Caroline races into the living room, picks up an armful of files and her pencil case and skips out through the porch, calling – 'You know where I am.'

The sun is already shining when Baldev reaches the rutted track through Badger's Dell. The walk has, surprisingly, taken less than three hours. After the long, steep climb out of Weatherhope, the descent to the city and the hike across the centre and out to the western suburbs was relatively easy. The ring road was almost deserted. He saw a number of rats and an urban fox. His light-headedness from lack of sleep is almost pleasant. Like being stoned. The plan is to hang out at good old Derek's place, whilst keeping an eye out for Aunty Joan's car leaving next door's, whereupon he will slip round and see Caroline. Alone.

Derek's porch is full of bottles and cans to recycle. The door is open but Caroline knocks and waits. A blue tit is pottering on the vintage headlamp rigged up as an outside light. The sky is blue and cloudless. The forecast said it could get hot.

Derek's woolly grin appears round the door. 'Hi.'

'Breakfast!' Caroline holds up the bagels.

'He's having a shower. He didn't have time at his mother's. Lofty!' Derek saunters off again.

'Caroline.'

Caroline turns, and jumps. Baldev is standing wanly on the drive under Derek's unpruned bushes.

'This is fate, this is. You being out here like this.'

Caroline looks back at the doorway, flustered, then approaches Baldev uncertainly. 'We're about to have breakfast. Me and Lofty and Derek.' She holds up the bagels.

'I've come to see you,' says Baldev.

Caroline twizzles the bagel bag by the neck, looking deeply uncomfortable.

'I'm sorry I didn't come and talk to you earlier. I mean, about...' His eyes travel to somewhere around Caroline's navel.

'Oh, God!' Caroline looks over her shoulder. There is the sound of happy whistling. 'I'm not, any more,' she hisses.

Baldev's mouth drops open.

'And nobody knows. *You're* not supposed to know. It's none of your business,' she hisses, again.

Baldev's shoulders visibly lift.

Lofty swings out of the porch, still towelling off his hair, and stops, seeing the two.

'Forget it, Baldev,' says Caroline loudly.

Lofty leaves the towel on a prickly shrub and lopes towards them.

An approaching vehicle is almost up to Derek's drive. Baldev and Caroline turn to look.

Lofty cranes his neck over the greenery and spots a taxi. 'Who's that?'

Caroline catches a glimpse of the passenger's profile. 'Oh my God.'

Darshana drags her baggage through the angles of Joan's porch: a large suitcase on wheels, a holdall slung awkwardly over one shoulder, too full to do up the zip. She staggers into the living room with Wesley wagging after her. The blinds have filled the room with white light. She smells coffee.

Joan is calling, 'Hello? Hello?' from the bathroom.

Wait till she comes out. *Surprise!*

Joan never used to be so disorderly. It's like when she came in with Caroline only worse. Abandoned cups and glasses around the fireplace, smeared plates on the carpet. She notices that the spare bed is unmade and that Caroline's pink nightie is coiled on the pillow like a meringue.

The toilet flushes and Joan appears in the doorway, silhouetted against the sunny hall. She is wrapped in a man's light cotton dressing gown. She has lost weight.

She is tanned and fit, and without her glasses looks much younger. Her hair is short, shaped into points in front of her ears then full and floppy on top. She is brushing it out of her eyes.

Darshana smiles. 'You look terrific.' She lets go of the case, lets her holdall thud to the floor. The forecast for today is *hot*. They'll end up sunbathing in deck chairs, like old times. She indicates the nightdress. 'Caroline's here, isn't she?'

'Darsh!' Joan stares at the yellow mini-skirt, the bright sun top, the roll of hair descending uncontrollably, the smiling face smeared grotesquely with eye shadow, lip-gloss and uneven foundation. 'What are you doing here?'

Darshana does a very big shrug and an ecstatic sigh. 'I've arrived.' She feels Wesley's welcoming lick on her ankle.

'But – what's all this stuff you've brought?'

'That's what I mean,' says Darshana.

'I don't know what you mean.'

'I'm coming to live with you. As planned.'

'You can't be serious, Darsh.' Joan perches on a chair-arm and again pushes her hair out of her face, looking bemused.

'You said you wanted this, in Morecambe.'

'Yes but you didn't do it, Darsh.' Joan's voice raises a little. 'You let me down, if you remember.'

'I know, I know. I know how I've been,' Darshana blusters, as Wesley heads for the porch to greet the further visitors, 'but you know it was because of the children. Anyway I'm here, now. At last.'

Caroline and Lofty stop short in the living-room doorway. The scene looks private. When Baldev rushes up behind them Caroline puts out an arm to block his entry.

'It was never the children,' Joan is saying. 'It was you, not being able to accept who you are.'

272

'I'm your best friend, that's who I am.' Darshana's voice cracks. 'And you're mine.'

'What about the sex, Darshana?'

She flinches.

Baldev strains over Caroline's shoulder, not to miss anything.

'Friendship has nothing to do with sex,' his mother gabbles. 'When you're students it's different. That was a different set-up.'

'What do you call last New Year, then? What happened on your last birthday? What was it that we did in Morecambe?'

'It doesn't count if you've had a drink.' Darshana's voice rises, panicky. 'Things that happen at a party are not real life.'

Joan steps closer, looking hard at her eyes. 'Are you alright?'

'I'm fine,' she shrills.

'Have you been drinking?'

'I'm absolutely fine.'

Joan takes Darshana by the shoulders. 'You're not fine, are you?'

'There's not a problem, Joan. I'm here now.' She grips onto Joan's forearms. 'So... so you don't need to go to America.'

'Sit down, Darsh. On the settee.'

The bedroom door opens quietly.

Darshana, hearing someone, calls out for Caroline, over and over.

In the porch, Caroline grasps Lofty's hand. 'Mum,' she whimpers, 'she's going really weird.'

Joan gives Caroline a reassuring look and motions her to stay outside.

Baldev pushes past. 'Mum?'

But Darshana is clamped to the lapels of Joan's bathrobe, burbling and shaking.

'It's okay, Darsh.' Joan pats her shoulder ineffectually.

Baldev reaches the hearthrug and repeats, more assertively, 'Mum!' He is unsure of what else to say. He thinks of his dad, and feels guilty.

Joan continues to pat, while craning her neck over the back of the settee to mouth a warning at Beatrice, who is hovering uncertainly in the hall. Not understanding, Beatrice comes into the living room, unselfconscious in Joan's pyjama top and a pair of knickers. 'Is there anything I can do?'

Darshana emits a sob and grasps Joan about the neck. *'Don't leave me.'*

Baldev bends his gangly frame, tries to catch his mother's eye. 'Don't worry about the clearing up, Mum. It's only a bit of water. We'll have it straight again by tonight.'

His mother continues to weep loudly, quivering and gulping air.

Caroline, in Lofty's willing arms, says again – 'Mum, that's like, really weird crying.' She takes the opportunity to push her face into Lofty's jumper.

Baldev is backing towards the porch. 'I ought to get back and start helping.' He trips over Wesley. 'I'll get the bus back. No problem.' Then he remembers he has no money. He turns to ask Lofty for some cash and finds Caroline burrowed into his friend, her arms wound around Lofty's body, hands wedged deep into the back pockets of his jeans.

'Maybe we should get Doctor Steed,' says Caroline, her voice muffled and trembling.

Baldev, edging past them, shoots out of the house.

'I'll do it.' Beatrice whips her mobile out of her bag, glad of a task. 'Gimme the number. I'll do it.'

Chapter 28

By late afternoon the heat has tranquilised the city, after last night's rioting, into a peaceful slumber. Returning to war-torn Henry Place, Beatrice finds all her windows smashed. A half-brick is lying on the bed next to her miraculously unmarked laptop. Propped on the mantelpiece is an envelope in which she finds a cheque for fifty per cent of the month's rent, and a note. He says he's sorry to have missed her. He has to get back for something on Saturday night. He's left her the coffee percolator as Fenella has got one. She should enjoy the rest of her weekend. Maybe phone him some time.

Joan is already knocking about in the narrow kitchen, sweeping up glass. She comes through and puts an arm around Beatrice's shoulders. 'I've emptied your food cupboards into carrier bags. I'll take this lot with me now and get my shopping done. I won't be gone too long.' She strokes Beatrice's cheek. 'I'll see if they'll let me park a bit nearer when I come back.'

Beatrice spends two hours packing. She puts the memory-stick containing her entire collection of images into a leather peggy purse on a long string and hangs it around her neck for safety. Then she carefully positions her folio flat in the bottom of a cardboard box and secures it with layers of books and files. Through the broken windows she can hear pigeons scrabbling in the gutter, but there is an eerie absence of ball games, that Sunday afternoon racket of children playing in the street. Finally, sitting tiredly on a box of books, she phones the agency.

'Beatrice! Good evening.' Chaz is ever cheerful. 'How was your weekend?'

'Fine thanks, Chaz. I'm calling about tomorrow.'

'Er, we've actually got you booked in Monday to Friday at Braithwaite…'

'I know, Chaz. But you know what it's like there.'

'Well, obviously we've seen the papers. It must have been a difficult week for you. I'm sorry about that. A lady colleague did try to phone you to see how you were.'

'It's not really about the murder. I got a full day's pay for half a day's work, so that was okay. But I want you to move me, Chaz.'

'The problem with that is, we'd have to take you off the higher rate that we've been able to offer you at Braithwaite. You'd be back down to, lets see…'

'I know, Chaz, but I'm through with all this.'

'Ah.'

'I live on the street where the riot was. They nearly got my laptop with a brick.'

'That's terrible.' Chaz sounds genuinely sympathetic.

'I was staying with a friend, fortunately.'

'You're moving then, I take it?'

'This friend's offered me to stay at her place till the end of term. It'll save me some money. That's why I don't care about the incentives. I just want to have a hassle-free four weeks before I leave this country.'

'These things don't happen where I come from, you know,' says Chaz.

'Where's that, Chaz?'

'Somerset.'

'I'll have to go there some time.'

'I'll tell you what we can do for you, Beatrice. How are you for getting to Leeds?'

'I guess I can get a ride to the station then go by train.'

'I can sort something out for you starting tomorrow. I'll call you within the hour. Leave it with me.'

As before, a red and white tape is tied across Henry Place like an ineffectual sticking plaster. A pink, stocky policeman with a ginger moustache is patrolling the street in the pleasant evening sun. He stops a few doors along from number forty-seven at the high, narrow former chapel sandwiched between the houses, its roof a blunt triangle jutting above the rest of the terrace. He notices, above the Arabic signboard, the trefoil in the brickwork and the words Wesleyan Chapel, 1902. Climbing the steps to the arched doorway he peers through one of the diamond-shaped holes where the glass has been knocked in and sees dozens of rolls of carpet, stacked vertically. After checking the padlock on the door he returns to the pavement and saunters back past the ladders, the hammering, the systematic boarding-up of windows, the women bobbing about on thresholds like worried hens, sending out their children to tread carefully through the glass and bring cups of tea to the workers. Reaching the corner shop, the policeman helps the Ahmeds load a van with the stock they've been able to salvage from the burnt-out shop.

When Joan returns, this time trying to get closer than the pub car park, the policeman waves her down. 'Can't let you drive down there.'

'I wouldn't want to, now I've seen the glass.' Joan sees Beatrice crunching down the pavement wearing her rucksack and carrying a black bin-liner, and calls, 'Sorry, we'll just have to load up from here.'

'Don't apologise; I'm really grateful for this.'

An elderly white man in braces and slippers comes out of the shop, having succeeded in buying a pint of milk. Seeing the policeman he comes over. 'One day, when they've pulled down the last of them mills,' he waves his milk carton at the horizon, 'that mosque will be the only thing on the skyline. A bloody Statue of Liberty for Yorkshire.'

'Excuse me while I help these two ladies, sir.' The policeman makes a return trip to the bedsit, bringing back the heaviest box of books and heaving it into the Astra's boot.

The old man is still loitering, grim-faced. 'You're doing right, love,' he says as Beatrice passes. 'I wouldn't be staying around here if I was an outsider like you. But this street is *my birthright*,' he announces to the world.

Beatrice gets into the car and Joan starts the engine.

The old man is standing on the curb, holding his milk carton in the air like a flaming torch, addressing the empty street. 'Enoch Powell was right!'

Beatrice pulls at the seatbelt. 'Who's Enoch Powell?'

'Don't listen to people.' Joan turns the car, wincing at imagined glass under the wheels, and heads out of Henry Place. 'This kind of thing upsets Darshana. People associate her with it. She'll tell people she's from Surrey, or a Hindu, or an atheist, but she never feels she can shake it off.'

Beatrice slips a hand onto Joan's knee. 'Don't beat up on yourself about Darshana.'

'It's okay. I'm not.'

'I must say, her husband was very odd. The way he took her and her luggage from us as though we were simply delivering his mail.'

'I don't think Walter's coping very well,' says Joan sadly.

'At least she'll sleep all afternoon, according to the doctor.'

'Pah. Never mind tranquilisers. She needs admitting somewhere.'

Beatrice's hand creeps up Joan's thigh. 'Seemed like the vicar and that harp teacher had things under control.'

Joan completes a change of gear then lays her hand on Beatrice's. 'Oh, the village will rally round. They won't be short of helpers to clear out their ground floor. Folk want to see what you've got.'

They pass a line of police vans on the brow of the hill where the sun is setting pleasantly.

Joan sighs sadly, finally, again. 'She's never managed to be true to herself.'

'That's always difficult,' says Beatrice.

'Shoo, darling.'

Russell turns from the late-night cricket replay and sits up with surprise. Entering his garage den behind his mum is Baldev's mother, puffy-eyed, make-up smeared and looking kind of dazed. Distractingly, Darshana seems to be dressed for the beach, her golden bosom bursting out of a halter-necked sun-top, her legs emerging like succulent hams from a bright yellow mini skirt, the roll of flesh at her waist as enticing as a doughnut. Russell's fascinated stare returns to Darshana's breasts as his mother steers her to sit on the camp bed.

'Darling, shoo! Shoo!'

Mumbling assent, he gathers up his crisp packets and magazines, flits past his mother and, with a last good look at the breasts, scoots off down the stairs.

'It's nice and private up here,' Clarissa explains.

Darshana stares, unseeing, at the TV screen.

Clarissa quickly lets down the blind to cover the black square of window then crouches in front of Darshana, giving a gentle push to the fat, shiny coil of undone hair until it slips backwards off her shoulder like a cat tumbling from its perch. Clarissa's hand lingers in its place. 'Shh,' she stage-whispers. 'Everything's going to be taken care of.' She grasps Darshana's hands in her own and stares intensely into her eyes. 'I'll sort everything out. You don't need to worry.'

Darshana gulps. Clarissa's hair, now almost entirely free of the clasp which earlier held it in a bun, has formed an electric frizz around the circumference of her face as though she has been plugged in and switched on.

'I can't cope on my own.' Tears trickle again down Darshana's puffy cheeks.

Clarissa fishes a cloth hanky, ironed and folded, from a copious pocket, shakes it out and wipes off Darshana's face, which she then cups in her two hands. 'I *understand.*' Darshana feels Clarissa's breath on her face, and smells peppermints and something doggy.

'Some people need looking after, while other people are looker-afterers,' says Clarissa earnestly. 'You're married to someone who can't look after you. He needs looking after himself.'

This afternoon's image of Walter standing helplessly in the flooded living room in his wellingtons makes Clarissa tut again. When Bill Steed showed up at the Chatterjee-Foxes' for a further check on his patient and saw the continued chaos, he was fully in favour of Clarissa's plan to whisk Darshana off. The vicar was capably looking after the rest of the household.

Clarissa plonks herself next to Darshana, throws an arm around her shoulders and pulls Darshana's head onto her flat chest. 'I'm the *looking after* type, myself.'

Darshana's nose is pressed into Clarissa's pullover. She makes a muffled noise, turns her face up to Clarissa's chin. 'But you've got your husband to look after.'

Clarissa whinnies. 'He's completely self-sufficient, my husband. It works terribly well. I do feel that the way to make a *Christian* marriage work is to spend very little time together. I think that's been your problem, Darshana. Not being Christian.'

'I'd like a vodka.'

Clarissa tilts back Darshana's submissive face. 'You'd better not have vodka after all those sedatives.'

'But I'm an alcoholic.'

'Nonsense. You're just ever so upset. We'll soon have you better. One should rely on God you know. Not

280

alcohol. Nor husbands. Spiritually, I mean.' Clarissa lands a big, firm kiss on Darshana's mouth.

Darshana emits a huge sigh.

On the edge of Clarissa's vision a man is slowly rubbing a cricket ball up and down his inner thigh. She reaches behind the bed, yanks out the plug of the TV and situates herself in a position from which to continue offering Darshana comfort. Beneath the weight of two bodies the camp bed's middle section slowly, inevitably collapses.

Chapter 29

The woman leads the way, her enormous dress caught on the ridge of her bottom, the hoiked-up hem revealing calves that dimple with each tread. 'It's been a long time since your last session,' she says. 'Come on through.'

Maria would call her an Amazon.

Joan asks for a full body massage.

The woman begins by trawling her fingers through the bristles at the base of Joan's neck. 'You're looking very well. Where are your glasses?'

'Contacts. I've got the ones that make your eyes look more blue.'

The woman sweeps aside the quiff flopping over Joan's forehead and begins circular motions on her temples. 'Been doing sunbeds?'

'Been on holiday. Feels like a long time ago now the schools have started back.'

'How far on are you with going to America?'

'I've been and come back,' says Joan. 'Went with my daughter.'

'Ah. I thought your aura was looking well.' The woman makes downward strokes on Joan's neck. 'Best I've ever seen your aura. Sort of pale pinky. About two feet of it sticking out all round you.'

'That's good news,' says Joan. 'That's very good news.'

'Find any romance, while you were over there? The man of your dreams?'

'I'm a lesbian.'

'I thought that was coming.' The woman changes to rolling her knuckles on Joan's shoulders. 'Turn over so I can do your back.'

Joan flips over. 'That's great. That's super.'

The woman presses hard with her thumbs. 'So you think you'll stick with your job after all?'

'You're all behind. I've left that job. I've got a deputy-headship up in the Dales. I'm looking for a house up there.'

'I knew there was something else.' A wet gust of wind splats on the window. 'There's already a wind, isn't there. September's autumn, really.' The woman undoes Joan's bra, tips oil into her palms and begins kneading her tanned back. 'So. That must be a change.'

'You're not wrong. The only "special needs" we have to deal with up there is "the challenge of excellence".' Joan groans. 'This is super, this.'

The Arts Centre café is quiet on a Sunday afternoon except for the rustle of large newspapers.

Terri's raven hair is showing grey at the roots. Her skirt is short, red, sprayed-on, and although the weather has turned, her legs are still tight-less and slightly streaky, a deeper orange at the knee. 'More like Leeds, this.' She sinks back into the sofa. 'More of a café-bar.'

Joan sets down the tray of cappuccinos and muffins and adjusts her leather baseball cap. 'Beatrice introduced me to this place.' She knocks on the table. 'Very Ikea. The films are a bit crap though.'

'Arty.' Terri pulls a face.

'S'nice for meeting up, though.'

'To be frank, I found Bee-tricks a bit stand-offish,' says Terri.

'You didn't get to know her. She's a very nice person. Very open and honest, mostly.'

Terri reaches for her cappuccino. 'You look great, Joan. Jeans & DMs. Very good.' She cackles. 'Don't get the wrong idea, mind. I'm not after you again.'

Joan grins, picks up a muffin.

'Cheers.' Milk froth attaches to Terri's lip. 'So. Is it on-going with her?'

'Nah. Just good friends. She's got a life, over there.'

'Well, why don't you move over? I thought that's what you wanted.'

'I've got my new job.'

'But I thought you wanted to be an artist.'

'I *am* an artist. I'm paying an agency to do me a website. It'll have all my pictures on it. Beatrice's friend Maria is going to put my website address out all over the place. She's very up on all that.'

Terri sighs wistfully. 'Better weather over there.'

'Go yourself, Terri. I love my new job.'

'Hell.' Terri puts her cup down. 'It's time I got myself something better.' She gets out her cigarettes.

'I thought you were enjoying being a supply teacher.'

'Novelty's worn off. Having a lie-in whenever you want's all very well, but there's no security in it.'

'They still haven't filled yours or Chantelle's posts, you know. They'd have you back like a shot.'

'No fear.' Terri fiddles with her lighter. The woman at the next table notices and looks disapproving. 'Actually I'm thinking of opening a little teashop or summat in *Last of the Summer Wine* country. Near my mother.'

'Wrong end of the Pennines for me. I'm more partial to James Herriot country.'

Terri grimaces. 'Out of my league. Come on – stand on the steps with me while I have a fag. Bring your drink out.'

Outside, the breeze is bracing. Joan sips her cappuccino. 'I see they got Chelsea's killer.'

'The mother.'

'Might have guessed it'd be drugs. Just went berserk and did her in. I emailed Beatrice the news link.'

Terri takes a long drag. 'Speaking of going berserk.'

'I haven't seen Darsh since that day.'

'Do you know anything?'

'Oh yes. We've heard things via Lofty. She spent the summer with the Woolfs at their house in France and now she's back at Walter's as though nothing ever happened.'

Terri exhales over her shoulder to be considerate. 'So you haven't heard she's joined the Anglicans?'

Joan sputters. 'Flipping heck.'

'She's with Clarissa. Thick as thieves, apparently.' Terri rolls her eyes.

Joan stares into the traffic, pulling on her fringe. 'She hasn't moved on, then.'

A spiked finger wags at Joan. 'Darshana made your life hell. Don't get sucked back in.'

'No way.'

'She's Clarissa's problem now.' Terri taps ash onto the pavement.

'Darsh needs to deal with her issues,' says Joan.

'You sound so American.'

One of Derek's vintage cars is propped up on breezeblocks, its wheels lined up against the porch. Hearing someone skipping up the path, he eases his head out from under the exhaust. His mass of hair, stuffed into a knitted hat, bounces on his head like a wobbly growth.

'Long time no see,' he hollers at Caroline. 'How was Vermont?'

'We did both. Vermont and Disneyland Florida. It was fantastic.'

'I wish I could give Lofty a reward like that, for his A-levels,' says Derek. 'Your mum got herself a great tan.' He silently observes that Caroline looks her usual pasty self, only not as skin-and-bone.

'I have to wear factor thirty,' she says, reading his look.

'And congratulations on your GCSEs.' Derek presents an oily hand and swings her arm up and down like rope. 'All As and Bs. Very, very intelligent.'

Caroline finds Lofty round the back, attempting to light the barbecue, poking at the coals for any sign of red. He catches Caroline in a big hug. The blustery wind is laced with rain. They have a long, messy kiss, getting wet.

Caroline pats the small pendant-shape of her camera under the big sweater she took from her dad's drawer. 'Got my holiday photos.' Her hands retract inside the sleeves and she clasps her arms round herself and hurries to shelter inside the back door. Flurries of ash catch on the wind as Lofty continues to poke and blow to no avail. After a minute, Caroline makes her teeth chatter loudly.

Lofty's fringe is sticking to his forehead. 'We might have to give up on this idea.'

'If you like.'

Lofty immediately chucks the poker into the tray, grabs the unopened packet of burgers and lopes into the bungalow. 'It was meant to be our last meal together though.'

'Not to worry, I'll put them under the grill.'

'No – Dad'll go mental if we cook meat in his grill-pan. Let's go over to yours.'

Joan has started packing up books and ornaments for the eventual move. Caroline picks her way between boxes in the living room to where Joan's laptop is propped in a chair, and hooks up her camera. 'Hey Lofty – I'll just show you some of my photos. Wait a second. Here.' She opens a slide show. 'These are Vermont. It's mostly Maria's, and the lake, and these really cool people who live in her house.'

The first picture shows Joan and Beatrice clinking beer glasses, the backdrop a blur of bodies and colourful bunting. 'That was Maria's birthday party. It was totally awesome.' The next is a close-up of Beatrice and a black woman cheek to cheek. Two smiling mouths with perfect teeth. They look somehow similar, though the older woman's shorn, spiked hair is all-over silver.

'Who's that?' asks Lofty.

'Maria. She's Beatrice's partner.' Caroline clicks quickly through the images. 'And I've got a video on my iPhone of some gay guys snogging.'

Later, as Caroline is fixing up her mother's grill-pan with tin-foil, Lofty says, 'Russ phoned.'

Caroline clips the foil neatly with scissors. 'About Baldev, I suppose.'

'Do you want to hear it?'

'I suppose.'

'Well, his dad's sending him to cramming school down south to retake his A-levels.'

Caroline spreads four burgers on the grill-pan.

'You pay them loads of money and get one-to-one tuition, so you, like, get 'A's in everything,' says Lofty.

'He must still want to go to university then.'

'Mr Bloom at school wrote to the unis he'd applied to saying he'd had family problems, so he's having some offers held for a year.'

'Jammy.'

'That's what they're paying for when they send us to these schools.' Lofty turns from the kettle with two steaming mugs. 'We get the service.'

Caroline pulls a face. 'That's what my mother says.' She strikes a match and holds it under the grill. The gas puffs into blue flame. 'Where are Bal and Luke living?'

'Back home in Weatherhope. Back to normal.'

'So Uncle Walter's paying for Bal to go to cramming school.' She slides the burgers under, noticing through the steamy window the green blob of her mother in a raincoat. 'Even though Bal's not his real son. That's really kind of Uncle Walter.'

'Feels guilty I expect.' Lofty kicks the fridge door closed and sloshes milk into the coffees.

The back door opens and Wesley waddles in, wagging drips onto the cupboards.

'We're having burgers. Shall I put you some under?'

Joan is shaking her brolly with her back turned. The kitchenette feels crowded and intimate. 'I don't want to be in the way...'

'Coffee?' asks Lofty.

Joan glances at her daughter and sees Caroline already throwing a couple more burgers under the grill. 'Milk and one sugar. Thanks.' She peels off her coat.

'We were just saying, all parents are guilty,' says Caroline.

Lofty looks surprised. 'I didn't say that.'

'Well, don't you agree?'

'I do,' says Joan. 'I agree with you. Putting children on this earth is almost a sin. Look what we do to you.'

Having her mother agree so readily turns it into something childish, obvious. Caroline goes red, and stares intently at the droplets running down the windowpane into the pink beginnings of mildew.

'How's your new job going?' Lofty asks.

'Marvellous,' says Joan. 'Absolutely great.'

Caroline pokes at the burgers, screened by hair.

'So when is it you go off to Durham?' Joan asks Lofty.

'Tomorrow morning.'

'Coz we might be getting a camper van after I've moved, mightn't we, Caroline? We might be up your way, one half-term.'

'I wouldn't mind seeing what Durham's like,' says Caroline. 'It's got to be better than this dump. Here,' she turns to Lofty with a dazzling smile, 'they're nearly ready. Pass me the bread rolls.'